DIE FOR ME

CYNTHIA EDEN

DIE FOR
ME

A NOVEL OF THE VALENTINE KILLER

Montlake
Romance

The characters and events portrayed in this book are fictitious. Any similarity
to real persons, living or dead, is coincidental and not intended by the author.

Text copyright © 2013 Cindy Roussos

Published by Montlake Romance
P.O. Box 400818
Las Vegas, NV 89140

ISBN-13: 9781611099140
ISBN-10: 1611099145

This book is for all of the amazing romantic suspense readers out there. I hope you enjoy the story!

- 1 -

It had taken Savannah Slater a long time to die.

New Orleans police detective Dane Black stared down at the dead woman, noting the series of shallow cuts that lined her arms. Then his gaze rose to her chest. She'd been stabbed in the heart, and it looked as if the killer had twisted the knife once he'd plunged it into her chest.

Hell. The scent of blood and death was heavy in the air. Behind him, Dane could hear the sound of retching, no doubt coming from the fresh-faced uniform who'd found the body tossed like garbage near the edge of the park.

Even Dane's stomach had knotted at the sight of her body, and he'd sure come across his share of twisted shit when he served his tour in the Middle East.

"You ever seen anything like this?" The uniform had gotten enough control to voice the question. "I mean, Jesus Christ, it looks like someone tortured her."

Because someone had. Her wrists had been bound with rope, her ankles tied with the same thick hemp. Duct tape covered her mouth—no doubt to muffle her screams while her attacker worked on her.

It hadn't been an easy death. Not with all of those slices on her arms. Some deep enough to sever veins and tendons. But those wounds hadn't killed her. The perp had just been playing with her until the moment he drove his knife into her heart.

Dane leaned forward. The victim's right fingers were curled around something. His eyes narrowed. It looked like…Savannah Slater was holding a bloodred rose in her right hand.

Hell no.

Dane's back teeth ground together as he stood. Savannah Slater had been missing for just over seventy-two hours. When the reporter hadn't shown up for work, her boss had started hunting for her. Hunting was what they did best at the *New Orleans News Journal.*

Dane had thought the reporter might have just gone in deep for a story. He'd figured that she'd turn up with a cover-grabbing headline.

She'd be grabbing the headline, all right. Only he'd never expected this…

*Just a few days until February fourteenth. Valentine's Day. And with the way she was killed…that knife in the heart…and that rose in her hand…*The press would flip when they made the connection. "Yeah," he finally said slowly, "I've seen something like this before." Not up close and personal, but he'd heard the stories. Stories of other women who'd been tortured and killed. *Just like Savannah.* But not in New Orleans. Those killings had happened years ago, way up in Boston.

Not down in his city.

He studied her body again. The wounds on her arms were deliberate and far too perfectly placed.

"Why'd the prick dump her here?" Dane's partner demanded. Mac Turner ran a hand over his cleanly shaved head. Sweat glinted lightly off his dark-coffee skin. "My niece plays at this damn park. Any kid could have found the body." He exhaled. "Dumping a body for a kid to find. Another sick freak on our streets."

"He left her here because he wanted attention." The perp hadn't wanted to wait several days or weeks for the body's discovery. This was an in-your-face dump. They'd been lucky, though, that no curious six-year-old had stumbled upon it. The reporter had been found just after dawn by a jogger.

Dane stared down again. Savannah Slater's dark hair feathered over the ground. She'd been beautiful. By all accounts, she'd been well liked, had a great family, lots of friends.

Such a waste.

A crime tech took a photo, and the flash lit up the scene.

"Sometimes I hate this job," Mac muttered as he turned away.

Sometimes Dane did, too.

The uniform, looking like he might be sick again, stumbled back. His horrified gaze was still on Savannah—hell yeah, the sight of her tortured body could make a person gag. That hole left in her chest was huge. But this wasn't Dane's first ball game, not by a long shot.

He studied the scene with clinical eyes. *Duct-taped her mouth. Bound her wrists and ankles.* The flesh around her wrists was bruised a dark brown. How long had she been bound? The whole time she'd been missing? She wouldn't have been able to fight back that way. She would have been the perfect prey.

After one final look at the victim, Dane headed for his car, his shoulders hunched. Before he'd taken even five steps, the roar of oncoming vehicles reached him. His head lifted, and he saw a news van rushing way too fast around the curve up ahead.

Sonofabitch. The feeding frenzy had already started. The first van was followed by another, and another...*and another.*

"Cover the body!" he barked. "And make sure no one contaminates my crime scene." He'd put up tape, done his best to block off the area, but if some overeager reporter came stumbling through...

He'd arrest the jackass.

Then the reporters were there, swarming with their microphones as the cameramen lumbered behind them.

Dane took a deep breath, tasted death once more, and prepared to face the sharks.

— — —

"Today authorities discovered the body of missing *New Orleans News Journal* reporter Savannah Slater..."

Katherine Cole glanced up at the small TV located just inside of Joe's Café. Her hand curled around the cup of coffee that Joe had just slid across the counter to her.

Savannah Slater. The name whispered through her mind.

"Such a damn shame." Joe shook his head.

Katherine blew on her café au lait and nodded.

A female reporter's face—sad, tense—filled the screen. "Skywatch Five has uncovered exclusive details about Savannah Slater's attack." An image of a crime scene flashed on the screen. Katherine could see police officers moving quickly behind a line of yellow tape. "Savannah Slater was missing for over seventy-two hours, and it is believed that she was held and tortured during that time."

Katherine's stomach knotted even as her skin chilled. *The world is full of sick psychos. Just another monster hunting in the dark.*

Another face appeared on the screen. A man. Handsome. Pissed. He glared at the camera and said, "I have *no comment* at this time. The investigation is ongoing."

The news cut back to the reporter. "While lead detective Dane Black isn't talking, Skywatch Five sources have revealed that Ms. Slater was found bound, her wrists and ankles tied with thick rope, in a local park. Duct tape covered her mouth, and she had been stabbed directly in the heart."

Katherine's heartbeat seemed to stop.

The reporter continued, "A single red rose was found clutched in Ms. Slater's right hand, and with this crime occurring so close to Valentine's Day, police at the scene seemed especially tense."

The coffee mug slipped from Katherine's hand and shattered on the floor. *No, please, no.*

"Katherine? Katherine, you okay?" Joe frowned at her.

She stood, stumbled back, and rammed into Ben Miller, another frequent early morning patron of the café.

His hands wrapped around her shoulders to steady her. "Did you get burned?" His brown eyes were worried.

Shaking her head, she hurriedly pulled away from him. Moving away was instinctive for her.

She'd been coming to the small café since she moved to New Orleans, and she usually talked to both Ben and Joe each morning.

She didn't want to talk then. And she didn't want either of them touching her. Katherine's gaze flew back to the TV.

"Viewers may remember another killer who bound his victims in a similar way, before he stabbed them in the heart," the reporter continued, eyes piercing through the screen. The lady had done her homework. "Michael O'Rourke was suspected of torturing and murdering four women in Boston. He was dubbed the Valentine Killer because he always stabbed his female victims in the heart and left each victim holding a red rose in her palm." A dramatic pause. "His last kill was almost three years ago, and though several manhunts have been conducted as authorities tried to track O'Rourke, he has never been captured. Several law enforcement officials with the Boston Police Department have even theorized that the infamous killer may have taken his own life in order to avoid facing a lifetime behind bars."

"I remember that guy," Ben murmured. "A sick sonofabitch."

Yes, he had been.

The reporter was still talking. "With Valentine's Day just a few days away, police would not speculate as to whether the killer was Valentine or a copycat who could be looking to emulate his crimes."

The room went dim. A dull roar filled Katherine's ears, and she was pretty sure she was about to faint. "I-I'm sick, Joe. Sorry... got to...go." Then she turned and ran—or weaved—and barely heard Joe and Ben as they called out after her.

Her hands slammed into the door, and then she was outside. The warm air—it always seemed to be warm in New Orleans, even in February—hit her like a slap, but it couldn't banish the chill from her bones.

Savannah Slater had been stabbed in the heart. Katherine *knew* Savannah. And with the story that Savannah had been pursuing, there was no way the manner of her death could be a coincidence.

A message, yes, but anything else?

No, no, *no.*

This wasn't happening. It couldn't be.

A nightmare. Maybe she was dreaming. Or maybe the bastard had hunted her down. He'd told her...*I'll never let you go.*

Cars buzzed on the streets. Katherine locked her arms around her stomach and looked to the left, to the right.

So many people. *Too* many.

And Valentine's Day was creeping ever closer.

Please God, no.

She didn't want to live through this hell again. She couldn't.

- - -

With determined steps, Katherine entered the police station. Voices shouted, phones rang, and chaos filled the air.

She held her purse close as she made her way up to the main desk. "Um, excuse me…"

The cop didn't glance up.

Katherine cleared her throat and tried again. "*Excuse me.*"

Bushy brows rose as the guy focused on her. "Something I can do for you, miss?"

"I need to see Detective Black, please. Dane Black." Thanks to the news report, his name was branded in her mind.

The cop pointed to the left. "Take the hallway, second turn on your right. His desk is number four."

"Thank you."

"You're gonna have to sign in first, miss." He pushed a clipboard toward her. "And I'll need to see your ID."

She scribbled her name on the page. Handed him her ID. He barely seemed to glance at it before handing the license back to her. Then Katherine straightened her shoulders and turned away from him. Her heels tapped on the tiled floor. With every step she took, her heart beat harder.

The hallway stretched forever. For-freaking-ever. She wanted to walk faster, to run to Detective Black, but she forced herself to keep it slow.

Don't draw any more attention than you have to.

The second turn led to a giant room that housed half a dozen desks. Some were occupied. Some empty. She counted as she walked forward. One. Two. Three. F—

"Look, I don't care who the hell you are," the big male with black hair snarled into his phone as he stood near desk number four. "I want to know who leaked you that information, and I want to know *now.*"

She tensed at the fury in his voice.

"You weren't *helping* anyone. You were trying to up your ratings, and now I've got a city in a panic because you all but told them the Valentine Killer was hunting in New Orleans." His fingers tightened around the phone. "When I find out who leaked the info to you, I'll nail his ass to the wall." Then he slammed down the phone.

He spun around and faced Katherine, and she jerked back.

Detective Black's eyes—a deep, dark blue—widened when he saw her. "Who are you?" he asked. The light drawl of the South in his voice.

She swallowed and tried to loosen her death grip on her purse. "My name's Katherine Cole, and I wanted to talk to you about Savannah Slater."

He blinked. The detective really was a handsome man. His features were strong, almost rough, but still handsome. Square jaw. High cheekbones. A nose that looked like it had been broken a time or two. She noticed that a faint scar curled under his lower lip.

She tilted her head back to better study him. The detective towered over her. He had to be at least six foot two, maybe three, and had wide, strong shoulders.

"What do you know about Savannah Slater?" he demanded, and he didn't exactly sound friendly.

I know too much. But she couldn't tell him that. The last thing she wanted was to find herself shoved into one of the cells at the police station. Well, actually, that wasn't the *last* thing.

"I have a few questions," Katherine whispered.

More phones rang. Detective Black swore and grabbed her arm. "Come with me." He hustled her toward a small room in the back. Not a cell, just some kind of interrogation room. She'd been in rooms like that one before. He pushed her inside and slammed the door shut behind him.

"You're a reporter." Detective Black glared at her, and his firm lips tightened even more. "Look, I'm not giving you a quote, I'm not giving you a scoop, I'm not giving you *anything* now."

He was too close to her. Her back was against the wall, and he stood inches away. Katherine didn't like getting this close to people. Especially men. That was one of the issues she'd been working on with her shrink. Before she ditched said shrink.

She exhaled and said, "I'm not a reporter." Her voice was stronger now.

"Then why are you in my precinct?" he asked. His gaze raked her body, and she didn't like that too-assessing stare.

"Because I need to know about Savannah." Truth. *I need to know so I can decide if I need to run.* Just when her life had started to get settled. The nightmares hadn't stopped, but she'd almost felt…normal.

She should have known better.

"You're out of luck." He didn't sound a bit apologetic. "'Cause I'm not talking about my case." A faint drawl rolled lightly beneath his words.

"Fine. Then I'll talk." Her own words were clipped and gave no hint of an accent. She'd worked hard to lose that Boston tone. Katherine licked her lips, and Black's gaze darted to her mouth as she said, "On the news, the reporter said that Savannah's wrists and ankles were bound. Did the killer tie a handcuff knot with thick hemp rope? Because Valentine always used a Mexican handcuff knot—"

"Fucking news," the cop muttered. "Look, we have no reason to believe the Valentine Killer is linked to this crime, got it? So if you think you're coming down here to spin some bullshit story and jerk me around—"

"I'm not jerking you around." Dammit, she was trying to *help.* Because she hadn't helped before. She'd done nothing, and women had died. *Not again.*

If there was any chance this was Valentine and not a copycat, she had to speak out. She'd never bought the idea that Valentine had killed himself. Sure, she thought some of the cops back in Boston wished that the killer had taken his own life, but she didn't believe that theory. It was a too-easy, too-neat theory to cover up the fact that the cops had never come close to catching Valentine. And, to her, he *was* Valentine. Not Michael. Never Michael.

Michael was the man she'd agreed to marry.

Valentine was the monster who'd stolen everything from her.

Keeping them separate was one of the ways she'd managed to stay sane after her life had turned into a nightmare.

By the time the cops had arrived at her house three years earlier, Valentine had been long gone. He'd just vanished and no amount of tracking had been able to find him. Until now? Because if Valentine had come out of hiding, if this was really him, then she had to speak, and screw what her handling officer with the Program thought. When she'd called him after leaving the café, he'd told her to stay away from the precinct. To keep a low profile and ignore the death.

But ignoring death wasn't easy. She had the nightmares to prove it.

"If it's Valentine," she was now telling Detective Black, "then there should be eleven slices on Savannah's left arm and ten on her right." A precise twenty-one. The cops had never leaked that particular detail to the press. "Valentine always gave his victims those wounds because…because he had the same slices on his own arms."

The cops hadn't made the connection with the wounds. She had. When they'd made her stare at the pictures, over and over again, she'd realized that those wounds were in the same pattern as the scars on Valentine's arms.

Silence beat in the small room. Then Detective Black leaned in until only a breath seemed to separate them. "*Who the hell are you?*"

"I told you. I'm Katherine Cole." *Say it until you believe it.* "And I just want to help you find out if this is the Valentine Killer or if it's just some wannabe trying to grab a headline."

His gaze searched hers. She wondered what he saw there. No emotion, surely. She'd gotten very good at burying her emotions.

"This *wannabe* tortured a woman for hours."

She didn't blink.

"He drove his knife into her chest. Sank the blade into her heart."

Her own chest ached. Katherine swallowed the bile that rose in her throat. Sweat slickened her hands. "Call your medical examiner. If he hasn't already done it, then get him to count the slices on her arms."

He grabbed her wrist. His hand was warm, almost hot, and when his long, strong fingers closed around her, she thought the usual fear would hit her. But it didn't, and that fact shocked Katherine to her core.

Detective Black gazed into her eyes. "I get the feeling you're a dangerous woman."

She didn't even have the breath to speak right then.

He pulled her toward the small table, pushed her into the wobbly chair. Katherine sucked in a deep breath that she really needed and tried to calm her racing heartbeat.

Then she saw the flash of silver handcuffs.

"Wait!" Katherine began, frantic. "What are you—"

He locked one cuff around the wrist he still held. Then he locked the other cuff to the leg of the table. "It's bolted down," he told her, giving a half grin that flashed the dimple in his left cheek, "so you're not goin' anywhere, lady."

"I'm trying to help you!"

His fingers stroked over the skin of her inner wrist, an almost absent gesture, then he pulled back, taking that seductive warmth with him. "We'll see."

He turned toward the door with his broad back stiff.

Katherine realized he was going to just leave her there. Cuffed. "You can't do this!" She knew her fear broke through the words.

"Watch me," he tossed over his shoulder without glancing back.

"*Please.*" The plea slipped out, but she couldn't help it. She couldn't stand confinement. Being cuffed, yeah, that sure counted as confinement to her. And she felt like she was far too close to freaking out.

He stopped and looked back. A frown pulled his dark brows low. "Relax," he told her, his voice softening just a bit. "I'll visit that ME and be right back for you."

He was checking out the story about the number of wounds. Okay. That was something. "Just hurry, okay?" Katherine tried to calm her racing heartbeat.

His gaze held hers. Then he left her. The door clicked closed quietly behind him.

She glanced around the room and finally saw the long mirror that ran the length of the left wall. A two-way mirror, she was sure.

So the cops could watch her.

She stared at the mirror and saw the dark-haired woman with too-pale skin staring back at her.

Katherine Cole.

Say it until you believe it.

— — —

A thin, white sheet covered Savannah Slater's body, hiding her from the chest down.

Dane gazed down at her, his jaw tight. "Ronnie, how many slices did you find on the victim's arms?"

Dr. Veronica Thomas glanced up at him. Freckles stained her cheeks, and her bright blue eyes were narrowed behind her glasses. "I'm working on the report now. It's *only* been four hours. And do you know how many stiffs I've got down here?" She lifted her pointed chin. "Go back upstairs. Get some coffee. Yell at a reporter for leaking the story, but give me some time, got it?"

He crossed his arms. "Eleven slices on her left arm." *Be wrong.* "Ten slices on her right."

"You counted on-scene, huh?" She pushed up her glasses. "Well, why ask, then? She was—"

"I didn't count on-scene." There'd been too much blood covering her, and he hadn't wanted to touch her until the techs had a chance to do their job. By the time the techs got to work, he'd been busy keeping the press away from the victim. He'd busted ass, and someone had still gone behind his back and leaked info to the vultures.

She blinked. "Then how'd you know?"

Every muscle in his body seemed to lock down. "I'm right." Not a question.

She nodded. "Yes, you are." Ronnie picked up a clipboard. "The wounds on her arms are meticulous, every slice exactly one inch apart. Like the killer was following some kind of pattern." A sad sigh drifted from her lips.

An image of Katherine Cole floated through his mind. Pretty face. Golden eyes. Full red lips.

Cold-blooded killer?

Or, at the very least, she could be an accomplice to a killer.

A woman that gorgeous *would* be deadly.

Ronnie walked around the table. "How'd you know, Dane?" Now suspicion had entered her tone.

"Because a woman walked up to my desk five minutes ago and told me."

"You're kidding." Ronnie's voice had risen two octaves.

"No, not this time." He shoved his hand through his hair. "This case is priority, Ronnie. Get me the full report and get it to me yesterday."

She nodded, eyes wide.

He turned away and pushed open the door that would take him away from the ME's office. The scent of bleach and death followed him. Hell, he didn't know how Ronnie could stand that place.

He hurried up the stairs, not bothering with the elevator. The ME's office was located in the building right behind his precinct. "The death rooms," as the cops called the place.

Please. Katherine's voice drifted in his mind. Breathy, sexy, and almost…desperate.

Killers could be very, very desperate indeed.

The sunlight hit him as he raced between the two buildings, burning bright and hot as it always did in New Orleans. He hurried inside the police station, grunting a greeting at the uniforms he passed.

When he reached the homicide unit, Dane found Mac sitting on the edge of his desk.

Mac pointed toward the interrogation room. "There a particular reason you got that kid guarding the door?"

Dane spared a quick glance at the door in question. The uniformed cop was exactly where Dane had stationed him.

Squaring his shoulders, Dane said, "He's keeping an eye on a suspect."

Mac arched a brow. "I saw the suspect." A low whistle escaped him. "I would have kept an eye on her for you. You could've just asked me nicely."

Yeah, he was sure Mac would have been only too happy to keep company with Katherine Cole. "I think she knows who killed Savannah Slater." He paused a beat. "Or maybe she even did the deed herself."

Surprise slackened Mac's face. "You're shitting me."

But Mac didn't actually sound disbelieving. More like sad. After working together for eight years, both men knew that even the most innocent faces could hide killers.

Dane started rolling up his sleeves as he headed for the interrogation room. Mac fell into step behind him.

"So who's good cop?" Mac asked, voice flat, as they neared the door.

Dane thought of Savannah Slater's broken body. "Neither one of us."

After one look at Dane's face, the uniform quickly moved out of the way.

Dane opened the door.

Katherine looked up at once, and she was just as damn beautiful as before. Heart-shaped face. Glass-sharp cheekbones. Tiny slip of nose. Lips made for sin.

And those eyes. One look into them, and he'd felt like he'd been punched in the gut.

But he knew all too well just how deceptive innocence could be.

Such a perfect face. But was it the face of an angel or a sadistic killer?

Time to find out.

– 2 –

Valentine was back.

Katherine got her answer from the look on Detective Black's face.

Twenty-one slices.

When Detective Black came back into the room, his eyes glittering with a barely contained fury, Katherine knew her carefully constructed world was about to be ripped apart.

"How did you know?" He was trying to sound cool, she got that, but his eyes revealed the truth.

Another man followed behind him, a guy about two inches shorter and thirty pounds lighter than Detective Black. Both men were in their thirties, but this guy's face was much softer than the other—

"How did you know?"

Katherine swallowed. "I told you, that's what Valentine did. He always left that exact number on his victims."

Detective Black sat in front of her. He'd rolled up his sleeves, and she could see the black edge of a tattoo on his right arm. It seemed to twist around his flesh like a snake.

"And how would you know what Valentine did, miss?" The other guy wanted to know. His voice was carefully curious, a little bland, but she could feel his tension, too. "I mean, those crimes happened all the way up in Boston, and we're way down—"

"I'm from Boston." That truth just slipped out.

Wrong story. *Say it until—*

"Are you now." Detective Black leaned toward her, seeming to swallow all the space with his bigger body. "Why doesn't that fact surprise me?"

She lifted her hand, only to have it jerked back by the handcuff. "Is this confinement necessary?" Katherine glanced down at the cuff. "I came here to help you."

"Is Valentine killing in my city?"

I think so. God help us all. "You need to call Detective Sean Hobbs. He worked the case up in Boston. Talk to him. He can—"

"Did *you* kill Savannah Slater?" Detective Black's cold question blew right through her words.

"No, of course not!" Fury hardened her voice.

His eyes narrowed on her, and she almost felt as if he could see right into her soul. Almost, until he asked, "Were you present when she was killed?"

"No!" Not for this kill. Not this time.

"Then where were you? Because, Ms. Cole, we're sure as hell gonna need an alibi from you."

Her lips trembled. She didn't have an alibi. She'd been alone all weekend. At home. And she had no close neighbors. No one to vouch for her.

The interrogation room door flew open. "*This interview is over,*" a familiar voice blasted.

Katherine looked up and found her handler standing in the doorway.

Detective Black leapt to his feet. His chair slammed to the floor behind him. "Who the hell are you?"

Her handler yanked out his ID. "I'm Anthony Ross, and this woman is coming with me."

The detective snatched the ID for a closer look while the man Katherine assumed was his partner cursed. Black and Ross were about the same size, and they were standing toe to toe.

"You're a U.S. marshal?" Detective Black asked, and there was no missing his shock.

Ross reached for her hand. "Come on, Katherine."

"I can't." She lifted the cuffs.

Ross closed his green eyes for a moment. "You are kidding me." His gaze snapped open and locked on the detectives. "Why is she cuffed? *Why?*"

"Because she knows far too much about my murder victim." Detective Black wasn't backing down. "Either she was *there* or she knows—"

"Katherine wasn't there. I can verify her whereabouts for the last forty-eight hours."

Sweet of him to lie. But the marshal had ulterior motives. ,

He wanted to get her out of the precinct.

Ross held out his hand. "The. Key."

But instead of handing him the key, the Detective Black stalked around the table and knelt beside Katherine. She tensed. *Too close.*

She stared down at him. His head was tilted as he stared at the cuffs. His hair was dark, so thick, and a little too long. His profile was strong, and from this angle, there was no missing the fact that someone had definitely taken a few swings at his nose.

And he smelled nice. Not a cologne scent. Just…man.

He slipped the key into the lock and the cuff opened with a quick *snick*, but the detective didn't back away. Instead, his fingers smoothed over her wrist, stroking lightly, right where the cuff had bitten into her skin.

Now his head tilted back so that he met her stare. "If you don't tell me what's going on," he said, his gaze searching hers, "then how am I supposed to keep you safe?"

Safe. Sometimes she wasn't even sure what that word meant anymore. Her tongue swiped over her too-dry lips. "You can't."

His fingers tightened around her wrist. "You don't know me well. Not yet." *Why did that sound like a promise?* "But believe me when I say that I could protect you from anyone or anything out there."

Detective Black was a good cop. She'd heard the stories about him before. Seen his high-profile busts on TV. Not a glory hound, but a cop the media seemed to love.

So her smile was sad when she stood and pulled away from him. "I have to go now."

"Damn straight," Ross said, and then he was the one catching her hand. "And if you have any other questions for Katherine, you route them through *me*."

Detective Black rose slowly. "You're not a lawyer."

"And she shouldn't be your suspect," Ross snapped right back. "So do your job and get out there and find the killer."

He tried to pull her through the doorway.

Katherine dug in her heels. She glanced back at the detectives once more. She'd come here for a reason. "Call Boston. Talk to Sean."

"*Dammit, Kat,*" Ross muttered. "We need to *go*."

This time, she went with him.

And she hoped that the cops would be ready to face the hell coming their way.

– – –

20

"Well, well, well..." Mac blew out a hard breath and shook his head as he stared out the open interrogation room door. "What the hell was *that*?"

Wrong question. "We need to find out why the U.S. marshal's office is protecting her." He could still smell her sweet scent. All around him.

Her skin had been softer than silk.

A killer? He didn't know, not yet. But now a marshal was involved, and that mixed up the case even more.

A marshal. Protecting a woman who knew far too much about one of the most wanted men in the United States.

He shoved by Mac and rushed back into the bull pen. His captain was coming out of his office. Harley Dunning's round face was even redder than usual. "You want to tell me why I got the *marshal's* office on my ass?"

Dane grunted as he sat down at his desk. "Ten minutes, Cap. Just give me ten minutes..." Sweat trickled down his cheek as he grabbed for his phone. He hit the button for the station operator. "Yeah, yeah, look, it's Detective Black, and I need you to connect me to the Boston PD, to one Detective Sean Hobbs." His heart thudded in his chest. "*Now.*" He was connecting the dots as quickly as he could.

"What's goin' on?" Harley demanded as he closed in on Dane.

Mac answered, "Our suspect gave us a tip, right before the marshal with the shiny badge dragged her away."

"A tip?" the captain pushed.

"Yeah." Dane grunted as he waited for the connection. "And one we're damn well checking out."

The marshal's involvement meant the woman wasn't just some bullshitter off the street. And her eyes—those beautiful, golden eyes—had been full of determination and fear.

There'd been no missing the way her voice broke each time she mentioned Valentine.

The marshal wanted to protect her, but Dane wasn't about to let that guy stand in his way. He had a murder to solve, and if Katherine Cole was involved, she wasn't getting away from him, marshal or no damn marshal.

To stop a killer, Dane would be willing to use anything or anyone.

No more blood. No more torture. He would do anything necessary to bring the killer to justice.

– – –

"No more talking to the cops, Kat," Anthony Ross said. His hands tightened around the steering wheel as he guided them through the thick New Orleans traffic. "What the fuck were you thinking?" He stopped the vehicle, and a trolley whizzed past them.

Anger stirred in Katherine's gut, slowly breaking through the ice that had encased her ever since she saw the news footage earlier that day. "Don't call me Kat. I told you that before." Because *he'd* called her that.

She saw him slant a quick glance her way.

"And as to what the fuck I was thinking…" She sucked in a sharp breath. "I was thinking the cops needed to know who they were dealing with."

"So you put yourself up as a target? Dammit, Kat—Katherine." He corrected himself quickly. "You know this can't be some random attack. A kill like this, basically right on your front doorstep—"

Her jaw dropped. "But you told me—when I called you—you said—"

"I was just trying to keep you calm until I could get to you!" His hand slapped against the steering wheel. "I wanted to keep you safe."

Detective Black had promised to keep her safe.

She glanced down at her clenched hands. "Savannah Slater had eleven knife wounds on her left arm and ten on her right."

Silence. She looked over and saw a muscle jerk along Ross's jaw.

"Would a copycat know about the number of wounds?" Katherine asked.

He exhaled, and the lines on his face deepened. "Only if he saw the confidential reports from the bureau or the Boston PD. The press never knew about the exact number on the victims."

She'd thought as much. There were no coincidences in this world. She'd learned that long ago. The wounds…the rose…the bindings…"If he's killing here, then he knows that *I'm* here, too."

"We don't *know* that yet. Hell, we don't know anything for sure at this point." Ross wasn't taking her straight home. They snaked through the city, following a route she knew was meant to confuse or lose any tails. *Just in case anyone is following us.*

He wouldn't want to lead anyone back to her house on the outskirts of the city.

"I'll drop you off, and then I'll do some checking on my own. I'll find out what's happening here," Ross promised. His knuckles whitened as he held the wheel. "But Katherine, if it looks like it really is him or even a copycat who knows about you…"

He paused, but she knew what was coming.

"You'll need to be transferred again," he said flatly.

Another transfer. Another name. Another place.

Another life.

She turned away from him and watched the blur of buildings pass. "Will I ever get to be me again?"

She couldn't really remember that woman. A woman who'd been so blind. A woman who, for all purposes, had died three years ago.

"It's just not safe, not until Valentine is in custody."

She didn't speak again. Not until Ross pulled into the long drive that led to her house. "I...ah...left my car at Joe's Café." She flushed with this confession. She'd been so shaken that she'd walked all the way from the café to the precinct. "Can you get someone to—"

"I'll get someone to bring it to you." He killed the engine. "I want to come in and check the house."

Right. But she didn't move. Her gaze raked the house, the yard.

She'd been living in New Orleans for just over a year. Opened her gallery. Gotten into a seemingly normal routine. She'd even started dating someone.

Now she was supposed to abandon everything. Again.

And do what? Run forever? While more bodies piled up?

No.

"I'm done," she told Ross, and climbed from the SUV. She shut the door on his shocked tumble of words.

Then she began walking toward the house. One determined step after another.

His door opened with a squeak and then slammed behind her. "Kat, Kat—you can't mean this! It's too dangerous! It's—"

She glanced back at him. "Don't call me Kat." Not a weak voice. Cold and flat. "And I'm going to do what I want to do. What I *need* to do."

No more running.

"If Valentine wants me, then he can come and get me." *And stop hurting others. Just—stop!*

Gravel crunched beneath Ross's footsteps. "You got some kind of death wish?"

She laughed, but it sounded hollow. "I guess I do."

– – –

"Holy shit." Mac's curse heaved out on a hard sigh. "That's *her*."

Dane stared down at the computer screen. While he'd been waiting on the Boston PD to fax over the case files, he'd started doing his own research on Valentine.

The Internet was such a handy bitch. With a few clicks of the keyboard, a guy could find almost anything.

Including pictures of one Katelynn Crenshaw. The photo had been snapped by a reporter right after Katelynn discovered her fiancé carving up his latest victim.

Right in their basement.

Her hair was longer and blonde in the picture. Her skin golden, and not the pale ivory it had been today. Her body was fuller, filled with lush curves.

But her eyes were the same. No mistaking those eyes. Or her lips.

"No wonder she knew so much about Valentine," Harley said as he crowded in near the computer screen. "She was screwing the guy."

Dane's shoulders tensed. The captain could be a real ass some days. "She told the cops everything she'd seen and spent months working with them as they tried to catch the guy."

He remembered the details now. Like the rest of the nation, he'd caught the images on TV about the Valentine Killer. Katelynn had come home early and found blood in her kitchen. She'd called 911 and gone looking for her fiancé. She'd found him in the basement, carving up Stephanie Gilbert.

By the time the cops arrived, Valentine had disappeared. He had left Katelynn unharmed and he'd just…vanished.

No more bodies had been discovered after his disappearance, so the Boston cops had started to think the guy might have killed himself. Some profiler appeared on one of the major network channels spewing about how a serial killer like Valentine couldn't go dormant for so long. Since he wasn't attacking, the profiler had said the guy might have turned his rage on himself. *Suicide.*

Bullshit.

From what Dane could tell, the profiler needed to think again.

"Was she in on it, do you think?" Harley asked. "She had to know what a twisted freak he was."

Sometimes you couldn't see the monsters right in front of you. No one had believed what a twisted SOB his old man had been, not until it was too late. "If this is really is Valentine, he's here because of *her.*" He'd tracked her, all the way down the Eastern Seaboard. This was one man determined not to let go.

"Yeah, well…" A chair squeaked as Mac rolled away. "You can sure bet that U.S. marshal will have her out of town as fast as he can." Mac exhaled on a hard sigh. "They're gonna want to keep her safe so they can pull her out at trial."

"Trial?" Dane repeated and forced his gaze off the picture of Katelynn. *Katherine.* "There's no trial to worry about now."

"Just because no one else has caught him," Harley interrupted smoothly, "doesn't mean *we* can't."

Harley might be an ass, but the guy had never been afraid of a challenge. He also loved getting his face splashed in the papers. If his department took down Valentine, he'd be able to wallpaper his office with all the news stories.

"Here you go." Detective Karen James handed a fat stack of papers across the desk to Dane. "All your info from a Detective Hobbs in Boston."

Not all. Sean Hobbs had promised to copy the rest of the files and overnight them. This two-inch stack was just the beginning.

Dane began to flip through the pages. Valentine had been one grisly bastard.

And he had only one weakness.

"Dane."

He looked up at the captain's voice.

"I don't want her leaving the city," Harley said. "Whether we're dealing with the real deal or some copycat, that woman is linked to these killings."

"All of the guy's victims in Boston were blondes," Dane said.

"And now we've got us a dead brunette," Harley cut in.

Dane met Mac's thoughtful stare.

"Katherine's a brunette now," Mac said.

Yes, she was.

When he'd first found Savannah's body and seen her clutching that rose, Dane had made the connection to the Valentine case just like the reporters had. He'd remembered that Valentine liked to bind his victims and then stab them in the heart.

But as for all the small pieces, the facts, the profiles…that was what he needed to discover if he was going to find out what the hell was happening now.

"Read that report. Start piecing together all that you can on Valentine," Harley ordered. "We have to work fast, because if it is him, the bureau will be down here trying to take over my case."

No missing the *my*.

"We all know you have a way with the ladies, Black," the captain continued. Detective James, who'd stayed around to shamelessly eavesdrop, snickered at that. Harley ignored her and pointed at Dane. "So I want you to use some of that charm and keep Katherine Cole in New Orleans, you got me?"

Dane nodded. "Don't worry, Cap. Katherine's not going anywhere."

Because she was the key to the case, and he'd be damned if he let the bodies start to pile up in his city.

Valentine had a weakness, all right, and Dane would be using that weakness against him.

Katherine, you're not getting away.

Not when he needed her so badly.

— — —

The house was clean. No, more than that. *Immaculate.* Fresh paint on the shutters. The windows gleamed as if freshly polished. There were no leaves or any debris anywhere in the front yard.

Dane stared up at the house. Katherine Cole's house. She had no close neighbors. No one to see what was happening at her place.

No one to hear the screams.

He raised his hand to the door and knocked hard with his fist.

While he waited, he exhaled slowly and wondered what kind of sweet talk he should use.

Then Katherine Cole opened the door. She stared at him with her wide, lost eyes, and he just said, "Help me catch the bastard."

She nodded.

- 3 -

The house smelled like her. Fresh strawberries. Sweet. Heady.

Katherine led him into the den, a den that looked like something out of a glossy home magazine. Picture-damn-perfect, but without a single personal touch. No photos. No mementos.

"You know who I am." She turned and faced him with her chin up.

He inclined his head. "Katelynn."

"No!" she snapped as she shook her head, sending her dark hair sliding over her shoulders. "I..." She cleared her throat. "I go by Katherine now."

Right. Best to lay the cards on the table. "You planning to leave town?" Dane asked as he raised an eyebrow.

"That's what Ross wants."

The marshal was going to be a problem. "And what do *you* want?" he demanded as he strode toward her. He gave her credit. The woman didn't back up.

Her breath whispered out over her lips. Sexy lips. "I want my life back, Detective Black."

He closed in on her. Inhaled more of that sweet scent. "Then work with me," he said. "Stay here in New Orleans. If this really is Valentine, help me to stop the bastard." He said "if," but the truth was that he already suspected they were facing the real deal. The crime scene had been so perfect, and those wounds on the victim's arms had been an exact match to the other killings.

Katherine stared up at him. She was small, no taller than five foot five, and she tilted her head as she met his eyes. "I will help you." Firm. "That's why I came to the station. Why I told you to contact Sean." Her stare didn't waver. "I've already let Ross know that I won't be leaving town."

His captain would be shit-eating-grin happy over that news.

Her eyelids flickered. "Believe me, I want Valentine stopped as much as you do." Her laugh was bitter, broken. "More than you do, okay? *More.* I want the guy caught and locked in a cage for the rest of his life."

Bloodthirsty.

"So I'll be staying here, Detective—"

"Dane." Not just detective. They were going to be working together, working *very* closely together, and he wanted her calling him by his name.

She blinked and nodded slowly. "I'll be here, Dane. This time I won't run away."

He realized that this Katherine wasn't the same as the broken woman in the photograph. Determination tightened her features and kept her back straight.

A fighter.

Good. She'd need to be.

He'd wondered just what kind of woman Valentine had lost his heart to. Now he knew.

And Dane realized that he'd been right about Katherine all along. She could be a very dangerous woman indeed.

- - -

Dane returned to Katherine's house that night and watched her from the shadows. Now that he knew her relationship to Valentine and with one woman already in the morgue, he couldn't bring himself to leave her unguarded.

There was just something about Katherine Cole...

She was working her way right under his skin.

Was this the way it had been for Valentine? The question whispered through his mind. Had Valentine met her and not been able to get her out of his head?

She's in my head.

If he weren't careful, the situation could be deadly.

Headlights lit the area as another car approached. The vehicle slowed and then braked at the end of Katherine's drive. Dane tensed, then saw a guy in a three-piece suit hurry out of his fancy sports car.

He ran a hand over his face. He hadn't expected Katherine to have a date, but it looked like the lady had planned a night out on the town. For some reason, the sight of the jerk in that overpriced suit pissed him off. Katherine, dressed in a form-fitting black dress that hugged her body like a sweet glove, smiled at the bozo when she opened the front door and even let the guy kiss her cheek.

Bastard.

Dane wrote down the bastard's tag number and called it in while he trailed them to a high-end restaurant. In less than five minutes, he knew that Katherine's date was Dr. Trent Lancaster, a local shrink.

Jeez, a shrink? He'd never liked the head case doctors. They analyzed everything to death.

The guy's hands were a little too clingy as he led Katherine toward the restaurant. And Dane realized he was gripping his steering wheel a little too tightly.

Just a case. Just a case. Breathing deeply, he forced his hands to relax. Then he pulled out his phone and called Mac. One ring. Two. The shrink and Katherine disappeared into the restaurant.

Mac answered on the third ring. Dane could tell by the background noise that his partner was still at the station. Perfect.

"Run a check for me," Dane said without bothering to identify himself. "Find out every bit of intel you can on Dr. Trent Lancaster." His fingers tapped against the steering wheel, and he kept his eyes on the restaurant's entrance.

One of Katherine's lovers had been a killer.

Was another?

– – –

This wasn't working. Katherine forced herself to smile at Trent. He was talking about an article he'd written, something about behavioral regression, and she wanted to just drop her head and bang it on the table. Hard. Over and over.

Not working.

Had she really thought she might be able to sleep with Trent? That tonight would be the date that finally took their relationship to the next level?

Her body was so amped up that she felt as if every muscle trembled, and her eyes couldn't seem to stop searching the room.

Someone's watching me. The tension in her belly told her that.

"I was thinking that we could rent a cottage at the beach for a few days," Trent said, his voice with that smooth, perfect tone that no doubt lulled many of his patients. "It would give us a chance to get to know each other even better."

Can't, Trent. The instant denial sprang to her lips, but she managed to bite it back. *My serial-killer ex might be in town.*

She also choked back the slightly hysterical laughter that rose within her.

"Uh, Kat?"

She flinched. "Katherine. Not Kat, remember?" Because whenever someone called her Kat, she heard Valentine's voice in her head.

Trent blinked.

Great. Now she was being a bitch to her date. Trent didn't deserve that kind of treatment. She forced a wan smile. "I'm sorry, Trent, but I'm just not feeling well tonight." She should have canceled the date.

His handsome face immediately crinkled with concern even as he inched back from her. The instinctive response of a guy who was preparing for something he didn't want to hear. Then he cleared his throat and asked, "What can I do?"

She rubbed her throbbing temples. "I think I need to go home." Too many people were there. Watching. So many eyes had been on her after the Valentine case exploded.

So many people, judging her.

As she sat there, Katherine still felt like she was being judged. "Please," she whispered. "I want to go home."

"Of course." He reached for her hand, and she had to fight the instinct to recoil. His touch felt cold, clammy.

What would Trent do if he knew who she really was? Would his eyes look so caring? Or would he start to study her with that clinical detachment she'd seen in the eyes of his partner, Evelyn

33

Knight? She'd gone to Evelyn to get help. To try to stop the night-mares and the paranoia. *Someone's watching...*

But from the very first, Evelyn had made her feel tense. Her questions had been designed to rip right through Katherine's skin.

I've already been filleted enough, thank you.

"Trent..." She reached for her bag but kept her eyes on him. This needed to be said. His grip was making her tense, and his eyes...they were looking for too much as he stared at her. "I don't think it's going to work between us."

His lips tightened a bit. "But we seem so compatible."

Compatible.

She knew Trent was used to women falling at his feet. He was handsome. Smart. Charming. The perfect gentleman. Pity she wasn't the perfect lady for him.

When he touched her, she didn't feel anything. She hadn't realized that was really a problem. For three years, she'd existed in that void, not truly *feeling* anything.

Then Dane Black had touched her. He'd been full of anger. Determination. Humming with wild energy.

And she'd wanted him. For the first time in three years, she'd actually felt something other than fear at a man's touch.

She'd thought Trent might be able to make her feel something tonight.

No dice. And he deserved better than to be strung along by her. "You're a wonderful guy, Trent, but trust me on this, I'm not the right girl for you."

A muscle jerked in his jaw. "You're just not feeling well," he said dismissively as he rose to his feet and signaled the waiter. "We'll talk about this after you're back to your old self."

"I'm sorry, Trent." She rose as well, and a few moments later, they were leaving the restaurant.

Trent might think all would be different in the morning, but nothing was going to change for Katherine. She knew she wouldn't be carrying through with her plans to sleep with him.

She couldn't. She just didn't want him, and she couldn't *make* herself want him.

– – –

The date had ended too soon. When Trent and Katherine had come hurrying out of the restaurant, Dane had tensed.

Then they drove right back to her house. They'd gone fast, maybe too fast, as he carefully tailed behind them.

Hell. He understood what that speed meant.

Why did that piss him off so much?

Dane clenched his jaw. He had no claim on Katherine. If she wanted to screw her shrink, then she could screw him all night long.

The thought burned right though him, but Dane locked his muscles and didn't move from his now-parked car. He'd found an old dirt road that ran alongside Katherine's property. A perfect place from which to watch and not be seen.

Katherine got out of the sports car. The shrink followed her. They went up onto the porch. The shrink pulled her close.

Asshole.

The guy put his hands on Katherine's smooth skin. Curled his palms over her shoulders.

Bastard.

Dane ground his teeth together. *You don't know her. She can have sex with whoever she wants.*

And she probably did.

But not that night.

Katherine pushed away from the shrink with a sad shake of her head. While the guy's hands fisted, she turned away and headed into the house alone.

Dane started breathing again.

The shrink watched her for a moment or two longer. Glared at the closed door.

Keep moving, jerk. Nothing to see here.

The shrink went back to his fancy ride. Cranked the engine. Drove away a little too fast.

Dane smiled.

The lights flashed on inside Katherine's house. Good. She was in safe for the night. Now maybe the tight tension that coiled his muscles would go away.

– – –

That had been awkward, but at least Trent knew where they now stood. It wouldn't have been fair to lead the guy on, not when she couldn't make herself *feel* anything for him.

But then, she hadn't felt very much in the past few years. Half the time, it seemed as if she were wrapped in some kind of fog, moving slowly through life.

You felt something when you were with the detective. The whisper slid through her mind. Katherine swallowed and turned toward the stairs. Right then, she didn't want to think too much about the dark and dangerous detective. Instead, she wanted—

She came to an abrupt stop.

There were roses on the stairs.

The breath froze in Katherine's chest.

Once upon a time, roses had been her favorite flowers. Then she'd learned just what Michael had been doing with the roses.

Buying a dozen roses...then leaving one with his victim and bringing the remaining eleven to her.

He brought them to me after each kill.

Her cheeks were wet now. Her hands were shaking.

And there were fucking roses on her stairs. *In my house.* "No," Katherine whispered. This could not be happening.

But there was something beside the roses. A small box. It almost looked like a candy box from one of those fancy chocolate shops that she'd seen in the French Quarter a few times. Slender, long...

She was walking toward the box. She should be getting the hell out of there, but it was as if she were being pulled forward, forced toward that box.

I'll look inside. It will just be chocolate. Trent could have left the candy and the flowers when I wasn't looking. He dropped them off when he was here earlier and I was getting my purse.

It didn't *have* to be from Valentine.

But he always sent me flowers after each death. She just hadn't realized that fact until it was too late. He'd sent her eleven roses, and his victim—each time his victim had the twelfth rose.

Her breath sawed out of her lungs as her gaze locked on those roses. Helplessly she began to count them.

One, two, three...

The scent of the roses was sickly sweet.

Four, five, six...

There were thorns on the roses. Thorns that would draw blood.

Seven, eight, nine...

Her heart beat so hard that it hurt her chest.

Ten. Eleven. Dear God, only eleven.

The twelfth rose was missing.

She picked up the box. Nearly dropped it because she was so scared and nervous. Then her shaking fingers lifted the lid off the box. Rose petals fell onto the steps. Then she screamed, a long, desperate sound, but one that also burned with rage because the sick bastard was back. He was playing his games with her—with his victims—all over again.

There was no chocolate in the box.

She dropped it. Jumped back.

Katherine whirled and ran for the door. *Get away, get away, get away.*

Because the nightmare of her past had found her once more.

— — —

The front door flew open and Katherine ran down the steps.

Adrenaline shot through Dane's veins as he jumped from his vehicle. "Katherine!"

She didn't seem to hear him. She was racing toward her little car, and even though he shouted for her to stop, she just kept going.

She jumped inside the small VW convertible. He saw the headlights flash on.

Dammit.

Dane leapt in front of her car, knowing the headlights would shine right on him. "*Katherine, stop!*"

The car's engine revved.

He held up his hands. "Stop."

The motor died away.

Slowly, Dane crept around the car. "Open the door." He knew she could hear him.

After the smallest of hesitations, she did.

"What happened?" he asked. She'd said she wouldn't run, but the woman sure seemed to be hauling ass.

She climbed from the car—and threw her arms around him. Katherine held tight to him, felt right against him, and Dane found himself wrapping his arms around her.

Pulling her even closer.

Her hair brushed against his nose, bringing him more of her scent, and her body pressed perfectly against his.

"Katherine…" He took a breath, almost tasted her. "What's going on?"

She tilted her head back to stare up at him, and, with the moonlight shining down on them, Dane saw the glint of tears in her lashes. "He gave me his heart," she said.

The shrink asshole? Or *Valentine*? He knew Valentine had been wild for her.

She swallowed. "Not *his* heart, though, is it? It's hers. The bastard left it on my stairs."

Understanding hit him. *Fuck.* He yanked out his phone. Called instantly for backup even as he kept a strong hold on Katherine. *Not getting away from me.* "What did you see?" he demanded as he waited for the line to connect. Maybe she was wrong. Maybe—

"A box was on my stairs inside. The third step," she whispered. "I opened it. Rose petals were inside. Rose petals and a picture." She drew in a ragged breath. "It was a photograph of Savannah's chest with a knife driven into her heart."

He glanced back at the house. The seemingly perfect house.

The call finally connected. He immediately barked, "This is Detective Dane Black. I need a team out at two-oh-one Byron West, and I need 'em fucking *now*."

His gaze darted around the darkened woods. *No one close to hear the screams.*

If he'd just stayed at her house instead of following after Katherine like a lovesick teen with a hard-on, he would've had the killer.

Had him.

But maybe the bastard had left evidence behind that they could use. Something that could help him track the guy.

"It's him," Katherine said, her voice a bit stronger now. "He wants me to know *it's him.*"

Dane had read more of the Valentine files before going to Katherine's. He knew Valentine had taken pictures of his victims. Pictures of their dead bodies, with knives driven into their hearts. Then he'd delivered the stark black-and-white photos. One had gone to a victim's parents. One to her lover. One to the FBI.

This time, the delivery had been made to Katherine.

He twined his fingers through hers. "Come with me." He had to search the scene. The killer could still be in her house.

"No, I can't go back in—"

"And I can't leave you alone out here!" Leaving her unprotected was not an option he would take.

She swallowed and straightened her shoulders. "Right."

He pulled out his gun and tightened his fingers around hers. "Stay with me. Every step, got it?"

A slow nod. "Got it."

He stalked toward the house. Her front door hung open, and light spilled onto the porch. Katherine was a silent shadow behind him.

He went in first, doing a sweep and keeping his gun up and ready. He saw the long-stemmed roses on her stairs, with the white box dropped next to them. Scattered rose petals trailed over the floor. He didn't open the box. No sense contaminating the scene any further, and Katherine—she didn't need to see that photograph again.

They swept the bottom floor first. Dane made sure his body guarded Katherine at all times. Into one room. Another.

No sign of an intruder. Nothing broken. Nothing disturbed.

Just a deadly present left behind.

Carefully they eased up the stairs. Two rooms waited up there. The first was filled with canvases, art supplies. Dark splashes of color—they almost looked like blood—coated the stark white canvases.

The second room—it was her bedroom. The scent of strawberries was stronger there. The four-poster bed waited inside. Her clothes hung perfectly in her closet. Her small bathroom shone with clean precision.

Again, no sign of the intruder.

At least, no sign he could see. Maybe the crime-scene team would have better luck.

The bastard's not in the house.

But that didn't mean the perp had left the scene.

Dane took Katherine back outside. They'd conducted the search in near silence. She'd been so close to him, her body had brushed against his with almost every step they'd taken.

On the porch, his gaze tracked along the line of trees. There were too many places to hide out there.

Dane wanted to race into the trees and find out if the bastard was still out there, hiding and watching, but he knew that keeping Katherine safe was the main priority. He couldn't leave her, and in the dark woods, he wouldn't be able to protect her.

So he kept her close, using his body as a shield, and he waited for his backup to arrive.

I'll find you, bastard. I'll stop you.

– – –

Shaking hands clenched into tight fists.

The detective wasn't part of the plan. *He* shouldn't be there. This wasn't about him.

It was about Katherine.

Rage built, *built…*

Katherine had been so afraid. She'd run, nearly tripping and slamming into the ground as she fled from her house.

This time, she couldn't pretend to bury her nose in the sand and ignore the death around her. This time, it would be up close and personal for her.

Every attack, every kill, every heart…*for Katherine.*

She wouldn't be able to act like her hands were clean anymore.

They'd never been clean.

Police sirens howled in the distance.

Time to go. Time to start hunting again.

The kill had been so easy. The rush better than sex. Life and death. Power and pleasure.

Pain. Fear. Release.

More, please.

The fun was just beginning.

— — —

Police cars raced onto the scene. Dane stepped away from Katherine. Almost immediately, she missed the warmth and security of his body.

She saw his partner emerge from a blue SUV. Uniformed cops swarmed the scene.

"There's a package on the stairs." Dane's voice rang out. "Don't contaminate it. We want the crime-scene guys getting it in *pristine* condition."

And the crime-scene unit was already there. She saw them piling out and pulling on their gloves.

"You searched the scene?" Dane's partner demanded as he loped toward the house.

"The house is clear, Mac," Dane said, but he pointed to the dark trees. "As for the rest of the place..."

"Let's get teams searching the woods!" Mac's order snapped out like a whip, and the uniforms scrambled to obey.

Dane grabbed the nearest uniform. Then he pointed at Katherine. "Watch her, got me? Make sure you stay with her, every damn second."

He was leaving her? She blinked. "Dane..."

But he was already heading toward the woods. Going after Valentine.

The uniform took up his position beside her, his body trembling a bit. "Did you—" he began, but his voice broke. "Did you really find a box from the killer, ma'am?" Sick fascination.

Don't feel. Don't think. "Yes, I did." She recognized the box and the message it conveyed. The box *and* the flowers.

He wasn't going to stop on his own, she knew that. He'd *told* her that.

I can't stop. I have to kill. You understand...

She kept her eyes on Dane as he headed into the darkness.

No, I don't understand. I never will.

Valentine might think she was his soul mate, but they were nothing alike.

Nothing.

She wouldn't let herself be like him.

— — —

CYNTHIA EDEN

Katherine sat in the back of the patrol car and watched as the evidence team *finally* came out of her house with the white box and the roses bagged for evidence.

She turned her gaze away. The other uniforms were piling into their vehicles, and the blue lights no longer lit up the scene. They hadn't found Valentine.

"What are you doing in there?" Dane's voice. "Dammit," he said to the uniform—her guard—who stood close by. "I told you to watch her, not to shove her into a patrol car!"

"It's okay, Dane," she said with a sigh. She was still in her cocktail dress, and the headache that fear had scared away before was back now, pounding like a drum in her temples. "I asked if I could sit in here." She slid her legs out of the car. Showed the high heels she still wore. "My feet were killing me."

His gaze dropped to her legs. "You're comin' with me," he told her, and his stare slowly rose to lock on hers.

Her brows lifted. "To the station? Tonight?" They'd been searching her property for *hours*. She'd been interviewed over and over again by Dane's partner. She'd told him every detail about her discovery.

Dane caught her arm and pulled her from the car. "I'm not taking you to the station."

There was a tightness to his mouth that hadn't been there before.

"He was in your house." He clenched his jaw as he said this. "If he'd wanted, he could have stayed inside and attacked you when you came home."

Valentine had never attacked her. "He never hurt me," she whispered.

"Before he didn't, but how the hell do any of us know what he's going to do now? Every report I read said he was psychotic and that he was totally fixated on you."

44

She flinched. She didn't want to think about that. Because if she did, then she'd feel the guilt again. So much guilt that it seemed to choke her some days.

"He targeted you tonight, and you are damn well getting police protection."

Did he think she'd refuse? She wasn't the crazy one. Despite what one of the profilers back in Boston had believed.

"Until we catch this bastard, I'm making sure that you have someone watching you, twenty-four seven." His eyes were lit with a stark intensity.

"Am I supposed to argue?" Katherine whispered. "I want him stopped. I want all of this to end." She'd told him that before. If they could catch Valentine, then she might be able to sleep through a night, just once, without the nightmares waking her.

"Good." He gave a grim nod. "Because your protection is starting right now." A brief pause, and the heat in his gaze seemed to burn brighter. "And you're gonna be spending the night with me."

- 4 -

"I thought you said that you had an extra room." Katherine's gaze swept around the small condo. She could see a kitchen. A den. And then…just one door that seemed to lead to a darkened bedroom.

She glanced over at Dane. Dark stubble lined his jaw. His hand rubbed across the stubble, rasping slightly. "I might have exaggerated on that," he said.

Katherine stared back at him. "Did you now?"

"Don't worry, I'll take the couch." He offered her a tired smile. "I do know how to play the gentleman."

Had she asked him to play a role? She didn't like it when a man pretended to be someone he wasn't. She'd rather see the frog, warts and all, than ever think she was with a Prince Charming again.

"Sorry you couldn't get any clothes from your place," Dane told her. His gaze was so watchful. She knew the guy was trying to figure her out.

Good luck with that.

"But the techs wanted to be thorough."

Right. Because her home was a crime scene once again.

Katherine kicked out of her high heels. Her toes curled into the thick carpet. The condo was nice, clean, and dominated by a flat-screen TV. The guy had to be a Marlins fan. She could see one wall was decorated with caps and a signed bat.

It was odd being in a man's place again. It was the first time since Boston that she'd actually gone inside a man's home. She hadn't even ever visited Trent's apartment.

"You can borrow one of my shirts for tonight." He eased past her and headed into the darkened bedroom. Katherine followed him. The carpet muffled their footsteps. "I'm sure the techs will have clothes for you by morning," he added.

"Or I'll just buy something." She kept her voice calm. She'd been doing her best to hold onto her self-control ever since she'd found the package waiting for her. *Don't think about it. Don't see that poor woman.*

But she knew the image would stay with her. She never forgot any of Valentine's victims. He wouldn't let her.

Dane was rummaging around in a drawer, and he pulled out an old T-shirt. THE MARINES. She blinked. "I didn't realize you were a military guy." The hair that brushed his shoulders sure hadn't clued her in. But the alpha attitude, yeah, that seemed to fit.

"Semper Fi," he murmured as he tossed her the shirt. "Uncle Sam paid for my college."

She caught the shirt, her fingers closing around the soft fabric. "In the marines...is that where you got the tattoo?"

He smiled faintly. "Yeah. I guess you could call it an initiation, of sorts." He lifted his sleeve to show her the twisting lines of a snake. "It's to remind me that danger's out there. And you need to be ready for it to strike at any time."

She didn't need any reminder for that. "Valentine...he was also in the military." Michael had even gotten medals for bravery. He'd seemed to be such a good, honorable guy.

He'd taught her just how false appearances could truly be.

Dane lowered the sleeve. "Take the bed," he told her, voice deepening as he closed in on her. "I'll bunk down on the couch." His body brushed against hers as he headed for the door.

At that light touch, she tensed, and her breath seemed to freeze in her lungs. Why was she so intensely aware of this man?

Her gaze lifted to meet his stare. His pupils were so big that his eyes looked almost black. And, suddenly, she had to ask the question that fear had made her forget before. "Why were you waiting outside my house tonight?" She wondered...had he been there to protect her? Or because he suspected her?

"I knew you were tied to my case." He lifted his shoulders in a small shrug. "So I wanted to keep an eye on you. Make sure you were safe."

Safe. That word again. She hadn't felt safe in a long time. "So you were just waiting at my house? You didn't see the killer come?"

His jaw hardened. "I wasn't at your house all night. I...followed you."

Her heartbeat kicked up. "Me and Trent?"

"Um, yeah. I followed you and the boyfriend."

"He's not my boyfriend."

"Does he know that?" A hard edge had entered his voice. "Didn't seem that way when he put his hands on you."

He'd seen that, too? *He'd been watching.* "We ended things tonight. Before I..."

"Before you found the little gift?"

A jerky nod. "Trent and I aren't what he wants us to be," Katherine said. Then, because she found that she could be truthful with Dane, while she felt she had to keep on her mask with so many other people, she added, "*I'm* not what he wants *me* to be."

"What does he want you to be?"

She glanced at the door. *Normal.* Hardly the type of thing she wanted to confess. "I think we should say good night."

The floor creaked beneath his shifting feet. "If that's what you want..."

No, what she wanted was to be normal. To be just like everyone else. *Not going to happen.*

She was barely holding onto her control, and she just needed to be alone for a while. Katherine didn't like for anyone to see her break.

He headed toward the door, then hesitated. "Will you have nightmares?"

Didn't she always? "I'll stay quiet."

Dane looked over his shoulder. "That's not really an answer, is it?"

"I don't have nightmares." She told the lie in a quiet voice. Then, because she had to say it, Katherine told him, "I know what you want."

His gaze dipped over her. A careful mask concealed his expression. "Do you?"

"You want to use me."

His gaze returned to her face. A banked heat lit the blue of his eyes, but he didn't speak.

She swallowed. "To catch Valentine. You're going to use me."

"Careful," he said, approaching her once more. His hand rose and curved under her chin. Her heart slammed into her ribs. This was the wrong time, the wrong place, but she was suddenly, intensely aware of the detective.

Aware of a man in a way that she hadn't been in a very long time.

Dane's eyes narrowed. "Your Boston just slipped out. You'd done so well at ditching it."

Her breath rushed out on a soft sigh. His touch was making her nervous when she already felt as if she were barely holding things together. She stepped away from him.

One brow rose as he noted her retreat.

"Good night, Dane."

After one last, unreadable stare, Dane backed quietly out of the room. The door shut behind him with a soft click. Katherine thought about locking the door. But she knew that locks weren't much good in this world. Real monsters knew how to get past most locks.

The monsters that always came for her sure did.

She stripped, put on Dane's shirt, then climbed into the bed. King-sized, it smelled of him. A slightly woody, masculine scent. The sheets were soft against her, faintly cool.

She closed her eyes.

And saw the dead coming for her.

– – –

Dane opened the bedroom door. The hinges squeaked quietly, but the woman lying in the bed didn't stir. Faint rays of light spilled through the blinds, onto his bed. *Onto her.*

Long, slender legs. Legs that seemed to stretch for miles.

Her head was turned toward the door, her thick lashes closed.

He'd stayed awake for a while last night, alert to every rustle from his room. It would only have been normal for her to have nightmares after the little gift she'd received, but Katherine had kept her word. She hadn't made a sound.

But had she stayed quiet because no nightmares came to her? Or because she knew better than to cry out?

He took a step toward her. The groan of the floor wasn't so quiet beneath his foot, and her eyelids flew open. He saw the fear in her gaze, confusion, but then her golden eyes swept around the room. Her breath panted out for a moment, and then she whispered, "It happened."

If by "it" she meant that her ex had come to town and started killing, then yes, that had happened.

She was wearing his shirt. The faded fabric had never looked so good.

Dane cleared his throat. "Sorry to wake you, but I, um, made some breakfast so I wanted you to eat while it was warm." As a rule, he *never* made breakfast for anyone. That would be why the eggs were so runny, but he'd tried.

She blinked. "You cooked for me?"

He'd never blushed in his life. A good thing, or his cheeks would have stained right then. "It's nothing fancy. Just eggs and orange juice. I figured you could use something to help you get going today."

She still had confusion in her eyes, but the fear had faded away. "Thank you." Katherine rose from the bed. He cast one more look at her legs—*gorgeous*—then forced himself to turn away from her.

She followed behind him with soft steps. He'd even managed to set the table for her. Her eyes widened when she saw the plates and napkins. Why the huge shock? Hell, he wasn't that bad of a host.

Okay, he usually was.

But this was different.

He pulled out a chair for her. She eased down into it with a murmur of appreciation. And the lady was even champ enough to eat his runny eggs without complaint.

He sat across from her and wondered where in the hell he should start. He'd handled things the wrong way with her at the beginning. When she'd first come into the station, he'd been too harsh. He was lucky she hadn't hauled ass out of town.

And when the marshal found out about last night's little visit, the guy would be pushing once more for her to leave.

I have to keep her in New Orleans.

Because she was the key to the case. The killer had found her in New Orleans. He'd left the package for her, drawing her into his sick little game.

"You aren't eating," Katherine said quietly.

He blinked. Realized that, yeah, he'd just been staring at her. Dane quickly shoveled some eggs into his mouth. They tasted like shit.

How was she eating them?

Then he realized…*she just doesn't want to hurt my feelings.* Huh. Who'd ever cared about that before? He put his fork down. "You can stop," he said.

Too late. She'd already emptied her plate.

Now she sat back and watched him, her eyes giving no hint of her emotions.

His kitchen table wasn't exactly a prime interrogation spot, but he didn't want to question her like a suspect. He just wanted to understand her. "Why do you think he came after you?"

"Because he said that he'd never let me go."

Cold words. Brittle.

"Valentine said that I fit him. That he needed me." Her fingers drummed on the table. "He said that without me, he wouldn't be able to survive."

"When did he tell you all this?" This bit hadn't been in the case files that Sean Hobbs had sent to him.

"He told me while I stood in the basement of my home and stared at Stephanie Gilbert's body. The police were on the way, he had Stephanie's blood on him, and I thought he was about to kill me."

Every muscle in Dane's body locked down. He'd heard the story of her entering her home, finding blood, calling 911...then discovering that her fiancé wasn't the one who was injured.

By the time the cops had arrived on-scene, Valentine had been gone. Katherine—no, *Katelynn*—had been huddled on the floor of the basement, in shock.

"Did he try to hurt you that day?" He kept his question quiet and calm, choking back his own emotions.

"No, he never hurt me." Her gaze held his. "That's the part no one understood, right? He was a sadistic killer, but he never so much as even bruised my skin. I was with him...we were engaged for a year. A whole year."

And she hadn't known that a killer was in bed with her.

The doorbell rang then, and Katherine jumped at the pealing sound. "Easy," Dane said as he rose. He was wearing a loose pair of jogging pants, and he sure hadn't been expecting company at six a.m.

Because he was a suspicious bastard by nature—and because he was lead on a case that was linked to the biggest serial-killer investigation currently running in the United States—he damn well took time to grab his gun before he headed to the door. But a quick glance through the peephole showed him that a perp didn't wait on the other side of that door. Mac was there.

Dane opened the door. "What's happened?" And why hadn't Mac just called him instead of paying a dawn visit?

Mac shoved a newspaper into Dane's chest as he pushed into the condo. "Another damn leak, that's what hap—" Mac broke off as his gaze centered on Katherine—Katherine who looked sleep-tousled and sexy and seemed only to be wearing Dane's shirt. *'Cause she pretty much was.*

"I—uh...didn't expect that," Mac muttered.

Katherine leapt to her feet. "I didn't have anything else to wear."

Dane slammed the front door shut behind his partner.

Mac was looking at the table. The remains of breakfast. He fired a quick glance at Dane. "You cooked?"

Dane glared at him, but then his gaze dropped to the paper. To the headline that screamed at him:

Valentine Killer Leaves Grisly Gift.

Shit.

He scanned the article as his heart raced. This was the last thing he wanted. Didn't the press get it? The city didn't need to be in a panic. Panic just made it harder for the cops to do their job.

The reporter hadn't revealed Katherine's identity, and he could only hope it was because the reporter didn't know who she really was. But someone had sure gone to the press fast with this big reveal.

Too fast. The captain was gonna be spitting nails.

"The press doesn't know who she is," Mac said as he inclined his head toward Katherine, "but I think it's safe enough to say that our killer certainly does."

She stood behind her chair, her fingers curved over its back. Dane saw her knuckles whiten.

"Is he a copycat?" Mac asked her. "Or the real deal?"

Katherine's eyes widened in surprise. "A copycat?"

"How many people in New Orleans know who you really are?" Mac pressed. "We're gonna need all the names. Maybe someone got close to you *because* of who you really are. Maybe that person is killing—"

Katherine started to laugh. But the sound was cold and hollow. "What? You think I can only attract killers?"

Dane winced. Mac had never been a smooth one with the ladies.

Then Katherine shook her head. "You two know my identity. Ross knows. And my ex-shrink knows." She shrugged. "No one else. When you've got a past like mine, you aren't exactly eager to share it with the world."

Dane folded the newspaper and advanced toward her. "What about the boyfriend? He doesn't know?"

"I didn't want him to know." Her lips pressed together. "When you're dating, you don't always want your significant other to look at you like you're some kind of freak."

He sure wasn't looking at her like that.

"This isn't a copycat," Katherine said. "The cuts on the victim's arms...the *roses*...only Valentine knew that."

Dane knew his whole body had tensed. "What about the roses?" There had been eleven left at Katherine's house last night.

"Roses were my favorite," she whispered. "Valentine knew that. What I didn't know until after was that he gave me roses when he made a kill."

His heart was beating faster. Another bit of evidence that had never made the news. More confirmation that this was no copycat. It was the real fucking deal.

"It looked like a dozen..." Her lips twisted in a humorless smile. "When you see a bunch of flowers, how many people actually count to see if twelve are there? I count now, I always do."

Mac swore, obviously realizing, just as Dane did, where this was going.

"Eleven for me. One for his victim. And the roses came in perfect time with his kills." She raked a hand through her tousled hair. "When I found Stephanie that last day—he already had the roses waiting on the table for me."

And roses had been waiting for Katherine last night.

Real. Fucking. Deal.

"I'm...ah...going to get dressed now." She backed out of the kitchen with uncertain steps. "Do you know when I'll be able to go home again?"

Mac glanced at Dane. Dane opened his mouth to respond, but it was Mac who said, "I'm afraid we need you to come down to the station, ma'am."

Her face fell. "Right." Almost whisper quiet. "Of course you do." Then she turned away and slipped into the bedroom. The door closed with a soft squeak behind her.

Dane sighed and glanced over at Mac—and he found his partner glaring at him. "What?"

"Did you screw her?" Mac's voice was hushed. "Dammit, man, we *need* her!"

And Mac *needed* to watch that tone. Dane closed in on him. "I kept her safe for the night. I kept my eyes on her." Just like he was supposed to do. The captain had given him orders that Katherine wasn't to slip town, so he'd made sure that he was between her and any exit door.

"But did you keep your hands off her?" Mac tossed at him. "She was wearing your shirt! And it sure looked like you were having a cozy breakfast for two!"

Dane's back teeth locked. "Sorry—should I have put her in handcuffs?"

Mac swore. "Knowing you, that would have been foreplay." Snapped but quiet.

Dane glared at him. "Watch it."

Mac exhaled and rubbed a hand over his tired face. "I'm just saying we *need* her." Mac glanced toward the closed bedroom door. "We need to stay on that woman's very good side until we can figure out our plan of attack."

Dane already had a plan of attack. Find the killer. Lock him up. Make sure the jerk never hurt another woman again.

Simple enough.

"Some FBI profiler is flying in. Captain told him about Katherine, and the guy wants to talk to her."

Dane nodded. He'd make sure he was there for those questions. Actually, until the case was closed, he planned to stay as close as possible to Katherine.

He'd learn all of her secrets, and he'd use those secrets to catch Valentine.

– – –

So she'd spent the night with the cop.

Katherine walked out of the entrance to the building that housed the detective's condo. She was wearing the same wrinkled dress she'd worn the night before, and looking for all the world like she'd spent hours screwing.

She didn't deserve to be special. She didn't deserve the attention she'd gotten.

Katherine was weak, pathetic, so easily dominated by her fear.

She should die like the others. Crying. Helpless. In agony. She *would* die that way.

It just wasn't her time…not yet.

Someone else had already been selected to be the next kill. A woman with hair as dark as Katherine's. A woman with a smile as lying. A woman who also deserved the pain that she had coming.

Katherine could wait a while. She could enjoy the time with her new lover—because that time would be fleeting. One more kill, then Katherine would get to face the knife.

No escape this time, Kat. You won't be so lucky anymore.

57

- 5 -

The bull pen quieted the minute Katherine walked in. It wasn't even one of those gradual hushes that can happen as folks elbow each other and point to an object of attention. It was just utter and complete silence.

Katherine stiffened beside Dane, and his hold automatically tightened on her arm. She wasn't showing any fear, but he could feel the slight tremble that shook her body.

"What the hell?" he snapped at the cops in the bull pen. "I know you bozos have cases to work."

And, of course, everyone started talking again and trying to look busy, when really their attention was totally on Katherine.

"It's okay," she said, giving Dane a weak smile. "This isn't the first time I've been the freak in the room."

"You're *not* a freak." She was beautiful. Fragile. And in a body-hugging dress that showed all of her perfect curves.

She also had a spine that he was coming to realize was pure steel. Because she was already pulling away from him and glancing around the bull pen.

"Where do I head for interrogation?" Katherine asked.

Before he could respond, Dane saw a familiar face across the bull pen.

"Oh, now it's a party," Katherine said. "But I did expect him to show sooner."

The U.S. marshal had beaten them to the station and was storming across the big room. In seconds Anthony Ross was in front of them, and he grabbed for Katherine's wrist. "You should have called me." His voice burned with censure and heat. "I would have come to you immediately."

Dane put a hand on the guy's shoulder. "You're gonna need to ease back and watch that tone."

Ross blinked at him. "What?"

"I said back the hell off." He didn't want the marshal messing up *his* case.

Frowning, Ross released Katherine and backed up.

"Anthony..." Katherine sighed out his name. "Detective Black was already at the scene when I found the..." She cleared her throat. "He was there. He called in backup, and he made sure I was safe last night."

Ross's green gaze narrowed. "And just why was the cop there?"

Dane didn't like that suspicious tone. "Because she's tied to my case, and someone needed to keep an eye on her," he said, casting a disdainful glance Ross's way. "Since you weren't doing your job, Marshal, I thought I'd step in."

"I gave her a new identity," Ross said through gritted teeth. A muscle jerked in his jaw. "A new name, a new home. I got her away from Boston."

"But you didn't keep that identity secret, did you?" And that was why they had a dead body in the morgue. "Someone screwed up—either you or someone in your department—and the killer found her again."

Ross's angry gaze slanted back to Katherine. Dane knew every cop in the area was straining to hear as Ross said, "Kat, I can have you out of this town within the hour. No one will follow you. You don't have to worry about Valentine."

That would pretty much wreck Dane's plans. Katherine was bait for Valentine, and if they were going to lure the guy in, then they needed her.

Dane saw the captain heading toward them. The guy needed to move faster. Dane knew the last thing that Harley wanted was for the marshal to spirit Katherine away.

Then Katherine said, voice firm, "I told you already, Ross. I'm *not* leaving." Her shoulders were tense. "If I can stop more women from dying, then I'm doing it. I've got enough blood on my hands."

Hell yes. *Spine of steel.* Beneath skin of silk.

Dane bared his teeth in a tiger's smile for Ross. "Guess that means you're out of your jurisdiction, then. If a witness doesn't want protection from your department…"

"Do you want her dead?" Ross snapped at him. "Are you so eager to close this case that you'd risk her life?"

The bastard had just pushed too far. Dane stepped forward.

But then Katherine said, "It's my life to risk." She pointed toward the open interrogation room. "I suppose that's my space? Excuse me, gentlemen." She walked by them, her chin held high. "You can finish your little argument without me."

Mac smothered a laugh as he hurried over and followed her inside the room. He shut the door, sealing them both inside.

Dane was going to join them, but first, hell yeah, he'd finish this "little argument." He locked eyes with the marshal. "This isn't a pissing contest."

Ross didn't blink. "Good. 'Cause I don't need to piss."

Dane almost smiled. Under other circumstances, he might like the guy. Maybe. "That woman can help me find the killer."

"That *woman* is living on nerves and fear. She can't help you."

How could the guy not know her at all? Ross had been working with her for three years, but Dane felt like he knew Katherine so much better than the marshal did after just a day.

"You're just making her a target," Ross continued, his voice roughening, "and I'm the one who'll have to bury her body." His lips twisted. "Because there's no one else left. She's already lost everyone else who cared about her. Valentine made sure she had no one."

Dane frowned. He hadn't realized how truly alone Katherine was.

"He isolated her. He used her. And, eventually," Ross said, with a sad shake of his head, "he would have killed her."

Dane started to respond.

"I'm afraid you're wrong, Marshal," a new voice said. It was a slightly nasal voice, one belonging to a thin man who'd followed Harley across the room. The guy was in his late twenties, with curly brown hair, and he wore a rumpled, dark gray suit.

"Aw, hell, now the head case expert is here," Ross muttered as he ran a rough hand through his close-cropped hair.

The newcomer frowned at him. "Nice to see you again, too, Marshal."

"Captain." Dane jerked his head in a nod, ready for the intro with this guy. But he already had a pretty good idea who'd just joined their little party.

"This is FBI agent Marcus Wayne," Harley said with a wave of his hand. "He flew down—"

"As soon as I heard the details of Savannah Slater's death," Marcus cut in, speaking quickly. "I wanted to be on-scene immediately."

Wasn't that grand. "Are the feds taking over?" Dane bluntly asked his captain.

The lines near Harley's thin lips deepened. "This is *our* case. No state lines have been crossed, no multiple homicides. As far as I'm concerned, we're looking at a simple murder. Twisted, brutal, but *ours.*"

The captain was territorial about his cases. Good. So was Dane.

But Marcus shook his head. "I'm afraid there's nothing simple about this case. Either you gentlemen have got the real deal—and if you do, then you'll need me—or you've got a copycat who's out to grab some of Valentine's headlines."

"I really didn't need a fed to tell me that," Dane muttered, aggravated. He'd been working as a cop for more than ten years. "We might be a bit slow on some things down in the South, but we know murder."

"And *I* know murder." Marcus stretched to his full height. About five foot seven inches. "I know Valentine. I've studied his case inside and out. I can help you."

Or he could get in the way.

For now, Dane would be forced to wait and see how things played out.

Marcus glanced over at Ross. "I'm surprised you haven't been reassigned." He paused. "Or did you insist on staying with the case?"

Ross didn't answer.

Marcus glanced back at Dane. His assessing gaze didn't make Dane nervous. It irritated him. He was irritated even more when the guy rather pompously said, "Detective, you know I'll want to talk to her."

"The way you talked to her three years ago?" Ross cut in. "You *know* the woman hates your guts, man."

This was just getting better and better. "We're trying to get Katherine's cooperation here," Dane said, "not alienate her more." And if Katherine didn't like the profiler...

But Marcus shook his head. "You don't understand her. She isn't a victim."

"Oh, for the love of—" Ross threw his hands into the air. "Just because Valentine didn't slice her up," Ross snapped, "it doesn't mean the prick didn't hurt her. I've been there. I've heard the screams from her nightmares."

But she hadn't screamed last night. Dane wasn't sure if that meant her nightmares had stopped or if she'd just learned not to scream.

"People scream for all kinds of reasons," Marcus said, his nasal voice irritating the shit out of Dane. "And I've wondered for a few years now...what gets to her?"

Dane's gaze met the captain's. The bureau had seriously sent this prick down to them? They must have better profilers. Somewhere.

"I *know* Valentine," Marcus said, his voice cracking. "Give me a chance, and I'll prove it."

The captain nodded even as he avoided Dane's gaze. "You have your chance, but if you do anything to jeopardize this case, I'll personally kick your ass all the way back up to D.C."

Blinking rapidly, Marcus nodded. Then he hurried toward the interrogation room.

Before Dane could follow him, Ross grabbed his arm. "Watch him," Ross warned.

Dane lifted a brow.

"Three years ago, Marcus Wayne was convinced that Valentine had an accomplice in his crimes."

An accomplice? That was news to Dane.

"His superiors thought the theory was BS, as did all the cops on the case. So Wayne got bumped from superstar profiler down to desk jockey." Ross's gaze was glued to Marcus's back. "Want to know just who he thought that accomplice was?"

Hell.

"Katelynn," Ross said softly.

The captain swore. "I think I need to get ready for some ass-kicking."

Dane shook his head. "It will be my pleasure, Captain." If anyone got to toss that guy out, it would be Dane. But first he asked, "If his theory is shit, then why is he back on the case?" Why the hell had the FBI brass sent the guy down to New Orleans?

"Because the guy has connections in the FBI, strings that he no doubt pulled to get down here," Ross answered. "*And* he's the only profiler who has spent three straight years poring over Valentine's life."

Dane's brows climbed. "Even when he wasn't officially on the case?"

"The guy's like a bulldog. He doesn't give up, and yeah, you need to take that as a warning."

He would. Dane turned away from Ross and hurried into the interrogation room.

— — —

The woman didn't even know she was in danger. She walked out of her apartment. Took the elevator down to the parking garage. And never even glanced up from her phone.

Too busy texting.

Too busy to be afraid.

Her mistake.

Most of her neighbors had already cleared out for the day. Too bad for Amy Evans—she was running late.

She thought she was alone.

Her keys slipped from her fingers. Hit the cement floor of the parking garage. She swore and finally stopped texting. She bent down and swiped up her keys.

She was making this too easy. Five steps, just five, and Amy was close enough to touch.

One, two, three, four…

Amy never even had the chance to scream. Her body slumped forward on the ground. Her head slammed into the cement.

Amy's dark hair had fallen over her face. Such lovely, thick hair.

Hair just like Katherine's.

No, she hadn't been given the chance to scream. Not then. But there would be plenty of time for screams later.

- - -

When Katherine saw Marcus Wayne enter the interrogation room, she felt her heart stop.

His eyes were the same small, beady brown that she remembered. Judging eyes. Suspicious eyes.

Plenty of others had been suspicious of her before, especially once they learned who she was, but Marcus had been the only one to ever just flat-out say, *I think you're a killer, and, sooner or later, I'll prove it.*

He didn't buy that she hadn't known the truth about Valentine. He said she fit the profile too well.

She knew just what the guy could do with his profiles. She might not have any fancy degrees, but she'd spent the last three years doing her own research.

You're wrong. I'm not a killer. And I'll prove it.

"Hello, Kat," Marcus said as he came into the room and pulled out the chair across from her. "You're looking well."

Kat. She knew he'd used the name deliberately. With him, everything was deliberate. "And you're looking the same, Marcus." Same stuffed shirt. Same narrow view that only he was right.

He cleared his throat. "I'm going to be working with your detectives on this case. I thought we could all begin by going over Valentine's profile."

Was she supposed to believe that she was one of the team?

Katherine glanced up as Dane came into the room, but she couldn't read anything past the veil of his eyes. His partner was still in the room, leaning against a wall with his arms crossed. She had no clue what Mac was thinking. *Mac.* He'd told her to call him that when he'd entered the interrogation room. He'd seemed friendly.

Now Marcus was trying the friendly routine with her, too.

The atmosphere just made her more tense.

Then Marcus began to talk.

"Michael O'Rourke is highly intelligent, charming, and without any sense of remorse or compassion," he said flatly. "He's a chameleon. He can blend, mixing perfectly in nearly any situation—and has. He graduated at the top of his college class. Did a stint in the military—picked up demolitions training with his unit—and even received a Purple Heart when he was injured while saving two men on his team in Afghanistan."

A hero. A killer.

"He saved men?" Mac asked, his brows wrinkling. "Why the hell would he do that if the guy just gets off on killing?"

"Because those men didn't fit his victim type," Marcus answered. "They weren't the ones he was going after." A pause. "But being around that level of violence, I believe, encouraged the darker instincts within Michael."

He came toward me, flashing a wide smile. "Hi, I'm Michael. Michael O'Rourke." His eyes were so green. "And I think I'm in love."

"To truly understand him, we have to look at Michael's origins."

Katherine fought to keep her breathing slow and steady.

"Michael O'Rourke grew up in a single-parent home. His mother was a drug addict who sold her body whenever she needed some cash. She generally forgot about her son, and when she did remember him, she spent her time slapping him around."

That didn't match up with the story Michael had originally told her...

My mother? She died when I was just six. Such a beautiful lady, inside and out. She had the biggest smile...but one night, a man came for her. He attacked her in an alley. She was just going to get groceries for us. He was high on drugs. He killed her quickly, so she didn't suffer—or at least that's what the cops told me.

"When he was twelve, Michael's mother overdosed. He was the one who found her body."

Her funeral was beautiful. So many flowers. Roses were her favorites, too. She loved them just like you do. I like to think she was smiling down from heaven when she saw those roses.

"No father was ever in the picture," Marcus continued. His nasal tone was like nails on a chalkboard. "I doubt his mother even knew his name."

My father took care of me until I was nineteen. Then he passed away. A heart attack. But if you ask me, I think his heart stopped the day my mother died. He loved her so much...as much as I love you, Kat.

Her palms flattened on the smooth surface of the table. She'd believed everything Michael had said about his life. Why doubt him? Falling for him had been so easy.

Because he'd been perfect.

"Michael O'Rourke probably began torturing and killing animals when he was a small child."

She remembered how Michael had seen a man kicking a dog one day and rushed over. Stopped the man. Demanded, *"How would you like to be kicked?"*

He'd *never* liked to see animals hurt. Her eyes narrowed as she stared down at her hands and saw her memories.

"He is a sociopath. Not able to form any sort of lasting relationship with anyone or anything. He suffered so much abuse as a child that he now believes the only way humans actually express emotion is through abuse. So when he attacks his victims, he's both showing his control, his complete dominance over them, and he's also showing...well, the only emotion that he can."

Her back teeth ground together.

I love you, Kat. I didn't think it would be possible to care about someone the way I do for you. But you're different. You make me want to be better. To be someone else. His warm green eyes had stared into her own. *Marry me. Let's start over, together.*

"I suspect he originally approached Kat here..."

She flinched at the name. "*Don't* call me that."

"Is that because Michael did?" Marcus asked.

"You know he did."

"Just as I know he approached you because you fit his victim profile. You were the perfect victim for him. Right hair, right eyes, right age." He paused. "Right past."

Her gaze snapped to his. *Don't talk about that. Don't go there.* She would share what she knew about Valentine, but her own wounds—the wounds that had come long before she ever met Valentine—those weren't open for the world to poke and prod for their pleasure.

"The women he targeted were all damaged." Marcus's eyes weren't looking away from her. They were trying to look *into* her. "You could have been his perfect prey, but he didn't kill you. He didn't put you on his table. Didn't slice into your arms twenty-one times and then drive a knife into your chest—"

"*That's fucking enough.*" Dane had dropped his neutral expression. His gaze was blazing as he jerked Marcus's chair back. Marcus stumbled, nearly falling to the floor.

Katherine realized her chest was heaving. So much for her slow breathing technique. Her heart was pounding too fast.

"To understand Valentine, you have to know why he picked Katherine," Marcus insisted, tilting his head to study her. He was sweating. She could see the gleam of moisture on his temple. "I know why he picked you. You were his mirror. His perfect, broken mirror."

Dane grabbed the guy by the shirt. "The FBI actually sent you? Or did you just bribe someone up there?" He dragged the man toward the door. "Time to kick your ass back to D.C. You don't come into my precinct and start talking to her like that—"

"Because she makes you feel protective?" Marcus jerked free of his grasp. "She made Valentine feel that way too. He should have seen her as prey, but for some reason Kat's good at—"

"How many damn times does she have to tell you?" Dane snarled as he opened the door and shoved Marcus outside. "Her name is *Katherine*. Learn it, asshole." Then he slammed the door in the agent's face.

Katherine exhaled slowly. "Thank you."

Dane turned to face her. Mac hadn't moved. Maybe the guy was too shocked to move.

"I'm not real interested in what Agent Wayne has to say about Valentine," Dane said. "I want to know what *you* think. You're the one who knows him best."

If only. "I'm the one who never really knew him at all." Her nails—she always kept them short and unpainted—tapped on the tabletop. "But I'll tell you as much as I can." And, maybe this time, things would be different. Maybe Dane or Mac would pick up on some detail that she and the other cops had overlooked.

Maybe this time they would actually catch the bastard.

— — —

Marcus Wayne entered the small observation room. The police captain turned toward him, a glower on his face. "Smooth, Agent, real freaking smooth." The captain's jaw locked. "I want your ass out of my precinct."

"The purpose of my going in there wasn't to break Katherine Cole." *I know you hate being called Kat.* His gaze darted to the two-way mirror looking into the interrogation room. *Sorry about that, Katherine.*

"Then what was your purpose? To piss off Ms. Cole?"

"No, it was to bring out more of the detective's protective instincts." And those instincts had sure come out. "If Katherine is going to be of any help to us on this case, then she will have to trust Detective Black. Katherine isn't a woman who trusts easily." He was rather surprised that she could trust at all, given what had happened to her.

"Always playing your little mind games." The mutter came from behind him. The marshal. Marcus knew the guy was far from being a fan.

Marcus glanced over at him. "She'll talk more freely now. She'll tell Dane as much as possible because she sees me as the bad guy and him as her white knight." He didn't mind playing the bad cop. With his slight build and fresh face, it wasn't a role he got to play often. Pity.

"Maybe she'll just talk," Ross said, voice snapping, "because she wants to catch Valentine. She wants him off the streets just as badly as we do."

Marcus locked his jaw but didn't respond. Ross didn't get it. Katherine Cole was the safest woman in the world. Valentine could have sliced her and killed her a thousand times over. He hadn't.

She was special to the killer.

The trick—the real trick—was finding out *why* she was special. If she'd just trust the detective enough to let down her guard, then Marcus might finally be able to get inside Katherine's head and figure out how she'd managed to reach the heart of a sociopathic killer. A man who, for all psychological intents, should have no heart at all.

- 6 -

"I learned a lot about Valentine. After he vanished. I started putting all the puzzle pieces together so I could see the real man he was."

Dane sat across from Katherine. She was pale and perfect, seemingly an ice princess, but he knew the ice was just on the surface. And the ice was cracking.

He could also see the pain in her eyes. Hear it in her voice. The jerk from the bureau had pushed her too much. Stirred memories that had ripped into her.

I should have ripped into him.

When women were hurt in any way, his protective instincts became difficult to control.

"I've studied serial killers." Katherine's confession was hushed.

Dane glanced at Mac and saw that his partner had lifted his brows.

"When you realize you've been sleeping with one, you'll do anything to make sure you never get fooled again."

He had to unclench his fingers from the edge of the table. *Sleeping with one.* A surge of jealousy caught him by surprise.

"In some ways, I think he was like Bundy," she said. "So charming on the surface. So smooth. He always seemed to know just what to say or do in order to put people at ease."

That must have been how he'd lured in his prey. Back in Boston, he'd killed four women in all. Four women they knew about. Three before he met Katelynn Crenshaw, one after.

Her breath whispered out. "He told me once that I was his chance to be better." She looked down at her hands. "Valentine was a gifted artist. He could paint anything, sculpt anything. He could create so much beauty with his hands, but he seemed to be drawn to death." Her gaze rose once more. "That's why the marks with his knife were so precise. Not because he was a surgeon, which is what the cops in Boston first thought when they discovered the bodies, but because he was an artist."

The dead women might have been his art. His twisted art.

"Valentine was always punctual, never late for a date or a meeting, always well dressed, and he had perfect manners." Katherine lifted a shoulder in a weak shrug. "Some folks would say he was obsessive-compulsive, but maybe that's why he did such a good job of cleaning up the crime scenes."

"Except for the last one." Mac finally spoke as he stirred from his position near the wall.

"He didn't have a chance to clean up. I came home early." Her voice dropped. Dane saw the delicate movement of her throat as she swallowed. "And don't you know, I've asked myself a thousand times, what would have happened if I'd worked later? Would I be married to him?" Her fingers were trembling as she shoved back her hair. "Would he still be killing women who could have been me?"

Yes.

"Serial killers don't just stop. I learned that." She waved toward the interrogation mirror. "Agent Wayne, watching in there, he will tell you that. They can have dormant periods, but they never totally stop. They never stop unless they are *made* to stop."

– – –

Amy Evans was tied to the table. Duct tape covered her mouth. Her eyes were opening.

Her gaze quickly filled with terror. Helplessness. Tears.

The tears fell quickly. Behind the tape, Amy was moaning. Trying to talk. Trying to beg. Trying to plead for mercy.

But there would be no mercy for her.

The tip of the knife slid over her skin. The blade didn't cut her. Not yet, anyway. There was a pattern to the kills.

A method behind the madness.

The method had to be followed.

Amy had been stripped, and now the knife lifted to the middle of her chest. Carefully, still not breaking the skin, the knife eased over her flesh, creating the sloping pattern of a heart.

Amy thrashed. Struggled to get free. She was fighting more than expected.

"Don't make me rush."

The terror deepened in Amy's eyes.

The tip of the blade moved toward her left arm. Sliced into Amy's skin. Blood ran down her flesh.

There is a method…

Though not all murders are about madness.

— — —

"I know why the killer chose Savannah Slater."

Dane had left his chair and walked around the table to Katherine's side. At her quiet words, he tensed, then asked, "Why her?"

Her gaze slanted toward him, then Mac. "I didn't tell you at first because you both already suspected me."

Mac's right eyebrow climbed. Dane knew what the guy was thinking: *I still might.* That move was one of the guy's tells. After working together for almost ten years, the two had pretty much worked out the whole silent communication aspect of interrogations.

Katherine rolled her shoulders. "Savannah called me a few weeks ago."

Sonofabitch.

"She was working on a piece about the Valentine Killer. I don't know how she found me—I was supposed to be safe with my new identity—but she did. She wanted to interview me. Do some write-up about 'the other side of the killer.'" Her voice hardened. "I told her I wasn't interested in talking with her or any reporter. And I said she shouldn't ever call me again."

"*Did* she call you again?" Mac asked her.

Katherine gave a slow nod. "Yes."

Shit. "When?" Dane demanded.

Her gaze held his. "The day before you found her body."

Again, all he could think was…*sonofabitch.*

"I didn't answer her call. I recognized her number on my caller ID, but I didn't answer." Her shoulders straightened. "Do you think he had her then? Was he already killing her? If I'd answered, would I have been able to—"

The peal of a ringing cell phone cut through her words. She jumped. Mac swore.

And Dane got a real damn bad feeling in his gut.

Katherine fumbled and reached into the small purse near her feet. "I don't recognize the number. Sorry." She started to shove the phone back into her purse.

Dane took the phone from her and answered it. "This is Detective Dane Black."

Silence. The bad feeling twisted in his gut.

Then he heard a hiss of breath. A woman's scream.

Fuck. Fuck. Fuck. "Who the hell is this?"

Katherine froze.

"Kat—" A woman screamed. *"Make him stop!"*

Then the line went dead.

Mac hurried to his side. "Dane?"

But Dane was already moving. "We have to trace that call!" He hit the call-back button, but the line just rang, over and over again.

He burst out of the interrogation room. Harley and the FBI agent were rushing toward him.

"Who was on the phone?" the captain demanded.

His fingers were squeezing the phone too tightly. "I think it was Valentine's latest victim. A woman was screaming." His jaw locked as he revealed, "She asked Katherine to make him stop."

Ross followed behind the other men. "Savannah Slater was just found yesterday," he said. "There's no way—"

"Valentine waited months between kills," Wayne cut in. "He wouldn't attack like this, not so soon…unless something set him off."

"We've got to get a trace," Dane said. "Get the techs up here, get a track on the other phone's signal." *The woman was scream- ing…that means she's still alive.*

But she wouldn't be for long, unless they hauled ass much faster than this.

– – –

The phone was placed gently on the cement. "There, that wasn't so hard, was it? And you did so well."

Amy wasn't talking anymore. Tears had dried on her cheeks. Slices lined her arms. Eleven on the left. Ten on the right.

There was no hope in Amy's eyes. There'd been hope before, just a few minutes ago. Until they called Katherine together.

The tip of the knife slid over her chest. Amy's eyes were open. *No hope.*

"It's over now." The blade sank into Amy's heart. "At least, it is for you."

But not for Kat. Not yet.

The life faded from Amy's eyes. Such a beautiful sight.

The knife was wet with blood. So much blood.

There wasn't time to linger or to enjoy this work. A rose was carefully positioned in Amy's palm. Her fingers were forced closed around it.

The scene was set.

It wouldn't be much longer until the cops arrived. *I have to hurry if I want to get a good seat.* It was guaranteed to be one helluva show.

- - -

"That telephone number traced back to an Amy Evans." The captain's voice rang through the station. "She's thirty-one, brunette, dark eyes..."

A picture of Amy Evans was on the computer screen, being printed out, as Dane grabbed his keys and double-checked that his gun was holstered.

"Got the lock," the tech John Baylor said from a desk two feet away. "The signal is coming from two-oh-nine Jamestown Avenue."

The warehouse district.

The captain started barking orders, both to the men in the bull pen and to those listening on the police radio.

Dane rushed for the door, then hesitated for an instant as he glanced over his shoulder.

Katherine had inched toward the computer screen. She was staring at the image of Amy Evans, and Katherine looked lost and scared.

I'll save her. He didn't give Katherine those words, though, because it wasn't a promise he knew he could keep.

– – –

"I need to go with you." Katherine's voice was low, but when she spoke, the police captain immediately jerked his head toward her. Dane had already left, and Katherine knew the captain would be rushing out soon, too.

"Hell *no*," he barked at once. "I'm not sending you to a crime scene. You're too valuable to this case—"

"If the cops arrive in time," Marcus Wayne cut in, "and Valentine is there with his victim, Katherine could be the only one able to get through to him. He *called* her. Dane said the victim specifically asked for Kat to stop the killer." He nodded toward Katherine. "I'd say she's exactly the person you need on-scene. She's our only way to control Valentine."

"Please," Katherine said to the captain. "I want to help." Valentine had let his victim call her. So maybe—maybe—he had let Savannah call, too.

Could I have saved her?

"Hell." The captain gave a grim nod. Then he motioned to Ross. "You've been keeping her in check for years—so you *stay* with her, got it? I don't want her out of your sight. You stay behind my men and you keep her back, too."

Her breath rushed out.

"Yes, sir," Ross said. His hand closed around her shoulder. He leaned close to her. "Are you sure you know what you're doing? The whole purpose of witness protection is to keep you *away* from Valentine so that you're alive when it comes time for the trail."

But if they never caught him, there would be no trial. How could she keep hiding while others died?

She couldn't.

- - -

They went in quietly. Dane led the team as they slipped inside the warehouse at 209 Jamestown. It was a tactical call. They could have gone in with sirens screaming, but the captain worried it would make Valentine kill the woman that much faster.

Don't alert him. Just get close and take him down. Those were his orders.

So Dane slipped through the run-down warehouse. The place seemed abandoned. Filled with the scent of old dust and mildew. The windows were broken. A rat scurried across the floor.

But he didn't hear the sound of a woman screaming.

Be alive. Please be alive.

The cops were wearing bulletproof vests, but he barely felt the weight of his. His gun was gripped firmly in his hand. He motioned to the right, and Mac rushed into the next room.

He followed his partner, searching.

Five rooms so far...*all nothing.*

But John had been certain that the cell phone signal was coming from this address. As far as Dane knew, the man had never been wrong on any case. When it came to tech, John was king.

Dane went back into the narrow hallway and followed two cops up the stairs.

Then he caught the scent of blood.

Be alive. The thought slid through his mind once more.

At the top of the stairs, a door had been left open. Mac gave him cover while he hurried inside. His gaze swept the room—

And he saw her.

He rushed toward her with his heart racing in his chest. The scent of blood was strong in the room, heavy and cloying as it filled his nostrils.

Amy's wrists and ankles were bound. Blood soaked the floor around her. Duct tape covered her mouth.

Deep slices lined her arms. A deep hole had been dug into her heart.

Amy had been screaming less than thirty minutes ago. But now she was dead, and fury had his whole body tensing. His breath panted out, hard and fast, and he couldn't take his eyes off her frozen features.

Another victim. *Too late.* Dammit. He shook his head, hating the sight of her broken body. *We didn't find her fast enough.*

Dane backed away from her. Almost stepped on the smartphone that had been placed on the ground. Why the hell was it there? Had the killer dropped it? Dane tapped the transmitter at his ear. Before he came into the warehouse, he'd gotten wired so he could transmit out to the others. "We found Amy." He swallowed and said, "We're gonna need the ME."

He could already imagine the expression on the captain's face as he heard the news—an expression that would match Dane's own.

They hadn't arrived fast enough to save the victim, but the sonofabitch could still be close by.

"Keep searching," Dane ordered the men around him. "Every single room. Every crawl space. *Everywhere.*"

He led the men. They took their time, doing their best not to destroy any evidence. They searched room after room. Air-conditioning ducts. Closets. Storage spaces. Every damn place.

Then Dane headed outside with his men. Bright sunlight beat down on him. He saw the line of police cars that had assembled and saw the captain glaring at the scene. Uniforms had fanned out and were searching all the nearby buildings.

They won't find him.

Because the killer was just screwing with them all.

Harley moved to the side, and Dane caught a glimpse of Katherine's face. Just seeing her so close to the murder scene was like a punch to his gut. *No. She shouldn't be here.*

He ran toward her and the captain. He tried to hold back his anger, but it broke free as he glared at Harley and demanded, "Why the hell would you bring her here?" How could the captain not understand what the killer was doing? He'd called her, lured her there.

"Valentine wanted her out here for a reason," Harley said, his voice rough. "And she insisted on coming."

Dane was starting to think the woman had a death wish.

But the captain was right. The call to Katherine had been deliberate, and Valentine would have been too smart to use the victim's phone—knowing they could trace both the victim's identity and the phone's location through that call—*unless he wanted us here.*

The bastard was jerking them around.

Because he wanted to watch.

"The men need to fan out more." His gaze left the closer buildings and drifted farther away, then rose. "Get uniforms up there." He motioned to the buildings on the far right. "He set the scene, and he lured his players out here. I'm betting he stayed to watch."

Valentine liked to think he was in control of the game. A twisted game in which he was the only one having any fun.

Harley sent the uniforms scrambling. They rushed toward the first building that Dane had indicated, a four-story warehouse that would have given the killer a perfect view of the cop cars as they arrived.

"He saw us coming," Dane said. "He watched us every step of the way."

Katherine touched his arm—a light, hesitant touch. "She was dead?"

He nodded. The ME's van was already there. Ronnie would be heading in soon to check the body. "She was still warm."

Katherine's breath shuddered out.

His gaze shot over her head and landed on the marshal. "Take her back to the station," he told Ross. He couldn't leave the scene yet or he'd have been the one to take her. But Dane didn't like having her out here. She was too exposed. Whatever game Valentine *thought* he was playing, *he needs to think again.*

Ross nodded, even as his gaze drifted to the buildings on the right.

"Keep her safe," Dane added. The last thing he wanted to see was Katherine tied to a table. With duct tape over her mouth. And blood dripping down her arms.

The woman in there, with her dark hair and pale skin, could have been a substitute for Katherine. Would the killer be coming for her soon?

Dane glared up at the buildings. *You can't have her.*

- 7 -

Cops guarded the front door of Katherine's house. A patrol car was stationed at the end of her driveway. If she'd had any neighbors to scare, the poor folks would have been terrified.

But she didn't have neighbors. Because she didn't want them to get too close. She didn't want anyone to get too close.

"Do you know anything about the victim?" Katherine asked as her fingers curled around the cup of coffee in front of her. It was nearing eight p.m., and she probably shouldn't have been drinking coffee so late, but there were plenty of things she shouldn't have done in her life.

Coffee wouldn't be what killed her. Valentine? He just might be.

Ross gave a slow shake of his head. He'd been her shadow all day, a shadow she was grateful to have. "Her name is Amy Evans. She's divorced. Thirty-one." He expelled his breath in a rush. "I learned that, then got—"

"Sentenced to babysitting duty with me," she finished, shoulders hunching.

The kitchen chair groaned beneath him as he shifted his weight. She looked up and saw that his gaze had hardened. "Do you still have the gun?" Ross asked.

He was always Ross to her. Never Anthony, never Tony. He'd been her handler for three years. Given her two new identities in that time. But she always called him Ross because she wanted to keep distance between them.

Because she didn't trust him.

I don't trust anyone.

Not even the men with badges.

"Katherine."

She blinked.

"Do you still have the gun?"

He'd given her the gun the day he got her out of Boston. She didn't know if it was standard procedure to give a witness a gun. She doubted it, but there had been shadows in Ross's eyes. A story she hadn't been brave enough to ask about. He'd given her the gun and said, "*If the bastard ever finds you, don't waste a breath talking to him. Just shoot.*"

Her fingers curled tighter around the mug. "I still have the gun," she said. She most certainly still had it, and she spent ten hours a week at the firing range making sure she knew exactly how to use it.

In the years since her horrible discovery in that basement, she'd taken steps to make herself stronger. She'd become a damn good shot, and she'd spent countless hours hitting the mat in self-defense classes.

She wouldn't be caught unprepared if she faced a killer again.

"Is it loaded?"

She shook her head.

"*Load* the damn thing, Kat—Katherine. Keep that gun close, and if you need to…*shoot*. He came all the way down to New Orleans, didn't he?"

"He…he never tried to hurt me before—"

"He's a fucking psychotic killer. Just because he didn't before, that sure as hell doesn't mean he won't come at you with his knife this time."

Some of the hot coffee spilled over onto her hand. The burn lanced her skin, but she ignored the flash of pain. "He never wanted me to find out what he did. He told me that in the basement." So why would he be calling her now? Trying to lure her to crime scenes? Maybe Ross was right. Maybe she'd become one of his targets now.

"Keep the gun close," Ross told her again, his voice dropping, "and don't forget for an instant what he is."

Her gaze held his. "I can never forget."

There was a beat of silence, and then she heard voices. Cops on her porch, talking to Dane. She pushed aside the coffee and hurried into the den just as he entered the house.

The faint lines near his mouth looked deeper, and there were shadows under his eyes. She knew from just one look at his face that he hadn't found the killer.

"He sent you a package after the last kill," Dane said.

The bloodred roses and the photograph to immortalize his kill. To show his masterpiece. Valentine had taken photos of his victims in Boston, too. The cops had tried tracking him down based on the paper and ink he used, but they hadn't found him.

"If the killer is sticking to his routine, he'll send you another package."

Her hand was starting to throb a bit now. She pressed her fingers against her jean-clad thigh.

"I'll be here if he comes. If anyone comes with any kind of package."

"I can stay—" Ross said immediately.

But Dane shook his head. "My shift." His gaze lingered on Katherine. "I've got her now."

Dane was going to spend the night with her. Again. At least she had an extra room he could use.

A room right across the hallway from hers.

Ross's fingers brushed down her arm. She instinctively stiffened, but he just said, "I'll be back in the morning."

She nodded.

He bent toward her. "Remember what I said." His words were a quiet whisper that Dane shouldn't have been able to hear.

But when Ross pulled away from her, she saw the suspicion on Dane's face.

"Detective," Ross said, nodding toward him, "if there's any threat—"

"Got you on speed dial," Dane said with a tight nod.

Then Ross was gone. Dane shut and locked the door, and the house that she'd always thought was too big for her suddenly seemed too small.

- 8 -

"What did he tell you?" Dane asked, voice curious. "He whispered to you, right before he left."

"I have a gun that I keep in my nightstand. Ross was reminding me that I needed to keep it close." *Use it.*

"You do," Dane agreed as his gaze swept over her.

She shook her head. "He never hurt me."

Three steps and Dane was in front of her. He reached for her hands. "He *tortured* those women. Don't tell me the guy wouldn't slice you if he had the—"

She gasped as his fingers tightened around the burn on her hand.

"What is it?" His gaze dropped. She followed his stare and saw the red streaks on her flesh. "What the hell happened?"

"I just...some coffee spilled on me." Katherine tried to pull her hand away. "It's nothing."

But he was tugging her toward the kitchen. Turning on the cold water. Holding her hand under the faucet. The icy water felt good on her skin. Or maybe it was his fingers that felt good. Strong. Tan and long.

She looked up. His eyes weren't on her. They were on her hand. On the water that poured over a small wound that shouldn't matter for anything.

"We need to put some cream on it, we need—"

"I've had worse burns." Plenty, back when she'd been a kid. "I'll be fine." Because being so close to him was making her nervous and edgy, she pulled away.

He turned off the faucet.

She backed up and hit the counter behind her. Great. Not exactly any place to run. The kitchen was *small.* Or maybe he was just too damn big.

"Does the name Amy Evans mean anything to you?" Dane's gaze was watchful, hooded.

"I know she was the victim. I heard that at the station."

"But you didn't *know* her?" Dane pressed.

"I don't think so. I saw her picture on one of the computers down there, but I'd never seen her before."

"You're sure?"

What did he want? Did he want her to break? "I'm sure. Why?" Her breath caught. "Was she another reporter? Was she working on a story about Valentine?"

"No, Amy wasn't a reporter. She was a lawyer." He exhaled slowly. "We're checking her background, seeing what can tie her to—"

"Me," Katherine finished.

He nodded.

"Because the reporter knew me, you think this Amy did, too."

"We have to explore that possibility." His voice was a low rumble.

Goose bumps rose on her arms. "You checked my phone, didn't you? You saw Savannah's number."

He nodded.

"Was that Valentine calling? Did he have her then?"

"Yes." A hard pause, then, "The ME thinks she was alive then."

Her lashes closed. *Dammit. One missed call.* If she'd just picked up the damn phone, maybe she could have saved Savannah. Stopped Valentine.

Then Amy Evans would be alive, too.

The floor creaked beneath his feet. His hands closed over her shoulders, but this time he seemed to be holding his strength in check. "Her death isn't on you."

She looked up at him. "Isn't it?" Her guilt said that yes, it was. Savannah's death and so many others.

"You aren't the one doing the killing."

"In Boston, that didn't matter." So many people had come at her. Bricks had been thrown through her windows. Threatening phone calls had come constantly. She'd been given police protection because of the death threats.

Then, finally, she'd had to take on a new life in order to escape.

"This isn't Boston. Everything is different now. *Everything.*" There was a deeper note in his voice, one she couldn't quite interpret.

She stared into his eyes and wanted to believe what Dane was saying. She wanted it so badly, but for three years she'd felt like she was running from death.

A girl could run for only so long.

"I'm tired." The confession slipped from her. It was the truth, and she wasn't just talking about being tired of running.

His eyes narrowed.

Tired of running. Of looking over her shoulder. Of jumping at every creak and rustle.

And mostly tired of not *living.* Of watching everyone else around her be happy and fall in love and get married and have their kids.

She'd watched them all. Life had passed her by. She'd finally forced herself to date again, with Trent, but that just hadn't worked. She hadn't wanted him.

When Trent touched her, she tensed. She got too nervous and anxious, the way she did with nearly every man who came close to her.

Every man except Detective Dane Black.

Her gaze slid over him.

He wasn't classically handsome, she knew that. He was big and muscled. Strong. He still had his holster on—she could see the outline of his weapon. He was a dangerous man, with a dangerous job.

But he made her feel safe.

When no one else—not even Ross—had been able to make her feel that way.

"Be careful." Dane's words were low.

Her gaze jerked back up to his face.

"There are some lines that you might not want to cross."

She felt her cheeks heat, and she wondered just what her expression had given away. This was the point where she should take a few steps back. Put some distance between them.

Go in her bedroom. Lock the door.

But she couldn't move.

"Sometimes," she whispered, "I feel like my life ended three years ago."

"It didn't."

He wasn't understanding. She'd been going through the motions for so many months. Thirty-six, to be exact. Pretending to live while her body was encased in ice.

She didn't want to pretend anymore. Valentine was back. This time he might come after her. She didn't want to die knowing only fear and pain.

Katherine wanted life.

She wanted Dane.

Her breath seemed to burn in her lungs as she forced herself to move closer to him. "You're staying here all night?"

He nodded. His gaze was hooded, and she didn't want him to look at her that way. She wanted to stare into his blue eyes and see need, lust, staring back at her.

She reached out and touched his chest. Her fingers were trembling, but maybe he wouldn't notice that.

"What are you doing?" Dane asked carefully.

If he had to ask, then she must be doing this wrong. She was rusty. Katherine swallowed and grabbed onto her courage as tightly as she could. "I was going to kiss you."

"Why?"

She didn't back down. "Because I want to." Then, since she wanted to be honest with him, Katherine confessed. "Because I don't want to die regretting that I didn't live."

"You *aren't* dying."

Amy Evans sure hadn't woken up that day thinking she'd die either.

"Will we break rules by kissing?" She offered him a smile that felt far too forced. "Fraternizing with a suspect? Is that against PD rules?"

"No." A stark pause as his gaze swept over her. "You're not a suspect."

Good to know.

"But you need to realize…" His voice had deepened. His fingers pressed a bit harder into her shoulders. "I might not stop with just a kiss."

She wanted to forget control and care and death and just *live* for a while. His chest was rock-hard beneath her touch. "And I might not want you to stop."

"Katherine…" Her name was a growl of lust. That same lust was in his gaze because he'd finally dropped his mask. *Yes.* That was what she needed to see. She needed to be wanted. Desired.

Just a man and a woman. That was what she wanted. In the next instant, his hands were on her. His mouth was on hers. Not a gentle, seeking kiss. Hot. Demanding.

At the first touch of his lips on hers, a dam seemed to explode within her. All of the needs she'd bottled up came crashing through her control. Her lips parted for him, and his tongue thrust inside her mouth.

She moaned, a soft, hungry sound. His hands slid down to hold her hips. Warm, strong hands, and his mouth…

The detective knew how to kiss.

She stood on her toes as she leaned into him. Her hands had curled around *his* shoulders and she was holding him tight. Her breasts were aching, the nipples tightening to hard peaks. She couldn't get close enough to him. Katherine knew she needed so much more than just a kiss.

Then he was lifting her up. Their mouths broke apart and she sucked in a sharp gasp of air. He sat her on the countertop and slid between her legs. His mouth was on her neck. Licking. Sucking the skin. Lightly biting the flesh.

A sensual current of energy seemed to pulse through her body. Her nails dug into his shirt. *I want the shirt gone.*

Her hands fumbled and slid under the material. Then she was touching his skin. Feeling the faint curl of hair on his chest. Feeling all of those sexy muscles. Hot flesh.

She tossed his shirt to the floor.

His fingers were on her thighs. They seemed to brand her through her jeans. Far hotter than the coffee, his touch singed her.

It hadn't been like this for her before. She hadn't wanted—

Katherine stiffened.

Don't think about before.

"Stay with me," Dane ordered her as his head lifted. His blue gaze was so intense, heated with desire. "Stay with me." Softer now. His lips took hers again. His tongue pushed into her mouth. His hand slid between her legs, to the juncture of her thighs. He stroked her lightly through the jeans.

Just think of Dane. Only Dane. Nothing else. No one else.

She didn't want nightmares to take this pleasure away.

Dane. She kissed him back. Slid her tongue against his. Nibbled on his lip. Sucked the small wound she'd made. Her legs rose and curled around his hips.

He kept stroking her through the fabric of her jeans, his touch growing harder. She wanted to arch against him, to push and demand more, but she didn't want the moment to end. This was the closest she'd come to actually feeling normal in—

She stopped the thought immediately.

Only Dane.

His lips lifted from hers. "Let's make the nightmares go away."

Yes, please. She was ready to shove those nightmares in a dark closet and padlock the door.

Dane eased back. "I want you naked."

She wanted him the same way.

"I'm not a gentle lover."

He seemed to be.

"I like sex wild and hot."

Sounded good to her.

"And you…you need more."

But Katherine shook her head. Didn't he get it? "What I need right now is you."

"Then baby, you've got me."

At first, she thought they might make love right there. But he pulled her off the counter. Led her through the kitchen.

Then it was her turn to lead. Up the stairs. To the room on the right. Katherine made sure to turn off the lights when she slipped into her room. She didn't want him to see her eyes…or her scars.

Not yet. For now, she wanted this to be only about desire. A man and a woman.

Nothing more.

She kicked off her shoes. Undressed with hurried, so-not-sexy moves. But in the dark, he couldn't see her clumsiness. He wouldn't see her stumbling around or notice her shaking hands.

He'd just see her shadow. The way that Katherine could see his shadow. A big, solid form filling the doorway.

Then he was heading toward her. Slow steps. She climbed onto the bed, pulling the covers back. "Um, do you want—"

"Just you." He kissed her again. "Just. You."

He was naked. Warm and solid and surrounding her. Part of her wanted to pull away, because, suddenly, this was too much. He was too much.

The whispers of the past tried to come for her once more.

"Tell me what you like."

His voice quieted the whispers.

"You." Her instant response. And it was true. There was something about him that got to her. An instinctive response.

He laughed lightly, and Katherine had the feeling that she'd caught him by surprise. She also liked his laugh. It sounded warm. A little husky.

"I like you too, Katherine." His fingers skimmed down her shoulder. Slid down to her wrist. He lifted her hand to his mouth and kissed the inside of her wrist. "But I want to know what gives you pleasure."

Pleasure was skating through her right then. A hum of pleasure because she'd felt the rasp of his tongue against her skin and her madly beating pulse.

"I want…wild." She forced the words out. "Hot." That had been what he said, right? If that was what he wanted, then she—

"We'll get to that," Dane promised. "But first, I think we need to focus on you."

And he was pushing between her legs. Putting those slightly callused fingertips on her thighs and easing them farther apart. She expected him to thrust a finger into her sex. She'd already tensed but…but Dane bent his head.

"I like focusing on you," he whispered, and then his mouth was on her.

She wasn't prepared for the sensual slide of his lips and tongue, and her whole body tightened. She arched her hips, not to get away from him, but to get so much closer to that wicked mouth.

Because he was giving her pleasure. Not reminding her of the past. Just making her feel—

Alive.

When her first orgasm hit, she choked out Dane's name. Her body bowed off the bed as the pleasure throbbed through her blood.

"And I fucking love the way you taste," he said, the words dark and deep.

Her heart slammed in her chest. The drumming filled her ears. She hadn't expected…that. Not so fast. Now all she wanted was—

Again, please.

"Ready for the wild part?" Dane asked, voice rough with lust. "'Cause I can't hold on much longer." A sensual warning.

The she saw that he was easing a condom over his erect length, and the guy was *very* aroused. She wondered if he always carried a condom around with him, or had he been planning on this?

Then his hands were reaching for her. His fingers curled around hers. Not holding her down. She hated to be held down, but…his fingers were twining with hers, not pinning her.

"Ready?" Dane asked.

She nodded, her hair sliding over the pillows.

"Then wrap your legs around me."

She did.

He'd promised her wild, but would he deliver on that promise?

Dane thrust into her. She gasped as her body tried to adjust. Three years. Not since—

"*Only. Me,*" Dane ordered. His fingers tightened around hers. Then he withdrew. Drove deep. Harder.

The bed began to rock beneath them. Her box springs squeaked. She wrapped her legs around him, tried to arch her hips, seeking a position that would let him slide in easier but…

The guy was *big.*

And it had been a long time.

Then his right hand pulled away from her. His fingers slid between their bodies. Pushed over the center of her desire.

He withdrew, then thrust into her.

Yes.

She stared up at him. Her eyes had adjusted a bit to the darkness, and she could almost make out his features in the dark.

Her cop.

Dane.

He hooked her legs up higher. Pushed harder. Deeper. Her breath heaved out and she arched against him, meeting him thrust for thrust. Again and again.

She came, her body tightening on a wave of pleasure as her orgasm shuddered through her.

Dane kept thrusting. The pleasure intensified, stealing her breath. She couldn't even call out to him.

"Want...more," he growled. Then he was kissing her. She was frantic for him. The pleasure was all she knew. He was all she knew.

They rolled across the bed. No, they were wrecking her bed, and she loved it. *Loved it.*

She was on top of him. Rising up and down, and her knees were sinking into the mattress. His hands were tight around her hips as he pulled her into his pounding thrusts. She wanted him to come.

Wanted the pleasure to last forever.

"Not...enough..." Then he had her under him again. Her legs were over his shoulders, and he seemed to be inside her even deeper than before.

Another thrust. Withdrawal. Thrust.

He'd promised her wild. He was giving her wild.

Dane stiffened against her. Shuddered. She almost wished the lights were on then, because she would have loved to see his eyes go blind with pleasure. Would the blue darken? Lighten?

Her breath rasped out. Her heart kept racing.

Pleasure still whispered through her body. So much pleasure. She licked her dry lips.

He eased her legs down. Stayed inside of her.

She wrapped her arms around him. Held him close.

Just sex. Just sex. The mantra repeated in her head again and again. They would part in a few minutes. The lust had been satisfied. The desire fulfilled.

But she didn't want him to leave her.

Only Dane. He'd made her feel normal again. Given her the pleasure that other women took with their lovers.

She hadn't trusted a man enough to get this close.

Why him?

But then he was pulling away, as she'd known he would. Heading into the bathroom without speaking to her. Katherine fumbled for the covers, suddenly feeling far too exposed even in the dark. Then she heard his footsteps coming back toward her.

He'd leave now. Go to the room across the hall. They'd have some awkward conversation in the morning and—

And he was climbing into bed with her.

She stiffened when his arms wrapped around her. She could have sworn...had he just pressed a kiss to her head?

"It's okay, Katherine," he told her quietly. "You're safe tonight."

Tears wanted to fill her eyes. Stupid tears. She hadn't let herself cry in so long. She wouldn't cry now. "Of course I am," she mumbled, hoping her voice didn't sound weak. "I've got a gun three feet away in my nightstand drawer."

He laughed at that. The same husky, deep laugh as before, and the sound seemed to warm her once more.

Yes, she had Ross's gun close by. And she had warm, strong arms around her. Someone to hold her in the dark.

Don't cry. Don't break.

She could still feel him inside her. Aftershocks of pleasure seemed to slip through her sex. But even better than that, she liked the way he held her.

Dane curved his body around hers.

Her lashes started to fall. She wouldn't be able to sleep with him there, of course. She'd wait a few minutes, then she'd tell him to head across the hall to the other room. She didn't want him there when dawn came. Didn't want him to see her in the light.

She'd tell him to leave soon.

Soon...

— — —

Katherine was sleeping with the cop.

Damn her. She was *screwing* the man. She'd just met him. So much for her ice queen routine.

The binoculars had given a perfect view into Katherine's house. She should have shut the fucking blinds in her kitchen. But, no, her kitchen lights had been blazing, and she'd let the cop put his hands all over her.

She'd twisted and pushed against him, looking desperate for his touch.

She was supposed to be the one who was special? She was just a whore. Katherine had shown her true colors.

She'd rushed from the kitchen with the cop. Gone upstairs but finally had the sense to turn off her light.

The binoculars were in the car now. No good anymore. Cops were at Katherine's door. A cop was in her bed.

She'll pay.

The fools thought Katherine was the target tonight.

No, Katherine wouldn't be getting this package.

A few moments later, the car's engine cranked up. The car slid slowly into the darkness. The cops didn't even give the vehicle more than a cursory glance as it drove down the street.

It should have been harder. The thought came instantly. But killing wasn't hard.

Especially when the world was full of such easy prey.

− 9 −

He woke to find Katherine curled around him. Her body was soft and sensual, she smelled lightly of strawberries, and her head was tucked onto his shoulder.

His hand was wrapped around her hip. Her leg rested on his thigh.

And it felt like he was in damn heaven.

Dane hadn't intended to have sex with her the night before. Hell yes, he'd wanted her. Most sane men would want a walking wet dream like Katherine Cole, but...

He'd brought the condom along just in case the relentless fantasy in his head actually came true. A guy could hope, right? He hadn't thought the lady would actually give him the green light. But then she'd looked at him with those big, deep eyes of hers.

And his self-control had been lost.

Pulling away from her would have taken more strength than he possessed. So it was a real damn good thing that the lady had been pulling him toward her. Not pushing him away.

He shifted his head on the pillow so he could look at her. She looked younger when she slept. Vulnerable. Her long lashes cast shadows on her cheeks.

He could see the smooth skin of her shoulders. Creamy and—

His eyes narrowed even as his hand lifted, and carefully his fingers skated over the tip of her right shoulder. The skin was slightly raised. Not in just one spot, but four. Four rough circles. Old scars that looked like—

"They're burns." She didn't open her eyes, but Katherine's body was suddenly tense beside him. "Cigarette burns, to be exact."

He'd seen a few burns like those before. Judging by the way they'd faded…"You were just a kid."

"I guess Agent Wayne was right about my shared history with Valentine. We both had really screwed-up childhoods." Her lashes were still covering her eyes, and he had the feeling that she was hiding from him. Or maybe it was just easier for her to talk without looking into his eyes.

"My mother was on drugs too—like his. And when she got high, she burned me."

His jaw locked. "How long?"

"When I was nine, I went into the foster care system."

Nine years. Had they all been hell? The scars said they had.

"The scars don't matter, okay? They're just marks on my body, nothing more." Her lashes lifted. The gold in her gaze seemed to shine even brighter.

"Are there more?" Because these marks pissed him off. He didn't want anyone or anything hurting her, ever.

"Not where you can see."

She tried to pull away from him, but Dane wasn't ready to let her go.

"You should have gone to the other room last night. After—" Katherine broke off and cleared her throat.

"After the fucking fantastic sex?" Because it had been incredible. The best he'd had, and Dane hadn't exactly lived a pure life.

Her cheeks reddened.

Damn, the blushing was cute. "You sure as hell aren't what I imagined."

Her lips parted in surprise, and her face seemed to pale. "You mean since I was the lover of a serial killer, you expected something else from me?" Then she shoved against him. "I'm not the freak show the papers said I was. I'm not twisted or depraved or—" Her breath heaved out. "I'm just *me*."

"Dammit, I meant—"

"The night's over," she snapped. "Time to return to reality."

He'd rather return to the night, but Katherine had climbed out of the bed and jerked most of the covers with her.

Since he wasn't the shy sort, Dane slowly rose to his feet. "I didn't mean that the way it sounded."

Katherine's head tilted back. Her hair tumbled over her shoulders. "Then what did you mean?"

"I didn't expect to touch you and go from zero to lust in about two seconds."

She blinked.

"I want you." The woman would be pretty blind not to realize that fact, considering the heavy arousal he'd woken with—the arousal that was plain to see right then. "But our timing is pretty screwed at the moment."

Her lips parted.

"If I weren't working the case, I'd be wining and dining you."

"You—" Katherine cleared her throat. "What do you want from me?"

Her trust. He had to have it in order to solve this case. But he couldn't say that. So he stuck with the truth that he could give. "I want everything you can give me." Because one time with her wasn't going to be enough for him. Last night had just been a taste. He was a starving man.

But before he could say anything else, the doorbell rang. Hell. He glanced at his watch. Seven o'clock. Not quite time for a shift change, and even if it were, Dane wasn't in the mood to leave. He and Katherine needed to clear the air some more.

But she was grabbing a robe and belting it. "What if they've found something else?"

She ran from the room, and he jerked on his jeans to follow behind her even though he already knew the cops hadn't found anything. He would have gotten a phone call if they had.

He stalked down the stairs after her. Before she could open the door, he caught her arm and pulled her back. Dane looked through the peephole and swore.

"Who?" Katherine demanded. "Who is it?"

He exhaled and raked a hand through his hair. "Your ex is on the doorstep." As far as Dane was concerned, Trent definitely fell into the *ex* category now.

All the color drained from her face.

Oh, hell. Dane grabbed her. "Not *Valentine.*" He had to be more careful. "Trent. The guy you were with the other night."

Her breath heaved out. Then her eyes widened in alarm. "Why is he here?"

Dane was rather curious to find out himself. He yanked open the door as one of the other detectives—he'd kept guards outside the house as lookouts—stepped in front of Trent to firmly push the guy back. "You can let him go, James," Dane said.

Karen James glanced back and gave a quick nod.

Trent rushed forward. "What the hell is going on here?" he demanded as his gaze flew to Katherine. "Why are there cops on your doorstep?"

"I—"

"She had a break-in," Dane explained. Hey, it was the truth. "The uniforms are just here as a precaution."

"Some precaution." But Trent was shouldering past Dane and reaching out to pull Katherine against him. "I was so worried about you when I saw the police car. I was afraid something had happened."

Dane's eyes narrowed. The shrink had about two more seconds to clutch Katherine, then he'd yank the guy back. One, tw—

Katherine pushed Trent away. "What are you doing here?"

Trent shook his head and finally seemed to realize that Katherine wasn't completely dressed.

His gaze snapped to Dane.

Dane lifted his brows. *Yep, I'm not completely dressed either.*

"*Katherine.*" Her name was a snarl now.

Dane didn't like that tone a bit.

"Who is he?" Trent demanded as he jerked his head toward Dane.

"That's Detective Dane Black. He's…working on the break-in."

"Doesn't look like that's all he's working on," Trent huffed out.

Katherine stepped away from him. "Why are you here?" she demanded.

Dane rather enjoyed the anger in her voice.

Trent sniffed. Sniffed? *What a prick.* And the guy's brows flew up. "I wanted to come by and talk to you. I wanted you to reconsider—"

"Trent." She sighed, shaking her head. "I told you, things are over for us. You're a great guy. But I couldn't give you what you needed."

"Could you give it to him?"

The low words had Dane's body stiffening. He took a fast step forward.

But before he could do anything else, Katherine lifted her hand, halting him. "We weren't exclusive, and as of our last conversation—right there on the porch—we were no longer dating at all." Her words were quiet and calm, but a faint pink had started to tint the tops of her high cheekbones. "I'm sorry if I misled you in any way—that wasn't my intention—but I'm not the right woman for you. I'm—"

"Damaged," Trent threw out. "I know that, okay? Evelyn warned me about you." He turned away and began pacing.

Damaged? The word echoed in Dane's head. Dane moved quickly, putting himself in Trent's path. "You need to get out of here," Dane told the guy, trying to hold back his fury.

Trent's head jerked up, and he almost slammed right into Dane. "What?"

"She's not *damaged*." Dane hated that word. Hated the pain that he'd seen flare in Katherine's eyes. "And she's not your concern." He waved toward the doorway. "Now get your ass out."

Trent's jaw dropped. His gaze swung to Katherine. "Kat?"

"She *hates* being called Kat," Dane said, never taking his glare off the man's face. "You should know that by now."

The wooden floor creaked beneath Katherine's feet. "Goodbye, Trent."

The guy stared blankly at her.

"*The door.*" Dane prompted.

Anger hardened Trent's face, but the doctor spun around and marched for the door. Dane didn't speak until the dumb-ass was good and gone. Then he turned to Katherine.

"You were sleeping with that guy?"

"No." She headed for the stairs. "Actually, you're the first man I've slept with in three years."

It was his turn to stare after her, with his jaw hanging like Trent's had been.

Her hand tightened on the banister. "I've got some trust issues. You know, because I'm *damaged.*"

He rushed after her, curled his hands around her shoulders, and made her look back at him. "You aren't damaged."

Her smile was sad. "You don't even know me, and if you did… you just might be afraid of me."

Then she pulled away, headed up the stairs, and shut her bedroom door behind her.

He didn't follow this time. He was too busy wondering about the haunted look he'd seen in her eyes.

– – –

Trent Lancaster marched into his office, rage burning through him.

Katherine had been half-dressed, with that smirking prick of a police detective at her side.

"Trent?" His partner, Evelyn Knight, entered his office, frowning. "What's wrong?"

He whirled to face her. He wanted to tell her that he needed to be alone, but he stopped when he noticed the stark concern on her face.

Good old Evelyn. He and Evelyn had first met back in their college days at Emory. They'd even dated back then, for a time, but soon enough he'd realized that they were better friends than lovers.

Evelyn had tried to warn him about Katherine. When he'd first begun to notice Katherine, Evelyn had said to stay away.

But Katherine's legs were killer. And her eyes...they always made him think of sex.

Then she'd stopped seeing Evelyn. There'd been no reason why he couldn't go after what he wanted.

He wasn't a man ruled by emotion so much as by basic needs. Katherine had certainly stirred up those basic impulses.

But then she'd gone and screwed the cop instead. Dammit.

"What's happened?" Evelyn glanced around the office. "What's going on?"

He sighed. "Nothing." He straightened his shoulders. He always had control at the office. He had control everywhere. "Katherine and I—we decided to end things."

Evelyn's gray eyes widened; then she nodded quickly. "That was the best decision you could make, Trent. That woman...she won't be ready for any sort of lasting commitment for a long time."

He hadn't exactly been in the mood for forever. In the mood for some good fucks? Yes.

"I shouldn't have told you as much as I did." Her rounded jaw hardened a bit. "*You* shouldn't have dated her."

"Yes, well, I didn't *date* her until you stopped treating her." So no conflict of interest. He'd been careful. He always covered his ass. The last thing he wanted was a lawsuit. After his divorce, he couldn't handle another cash-flow problem.

He'd almost lost the practice in that divorce. What had he expected? His ex was a divorce attorney. She'd known exactly how to hang him out to dry.

Thanks for taking everything, sweetheart.

Good thing Evelyn had been there to help him out financially. She was always there to help.

"Katherine still needs treatment. So much…" Evelyn exhaled. "But we can't help those who don't want to be helped, right?"

That was Evelyn's mantra.

He turned away and headed for his desk. His first patient would be in at ten o'clock. He'd focus, get through the day, then go find some sexy, dark-haired woman at a club. He'd screw her, pretend she was Katherine, and all would be right in his world.

Or mostly right.

He frowned. There was a white box in the middle of his desk, right next to a vase full of fresh roses. He *hated* flowers of any sort. Just because Valentine's Day was drawing near, it didn't mean he had to have damn roses in his office. Vendors were hawking the roses on every street corner of the city.

I don't want them in here.

Trent would have to make sure the receptionist knew not to put any more in his office. "When did this arrive?" he asked as he stared down at the package.

Evelyn was almost at the door. She looked over her shoulder. "When did what arrive?"

He held up the box. Shrugging, Evelyn said, "Maybe one of the secretaries brought it in." She left the room with her usual no-nonsense stride.

Trent studied the package as the scent of the roses filled his nose. The white box wasn't from their usual delivery service. There was no writing on it—it almost looked like one of the boxes from the bakery on the corner. Maybe it was a pastry delivery. One of the receptionists could be trying to get on his good side.

He slid his finger under the box's tab and lifted up the top. The box slid in his hand as he eased into his seat, and rose petals spilled onto the surface of his desk. "What the hell…?" Trent began.

Then he saw the photographs, and he couldn't speak at all.

His fingers began to tremble. The first photograph was a close-up of a woman's chest. There was so much blood. Someone had driven a knife into her heart. His own heart was racing so hard that it seemed close to bursting from his chest. His body felt ice cold as he stared at that horrible photo.

The second photo showed the woman's full body. The slices on her arms. The ropes that circled her ankles and wrists. The duct tape over her mouth.

Her eyes were closed, her hair tangled around her face.

A face he knew too well.

A face he'd once loved.

A face Trent had thought he desperately hated.

Amy. His ex-wife.

Nausea rolled in his stomach as sweat poured from him. *Not Amy. Not Amy.*

"Evelyn!" he roared, then dropped the photos and vomited into the trash can.

— — —

The elevator slowly ascended in the high-rise office building. Dane's eyes were on the blinking control panel lights. Just a few more floors until Lancaster & Knight Psychiatry.

"We'd just found the connection between them," Mac said at his side. "The mother was in to ID the body, and she mentioned Amy's ex to Ronnie…"

Amy's ex. Also known as Dr. Trent Lancaster.

"The lady told Ronnie that the divorce was bitter. Trent had a wandering eye, and Amy was out for blood in court."

Only Amy was the one who bled.

"Then the precinct got the call from the shrink's office," Mac said.

Two crime-scene techs were behind them. Silent. Watchful.

"And Trent got the photos," Dane finished. He'd headed over to meet Mac as soon as he got the order from the captain.

Katherine still had protection, tagalong uniforms who'd be with her for the day, while he had an appointment with the good doctor.

"Why didn't Katherine get the photos this time?" Mac wondered as he rolled his shoulders. "Why did she get the call but not the package?"

"Maybe our perp couldn't get to her because *we* were there." Made sense to Dane. *Did the SOB see that I was there last night?*

The elevator doors opened with a soft ding. Dane headed into the hallway, walking fast. Mac was right by his side. Mac shoved open the door of Lancaster & Knight, and two women near the reception desk began rushing toward them.

Dane and Mac flashed their badges. Relief washed over the women's faces as their shoulders slumped. They looked pale and shaken.

"Where's Dr. Lancaster?" Dane asked.

The one with short blonde hair pointed to the right. "In Dr. Knight's office." She grabbed his arm before he could pass her. "Please, can we go home? I don't want to be here any longer."

No, unfortunately, she couldn't leave. Not until he and Mac had questioned her. He inclined his head to Mac and saw his partner flash his trademark calming smile. That smile could work magic.

"Just let me ask you a few questions, ma'am," Mac began as he gently took the blonde's arm.

Dane made his way toward Dr. Knight's office. The door was ajar, but he rapped lightly on the heavy wood to announce his presence before he headed inside the room. A leather couch and two chairs were to the right. A gleaming desk waited to the left. A laptop and some wilting roses were on a corner of the desk.

A woman with sleek blonde hair, which was twisted into a coil at the nape of her neck, spun toward him. Trent was seated in a chair beside her, his head hanging low, his body shaking.

"I'm Detective Black," Dane said, offering his badge, "and I understand you found a package."

Trent's head jerked up. "*You.*" He surged to his feet. "*What the hell are you doing here?*"

Dane kept his expression blank. "I'm the lead detective on your ex-wife's murder case."

"You're in burglary."

"No, I'm a homicide detective." That was all the guy needed to know. *Because I could be talking to a killer.* As a guy with access to both Katherine and Amy Evans, Trent had made it to the top of his suspect list. Now, if he could just connect Trent to Savannah Slater...*One step at a time.* Dane narrowed his eyes. "Where are the pictures?"

Trent's shaking hand pointed to a door on the left. Dane headed for the door. He yanked on his gloves; then a quick twist of the knob revealed that the doctors' two offices were connected. The crime-scene techs followed behind him, and the acrid scent of vomit hit him immediately.

Hell.

He made his way to the desk and saw the scattered photos. The stark black-and-white images of Amy Evans's death. *Hell.* Dane studied the small white box. He'd already initiated a search to track the package that had been delivered to Katherine. So far, that search hadn't proved fruitful. He doubted this one would either. The nondescript package could have been purchased almost anywhere.

As for the rose petals and that vase of roses—*eleven roses in that vase*—he'd already started sweeps at the local florist shops.

The techs closed in around him. Dane knew they'd dust the box and the flowers for fingerprints. They'd dust the whole damn room. On a case this big, nothing could be overlooked.

Dane's gaze darted back to the photographs.

The photos hadn't been printed at some local drugstore. No tags were on the back of the images, no numbers that would lead them to a specific printer. But they could still analyze the paper and the ink.

Dane scanned the room. Nothing seemed disturbed or out of place. He hurried to the office's main door. The lock hadn't been damaged in any way.

He opened the door and found Mac with the two receptionists. "Did one of you put the package on Lancaster's desk?" Dane asked.

They both shook their head.

"He locked his office on Friday night," the redhead said, inching a bit closer to Mac. "And no packages came in that day."

Amy had still been alive on Friday. The package couldn't have come in then. Keeping his voice easy and calm, Dane asked, "What about this morning?"

The redhead shook her head. "The office stayed locked until Dr. Lancaster came in. No one went inside until then."

"He came in looking angry," the blonde said. "So we just stayed away from him."

Yeah, Dane was sure the guy had been angry when he'd arrived.

"Are there any security cameras on this floor?" Dane asked.

"No, the doctors specifically requested that none be installed," the blonde receptionist said. "They want to protect the privacy of their patients."

He'd talk with the guard downstairs. Maybe there'd be footage of the perp entering or leaving the lobby. Or maybe the guard would remember seeing *someone*.

Dane turned away and headed back to the two shrinks.

Trent was still seated. His face was even paler than before, and his hands were curled tightly around the arms of his chair.

"Dr. Lancaster," Dane began, "do you know anyone who would want to hurt your wife?"

Trent flinched. "Me." The answer was stark, and not at all what Dane had expected. "Everyone else loved her. I was the one who fucked things up and caused the divorce. I was the one pissed because she tried to take my practice."

"*Trent*…" Dr. Knight began, her voice high and nervous as she edged toward him.

"*I'm* the one with the motive. I'm the one who wanted her to disappear, so let's just cut through the crap, okay?" Trent shoved to his feet and swayed unsteadily. "I've been angry with her. She hated me, but that—" He broke off, swallowing. "I'd *never* do that to her. Not to anyone. It's *sick*." He was panting. "And Amy…she didn't deserve it." His shoulders slumped. "*I'm sorry, Amy.*"

Dr. Knight stepped in front of him. She was a pretty woman, with hard, gray eyes. "That's *not* a confession, Detective."

He hadn't thought it was.

"I was with Trent when he found the package. He's clearly devastated."

To Dane, it looked like the guy was heading into shock, but appearances could be deceiving.

Dr. Knight glanced at Trent but then moved closer to Dane. "I need to talk privately with you."

He moved back and let the lady lead the way. She led him to the lobby, where Mac was just finishing up with the women. Mac headed toward them.

"But—" Dr. Knight began.

"This is my partner, Detective Mac Turner." Whatever she wanted to say to him, she could also say to Mac.

Gray eyes darted between them, then briefly over her shoulder toward her office. "I could get into so much trouble for this."

"For what?" Mac asked, keeping his voice low.

"I saw the pictures of poor Amy." Her own voice sounded a bit broken. "But I've seen images like that before."

Dane didn't speak.

"When?" Mac asked quietly.

Dr. Knight glanced at the reception area. With her voice even quieter, she said, "I have a patient...*had* a patient...there's confidentiality, but I *can't* let anyone else die—"

"What about the patient?" Mac pushed.

"Have you heard of the Valentine Killer?" Dr. Knight leaned toward them. "Because he killed women, just like this. He bound them. Sliced their arms. Drove a knife into their heart. When I saw the rose petals scattered on Trent's desk, I thought of him." The phone rang, and she jumped. Her hand rose to cover her heart. "My patient is linked to Valentine."

Then she grabbed Dane's shirt. "I knew she was dangerous. I just didn't realize she would *kill*."

Dane didn't move a muscle. "Doctor, are you telling me a patient of yours committed this crime?"

Mac froze beside him.

Miserable now, Dr. Knight nodded. "I thought she had her impulses under control, but my gut told me she was dangerous." Dr. Knight's eyes were now glued to the floor. "Katherine Cole." The name was a hopeless whisper from Dr. Knight. "She was my patient. I'm afraid she's the killer."

- 10 -

The police officer trailing behind Katherine was in plainclothes—jeans and a dark T-shirt. He looked like a tired college student, just running into Joe's Café to grab an early morning bite to eat. He didn't even make eye contact with Katherine.

But she knew he was there. And she felt better for having him close by.

After Dane was called away, she'd dressed as fast as she could. She wasn't going to hide in her house. She would get out, do her normal routine, and if Valentine was out there...

Then maybe by being *out*, she'd be able to find him.

Katherine took her usual seat at the counter. Joe came over at once, his face drawn in lines of worry. "I'm glad you came back." He leaned toward her, and his gaze searched her face. "You ran out of here so fast the other morning, I thought something was wrong."

Just one or two things. Murder. Torture. The usual.

"I wasn't feeling that great." She offered him a smile. "I'm sorry if I worried you."

"You worried us both."

She turned her head, and saw Ben Miller on a nearby stool. Like Joe, Ben had always seemed friendly, but since she hadn't been in a frame of mind to make friends, she'd closed him out.

She'd closed everyone out. It had become habit for her.

Ben usually arrived at the café at the same time she did. A few years older than she was, Ben wore dark-framed glasses and always looked as if he'd just left the gym. Sweats, freshly washed hair. She suspected he worked out at the gym across the street, then raced over for Joe's famous breakfast. Joe really did make the best beignets she'd ever tasted, and after moving to New Orleans, she'd made it a point to taste every beignet she could.

Ben hadn't ever hit on her. He just ate, gazed at the news, then went about his business. He'd even brought his girlfriend with him a few times, a pretty blonde in spandex.

Katherine realized she should say something. Their concern was making her uncomfortable, especially since she was lying to them both. Her fingers tapped on the counter. "It was really nothing." The cop had to be listening in on this. "I just needed to get back home."

But it mattered to her that these two men cared about what happened to her. She wasn't just walking through life like a ghost after all.

Ben's dark brown eyes drifted over her face. "If someone's giving you trouble," he said softly, "you can tell me."

"Damn right." Joe slapped his apron on the counter. "You're a good lady. You come in here like clockwork, never bother anyone. If someone's bothering you, me and Ben will take care of him for you."

She blinked away tears. "Thank you." *I matter.* "But it's nothing, really. Just a little sickness." Her smile was more genuine this time. "Can I just have my usual, please, Joe?"

"Sure thing." But Joe hesitated, and his face became more serious. "I know about trouble, okay?" He reached into his pocket and pulled out a gold coin. "Seven years sober," he whispered. His fingers fisted around that coin. His gaze held hers. "When it's not easy, you have to remember: things *always get better.*" He gave her a firm nod.

She nodded back and forced a smile. *Things could get better, but how many people have to die first?*

The bell over the door rang, signaling a new customer. Katherine glanced over and saw a leggy blonde making her way to Ben's side.

"Sorry I'm late," she said as she pressed a quick kiss to Ben's cheek. "Spin class was a bitch."

The woman had an easy, casual confidence. Her fingers linked with Ben's. There was warmth and affection in her gaze. These two, they were normal. Happy.

I want to be like that.

Ben bent and whispered to his girlfriend, and the blonde laughed softly.

"I'll take that order to go," Ben told Joe.

Joe started to bundle up some beignets in a plastic container.

Ben and the blonde stood, but Ben cast Katherine one more glance. "Don't forget, if you have trouble…"

"What's going on?" the blonde asked, her eyebrows rising.

"Nothing," Katherine said immediately. The last thing she wanted was to pull these two into her nightmare.

The blonde's gaze was worried as it lingered on Katherine. Not worried in the jealous way. Just *worried.*

Joe pushed the to-go order toward Ben, and the couple headed toward the door. Katherine exhaled slowly. Her gaze swept over the diner. Joe had put out a few dozen red tablecloths for Valentine's Day. The red was dark—and it reminded her far too much of blood. Joe had also put bouquets of white balloons in each corner of the restaurant. His patrons were smiling, relaxing, obviously enjoying the decorations.

But those decorations just made Katherine tense.

Valentine's Day is so close.

The bell jingled again. She figured it was Ben and his blonde leaving, so she didn't glance back. But then she heard, "*Katherine.*"

Dane's voice.

She turned toward the door.

Ben and the blonde weren't outside yet. Dane and Mac had come into the café. They looked grim, determined.

Another kill? She stood on trembling legs. Oh no, please…

"Dane?" The blonde said his name in surprise. *She* glanced between Dane and Katherine. "Is everything okay?"

"Nothing for you to worry about, Maggie," Dane said as he gave her a quick nod. His gaze scanned over Ben. Then he hurried toward Katherine. His voice dropped, and he said, "You need to come with me."

"Katherine, is this a friend of yours?" Joe asked as his eyes narrowed suspiciously.

Ben had tensed.

Maggie also appeared nervous. "He's a cop," Katherine heard the blonde tell Ben. "He works with my dad."

Katherine slid off the stool. "It's okay, Joe. This is Detective Dane Black."

Dane tossed some money down on the counter. "Come on, Katherine."

She hurried to grab her bag. The plainclothes shadow was also rising to leave.

"But she didn't eat!" Joe called out.

It didn't matter. Suddenly she wasn't hungry.

Then they were outside. The rising heat hit her in the face, and before she could head toward Dane's parked car, he was pulling her away from the street and into the shadows on the side of the building.

"Do you trust me?" Dane demanded as his hands closed around her shoulders.

She tensed. Katherine didn't want to give him the harsh answer, but the truth was, she didn't trust anyone.

"I need you to trust me, Katherine."

She could only shake her head. "I'm sorry."

A muscle flexed in his jaw. "I think the killer has been very close to you, Katherine. Close all along, and you didn't even realize it."

Her skin started to feel icy.

"Amy Evans used to be Amy Lancaster."

The ice started to burn.

"As in Trent's ex-wife."

— — —

Dane led Katherine to the interrogation room, making sure to keep his hand light on her shoulder. They'd come in the back entrance to make sure no press saw them. Or rather, her.

Trent was just coming out of the captain's office, with Evelyn at his side.

Dane didn't glance their way as he led Katherine by them.

"Katherine!" Trent tried to hurry to her.

Mac pushed the guy back. "Sir, you need to back away."

Dr. Knight jumped in. "I told you, Trent, she's a disturbed woman."

Dane's teeth locked, and his finger skimmed over Katherine's shoulder. Her whole body had tensed, and he knew fury when he felt it, but Katherine didn't say a word to her ex-shrink. Though her eyes sure looked pissed.

Since she wasn't talking, he was more than happy to say, "Dr. Knight, why don't you keep those opinions to yourself for now?"

He walked right past the FBI profiler. He'd called Wayne in for this scene, and the agent's head inclined just slightly. Dane might not like the profiler, but he would use him.

He would use almost anyone to get his job done.

Ross was around too, but staying out of sight for the time being. Like the marshal would have let them bring Katherine into the station again without his okay.

When Dane had called him, Ross had been hesitant about the plan, but he'd finally agreed. Once he'd realized this gave them their best shot at stopping a killer, Ross had been ready to come on board.

Dane opened the door to interrogation room one and escorted Katherine inside. She eased into a chair and stared up at him.

He could see the fear in her eyes. Was she afraid he was setting her up? Evelyn had sure come across strong in her belief that Katherine was a killer, but he knew one thing that the shrink didn't know.

"You had an alibi when Amy Evans vanished," he said. "You were under surveillance. The cops were watching you."

Trent had been pissed when he left Katherine's place after their date. So angry that he'd gone out and gotten a little revenge on his ex?

Maybe.

Or maybe the plan had been to murder Amy all along, and to use Katherine just to raise suspicion about Valentine once more.

Dane had to see if he could connect the dots between their first victim and the not-so-good doctor.

His fingers brushed her arm. "Just stay here. I'll be back soon."

He might even be returning with an audience.

When he was at the door, he glanced back at her. Just that fast, it looked like her fear was gone. There was no trace of any emotion in her eyes.

Her hand lifted, and she tucked a strand of hair behind her ear. Then she rolled her right shoulder, as if pushing away a burden.

Dane left the interrogation room and kept his face set in hard, tense lines. He carried his own darkness. One that he worked so hard to hide from others.

"What's going on?" Trent demanded as Dane approached him. "Why is Kat here?"

Dane ground his teeth at the use of "Kat."

"According to your partner," Dane said, inclining his head toward Evelyn, whose eyes were worried, "*Katherine* may have important evidence to contribute to this case."

"What are you talking about?" Trent yanked a hand through his disheveled hair. "How could she have evidence?"

"You really don't know who she is?" Mac asked, cocking his head.

Marcus the profiler was watching from just a few feet away.

Trent shook his head.

"You ever hear of the Valentine Killer?" Dane said.

Trent's brows lowered. "Vaguely. I don't really follow the news." The guy actually sounded impatient. What a prick.

"Three years ago, a man named Michael O'Rourke killed four women in Boston." Four they knew of. "He kidnapped them, bound their hands and feet with rope, used his knife to slice their arms, then drove his knife into each woman's heart."

Trent stumbled back and bumped into the captain. "Like what happened with Amy."

Dane kept his stare on the man.

Trent's gaze darted to the closed interrogation room door. "Was Katherine a victim who got away?"

Mac pressed closer. "Katherine was the killer's fiancée."

Trent blanched. "*What?*"

Dr. Knight bit her lip. "Trent—"

"She found him right after he killed Stephanie Gilbert," Dane said. "Katherine is the one who called the cops, but they didn't arrive in time to catch Valentine. He vanished, and the FBI has been looking for him ever since."

Trent's chest rose and fell rapidly. His gaze turned to Evelyn. There was fury in his eyes. "You said she was *damaged.*"

"She is, and—"

He lifted his hand. His fingers were rock steady as his eyes came back to Dane's. "Was she in on the killings? Is that what this is about? Dammit, do you think she killed Amy?"

This was what they'd wanted. To see the doctor's reaction. To push him for a response. "What do *you* think?" Dane asked.

"I think I didn't know her at all. I thought she was vulnerable, hurt. She seemed to *need* me." His eyes squeezed shut. "Did I mention Amy to her? Did I show her a picture? I can't remember."

"It would have been easy enough for her to find out about your ex," Dr. Knight said. "Actually"—she looked stricken as she paused and confessed—"I might have even told her. I just can't be sure."

They had the doctor off-balance. Now it was time to move this into interrogation. Dane glanced at the captain, who gave a faint nod. "Let's go someplace private, where we can talk more."

Mac led Trent and Evelyn toward the second interrogation room, which was just a few feet from the one where Katherine waited. Trent's gaze darted to that room, again and again.

Neither the profiler nor the captain followed them into the room. They were going to watch from the observation area.

Once inside, Mac stood at his usual position near the wall.

Dane took a seat across from the two shrinks. *If anyone in the room was skilled at playing head games...*

He'd have to tread carefully.

"Do either of you know a Savannah Slater?" Dane asked.

Dane saw Trent's eyelashes flicker.

"The name is familiar," Dr. Knight murmured. Her brow furrowed, and then she inhaled sharply. "Wait, is she that poor reporter who was killed?"

"Yes, Dr. Knight—"

"Evelyn," she murmured, cutting through his words. "At this point..." Her smile was tired. "Just call me Evelyn."

"Savannah Slater was killed last week."

"In a manner very similar to your ex-wife's murder," Mac added, his gaze ever watchful.

Trent's shoulders sagged. "I knew her. And I knew Amy."

It was exactly what Dane had been hoping to hear. His gaze cut to Mac.

Mac's right eyebrow lifted.

Dane's gaze slid back to his suspect.

Trent licked his lips. "Savannah and I went out a few times. Nothing serious."

"When was this?" Dane kept his voice expressionless.

"About six months ago." Trent's hands pushed against the tabletop. "Maybe seven. We met in a club. She was smart and pretty." He paused, then added softly, "A long-legged brunette."

"Just your type," Evelyn whispered. "Just like Katherine."

"What is it that you're saying here?" Trent asked as he leaned forward. There was a harder intensity entering his voice.

Evelyn put a comforting hand on his shoulder.

"Are you telling me," Trent continued, eyes glinting, breath coming faster, "that you suspect Katherine was involved in these crimes? That she killed these women?" His eyes widened. "Why? Because she was jealous?" He looked around the room. "Okay, I *did* hook up with Savannah while Katherine and I were dating, but Katherine never really seemed to care that much what I did or who I did it with."

The guy was such a charmer. And he was sure doing a whole lot of talking.

Evelyn bit her lip. Oh, yeah, that lady had things she was dying to say. But probably couldn't, thanks to good old doctor-patient confidentiality.

Evelyn's fingers tightened around Trent's shoulder. "Are you going to question Katherine?" she asked.

Dane nodded.

"I should have stopped her." Now Evelyn's eyes were haunted. "When she told me about the nightmares and the blood she kept seeing, I should have stopped her." Her breath rasped out. "But I was too worried about my career, about losing everything that I'd built if I didn't keep my mouth shut."

Trent turned his head toward her and frowned.

Evelyn's shoulders straightened. "But I don't care what I lose at this point. I can't let anyone else get hurt."

Dane waited. Even Mac had taken a step closer to the table.

"I've spent hours with Katherine. Many hours..." Evelyn's words were soft. "She can seem so normal, but there were times I'd catch her watching me. She'd give me responses she *thought* she was supposed to give. All she was doing was pretending." Her voice was now a stark whisper. "When I told her what I suspected, Katherine stopped therapy."

"And you suspected—what, exactly?" Mac asked.

"That Katherine Cole has sociopathic tendencies. Her emotional responses are stunted, if they are there at all. She mimics the behavior of others, but…" Evelyn shook her head. "I'm not sure if she feels anything at all."

Dane maintained his expressionless mask. "So you think Katherine is as crazy as Valentine?"

Evelyn licked her lips. "I think she is just as *dangerous* as he is."

"But you didn't think she was an immediate threat to anyone, right? Because if you had, then you would have been obligated to report that to the police." Dane knew how doctor-patient confidentiality situations worked. He'd handled cases before in which a breach had been necessary. If there was no specific threat…

"Katherine never said she was planning to hurt or kill anyone." Evelyn's voice was still soft, but her shoulders straightened and she met Dane's stare head-on. "But I've been working with troubled patients my entire professional career. I know what I'm talking about here. I *know* that Katherine is a threat."

A threat who had an alibi for Amy's murder.

Trent swore.

"I *warned* you," Evelyn snapped at Trent, sounding both defensive and scared. "You didn't listen to me. The woman is dangerous, but you looked at her and saw some kind of broken damn princess. You *always* do that. You always go for the weak ones."

"Why was she even in therapy?" Mac asked quietly. "Why go to see you in the first place if she was just going to pretend with you?"

Her smile was sad. "Because Katherine *knows* that something is wrong with her. She knows that the impulses she has are bad. I honestly believe that she wants to stop herself, but she can't."

Not what Dane had been hoping to hear during this little talk. "Don't we all have the capacity for violence, though, Doc? Deep inside, just waiting to come out?"

"Well, yes," she admitted, "under the right circumstances, I suppose, but—"

"It's all about motivation, huh?" Dane asked, struggling to keep his voice mild. "I mean, it's about the trigger. And I've sure seen lots of triggers during my years in homicide."

Evelyn's frown had deepened.

"People can kill because of jealousy, lust, greed…" His gaze returned to Trent. "They can also kill because they're damn pissed off at an ex who cleaned them out. And maybe—just maybe—one night during a chat with a coworker, the perfect opportunity presented itself."

"What the hell are you talking about?" Trent demanded as he surged to his feet. His chair flew back and slammed into the floor with a crack.

"Easy." Mac was there instantly, locking a hard hand around the guy's arm. Mac could always move so much faster than people realized. The quiet, deadly type. One of the reasons he made such a great partner.

Dane also rose to his feet. "I'm saying to drop the act, Doc," he snapped as he dropped his own mild veneer. "You've known about Katherine's past for quite some time, so stop acting like you're shocked to discover her real identity."

Trent's gaze flew from him to Mac and then to Evelyn. Dane could almost see the wheels turning in Trent's head as the guy tried to figure out his next move.

Figure faster, jerk.

"Trent?" Evelyn whispered.

Trent gave a grim nod. His shoulders thrust back even as his chin jutted up in the air. And damn it all, he even gave that arrogant-ass *sniff* again as he said, "Hell yes, I knew. So what?"

And that was what Dane had needed to hear. "Well, that leads me to my next question. What is your alibi for both Saturday and Sunday? I want places, I want names. *Everything.*"

"You think he's a suspect." Evelyn rocked back in her chair. "But I just told you about Katherine."

"Yes, you did, but Katherine has an airtight alibi. She's covered for Amy's murder." His stare drifted between Trent and Evelyn. "Are *you*, Dr. Lancaster?"

– – –

"They sure lawyered up damn fast," the police captain said to Dane as the two men watched the shrinks huddling with their high-priced lawyers in the interrogation room. Lawyers who had busted ass getting down to the station.

"Figured they would," Dane said.

The more he learned, the more it looked like these murders weren't about a serial killer at all. They were about a jerk who wanted out of alimony payments. Had the reporter just been his setup kill? To make the cops to think Valentine was involved? Or Katherine? Hell, the guy could have learned all about Valentine if he'd gone through the notes that Evelyn had doubtlessly taken during her sessions with Katherine.

Just then, Trent glanced up and stared at the mirror. There was no missing the fury in his eyes.

The lawyers rose, followed by Trent and Evelyn. They said some final words and headed for the door together.

Dane and Harley moved to cut them off. As they met in the bull pen, another door opened. Katherine appeared in the doorway of interrogation room one as Mac escorted her out.

Perfect timing. Timing they'd planned.

Trent's gaze flew to Katherine. Then back to Dane.

"What's her alibi?" Trent demanded as he pushed his lawyer away.

Katherine flinched.

The captain locked a hand on Dane's shoulder. "This is what we wanted, remember?" Harley said under his breath.

Trent was just a few feet from Katherine now. "Where were you when Amy was being sliced open?"

Katherine's nostrils flared. "I was with the cops. They had me under surveillance."

Trent's head whipped toward Dane. "You're screwing the cop. *That's* why he's trying to pin these kills on me." His face was mottled with fury. "I knew what you were. I saw Evelyn's files. She thought your case was so damn special."

Evelyn gasped behind him.

Trent's gaze raked Katherine once more. "What made a killer spare you when he killed every other woman who looked just like you?" He paused and glanced between Katherine and Dane. "But you got to the cop, didn't you?"

Beside Dane, Harley had stiffened.

"I saw the way you looked at her this morning," Trent continued. "I *saw*. And I'll be damned if I let you two set me up."

His lawyer finally managed to haul the guy away. With a last, wide-eyed look at Katherine, Evelyn followed them.

"*My* office," Harley snapped. "Mac, you keep an eye on Ms. Cole for us."

Shit.

Dane turned away from Katherine and followed the captain. Harley slammed the door behind him. "Tell me that pompous prick is wrong."

Dane immediately said, "He's wrong. I'm not setting him up."

"Tell me that you *didn't* sleep with her."

Angry now, Dane snapped, "She wasn't a suspect. She's a consenting adult." Why the hell did he have to explain this? "We didn't do a damn thing wrong."

The captain slumped into his chair. "Hell, Black, you *know* better!"

"She's still not a suspect."

"If we go to court, that jerk's lawyer will have a field day about your involvement with her."

"We'll get enough evidence that it won't matter what BS story the guy spins."

"You'd fucking better!" Harley leveled his index finger at Dane. "Because if the killer walks, it's your ass on the line."

"I know how to watch my own ass," Dane said. He wasn't backing down, not from the captain, not from anyone. His record was spotless. Emotion didn't get involved in his cases. He did the job. He caught the killers.

Case fucking closed.

"Dane..." Harley slumped into his chair, and, just that fast, it wasn't simply the captain talking to him. It was a man who'd been his mentor for more than fifteen years.

Harley's eyes drifted to the framed photograph on his desk. A photograph of a blonde wearing a graduation cap and smiling as she stood next to her proud father.

Margaret Dunning. Harley's only daughter. She'd been at the café when Dane went in to get Katherine. She'd been nervous when she saw him.

Maggie knew Dane worked homicide. She hated homicide. Hated her father's job and the danger it brought.

"It's not just about the case." Harley's voice was softer now as he reached out for that frame. He glanced up at Dane. "You know you're the closest thing I have to a son."

They didn't usually talk about Dane's past. Or Harley's. They'd both tried to bury it.

"I don't want to see you get hurt." He put the photograph back down. "I don't want you getting in too deep with that woman, okay? She's got some dangerous ties."

"Katherine won't hurt—" Dane began immediately.

Harley's lips thinned. His cheeks reddened. "Even if Lancaster is the one killing in New Orleans, do you really believe that Valentine has just walked away from Katherine Cole? By all accounts, she's the only thing that ever mattered to the man."

\- - -

Trent had been reduced to living in a cheap motel room. The cops were at his apartment, tearing through every drawer and file he had.

By the time Trent left the police station and arrived back at his home, the cops had gotten a search warrant. They'd met him in the lobby of his building. His lawyer had said the search was BS, that the cops had just found an overly sympathetic judge who should never have granted the warrant, but there wasn't a whole lot Trent could do at that point. Someone had remembered him threatening Amy—and, yeah, back during the divorce, he'd made a few threats. Heat of the moment shit. He hadn't *meant* them.

But what he'd meant didn't matter. The cops had a witness to the threats. They had him tied to two victims, and now, thanks to that warrant, the cops were already in his fucking underwear drawer.

He walked the short length of his motel room. *This dump sucks.* His body was tense, his hands shaking. Amy was dead—*dead.* Sure, he'd nearly hated her by the end of their divorce, but he hadn't wanted her dead.

He'd wanted her out of his life, but still breathing somewhere else.

A slight rap sounded at his door.

Tense, he glanced over at the door. He'd told his lawyer where he was going. Told Evelyn. Poor Evelyn. The woman was a wreck—and so sure that Katherine was setting him up.

He should have listened to Evelyn when she tried to warn him. Should have stayed far away from Katherine.

But Katherine just hadn't seemed dangerous to him. If she was truly a killer, he should have seen it. But maybe he'd spent too many days counseling bored housewives and sullen teenagers. Maybe he'd lost his edge. Maybe he couldn't really see the sickness in people's minds anymore.

The rap sounded again.

Trent headed for the door. He glanced through the peephole, frowned, then yanked open the door. "What are you doing here?" he asked.

Evelyn walked inside, her steps determined, but her hands shaking. Her hair had come out of its twist. "It's my fault."

Trent sighed. "Don't worry, Evelyn. This will all be over soon. There's nothing to find at my place."

She shook her head. "I brought her into our lives."

"We can't save everyone, Evie," he said, using his old nickname for her. Trent pulled her against his chest, and for a moment he just held her.

He felt her nod. "I know." She lifted her head. Stared up at him. Tears glinted in her eyes, and she looked vulnerable.

Almost beautiful.

Trent stiffened. He wasn't going there. Not again.

He released her.

A furrow appeared between her brows. "Trent?"

He shook his head. "You should go home, Evie."

Evelyn's features tightened, but she gave a small nod. "You're right. We're both upset. We can talk tomorrow."

There was always tomorrow.

At the door, Evelyn glanced back. He couldn't read the emotion in her gaze, but then, she'd always been hard to read.

"I'm so sorry this has happened to you," she said.

His brows rose. His smile was forced. "My lawyer will have this handled in hours. The PD will be the sorry ones—sorry they ever messed with me." Or they would be, if he could actually afford a lawyer who gave a damn. The lawyer who'd come down to the police station was way over his budget and already threatening to walk.

But Evelyn bought his act. She gave a little wave and left.

He shut the door behind her, catching the faint scent of her lingering perfume. For a moment he just stood there, thinking about the mess of his life—and trying not to think about those black-and-white images of Amy's body.

But he couldn't get them the hell out of his head.

A knock sounded at the door again. Sighing, he turned back and yanked open the door. "Evie, look, I told you—" His words ended in a hard gasp.

A knife had been shoved into his chest.

Trent tried to speak but couldn't. He was shoved back, away from the door. Away from help.

He hit the floor. His blood seeped out. His body began to grow numb.

The door closed with a soft click, sealing him inside with his attacker.

"You're still alive," Trent heard. "I missed your heart."

The knife lifted.

"Don't worry, I'll get it this time."

- 11 -

Dane didn't come to Katherine's house that night. Mac did instead. He looked grim and determined, and he spent the night on her couch. He was the silent type, all right.

The next morning, as the sunlight trickled through her window, Katherine stood in the kitchen, glancing out at the line of trees near the edge of her yard. She was sipping her coffee when Mac entered the kitchen. He'd changed into fresh clothes, and his gaze was as watchful as always as it swept over her. "What can you tell me about Dane?" she blurted out when he'd had time to get his own mug of coffee.

"The captain told him to stay away." Mac was silent for several moments. Then he sighed and his face softened. "He can't be involved with you, not while he's trying to take down Lancaster."

"We're not *involved*."

"He sure looks at you as if you are."

She wasn't sure how to respond to that.

Then she heard raised voices outside her front door. Shouts. Her body tensed as she recognized one of the voices as Dane's. Whatever was going on out there, he sure sounded pissed.

Mac hurried out of the kitchen and yanked open the front door. "What are you doing here, man?"

From the shouts, Katherine knew someone else was out there with Dane, but she sure hadn't expected to see Evelyn.

Evelyn's eyes were wide and tear filled. A uniformed cop stood beside her with his hands wrapped around her arms, as if restraining her.

"Where is he?" Evelyn demanded.

Katherine frowned.

"*Where is he?*" Evelyn screamed. The reserved, always questioning, always watching doctor was screaming.

Katherine's gaze darted to Dane.

"It seems Dr. Trent Lancaster is missing." His voice was mild.

"Missing?" Katherine said, feeling lost.

"Innocent men don't run," Mac said. He stood beside Katherine with his arms at his sides

"He wouldn't run!" Evelyn's face was red and blotchy. "I went back to his motel this morning. Something happened to him, I know it!"

Katherine could almost feel Dane and Mac's silent communication. She'd noticed that they often spoke to each other in glances or raised brows.

"I caught her on the way up the walk," Dane murmured with a nod toward Evelyn. "She was racing for the door."

"Because *she* did something to him!" Evelyn pointed at Katherine. The cop tightened his hold on the shrink. "She killed him, just like she did the others!"

Katherine took a step toward her. "I had a guard at my house all night. How was I supposed to kill someone with cops all around me?"

Evelyn's eyes widened. She glanced at Mac, Dane, then the uniform. "Where is he?" Now her voice was hushed. Desperate. "*Where is Trent?*"

Katherine didn't know, but Dane's hard stare told her that he'd be finding out.

— — —

The smell of bleach hit Dane the instant the maid opened the motel room door.

Mac was behind him. "Thanks, ma'am," he murmured to the lady with the nervous hands.

The maid backed away.

Dane eased inside. His gaze went to the floor. He was staring down at concrete. The carpet was gone and the scent of bleach hung heavily in the air.

They both knew what this scene meant. Either Trent Lancaster had been attacked in this motel room, or he'd attacked someone there.

Someone had cleaned up that room, and it sure as hell hadn't been the maid.

Dane made his way around the room as he yanked on gloves and went to work.

— — —

Katherine forced her shoulders back as she unlocked the door to her gallery. Plainclothes cops were standing across the street, trying to blend in, but their avid gazes kept drifting to her.

The bag of beignets in her hand jostled a bit as she opened the door. She'd made a quick stop by Joe's Café on her way to the gallery. The gallery was in the Quarter, in a hundred-year-old building that had been partially renovated and rented out to her. *Get back to your routine. Try to draw him out by acting normal.* That had been Dane's advice to her.

So she was trying to follow his orders.

The gallery was dark inside, and her hand automatically reached out to hit the lights.

Only the lights didn't come on. She pushed the switch again and again, but nothing happened.

Her body tensed. Short-circuits were common in buildings this old. She'd had a repairman out three times already in the past six months. Just because the lights weren't on, it didn't mean anything.

Get a grip. Right after she'd left Boston, she'd seen Valentine in every shadow. Heard him in every rustle of sound.

But he hadn't been there.

And just because her lights weren't working, it didn't mean he was here, either.

But he is in New Orleans.

Her breath was coming out too hard and fast.

She noticed the alarm also wasn't beeping. That was normal, though, if the power had shorted. The alarm wouldn't work until she got the repairman in there.

Katherine turned back toward the plainclothes cops. They'd crept closer when she opened her door. "Can one of you go check the circuit breaker at the back of the building? I've been having trouble."

The shorter cop nodded and immediately took off toward the back. The second cop stepped toward Katherine. "You need me, ma'am?" he asked.

Her gallery was dark. The lights went off there all the time. There was no reason for her to panic.

Right?

"I-I'm fine. Can you just make sure he gets the lights back on?" She turned away from him. Katherine kept a flashlight in her desk. She'd get it, and if the cops couldn't fix the problem from the outside, she'd look around the gallery to see what she could do about the problem.

She took a few hesitant steps toward her desk. Her eyes strained, trying to adjust to the darkness.

Nothing looked disturbed or out of place or—

She wasn't alone.

The bag slipped from her fingers, and the beignets spilled across the floor.

A man was slouched in the chair to the left. He was so still and silent that she hadn't noticed him at first. Her breath heaved in her chest as she took another step forward. Her eyes narrowed as she strained to make out his features. There was a large window behind him, but the curtains were drawn, and only a faint trickle of light spilled inside. But she could just see his profile. The strong lines and angles of his face were familiar.

Trent.

Her thigh bumped into the edge of her desk, and she fumbled in the lower desk drawer. Her fingers slid under the drawer's false bottom, and she pulled out a small, black gun. Dane thought Trent might have killed his ex-wife, and now Trent was waiting for her inside her darkened gallery? Oh, hell no, that wasn't good.

"Trent?" Her voice was hoarse as she called to him. Her fingers were trembling around the gun.

Trent didn't stir.

She wished she could see more of him.

"Trent, how did you get in?"

He still wasn't moving.

"Trent, the police are outside." Instead of inching forward, she was now inching back. She was getting the cops, and whatever game Trent *thought* he was playing, well, the guy could think again. "You stay right there," she snapped at him. "Don't even think of coming at me. I-I've got a gun."

Then she heard a loud click—like a lock turning. Behind her.

Her whole body went into high alert. She started to whirl toward this new threat, but strong hands wrapped around her body, and she was jerked back against a hard chest.

"You aren't going to use that gun on me, are you, Kat?"

That low whisper had haunted her nightmares for so long.

It was a whisper she'd never been able to forget.

Valentine's whisper.

‒ ‒ ‒

"What do you think? Is the shrink in the wind?" Mac asked as he backed up and let the crime-scene techs take over the motel room.

Dane shook his head. "He left his wallet behind. All of his credit cards. His cash." What little there had been of it.

"A guy like him would have plenty of backup resources."

"No, the ex-wife got all the money in the divorce." Trent had gotten nothing. Dane's gaze swept over the room once more. He knew a crime-scene cleanup when he saw one, and this scene—it had been fucking thoroughly cleaned.

No blood drops. No sign of a struggle. Nothing at all.

He glanced at the door once more. They'd already put out an APB on Trent Lancaster, just in case, but the knot in his gut was telling him that he had to do more right *then*.

He and Mac headed outside. "We'll need to talk to Evelyn again." The woman had been damn near hysterical earlier, so sure that something had happened to Trent.

She'd been right.

Dane's gaze scanned the parking lot. They'd talked to the front desk clerk, and the guy had remembered seeing Lancaster pull up in his sports car. Apparently they didn't get a whole lot of Jags at that place.

Considering the financial mess the doc was in, Dane was rather surprised he'd even kept the ride.

But that fancy vehicle wasn't there now. Every cop in the city was looking for it, though. Dane slid into his vehicle.

Find that Jag and they'd find—

The radio crackled to life. Dane leaned forward. "Got a hit on that APB," he was told. "Your sports car was just spotted in a tow-away zone." The dispatch rattled off the address—an address that was too familiar to Dane.

"Hell." His breath rushed out. "That's three blocks from Katherine's gallery." He'd given the guards orders to stay close to the gallery.

They'd better damn well be close. "Send the cops in now!" Dane barked. "I want them standing by Katherine's side until I get there."

He raced down the road with a squeal of his tires. Why was Trent's car so close to Katherine's gallery? No damn way it was a coincidence. No fucking way.

He tried to get Katherine on the line. But her phone just rang and rang, then her voice mail picked up. Shit. "Katherine, get to the cops who are watching you. Stay with them. Got it? *Stay with them.*"

Then he and Mac burned rubber to get to her.

− − −

"Good girl. You don't need to answer that call. It's no one who matters."

His arms were still too tight around her. His face was behind her, his lips near her ear as he whispered, "And you don't need the gun. Trent can't hurt you or anyone else anymore."

Her gaze flew back to Trent. He still hadn't moved. Not at all. "The gun isn't just for Trent," she said.

He laughed behind her. "Oh, sweet Kat, you don't have to worry about me. I'd never hurt you."

She was supposed to believe a man who spent his nights carving up women? Katherine would love nothing more than to put a bullet in his heart. If he actually had a heart.

"I couldn't let Trent hurt you. I can't let anyone hurt you."

Then she felt the press of his lips against her neck.

Katherine shuddered.

"I'll *never* let anyone hurt you."

Fists pounded against the gallery's front door.

He laughed again. "I locked the door behind you. So we could have a chance to talk. It's been far too long, Kat."

"Not long enough." It was her turn to whisper. Then, because the cops were close enough to hear, she screamed, "*It's Valentine! He's here!*"

The pounding at the door doubled. "Ms. Cole!" She heard the frantic shout from one of the cops.

Shouts weren't going to help her. Bullets would.

She took a deep breath and knew that this was her chance. Katherine lunged away from him, then spun and fired—

Only the gun just clicked. Again and again.

No bullets came out.

And Valentine had disappeared into the dark shadows of the gallery. His laughter reached out to her. "Oh, Kat, did you think I didn't know about your weapon? I've been watching you."

She backed away and headed toward Trent. She reached down, trying to find a pulse.

But his skin was ice cold. And sticky.

Nausea rolled in her stomach.

The cops were still outside.

"I'm *always* watching," he told her, and he was still whispering. Just a whisper that made goose bumps rise on her arms. This felt like the nightmare she'd had dozens of times. "Remember that, and *stay the fuck away* from that detective."

A gunshot blasted.

Katherine screamed. Another blast thundered through the gallery. The cops were trying to shoot their way inside.

They needed to *hurry.*

– – –

Dane slammed on the brakes and jumped from his car. Katherine's gallery was ten feet away. Two plainclothes cops were in front, and they'd just fired at her window. Even as he leapt from his car, the shattering of the glass filled his ears.

"Fuck me," Mac muttered.

Dane ran toward the cops. "Circle around!" He looked back at Mac. "Make sure no one gets out the back entrance!" His heart was racing and his palms were sweating as he kept a death grip on his gun.

Katherine hadn't answered her phone. The cops had radioed and said they'd heard a scream from inside.

Be alive. He'd planned to use Katherine as bait to lure in Valentine, but he'd never planned for her to get hurt.

He flew through the window, crashing through the glass and heavy curtains—and almost landed on top of Trent Lancaster's body. The guy was slumped in a chair, and blood covered him.

There was a crash from the back of the gallery. He hauled ass into the back room, with the two plainclothes cops right behind him. He went in low and fast and came up with his weapon raised. "New Orleans PD! Freeze!"

And he was staring down the barrel of a gun.

He had his weapon pointed at Katherine. She had her gun pointed right at him.

"Katherine!"

Her eyes looked huge. So stark and afraid.

"Lower your gun," he ordered her.

"Valentine was here," she whispered. Slowly, the barrel of her gun angled toward the floor.

Yeah, he'd figured that when he saw the dead body. "Did you see him?"

She glanced over her shoulder. The back door was open.

Mac stood there, frowning. "No one came out this way."

"He did," Katherine whispered. "When the cops started firing, he ran out the back."

Dane motioned to the cops. They immediately ran out to search the area. He wanted to search, too. Wanted to rush out and hunt down the bastard.

But he didn't want to leave her alone.

"He was waiting for me to find Trent."

Every muscle in Dane's body vibrated with tension.

Katherine's chin jerked up. "Go," she said. "I'm fine. Just *get him.*"

That was all Dane needed to hear. He was already running through the back door.

- - -

Katherine's knees sagged, and she hit the floor. He'd been there. *He'd been there.* And he'd killed again.

Sirens were blaring in the distance. Help was coming. Only the help was too late for Trent. *She'd* been too late.

Again.

She rose to her feet and forced herself to take one step. Then another. And another. The curtains had been shoved back, and light spilled in through her smashed window. In that too-bright light, she saw Trent's body. So much blood. His chest had been carved open.

There were roses beside him. A vase—one of the vases that she kept at the gallery but never used because she hadn't been able to force herself to actually *buy* flowers—had been shattered near Trent's feet. Fresh roses, the same color as blood, were strewn over the floor.

I'm always watching.

Her nightmare was never going to end.

She started walking again. She fumbled with the locks on the front door. Why hadn't she heard him set the locks? Then she was out in that bright sunlight. The gun was in her hand, the stupid, useless gun that should have ended Valentine's life.

He'd gotten away. She'd been frozen with fear and he'd slipped away.

Get away from the death.

She put one foot in front of the other. Walked.

One foot.

In front of the other.

Do you love me, Kat? The voice from her past whispered through her mind.

She could hear the echo of her own laughter. *Of course I do. I'm marrying you, right?*

She'd been so confident. So certain.

One foot.

In front of the other.

You love all of me, right?

He'd been teasing her, or so she'd thought.

The good and the bad? You'll stay with me, for better or worse?
She'd kissed him. *That's what I get to promise in the vows.*

One foot.

In front of—

"Katherine?"

Her chin snapped up. It was Joe's voice. She was in front of Joe's Café. Joe and Ben were both there, both rushing toward her, then freezing when they saw her gun. They shouldn't be scared. There were no bullets in her gun. Valentine had taken them away.

Like he'd taken everything away from her.

"Katherine, what's happened?" Joe demanded.

I'm in shock. She realized it because she'd been this way before. She could hear the scream of police sirens getting closer now. Because she'd walked two blocks toward them? She didn't remember walking that far.

Ben reached for her arm. She flinched and her confession slipped out: "I don't like to be touched." Except by Dane. She didn't mind his touch.

He nodded and his hand opened. "Give me the gun," he said.

Her fingers tightened around the handle of her weapon. "He's…he's coming to hurt me."

Ben stared into her eyes. Behind the lenses of his glasses, his brown gaze was deep. Worried. "I won't let anyone hurt you."

Easy to say. He didn't know her. Neither did Joe. And Joe was coming up on her left. Looking just as worried as Ben.

"*Katherine!*" The roar of her name didn't make her flinch. She heard the thunder of footsteps rushing toward her.

Then she realized Ben and Joe weren't the only ones there. A small crowd had formed. Fearful folks gazed at her and her weapon.

A hard hand closed around her shoulder. "It's all right!" Dane's thundering voice carried easily. "I'm a police officer. The situation is under control."

He was lying. Nothing was under control.

Katherine turned into Dane's arms. He took the gun. Led her away.

And even though Joe called her name, she didn't look back. She was too afraid of the horror that she'd see on his face.

– – –

Katherine sat at Dane's desk, her shoulders hunched forward, with a cup of coffee—the bad shit that most of the cops avoided—cradled in her hands. She hadn't spoken much, or actually at all, since he'd brought her in to the station.

Dane and Mac had searched her gallery. The PD had hunted for blocks, roping off the area, but there had been no sign of Valentine. The guy's face—an image provided by the Boston PD—was being flashed on every TV in New Orleans. But the man had vanished.

"Did you actually *see* Valentine?" The quiet question came from Marcus. The profiler had shuffled up beside Dane.

Katherine didn't stir at the man's question. She hadn't stirred at anything.

Dane inclined his head to the nearby uniform. "Keep an eye on her," he ordered.

The sandy-haired man immediately stepped toward her.

Dane hauled the profiler into the nearest empty interrogation room. "What the hell are you implying?" Dane demanded as soon as the door shut behind them. "No, dammit, I didn't *see* Valentine. The bastard was there, he dumped the body, he terrorized her, then he got the hell out before the cops could get to him." Valentine was good at getting away. Too good.

Marcus swallowed quickly. "I just meant we only have Katherine's word—"

"She's in shock. Did you *see* her? Did you actually look at the woman? She's barely holding it together." Because she'd been alone with her worst nightmare. Trapped. And that knowledge pissed him off. He should have been with her. He'd said he would protect her.

"If the guy had wanted," Dane muttered, the fury he felt directed at Valentine and at himself, "he could have killed her right then."

Marcus shook his head. "That's not what he wants." Now his voice was far more confident. "That's *never* been what he wanted."

"Then tell me. Make me understand. Just what is it that the prick wants?"

"Katherine."

He'd had her, been alone with her in that dark gallery. But from what Dane could tell, the woman didn't have so much as a scratch on her.

"I should have realized he'd go after Dr. Lancaster," Marcus continued.

Was that *guilt* in the man's voice? Dane studied Marcus and saw that, yes, it was.

"One of the reasons I thought Katherine was originally a participant in the killings was...well, it was because she was tied to one of the victims in Boston."

"Tied how?" He'd gone over Hobbs's report and hadn't seen a connection.

"Katherine and Stephanie Gilbert, the final victim in Boston, were both foster children at the same home years ago."

Katherine had walked in on Stephanie Gilbert when Valentine was killing the woman. No, *after* the kill.

"From what I could gather, she and Katherine stayed in the same home for two months. Just two, but during that time, Katherine went to the hospital twice. Once for a broken arm, and once because she'd been stabbed in the right thigh with a kitchen knife." His lips tightened. "Stephanie was relocated after that, sent for additional therapy."

Dane lifted his hand. "What are you telling me? That you think Katherine *wanted* Valentine to target Stephanie because the woman had hurt her when they were kids?"

"That was one possible theory."

"It's possible bullshit."

Marcus flinched but held his stare. "Do you know what a killer's signature is?"

"It's the way he kills," Dane said instantly. "The slashes on the arms, the carving of the chest. All of that shit is Valentine's twisted signature."

"A killer's signature doesn't change over time. The signature is what the killer *has* to do in order for the kill to give him a feeling of completion. Satisfaction."

Twisted fuck.

"With Valentine, part of his signature is that he's controlling his victims. He's tying them up, torturing them, *dominating* them. He's punishing those who wind up on his table, the same way he was punished by his own mother. That's why he re-creates the same wounds on their arms." He paused. "Three years ago, I thought Katherine might have been involved in the Gilbert murder—"

"Didn't we decide that was BS?"

The profiler's cheeks flushed. "I've been working the Valentine case for three years. *Three years.* I now believe that with the murder of Stephanie Gilbert, his motivation changed."

Dane's brows snapped up.

"Gilbert's attack wounds were more savage than those of the other victims, showing a more emotional response. I think Valentine was angry with her because he *knew* what she'd done to Katherine. As far as Valentine was concerned, Katherine didn't deserve any punishment."

"What did she deserve?"

"Protection."

That wasn't the answer Dane had expected.

"Trent was here yesterday shouting at Katherine. Threatening her."

"But Valentine wasn't here. He wouldn't have known—"

"Control, Detective. Remember…control. Valentine will always want control over Katherine, so I suspect that he has been watching her, and those around her, very closely for some time." Marcus's breath shuddered out. "With Lancaster, Valentine crossed a lot of lines that he hasn't crossed before. He broke his own rules."

"He took the body to her."

A slight nod. "He wanted to give her a present. Lancaster upset Katherine, Valentine perceived that the shrink had *hurt* her, so he—"

"Hurt the bastard back."

Another nod. "Katherine changed Valentine. Perhaps more than I realized. Until Trent, his victims—those we know of—have been female. This evolution is showing that he feels he has no boundaries. He can and *will* attack anyone he perceives to be a threat to Katherine."

"Hell." Dane jerked a hand through his hair. "Savannah wanted to do a story on Katherine—"

"And Katherine refused, but the reporter kept pushing her." Marcus's lips tightened. "Another threat to Katherine that had to be eliminated."

So how the hell had Amy Evans been a threat to her?

Marcus must've had the same thought. "If you dig, I think you'll find a connection to Amy."

A light rap sounded at the door. Then the captain came in. His face was tense as he stared at Dane. "The sonofabitch was in her gallery?"

"Yes."

"With fucking cops right outside? Why the hell weren't the uniforms able to stop him?"

"Because the uniforms didn't see him. Katherine went in alone, and when she realized the lights weren't working, she sent one of the cops to check her breaker box." The cops should have damn well been *in* that building with her. They'd made a mistake that no one would be repeating. "He was waiting for her."

"He had to get close," Marcus said. "He had to let her know he was there, taking care of her."

The captain's eyes narrowed. "I want to know every single thing that man said to her. I want to know every detail."

Dane knew they had to question Katherine. She just looked so damn fragile that he wanted to wrap his arms around her and tell her that everything would be all right.

Even if the words were a lie.

"Bring her in," the captain ordered.

"I will," Dane said, "but I want the two of you out." They could watch. They could listen. But he wanted to be alone in that room with Katherine.

He had to make her relax, feel safe, and that wouldn't happen if the profiler and the captain were breathing down their necks.

Harley gave a grim nod. "Do what you have to do."

Dane knew the order for exactly what it was. But before he left the room, he had one more question for the profiler. "Why the fucking roses? What's their message?"

Marcus rubbed his chin. "Originally, the roses could have been a sign of remorse. He'd taken their lives, so he gave his victims a token to remember him. But when he met Katherine..." Marcus shook his head. "Roses used to be her favorite flower, did you know that? She revealed that fact in her Boston interrogations. She even kept a small rose garden behind the house she shared with Valentine. When Valentine found out about her love for roses, the guy must have seen that as another sign that Katherine was perfect for him."

Sick fuck. She *wasn't* perfect for him and never would be.

With his jaw locked, he headed out of the room and went straight to Katherine.

Her shoulders were still hunched, and she looked so beaten. He hated that. He tried to control his rage as he reached out and touched her shoulder.

She flinched and jumped to her feet. "No!"

All eyes flew to her.

Her breath came fast and hard. Her eyes seemed desperate. Then she focused on Dane and gave a little shudder. "I-I'm sorry."

He wanted her in his arms. Screw it, he pulled her against him. Held her tight and didn't care who saw them. She needed him. She needed to know that someone was there for her.

And he'd damn well be that someone.

"I wanted to kill him," she said, her stark whisper barely reaching his ears.

He wasn't surprised by her confession. Full truth, he wanted to kill the bastard too. The badge was the only thing holding him in check.

"But he took the bullets from my gun. He figured out where I kept it hidden, and he took my bullets."

The profiler's words whispered through his mind once more. *I suspect that he has been watching her.* He had been.

Katherine stiffened in his arms. She shoved against him, catching Dane off guard, and he stumbled back.

"Stay away from me!" she told him as dark color flushed her cheeks. "You *have to* stay away from me!"

"Katherine?"

"If you don't, he'll hurt you, too." Her whole body was stiff. Her eyes stark. "He told me. You have to stay away."

The bastard thought he'd be afraid? Dane grabbed her hands. "That's not happening. No one will keep me away from you."

He heard a gasp, then looked to the side. Evelyn Knight had just been led into the bull pen. Her tear-filled gaze was on him. Katherine. Their linked hands.

Mac hurried forward and tried to steer Evelyn away, but she wasn't moving. She just stared at Katherine.

Katherine pulled away from Dane again. She wrapped her arms around her stomach and rocked back and forth as if trying to soothe herself.

The silence in the bull pen was deafening. Dane cleared his throat. "Come on, I need to talk to you in interrogation."

Katherine didn't flinch. Didn't even look at him. She just turned woodenly and headed for interrogation room one.

Evelyn was still there. Watching.

Katherine paused in front of her. "I'm sorry about Trent."

A tear leaked down Evelyn's cheek. "I don't think you are, Kat."

Dane stiffened.

"I'm not sure you can actually be sorry about anything, especially something as insignificant as another person's life." Another tear trickled down her cheek.

Dane stepped in front of Katherine. "Take her *out* of here, Mac," he ordered.

Evelyn's shoulders straightened. "Because I'm the one who's out of control, right?" Her tear-filled eyes found Dane's. "Why can't you see what she is? Trent couldn't see either. Now it's too late."

Then she was gone. Being led—pulled—away by Mac.

Dane turned back to Katherine. He saw a woman struggling to hold on to her self-control. Was she a monster?

No, he didn't see it.

But he knew, based on his own life, that monsters could hide anyplace.

– – –

"I *need* to see him," Evelyn said. The tears wouldn't stop flowing. The detective named Mac was trying to force her out of the station, but it wasn't happening.

She needed to see Trent.

One more time.

"He's in the morgue. You don't want—"

"Yes, I do." She lifted her chin. "Someone has to identify the body, right? Or did Katherine do that already?"

"You ever been in a morgue, ma'am?"

"I'm a doctor—I have a medical license. I've seen plenty of bodies." And she knew where the morgue was located. So she headed for the elevator. She couldn't look at Katherine anymore.

The woman was standing there, offering her apologies.

I don't believe her.

But before she could get in the elevator, the detective moved to block her path. "You can't see him yet."

"I *have* to see him."

He shook his head. "No, ma'am, not yet, you don't. Once I get the clear from the captain and the ME, then I'll take you down. You should go home. Get some rest. We'll call you."

They'd call her to see Trent's remains.

Trent. He'd been far from perfect, she knew that. But he'd also been her best friend.

"I'm not leaving until I see him."

Mac swore. "Then go down to the lobby. Stay there, hit the cafeteria. Just don't come back to the bull pen. I'll find you."

The elevator's doors opened.

Mac walked away from her. Probably heading back to talk to Katherine.

All the cops wanted to talk to Katherine, but no one ever arrested her. No one seemed to see past her surface.

Only I do.

Evelyn's steps were wooden. In a few moments, she was in the lobby, but she heard raised voices. She turned her head and watched the crowd through the windows.

Reporters. All pushing and asking questions of the uniforms outside.

She headed toward them and shoved open the doors. The sun was bright, shining.

"Is it true that Valentine has claimed another victim?" one reporter asked a cop who was heading toward his patrol car.

The cop didn't respond.

Valentine.

The reporters just didn't understand. Valentine was only part of the story. Katherine was the rest.

But no one knew about Katherine. Not the real Katherine.

Only I do.

Evelyn's gaze swept the street, and she saw the news vans that were parked near the station.

Her heart began to beat faster. Maybe it was time for everyone to know the truth.

- 12 -

The door closed behind Dane with a soft click. Katherine took a slow, deep breath, then glanced toward the two-way mirror. "Who's watching this time?"

"The captain and Marcus Wayne."

She stared at the mirror. The numbness was starting to wear away. Now she just wanted to scream. To rage. To do *something*. "He was right there. Do you know how many times I've imagined what I would do if he was right in front of me?"

Kill him.

She'd wanted to.

Dane pulled out a chair for her.

She didn't sit. She started to pace, her body far too tense right then for sitting. Now that the ice was cracking around her, Katherine's whole body seemed filled with desperate energy.

"Did he look the same? Has he changed his hair or—"

She whirled toward him. "I didn't see his face. He came up behind me." Her hands lifted, curving around her body in mimicry of his. "He had his mouth at my ear."

Dane stepped closer to her. "You're sure it was him?"

"He was whispering to me. I remembered his whisper." Because he'd whispered to her so many times before. Only she hadn't realized that the one sharing his secrets with her was a killer. "I had my gun, and I was going to turn and shoot him. But he'd taken my bullets." She rubbed her temples. They were throbbing so badly. "I told you that, didn't I? That he took my bullets?"

"Yes, you told me." There was no expression in his voice.

Her hands dropped. She studied him, suspicious. "You believe me, don't you? I had bullets in that gun! I was going to stop him!" Then she whirled toward the mirror. "Marcus! I don't care what you think—I *didn't* let him get away! I wanted to stop him!" She slammed her hand against the mirror. "I want this over."

Then Dane's reflection was behind hers. He reached for her again.

She whirled around to face him. "Don't. I-I can't!"

And that hurt. Because Dane…he'd been the one person she could touch without feeling the instinctive urge to withdraw. Only now… "I can still feel him on me." It made her feel dirty. But what was new? Ever since she'd walked into that basement, she'd felt that way.

Nothing could change that.

"He's not here, Katherine." Dane put his hands on her shoulders.

His touch was warm and strong, and she wanted to shove him away. "He's always here." Didn't he get that? "Always watching."

She saw Dane's gaze cut to the mirror.

"You need to get off this case." She wouldn't have his death on her conscience. "You need to stay away from me."

He didn't back away. He crowded in closer. "Why? Because Valentine might come after me?"

"There's no 'might' about it. He said he would! He told me!"

Dane actually smiled, and the sight chilled her to the bone. "Good. Let the bastard come."

"I don't want any more deaths on me!"

His gaze searched hers. "That's what you need to stop believing. None of the deaths are on you. They are all on him. Every single one."

But Katherine could only shake her head. "Tell that to Trent. If he'd never met me, he'd still be living."

— — —

"Still think she's working with Valentine?" the captain asked him.

Marcus Wayne didn't take his gaze off the couple before him. There seemed to be genuine guilt in Katherine's voice. Of course, sociopaths were often skilled at mimicking emotions.

Michael O'Rourke was certainly skilled in that area.

"Katherine Cole is a very complex woman."

She'd pulled away from Dane. It was obvious from his expression that the detective hadn't wanted to let her go.

Like Valentine, he seemed to be getting pulled in by Katherine. Valentine wanted to protect his Kat. It seemed the detective wanted the same thing.

"I'd like to see the detective's personnel record," Marcus said.

From the corner of his eye, he saw the captain stiffen. "Why the hell do you want that?"

"Because Katherine just told us that Valentine may target your detective. It only makes sense that I learn everything I can about him." The words were partially true, but more, he wanted to understand why Katherine was drawn to Dane Black.

First Valentine, now Black. Both men were highly protective and, judging by what he was observing, possessive of her. Did the men share other traits?

Perhaps he could actually learn about Valentine by studying Black.

— — —

"Katherine, look, I need to—"

The door flew open. Mac stood there, his face tense. "Dane, I need you. Now."

Katherine stepped forward immediately. "Has something happened?" *Please, not another victim. Not another...*

Mac's gaze swept to her. He must have read her fear because he said, "It's not another victim."

Her shoulders sagged as relief hit her.

"Dane, *now*."

Dane marched toward him. He bent his head near Mac's, and Katherine strained to hear their whispers. She caught "...reporters...she's talking to them now..."

Who was?

Dane swore and glanced back at Katherine. "Stay here, okay?"

She was tired of hiding. Hiding hadn't done her any good. Valentine knew exactly where she was. "Who's talking to the reporters?"

A muscle jerked along Dane's jaw. "Please, stay here."

Then he was gone. Leaving her, and no way was she just going to stand there. She couldn't. Her body was vibrating with desperate energy, and every time she had even a second to think—

She saw Trent's body.

Katherine hurried to the door, but Mac blocked her path. "You should stay here, ma'am."

"Am I under arrest?"

Mac shook his head. "No."

"Then I'm going with Dane." She rushed past him and caught Dane just as he was leaving the bull pen. "Wait!" she called.

Dane turned and reached for her, but seemed to catch himself. His hands fisted. "I've got to go outside and do damage control.

You need to stay in here. The vultures are circling, and I'm not giving them your blood."

Everyone else had bled. Savannah. Amy. Trent.

Maybe it was her turn. "I'm coming with you, and unless you want to cuff me and toss me into a cell, then you can't stop me."

His jaw locked, but he turned and stormed away. No cuffs. No cell.

Every step she took after him made her feel stronger. The ice was falling away, crashing at her feet.

Valentine's touch was still there, his whisper running through her ear.

But…

I won't let you win.

Then Dane was heading outside. She could see the crowd of reporters. None of them were looking her way because they were too focused on someone else. Someone right in the middle of the throng.

Katherine hurried down the steps outside the PD, trying to catch up to Dane. Then she heard a familiar voice. A voice that halted her.

"I know I've put my professional career in jeopardy…"

The reporters shifted a bit, and Katherine was able to peer through the crowd. She could just see the top of Evelyn Knight's blonde head, and she heard the woman say, "But I couldn't stay quiet any longer. Sometimes there are things in this world—people—who are more important than a career." She pulled in a breath and pointed at Katherine. "My colleague and friend, Dr. Trent Lancaster, was one of those people. Last night, he was brutally murdered by the Valentine Killer."

The reporters began firing questions.

Raising her voice, Evelyn kept talking. "The police won't tell you the truth. They don't want you to know Valentine is here, killing in their city."

"What. The. Fuck." Dane's snarl was lethal. Then he rushed toward Evelyn and the reporters.

Katherine didn't move.

"Valentine is here because he followed the one woman he loves. Katelynn Crenshaw is living in New Orleans."

"How do you know that?" A reporter's yell carried over the frenzied questioning voices.

"I was treating her." Evelyn's stark confession.

"And this interview session is *over*." Dane shoved away a handful of microphones. "Dr. Knight, you need to come with me *now*."

"Detective Black knows the truth!" Evelyn yelled, her face flushing as she stared into the crowd of reporters. "He knows Katelynn is here. He knows—"

Dane caught her elbow in his hand. He ignored the reporters' questions and began pushing Evelyn up the steps.

Evelyn's gaze darted to the left and met Katherine's.

"Where is Katelynn Crenshaw?" shouted a reporter.

A car braked near the front of the station. Katherine's marshal jumped out, took in the scene in one wild glance, then started running toward her. Evelyn yanked her elbow from Dane's grasp, turned back to face the reporters, and pointed at Katherine. "Katelynn Crenshaw is right here!"

At first there was only silence.

Then more questions erupted. Her instinct had always been to run. To hide. But now she had the perfect opportunity to say what *she* wanted to say. "Yes, I'm here."

The reporters moved instantly, rushing to swarm around her. Their camera lenses locked on her. Their microphones were suddenly in her face.

"Katherine!" Ross yelled. She knew he wanted her to stop.

But she knew she couldn't.

The reporters were shouting their questions, one after another in a dizzying blur. She ignored them and stared into the camera nearest her. She wanted a message delivered, and the media would be her delivery service.

"I'm here," she said again and lifted her chin. "So if you're hunting because of me, then come for *me*. Not anyone else. Just me."

She heard low, vicious curses, and then Ross put his hand around her shoulders, pulling her close to him. "I'm U.S. Marshal Anthony Ross." His voice boomed out. "And all future questions had better be directed at me and my office."

There wasn't a need for Katherine to say more. She knew her clip would air on TV, again and again, and that was exactly what she wanted.

Give the killer a challenge. Give him me.

Ross bent his head. His lips brushed the shell of her ear as he whispered, "Why?"

But he knew. He had to know.

So she pulled back, gave him a grim smile, and said, "Because someone has to stop him."

And she was tired of having blood on her hands.

Then Dane was there. Face locked in angry lines. Jaw tense. As Ross turned back to the reporters, Dane glared at Katherine. "You put yourself out there as bait."

Yes, she had. But why was that so surprising? They both knew that he'd planned to use her as bait from the very beginning. There was no reason to pretend otherwise.

Now they'd just see what Valentine did next.

— — —

Dane pretty much dragged Katherine back inside the station. Cops were watching them with wide eyes. The captain was staring at her, shaking his head. Evelyn was seated near a desk, with two uniforms glowering down at her.

Dane didn't stop walking. He pulled Katherine with him, then pushed her inside the interrogation room that was becoming too annoyingly familiar to her.

"Dane, look, I—"

He slammed the door behind him. His mouth crashed down on hers.

She should push away from him. Should tell him to stop. She shouldn't wrap her arms around his shoulders and yank him closer. She shouldn't open her mouth wider. Shouldn't kiss him harder.

A dozen cops waited outside. The vulture reporters were salivating at the chance to tear her apart.

She shouldn't be doing this.

But she needed him more than she needed air right then.

"Dane." She forced herself to speak. To grab onto the self-control that was shredding.

His fingers were wrapped around her hips. Holding tight. His head lifted. His blue gaze blazed. "You think I'll just stand back and let you get hurt?"

She hadn't thought about what Dane would do. She just wanted to stop the killing. To get the murderer's attention. Katherine made herself take a deep breath. Her gaze drifted from him—she couldn't stare into his eyes right then—and landed on the two-way mirror. Her body tensed. "Is anyone—"

"There are no suspects in here, so no one's watching. It's just us." His breath expelled in a hard rush. "Bait. You put yourself up as fucking bait." His fingers bit into her hips. "Why? Do you want to die?"

There was a rap at the door. "Dane?" Mac's voice.

"Give me a minute!" Dane snarled back. Katherine realized he'd pinned her between his body and the door. His muscled frame pressed against her. She should have felt trapped. Should have been angry, afraid.

But Dane had never made her feel fear. Her heart beat too fast. Adrenaline spiked in her blood. But it wasn't fear driving her, not with him.

"Whatever I have to do, I'll keep you alive." His words were a vow. "Just don't *ever* do something like that again."

Then he was kissing her once more. A kiss that was still angry, still rough with desire, but also…desperate.

She knew desperation when she felt it.

When he released her, Katherine's breath panted out.

He took a step back. Clenched his hands into fists and seemed to be fighting for his own self-control. "If the killer comes after you, he'll have to go through me first."

She couldn't allow any weakness. Dane was a weakness. She needed to separate from him while she still could. She turned her back on him and reached for the door.

She twisted the doorknob.

His hand flew up and slammed the door shut. Then he leaned in behind her. His breath brushed lightly over her ear. Ross had been this close to her on the steps outside the police station. Only she hadn't felt this desperate tension in her body then. Too much awareness. Too much need.

It was only for Dane.

Her heart raced even faster in her chest. "You don't know me," she said again—because he couldn't. She didn't want him to know the secrets she carried.

He backed up a step.

They stared into each other's eyes.

"Stay here." His words weren't an order this time, but almost a plea. "If you don't agree to stay on your own, I *will* put you in protective custody—or else the marshal will take you away. You know Ross isn't going to just let you walk out of the station alone."

No, he wouldn't. He wouldn't consider his job over.

Even if she did.

"Okay." The agreement slipped from her.

Dane heaved out a hard breath. Then he nodded. His gaze swept over her face. "Thank you."

Dane might think he was going to be her protection, but the truth was, she'd only agreed to stay for one reason.

To keep him safe.

Because Trent hadn't been a random victim. She'd dated him. The only man she'd dated since Valentine.

And Trent had gotten a knife thrust into his heart.

So what would happen to Dane? To the man that she'd actually slept with?

"I'll stay," she whispered once more, because she owed him. He'd made her feel alive again.

- - -

"You do like to watch, don't you, Wayne?"

Marcus Wayne jumped at the police captain's low, drawling voice. He hadn't heard the other man come into the observation room. He'd been so absorbed by the detective and Katherine...

But the detective was leaving the interrogation room now. Katherine was all alone.

Marcus glanced over his shoulder at the captain. "I was here when they entered the room." Pure chance. He'd just wanted a quiet place to think. He certainly hadn't expected to see what he'd witnessed.

The woman he'd just seen in that room didn't fit the profile he'd created in his mind. Katherine actually seemed to be trying to protect the cop. To protect everyone but herself.

It didn't fit with what he knew.

Have I been wrong about her?

"You could've walked out when they entered." The captain was glaring at him.

"Then I wouldn't have learned more about Katherine." There had been real pain in her voice. Real emotion on her face.

He'd always thought she was a bit of an actress, but she'd seemed so genuine this time.

Voices spilled into the room. The captain had left the door open. The captain stalked toward him. "Whatever the hell is going on personally between that woman and my detective is none of—"

Marcus waved that away. He didn't care if they screwed each others' brains out. That wasn't the point. "She cares about the other victims. Empathizes with them."

Katherine had always been on guard with him. She'd never let him see past her facade.

He'd just glimpsed past the brittle image. Detective Black had battered his way right through that facade and gotten to the real woman inside Katherine.

He needed to check his files on Valentine's victims again. He'd thought there was nothing different about Katherine. No reason for Valentine to spare her. But now—

"*What the hell are you doing in here?*" Marcus flinched at the snarl.

"I found him here watching you and Ms. Cole," the captain said as he continued to glare at Marcus.

Marcus cleared his throat.

Dane marched toward him. "Enjoy the show?"

"It was illuminating," Marcus confessed.

Dane lunged for him.

The captain stepped in his path. "Easy, Black."

Detective Black had an anger management issue, obviously.

Why is Katherine so drawn to him? That was another part of the puzzle.

There was so much more going on here.

"Your profile is shit," Black snapped. "Katherine was never involved in any of the killings—she was as much of a victim as anyone."

Marcus glanced through the two-way mirror at Katherine. He realized then that Black had left the interrogation room door open, giving Katherine the chance to leave. But she wasn't leaving. Marcus exhaled slowly. "Before Dr. Lancaster, Valentine had never killed a man."

His gaze couldn't leave Katherine.

Trent Lancaster had been dating her. At the station, he'd savaged her with a verbal attack that a roomful of cops had witnessed.

Then he'd been killed. Executed.

And taken to Katherine's gallery.

Delivered. Almost like a present. With Valentine's Day so close, did the killer believe he'd just given Katherine the ultimate gift? Proof of his devotion? Valentine had obviously wanted to make contact with Katherine. He'd wanted her to appreciate his gift.

Possibilities began to roll through Marcus's head. He pushed past the cops and hurried toward the bull pen. Dr. Knight was there, glaring at the uniformed men.

Black followed on his heels. Good. He wanted the detective to hear this exchange. Black was good at reading people. The guy would have made one hell of a profiler. *Better than me.*

"Why do you think Valentine never tried to hurt Katherine?" Marcus asked her.

Dr. Knight turned toward him. "Who are you?"

"I'm FBI Agent Marcus Wayne." He stared down at her. Pretty, composed, and from what he'd learned in his preliminary background investigation, very, very smart. But she'd also just potentially thrown away her psychiatry license.

Not so smart.

Why would a woman like her take that risk?

"Well?" he pressed.

Black and the captain joined him at the small desk.

Dr. Knight's gaze darted around the circle that surrounded her.

"He saw something in her," Dr. Knight said slowly. "Something that stopped him from killing her."

Exactly what Marcus thought. Only, before, he'd believed that Valentine had spared Katherine because he recognized a kindred spirit in her.

But what if it was something else?

Marcus glanced over his shoulder at the interrogation room. What if, when Valentine looked at her, he hadn't seen a victim or a killer? What if he'd seen...

Hope?

Katherine was a mirror for him, yes, but instead of reflecting darkness back to him, maybe she'd shown Valentine a glimpse of what life would be like, if he had been normal.

Katherine had loved Michael O'Rourke. Had that been the first time in Valentine's life he'd ever actually been *loved*?

Perhaps through Katherine, Valentine had seen his chance to reach for happiness. To have what others around him seemed to enjoy. A wife. A home. A life that didn't involve beatings and punishment. Katherine had given Valentine the promise of everything he'd ever wanted.

And if Katherine truly was that one perfect glimpse, that one chance Valentine had for a connection with another person, just what would the killer be willing to do in order to ensure that Katherine always stayed safe?

The answer, to Marcus, was obvious.

Anything.

– 13 –

The historic building in the French Quarter sat, stark and silent, near the end of the street. The glow from a nearby streetlamp fell on the entranceway, softening the hard lines of the building just a bit. Dane hadn't wanted to take Katherine back to her house—not after the big disclosure Evelyn had made to the reporters, and he also hadn't wanted the media following them back to his place.

So they'd sneaked out the back of the station and taken refuge here. The apartment would give them a chance to decompress—safely—for a while.

Dane held open the car door as Katherine climbed out of the car and glanced up at the safe house. "Whose place is this?" she asked.

"It belongs to a friend of the captain's." Harley was a man with plenty of connections.

The scent of the Mississippi drifted on the wind even as faint jazz music teased his ears.

Katherine glanced down the street. "Do we have guards?"

Yes, guards she wouldn't see if the men did their jobs right. He gave a grim nod.

He unlocked the street-level door, then led her up the stairs toward the apartment, making sure to set the security system behind them.

The place had been remodeled after its sale to some celebrity—a guy who'd later gone bankrupt. Now the luxury apartment seemed to sit vacant most nights.

Not tonight.

They reached the top floor. Again Dane set the security system—a secondary system now. One of the reasons this place was so perfect for tonight was the state-of-the-art security that it offered.

Katherine stepped into the apartment, then paused in the middle of the living room, her shoulders stiff, and gazed around. "What happens now?"

Now I keep my hands off you. It was what he should do. He was already getting too involved with her.

Katherine glanced over her shoulder at him. A woman truly shouldn't have eyes like that. Eyes so deep and beautiful. He'd never seen a woman with golden eyes before. Not until her.

He locked the door and didn't take a step toward her. "Now you go take a shower and get into bed. It's been a hell of a day."

No emotion flickered in her gaze. "Yes. It has been."

She needed to walk away. Because he wasn't smelling the river then. He was catching her scent. Remembering her taste. It was so hard to keep from touching her. Her skin was like silk. He could caress her for hours.

Katherine walked away. The shower kicked on a few moments later. He heard the spray of water from the next room.

His breath rushed out. Sonofabitch. He wasn't used to turning away from a woman who looked like a wet dream.

But with her…it hadn't just been sex.

The woman was lethal, in more ways than one.

Dane shoved his hand into a pocket and yanked out his phone. He dialed his partner's number, and as he waited for Mac to pick up, he glanced out the window. Only the night stared back.

"Shouldn't you be busy with your lady?" Mac muttered, sounding slightly annoyed. Voices buzzed in the background.

He was trying *not* to be busy with her. "We're secure at the safe house."

"And I'm getting ready to make sure that Dr. Knight gets home and away from the station."

The woman had still been there when they left. "She still insisting on seeing the body?"

"Yeah, and Ronnie's almost ready for her."

Ronnie had told Dane that she'd have a report ready on Trent Lancaster by dawn. Maybe the killer had left some evidence they could use.

"How are you doing?" Mac's voice had dropped.

Dane frowned.

"I saw your face," Mac said softly, "when Katherine stepped in front of the cameras."

Dane's jaw ached, and he forced himself to unclench his teeth. "I didn't know she planned to make that move." He'd wanted to yank her back, to shield her with his body.

"Wasn't the plan to use her?"

The plan hadn't been to destroy her life—and now, because of those few moments on camera, the life she'd built as Katherine Cole would be gone.

The door opened behind Dane. His shoulders stiffened. "I've got to go, Mac. See you at tomorrow's briefing." He ended the call, then slowly turned around.

Katherine's wet hair trailed down her back. She had a white towel wrapped around her, covering her from breast to thigh. Her eyes were on him.

Her scent was pulling him in. *She* was pulling him closer, and the woman wasn't even moving. "Do you need anything from me tonight?"

Her smile was sad. "Chase away my nightmares?"

"I thought you didn't have nightmares."

Katherine averted her gaze. "I lied."

He knew that. "What are your nightmares about?"

Her gaze held his. "I'm back in my old basement. Valentine is there. He's wearing his black apron—he always wore that apron when he painted. Only he's not painting. And the red on that apron...it isn't paint. It's my blood."

His muscles turned to stone.

"I'm on his table." Her voice was flat. "My hands are tied. My mouth is taped shut. I can't scream. I can't move. And I know he's going to kill me." She rolled her shoulders, as if pushing the image away. "That's one of my nightmares. I have plenty more."

He wanted her in his arms.

"Don't pity me." Her voice snapped like a whip. Not flat now, but furious. "Pity isn't what I want from you. You were the only one who didn't look at me with pity in your eyes!"

Before he could speak, she spun away.

He wanted to grab her arm. Even reached out to her.

But then his hand fisted.

Stay on guard.

He watched her walk away. And he didn't follow. His cock shoved at the front of his pants. He could taste her in his mouth. But he didn't follow.

Because Dane was coming to realize that he didn't just want sex from Katherine. He was starting to want...*everything.*

If he had his way, he'd get it.

— — —

Ronnie whistled softly as her tennis shoes moved over the tile in the morgue. It was edging close to midnight, and the place was pretty much deserted.

Dead quiet.

Normally she didn't mind the quiet, but tonight, she felt on edge.

She lifted the sheet that covered Trent Lancaster's upper body. Her gaze dipped over his wounds. This attack wasn't as controlled as the others. It was as if the killer had been enraged.

"I'm sorry you had to cross my slab," she whispered. She was always sorry for the bodies that found their way to her.

These people, they never died easily.

She'd seen deaths that still made her shudder.

She pulled the sheet back and reached for the tox screens that had just come in. A report for Savannah Slater and Amy Evans. Getting a tox screen was standard protocol, and—

What the hell?

Ronnie frowned as she read the results. Fentanyl. That was a seriously high dose. And for both victims?

She put the reports down and hurried toward Savannah Slater's body. She unzipped the heavy bag that enclosed Savannah—the woman's body was due for transport soon—and Savannah's pale flesh was revealed. Ronnie grabbed a small flashlight and began to shine the light over the victim's body.

Fentanyl was like morphine, and with a dose that high, Savannah would have been unconscious. Easy prey.

The question was…just how had she been given that dose?

I missed something with her. I missed it.

Ronnie's flashlight swept over Savannah's arms, lingering near her veins. No puncture wounds. But maybe the slashes had hidden an injection site.

Maybe...

The flashlight rose. Ronnie swept it over Savannah's neck and saw the small brown mark. So tiny.

She leaned closer. Her heart beat faster.

The injection site. So incredibly small. Placed right above the jugular so the drug would have been pushed into the victim's system immediately.

Savannah never had a chance.

"Dr. Thomas?"

She jumped at the deep, rumbling voice—a voice that was all too familiar to her. She spun around and saw Mac standing in the doorway.

A slightly disheveled blonde woman was next to him.

"Dr. Thomas..." Mac was formal only when others were around. When they were alone, it was quite a different story. "Are we clear to view Trent Lancaster's body?"

Her gaze darted to the blonde once more. Right. Right. That was Evelyn Knight—she'd heard rumbles about her from some of the uniforms who'd dropped by earlier. Evelyn had gone on the air and outed Katherine Cole.

She hadn't expected Evelyn to look so fragile.

Evelyn's shocked gaze was on Savannah Slater's body. Ronnie jumped to attention and hurriedly covered Savannah once more. "Yes, yes, of course. Give me just a moment."

She took a deep breath. She wanted to race over to the body of Amy Evans and search for a puncture wound, but word had come down from the captain that she was to make sure Evelyn saw Lancaster's body.

Apparently the woman had said she wouldn't leave the station until she saw Trent.

After her outburst to the media, the captain was trying to placate her.

Ronnie knew that Harley's placating moves rarely lasted long.

Evelyn's high heels tapped over the tile. "Which one? Where is Trent?"

Ronnie quickly adjusted a new pair of latex gloves. "He's here." She pointed toward the sheet-covered body. "And, Dr. Knight, I'm very sorry for your loss." Ronnie had said those words hundreds of times—but she meant them. She hated seeing people in pain as they viewed their loved ones.

Evelyn's eyes teared up, but she gave a grim nod.

Carefully, Ronnie pulled down the sheet, revealing only Trent's face. His face was uninjured—actually, it looked almost as if the man were sleeping. Evelyn didn't need to see the rest of his body. There was no reason for her to have those images in her mind.

A sob choked from Evelyn. "He was—he was my best friend."

Ronnie pulled the sheet back into place. Then she put her body in front of Lancaster. It was a distancing technique that she often used. Show the body, get the focus of the grieving party, help him or her to leave the morgue.

The morgue was no place for the living—well, for most of them, anyway. Ronnie had always felt strangely at home there.

Helping those who deserved their justice.

"Did he suffer?" Evelyn asked, lifting her chin.

He had, but there was no need for Evelyn to know that. Ronnie's gaze cut to Mac, and he gave a barely perceptible nod, then reached for Evelyn's elbow.

"It's time to go, Dr. Knight."

"He suffered, didn't he?"

All of Valentine's victims had suffered. Evelyn would know that.

"I'm going to take you home," Mac told Evelyn. "You need to get some rest."

A tear slid down the woman's cheek. "I don't understand what's happening." But she let herself be pulled away.

Mac glanced back at Ronnie. His gaze swept over her. *I'll be back.* He mouthed the words.

It was her turn to nod.

She didn't think anyone knew about her relationship with Mac, and she wanted to keep it that way. Being gossiped about wasn't her thing.

The doors swung shut behind Mac and Evelyn.

Ronnie waited a few moments, until she was sure they were gone. Then she reached for her flashlight.

She thoroughly searched Trent Lancaster's body but found no sign of an injection.

Then she checked the body of Amy Evans.

Amy had the same small bruise on her neck that Savannah did. The drug had been sent right into her.

Ronnie frowned as she stared down at Amy's body. Amy and Savannah were both slender women, and both barely five feet five inches tall. As far as she knew, Valentine had never drugged his earlier victims.

He'd charmed them, seduced them into coming with him.

But he'd drugged these two.

She tossed her gloves and reached for her phone. Her temples were starting to pound. "Hey, Mike? Yeah, it's Ronnie. I want a rush on the Lancaster tox screen, okay? I need that report as soon as possible."

This could very well be the break that the PD needed. They could trace the drug and find their killer.

— — —

Katherine awoke with a scream. Her heart was pounding, her body tight with fear and slick with sweat.

She'd been back in her basement again. Tied down on the table. Valentine had been over her with his knife gripped in his hand. She'd wanted to beg him to let her go, but duct tape had covered her mouth. She hadn't been able to scream. Hadn't been able to beg.

Then he'd lifted the knife over her.

That was when she awoke.

Katherine climbed from the bed. The T-shirt and old jogging shorts she wore—clothes that had been brought to her, courtesy of the PD—seemed to stick to her skin. The bedroom was too small. Closing her in. She had to be outside. To feel fresh air on her cheeks.

To clear the scent of blood and death from her nose.

Katherine opened her bedroom door with barely a sound. The hallway and living room were dark, but her eyes quickly adjusted, and she didn't bother turning on any light. She didn't want to wake Dane.

She'd just go out on the balcony for a moment. Breathe air that didn't taste like death. Then the chill would finally be chased from her bones.

Until the dreams came back.

"What are you doing?" His voice rumbled from the darkness.

Katherine jumped, her hand just inches from the balcony door. She spun around as a lamp flickered on. She saw Dane sitting in an oversize chair to her right. His hand was still on the lamp. His eyes were on hers.

She swallowed. "I just needed some fresh air."

His gaze weighed her. Then Dane gave a nod and rose to his feet. He was wearing just a pair of jeans that clung loosely to his hips. "I'll come with you," he said, picking up the gun that she hadn't noticed beside the lamp.

Dane tucked the gun into the back waistband of his jeans. The muscles of his chest and shoulders rippled, reminding her of his strength.

She stared at him a moment, lost in the shadows that slid over his skin. Dane Black was a dangerous man. Strong and deadly. So why didn't he scare her? "Have you killed before?" The question slipped from her.

"Yes," he said flatly. He took a slow step toward her.

"That's what happens in the line of duty." The words tumbled from her. "You were probably trying to—"

"I killed my father when I was seventeen."

She fell back against the door. "What?"

He took another step. "You think you're the only one with secrets, Katherine?" Dane shook his head. "We all have them." His hands reached around her. "You have to move for me to open the door."

Oh. Right. She stepped to the side and he opened the door. The wind blew off the river, lifting her hair. She turned into the wind and stepped onto the balcony, wrapping her arms around her stomach.

"Aren't you going to ask me why?" Dane's deep voice followed her onto the balcony.

She stared below, at the darkness of the twisting New Orleans streets. Danger was everywhere. "Why?"

"He was an abusive SOB who thought I'd let him use me as a punching bag for the rest of my life."

She didn't speak. She hadn't expected this from Dane, hadn't realized—

He's like me.

"I was tired of taking his hits. Tired of having his fist slam into my face." He rubbed his fingers along the bridge of his nose. The small bump suddenly took on a new significance.

Katherine's hands curled along the wooden railing of the balcony.

"My mom left when I was ten," Dane continued. "I didn't blame her. He'd been hitting her. He didn't hit me. Just her."

"She left you with him?" Anger boiled inside her body.

Dane came to stand beside her and stare out at the glittering city lights. "Maybe she thought it was just her who he'd hurt. I saw her bruises all those years, I heard her crying…"

"Why didn't she go to the cops?" Instead of leaving her son.

"Because he was a cop."

Her heart beat faster. Cops hunted the monsters. They weren't supposed to be the monsters.

"So one day, while he was off working a case, she packed her bags and got the hell away from him. The bus dropped me off after school, I walked home, and she was just…gone. Without her there, it was only a matter of time, I guess, until he turned all his rage on me."

He'd been ten when his mother left. Seventeen when he killed his father. So many years. So much pain. The whisper of that pain was in his words. Her left hand moved a few inches. Her fingers brushed over his.

"I tried to tell his partner what was happening. Maybe he didn't want to believe me. Not at first."

A kid's word against a cop.

"Then my dad started drinking. He got into fights with suspects. Put another cop in the hospital. The more he drank, the more he lost control."

Her hand was entwined with his now.

"One night, he broke a whiskey bottle and came at me, swinging." His free hand rose, and his fingers slid over the faint scar beneath his lip. "He was screaming about how my mother left because of me."

She turned away from the city. Stared up at his profile. So hard. Jaw locked.

"I knew he wasn't going to stop. He was going to kill me. He wanted to kill me."

"I'm sure he didn't." Her own voice was sad.

"I punched the bastard as hard as I could. Slammed my fist into his jaw. He was at the top of the stairs. He stumbled back, lost his footing. By the time he hit the third step going down, the whiskey bottle had embedded in his throat."

Her fingers tightened around his.

"His partner was the first one on the scene. I was bleeding and had bruises—I always had them back then—and my dad stunk of booze. His knuckles were bloody from where he'd been punching me. The neighbors finally came forward and talked about the yells they'd heard for years. The fights they'd seen." His lips twisted. "It just took him dying for them to be brave enough to come forward."

A lock of her hair slid over her cheek, blowing with the wind. "What did his partner do?"

"Harley?"

Harley Dunning? Katherine gasped.

"Harley told me he was sorry. Said he should have helped me sooner. He got me out of that house and brought me to live with him." He gave a little roll of his shoulders. "Then he turned me into the one thing that I always thought I'd never become." He met her gaze. "A cop."

He looked back out at the city. "So yes, I've killed."

"What happened to her?"

Dane's head turned toward her.

"Your mother. Did you ever go find her?"

"She left me. There was no point." He shook his head. "I don't want you thinking I'm some kind of damn hero. I'm not perfect, far fucking from it."

And that was a good thing. "Perfect's a lie. I thought I had perfect once. Now I want real. I want good, bad, everything in between." She stood on her toes and pressed a quick kiss first to the scar beneath his lip, then to Dane's mouth.

"Katherine…" Her name came out as a growl.

Her turn to confess. "In three years, I never wanted a man. Not until I met you."

His fingers tightened around hers. "What?"

"It was like part of me was dead. I was cold inside. I went through the motions. Even attempted to date some guys." *Trent.*

He released her hand. Then his fingers were closing over her shoulders, pulling her back against him. "I'm trying to do the right thing with you."

"I've got a killer on my trail. I'm more concerned with feeling alive than I am with what's *right*." Didn't he understand that?

"You're *staying* alive." She couldn't hope yet. For years she'd been living with the threat of the grim reaper. Katherine pulled in a deep, steadying breath, then slowly eased away from him and began to walk back toward the open door.

"No one in three years?"

She'd just reached the threshold when he came up behind her. His arms closed around her. "Why me?"

She didn't turn toward him.

His mouth was on her neck. He kissed her sensitive skin. Katherine felt the light rasp of his tongue. "All of those men out there, why the hell did you pick me?"

She looked back into his eyes and told him the truth. "You make me feel safe, Dane."

His mouth took hers. Not tame any longer. Not gentle. The need had burst free. He kissed her with a wild hunger. The same hunger that she felt.

Then she was being lifted into his arms. He was carrying her inside the house, locking the door behind them. The faint light from the lamp illuminated the hallway as he took her back to the bedroom.

Her arms were around his neck. Holding so tightly. She wasn't letting him go.

Chase away the nightmares.

Feel alive.

Then he was putting her on the bed. "I tried," Dane told her, his voice deep and dark. "Why the hell can't I hold back with you?"

"I don't want you holding back." She wanted everything he could give.

Every. Single. Thing.

His hands hardened on her. "You need to be careful what you wish for." He stripped off her shirt. His fingers went to the waistband of her loose shorts.

Then he was discovering that, no, she hadn't bothered with underwear.

"*Katherine.*" A rumble of raw lust. He tossed her clothes off the bed.

She started to smile up at him, feeling a heady rush of what might have been happiness in that moment.

He took the gun from the back of his jeans. Put it on the nightstand. "I need you. I sat in that chair…" His words were a heated whisper. "Two hours…thinking about you…"

"You should have been with me."

"Wondering…" Now his hands were on her thighs. Pushing them apart. "Just how you'd taste…"

He was climbing onto the bed. Pushing between her legs. His gaze was on her sex. Seeing every inch of her.

Then he leaned forward and put his mouth on her.

Katherine wanted to look away, but she couldn't. His dark hair was a stark contrast to her pale thighs. His lips were on her, his tongue *in* her.

Her breath caught in her throat. She lifted her hips toward him. She just felt. His tongue. His lips.

"So good…" Dane muttered, the words rumbling against her and sending a pulse of pleasure through her. "So…damn… good…"

Better than good. Her body was tightening as his finger slid into her sex, his tongue licking across the sensitive center of her need.

She came in an eruption of pleasure that burst through her whole body. Pleasure that shook her, twisted her, hollowed her out.

Katherine realized that her hands had grabbed the sheets. Fisted the fabric. Her breath was gasping out, and her heart pounded in her ears.

Dane was watching her.

"Dane…"

"I like the way you taste."

She wanted him inside of her.

He still had on his jeans. He needed to ditch those.

Her hands slid down between their bodies. She undid the snap and eased down his zipper. His cock was big and heavy, and her fingers stroked over him.

"*Katherine.*" There was such need in his voice.

The same need that she felt.

"I don't want to wait." She wanted the pleasure—she wanted him. Right then.

He reached into his back pocket. Pulled out a foil packet, and then he was positioning his aroused length at the entrance to her body.

Death had come too close to her that day. But at that moment, Dane was reminding her about life.

He thrust into her.

Her legs wrapped around his hips. He was still wearing his jeans, and the material rasped against her inner thighs, but she loved the rough friction.

He withdrew, then drove deep, over and over. And he kissed her. Thrusting his tongue into her mouth as he took her body.

Her nails scratched over his back. She didn't worry about being controlled or restrained or anything. She just felt.

Alive.

Then his mouth was on her neck. Licking. Sucking the skin. Scoring her lightly with his teeth. She arched toward him as the pleasure built within her, spinning her higher and higher.

Then her climax hit, stealing her breath, and the explosion rocked through her—the most powerful release she'd ever felt.

Katherine held tight to him, and in the next instant, he was shuddering above her. His eyes seemed to go blind, and he held her so tightly.

As if he'd never let her go.

Slowly, so slowly, their heartbeats eased back to a more normal rhythm. He eased away from her, and she fought the urge to reach out and hold onto him.

Dane disappeared into the bathroom. She heard the splash of running water.

Her eyes squeezed closed. When the pleasure ended, reality came back far too soon. She would have rather just stayed with Dane longer, curled in his arms, so she could pretend—for just a little while more—that death didn't stalk her.

Then the bed dipped beneath his weight. Her eyes flew open in surprise. "Dane—"

"Shh....let me take care of you." A warm cloth slid over her sensitive skin. She gasped at the contact, soothing and arousing at the same time.

Was it wrong to already want him again?

She felt like she needed, wanted too much with him. As if her feelings were out of control.

Maybe they were.

He started to rise. She grabbed his hand. "Stay." She wasn't sure just how much time they had left. Not with Valentine out there.

Watching.

Always watching.

She didn't want to be alone in the dark.

He slid back into the bed. Curled his arms around her. Pulled Katherine back against his racing heart.

She closed her eyes and hoped that—this time—she wouldn't dream of blood and death. Of a man who'd said he loved her even as he lifted a knife and prepared to take her life.

— — —

"You didn't have to bring me home," Evelyn said quietly as the detective walked her to her door. "I could have taken a taxi."

"The NOPD wanted to make sure you arrived safely." His voice was carefully modulated to show no emotion.

"The NOPD just wanted me away from the station." She rubbed her temples. She was so bone-tired then. Her shoulders slumped and she reached for the doorknob.

Only her door was unlocked.

Tension snaked through her suddenly stiff body.

"Dr. Knight?"

She glanced back at Detective Turner. "I locked my door." She *always* locked her door. Her heart beat faster.

The detective pulled his gun even as he pushed her behind him. Evelyn swallowed, and the image of Trent's sheet-covered body drifted through her mind. She reached out for the detective, moving on instinct, and her fingers curled around his shoulder.

"Stay behind me," he ordered.

She nodded, but he didn't see the move.

Then the detective slipped into her house. It was dark inside, quiet, and the thick carpeting muted the sound of their footsteps. The detective was methodical, searching every room, every closet, but no one was there. Nothing was disturbed.

They returned to the living room. With nervous hands, she quickly turned on all the lamps in the room. The detective watched her with a guarded gaze that she didn't like.

"Your alarm wasn't activated, Doctor."

"It should have been," she whispered, almost to herself.

He pulled out his phone. Called for a crime-scene unit.

"Why are you doing that?" She glanced back toward the door. It *had* been locked when she left that morning, right? She'd been so frantic to find Trent.

Surely she hadn't just run out and left the door unlocked.

"I want the door dusted for prints. I want fresh eyes in here looking at the scene." He put his phone back in his jacket. "You want to know why the crime team is coming?" He shook his head as if he didn't understand. "Lady, your partner was murdered by the Valentine Killer. You just went on the news and outed his ex-fiancée, a woman who was supposed to be protected with a new identity. Did you even stop to think for a second that you could be putting a target on yourself?"

A target? No, that wasn't possible. "Valentine wouldn't come for me."

"You sure about that?" He stepped toward her. "Then who the hell else do you think might have broken into your place tonight?"

Her heart was beating so fast and hard that she feared it would burst from her chest, but she tried to control her expression—an old habit—because she didn't want the detective to know how she truly felt.

"Valentine is killing in this town," he told her, giving another slow shake of his head, "and with your performance today, you just might have set yourself up as his next victim."

- 14 -

She hadn't planned for an early morning trip to the morgue, but that was exactly where Katherine found herself at six a.m.

When he'd been talking to her, Dane had called the place "the death rooms," and she thought the name was apt. The building behind the police station was cavernous, deep, and chilled. The place smelled of antiseptic and bleach, and she had no idea how the ME could spend so much time there.

"I could have gone back to my place," Katherine said as she pulled Dane to a stop beside her in the hallway. "You didn't have to bring me here."

"I want you where I can keep an eye on you."

"You can't watch me twenty-four hours a day."

"I fucking want to," he muttered.

She frowned at him. He'd gotten a call before dawn that sent him surging out of bed and rushing her to the morgue.

"Ronnie has something she needs to show me. She said it was important." He paused as his gaze swept over her face. "It's about Valentine, and I thought you deserved to hear the news that she has."

Katherine nodded, then she braced herself as Dane pushed open the swinging doors that led to the morgue.

A woman swung toward them. She wore a rumpled white lab coat and wire-framed glasses. Dark shadows lined the woman's eyes. "Great. I was beginning to wonder—" She broke off, her eyes widening behind her glasses as her gaze shifted to Katherine. "You're...her."

Katherine cleared her throat. *Her?* She'd gotten that wide-eyed stare plenty of times back in Boston. Now that she'd gone on the news and revealed her identity, Katherine figured she'd be getting it plenty more, too. *Deal with it.* She straightened her shoulders. "Yes, I'm Katelynn." The name felt foreign to her, wrong.

"This is Katherine Cole," Dane said in the next instant, voice hard. "Katherine, this is our ME, Dr. Veronica Thomas."

Before Veronica could speak, the doors gave a swish of sound behind them. Katherine glanced back and saw Mac pushing inside. There was a tense, hard look in his eyes.

She felt Dane go on alert beside her. "What's happened?"

"Took the shrink home last night," Mac said. "When we got there, her door was unlocked."

"Evelyn?" Katherine said as she rubbed her arms. How did Veronica stand that chill? "Is she all right?"

"She's fine. I left a uniform outside her place, but..." He exhaled. "She wasn't even one hundred percent sure that she'd set her lock and alarm. She told me she'd left that morning in a panic and couldn't remember."

"Was there any sign of an intruder?" Dane asked.

"No." Mac strode past them. Went to Veronica's side. Seemed to stand a little too close to her. "I got the techs to sweep everything, but there was no trace of anyone else there."

The goose bumps were still on Katherine's arms.

"I want to keep a uniform on her, just as a precaution," Mac said.

Katherine understood what he wasn't saying: *In case Valentine is going after her.*

Her gaze slid back to Veronica. The other woman was studying her a little too intently. When she realized that Katherine had caught her staring, Veronica gave a little jump.

"I found something last night. Something that could help with the investigation."

Veronica turned away and pulled a slab from one of the nearby lockers. Cold air brushed against Katherine's skin. Mac and Dane edged closer to the slab, but Katherine didn't move.

Veronica unzipped the bag, and her gloved fingers pointed toward Savannah's neck. "Take a look here." She shone a light on Savannah's neck and pushed a magnifying glass toward Savannah's throat.

Dane leaned forward.

Katherine edged back. Her eyes weren't on Savannah's neck; they were on her face. So still and pale. All the color bleached away. All of the life—just gone.

"I see the bruise," Dane said.

"Not just a bruise. An injection site."

Katherine's gaze snapped to Veronica.

"I didn't even realize what it was at first because it's so small, but once I got the tox screen back on her, I knew what to look for." Her voice rose with excitement. "The killer injected her with fentanyl, a high enough dose to knock her out for a good long while."

"Fentanyl?" Katherine repeated, lost. "What's that?"

"It's like morphine, but much stronger. With the dose that Savannah Slater was given, she would have been unconscious within moments." She licked her lips. "Helpless."

"I've heard of fentanyl, and that's not exactly an easy drug to get your hands on," Dane muttered as he eased closer to Katherine.

"No." Ronnie pushed her glasses higher on her nose. "You need a prescription. Doctors would have access. Nurses."

"Hot damn." Now excitement had entered Dane's voice, too. "We might be able to track the bastard through the drug."

Veronica nodded.

"We'll start a check, trace down the distribution—"

Katherine grabbed his arm. "Valentine never drugged his victims. They all came with him willingly." Her eyes were on Savannah's body. "He seduced," she whispered. "He didn't drug." That wasn't the way he'd worked in Boston.

"*This* killer is drugging his victims." Ronnie pulled out another body from a second locker. Unzipped the bag. Katherine took a sharp breath when she saw the woman's dark hair. Was that Amy Evans? Yes.

Ronnie was still talking. She used her magnifying glass and said, "Same injection spot. Same drug. Same high dose." Ronnie's gaze turned to Dane. "Both victims were unconscious when the killer took them."

"What about Lancaster?" Dane demanded. "Did he have the same injection mark?"

Ronnie shook her head and moved away from the slabs. She walked toward a sheet-covered body that waited on a table in the middle of the room. "I've got his tox screen running now, a rush order, but I checked thoroughly, and I haven't found any sign of an injection on his body."

Katherine turned and walked toward that table. She stared at Trent's covered body. A tremble shook her.

"I did notice something different, though." Ronnie's voice was contemplative. "The angle of the attack is different with him. The knife plunged into him deeper, harder. There was a hell of a lot more force used in this kill."

"Because he was angry," Dane said, coming to stand by that table, too.

Trent's face was covered by the sheet. Katherine didn't want to see his face.

Not again.

I'm sorry, Trent.

"Valentine was angry," Dane said again. "That's why the wounds were harder. He was pissed off."

At Trent.

At me.

Ronnie cleared her throat. "There are the exact same number of slashes on the arms of all the victims, the pattern is perfect."

"Because it's the same pattern that Valentine has on his arms," Katherine added. She'd seen those scars, touched them, so many times and not even realized... "He suffered, so he wanted his victims to feel the same pain he felt."

She had no doubt that Trent had felt plenty of pain before he died.

"We need to talk to the profiler," Mac said. "If our perp is drugging his victims, then his MO has changed."

Katherine turned away from Trent's body. The scent in that place was making her sick. No, just being there, so close to the victims...

They'd all suffered too much. And for what? Because Valentine had marked them for death.

But why them...*and why not me?*

"Katherine!" Dane called her name as she rushed for the door.

But Katherine just shook her head. She needed air. She was suffocating in there. She pushed past the doors, didn't wait for the elevator but rushed up the stairs.

Then she was outside. The back lot was all but deserted, and she sucked in deep gulps of air.

A hand wrapped around her shoulder. She knew the touch instantly. Dane.

She didn't turn toward him. "I want this to stop." What did they have to do?

"The drug is the biggest break we've had. We can track its distribution and run the bastard down."

"He didn't drug his victims—"

Dane caught her chin and forced her to look at him. "That was three years ago. Maybe something happened to him. Maybe he *has* to drug them in order to get them under his power. Whatever the reason, this is the break we need. We can find him."

She couldn't get those dead bodies out of her head. She would never be able to get them out. "He's always watching," she said. Her gaze darted around the parking lot. "He knew about me and Trent, so he killed Trent. He knows about us, Dane." Dammit, she'd been so selfish last night. Wanting to be with him because he made her feel *alive*.

Even though just being with her could make him dead.

Katherine shook her head. "He said I should stay away from you."

"And that's exactly why you're staying close to me. That bastard doesn't get to dictate to you. We're not playing his game."

Yes, they were. Didn't Dane realize it? With each body they discovered, they were just running blindly behind Valentine.

"I don't want you to be the next victim in the morgue," she said, and suddenly Katherine was the one holding on to him. Her nails sank into his arms. "I don't want that, do you understand?"

Not when she'd just started to care for him. He'd broken through her wall, and she didn't want him to die because of her.

"He's not going to catch me unaware. I'm the one who's going to catch him."

So confident. So determined.

She wanted to believe him, but she was afraid.

What if...

Dane kissed her. Hard. Deep. "You're not losing me, and I'm *not* going to let you go."

— — —

"I want you to stay at the station," Dane said as he checked his weapon. He was going to head back to Trent Lancaster's place and make sure the techs hadn't missed any detail. The more he learned about his victims, the more he could potentially learn about Valentine.

"No." Katherine's voice was quiet and determined and damn well not saying what he wanted to hear.

She was seated in his desk chair. He leaned over, caging her with his hands. "I have to know that you're safe."

"I can't keep hiding." Her chin lifted. Sexy. Strong. But driving him crazy when he just wanted to protect her. "He's never tried to hurt me, don't you get that? If Valentine wanted me dead, he could have just stabbed me in the heart at the gallery."

That wasn't the visual that Dane wanted in his head. But he knew she was right—he'd thought the same thing.

He had the opportunity. Plenty of time. Valentine could have easily killed Katherine before Dane arrived.

"I'm not going back to the safe house. I'm not going to hide at the station all day." Her gaze was clear. "Hiding won't draw him out. My being out there, walking around where he can see me—"

Where the bastard could watch.

"—that's when he'll be more likely to slip up." Her breath whispered out. "Just put cops on me."

The uniforms hadn't done her a damn bit of good before. This time, he'd tell them to stick shadow close.

"But I'm not going to cower in the shadows."

He could admire that. He did. He actually admired a hell of a lot about her.

If they hadn't been surrounded by a roomful of avid cops, he would have kissed her.

Again.

"I need to see Joe and Ben," she told him.

His brows climbed. "The guys from the diner?"

"After what happened yesterday, I just...I need to talk to them." She glanced down at her trembling hands. "They're the closest thing to friends that I have in this town. I feel like I owe them an explanation."

She didn't owe anything to anyone.

"So I'm going to the diner, then I'll go home." Her lips twisted. "Because I'm guessing my gallery is off-limits."

"It's an active crime scene."

"And the showing won't be happening. Not that any-one would want to come now, knowing who I am." Her lips twisted. "Or maybe they would. There's always the freak show aspect."

"You're *not* a freak." Just hearing her say that had rage pulsing through him. Katherine had worked hard to build her new life, but that life had been ripped apart by a few minutes of prime-time TV.

"Hendricks! Johnson!" Dane barked for the uniforms.

They rushed toward them.

He glared at the two men. "You're her shadow today, got it? Where she goes, you go."

The men quickly nodded.

"If *anything* happens, anything that makes her nervous or makes *you* nervous, then you get her to a secure location and you call me. Got it?"

More quick nods.

His gaze turned back to Katherine. "I don't like this." Just so they were clear.

"I don't either, but it's what I have to do."

Not be afraid. Take charge of her life.

Fuck. It would be so easy to love a woman like her. With a spirit that couldn't be broken.

So easy.

Screw the cops watching. He took her lips again. Then growled, "I'll come to you as soon as I finish my check at Lancaster's." And as soon as he started running down those drug orders.

She nodded. Her gaze showed no fear, but he knew Katherine was good at hiding her emotions.

Good at not screaming from nightmares.

Good at not breaking when death came.

What would she be like, he wondered, if she didn't have to be so careful? So good at staying on guard? He'd like to see her that way. The real Katherine.

One day, he vowed, he *would* see her like that.

– – –

The door jingled as Katherine entered the café. The morning rush was in full effect, and the place was packed with hungry customers.

The cops were behind her. They were staying about five steps away from her for every step that she took.

The café was still a sea of red with the tablecloths that Joe had put out before, but now, Katherine saw that Joe had added vases of roses to the tabletops. The sickeningly sweet scent of the roses hit her the instant she stepped inside.

So many damn roses. With Valentine's Day right around the corner, the roses were everywhere. And she *hated* them.

Katherine exhaled slowly and squared her shoulders. She'd come there for a reason, dammit, and she wasn't going to let some flowers stop her. When she approached the counter, Joe's head lifted. His eyes widened when he saw her.

"Katelynn."

Right. "So I guess you saw the news."

She eased into her usual seat at the bar. Ben wasn't there. Pity. She would have liked to talk to them both.

And tell them to be on guard.

Because that was part of the reason she was there. Not just to apologize for scaring both men yesterday, but also to warn them.

She'd told Dane the truth when she said these men were the closest things to friends that she had. Would that closeness cause them to be targets?

Katherine couldn't take that chance.

Joe's gaze swept over her face. He was guarded today, whereas before he'd always greeted her with a warm smile.

The smile was gone now.

"I saw on the news," Joe said quietly as he leaned toward her, "they found that man in your gallery."

She nodded.

It seemed as if the other voices had hushed in the diner. Or was that her imagination?

"Then you were walking here, with that gun in your hand..."

Katherine took a deep breath and leaned toward him. "There's a very dangerous killer hunting in this city."

"Valentine." The lines near his eyes seemed deeper.

"Yes. I had the gun yesterday—I had it because I was trying to protect myself."

"From the killer."

"He's a man who doesn't give up what he wants." Lucky her, she seemed to be what he wanted. Katherine leaned forward. "I want you to promise me you'll be on guard, okay? Don't go alone anywhere, don't stay at the café late by yourself. Just *be careful.*"

His brows climbed. "Is that why you came here today? To tell me to be careful?"

"I think he's been watching me." *I know he's been watching me.* "So that means he might have been watching the people in my life, too. You and Ben…you two have always been good to me, and I would never want anything to happen to either of you. You and Ben…you're the closest I came to having friends here."

Joe was silent a moment, then he turned away from her. Katherine's shoulders wanted to slump, but she held them upright with an effort. She hadn't exactly expected a warm reception, but she'd wanted to warn Joe.

A hot mug of café au lait was pushed in front of her. Katherine glanced up in surprise.

Joe held her gaze. "We're not close to friends. We *are* friends… Katherine."

Her smile trembled.

But then Joe was called away by another customer before she could say anything else to him. Katherine took a sip of the café au lait. She felt warmer now, and it wasn't because of the drink.

The bell on the door jingled, and Katherine glanced over, hoping to see Ben. Only Ben wasn't in the doorway.

Another familiar figure was.

Evelyn?

Tension knifed through Katherine as Evelyn's gaze seemed to laser in on her.

Katherine shoved to her feet. She tossed some money down on the counter. This was not the place to have a public battle. Joe deserved better than that. Evelyn had tracked her there, obviously. From their sessions together, Evelyn knew of Katherine's routine stops by the café.

She came looking for me.

Fine, but Katherine would take that battle away from Joe.

Evelyn marched toward her.

Katherine shook her head. "I'm not going to—"

"I'm sorry." Evelyn's voice was stark.

Katherine frowned, and she realized that mascara stains were beneath Evelyn's eyes. The woman's makeup was rubbed off. No, it looked like she hadn't put on any makeup since the previous night.

Fear was etched across Evelyn's face.

"I was out of control yesterday. So upset about Trent. I—" Evelyn sucked in a deep breath. Her shaking hands hit the counter, sending the café au lait crashing to the side. "I should never have gone to the media. I was just hurting so *much*."

This was an Evelyn that Katherine had never seen before. Usually the psychiatrist was so controlled.

But emotions were pouring out of the woman now.

Katherine slowly sat back down on the stool. A waitress slid a fresh mug of café au lait toward her.

"I think he was in my house."

"Something for you, miss?" the waitress asked, cutting in.

Evelyn looked blankly at her.

"Get her the same," Katherine said softly.

"When I got home last night, my front door was unlocked." Evelyn's eyes were bright with tears. "Is he coming after me? Because of what I did to you?" Her voice was a stark whisper that carried only to Katherine.

"I don't know what he's doing," Katherine said.

Another mug was pushed forward. Evelyn's hands were shaking so hard that she spilled more of the hot liquid. Katherine tried to help her wipe it up.

"I don't want to die." Evelyn wasn't looking at her as the shrink made the confession.

Neither do I.

"Should I leave town?" Evelyn took a sip of her drink. "Will I be safe then?"

Katherine drank some of her own café au lait as she tried to think. She'd tried fleeing and getting a new identity, but Valentine had still tracked her.

"I won't be safe then, will I?" The hope had bled from Evelyn's voice.

Katherine glanced at her. "Dane and Mac are going to find him. They found evidence of a drug he used on his victims—"

Evelyn's eyes widened.

"They're tracking it," Katherine said. "We just have to—" *Stay alive until they stop him.* No, she couldn't say that. Katherine drank more of her café au lait. She put the nearly empty mug back down. "Don't stay by yourself. Go to a friend's, a relative's. Get police protection."

"I have it," Evelyn confessed as her eyes cut to a man in a nearby booth.

Katherine's temples began to throb. Evelyn in Valentine's crosshairs? First Trent, now Evelyn. No wonder the woman was scared.

Katherine was terrified for her.

"Hearing about him was one thing," Evelyn whispered. "Our sessions, that was different." She grabbed Katherine's hand. Held tight. "I don't want to be one of his victims."

Katherine swallowed. The throbbing in her temples was getting worse. "Do you have relatives out of town you can stay with?"

Evelyn nodded.

"Then go to them." Just because he'd followed Katherine didn't mean he'd follow Evelyn. Maybe once she was out of town, his focus would shift back to—

Me.

"How have you done it?" Evelyn asked as she raked a hand through her hair. "All of these years, knowing he was hunting you..."

"It was hard to stay sane," Katherine confessed. "Guess that's why I wound up seeing you."

Evelyn blinked, as if surprised, and a ghost of smile tilted her lips.

The jingle came from the diner's door once more.

Katherine glanced over. This time Ben was in the doorway, with his blonde girlfriend by his side.

She had to talk to him. Needed to warn him, too.

"Excuse me," Katherine murmured, but the words sounded funny to her ears.

Katherine tried to stand up, but her knees gave way. She hit the floor with an impact that jarred her whole body.

Her hands pushed weakly against the tile, but she couldn't get up.

"Katherine?" Ben was rushing toward her.

"Katherine!" Evelyn crouched in front of her. "What's happening?"

The plainclothes cops were rushing up behind Evelyn.

Then Evelyn became a blur. Katherine's eyes began to roll back in her head. Her body shook, convulsing.

"She's seizing!" Evelyn yelled. "Call an ambulance!"

Hard hands were on Katherine, holding her down, but her body kept bucking. A rough, bitter taste was in her mouth, and her heart was racing so fast. Too fast.

"Katherine?" The voice came from her right. She tried to focus but couldn't see anything.

"Katherine, it's Ben. Hold on, okay? Joe's calling an ambulance right now."

Ben. She needed to warn Ben. "Kill…"

"What is she saying?" Ben asked. "Katherine, say it again."

"Run…" *Run from the killer. Valentine is in town. I don't want anyone else hurt.*

No one else under his knife.

But she couldn't tell Ben that. She couldn't say anything, because when she tried to speak, she started to choke.

"Clear her airway!" That voice belonged to one of the cops. Then a hand was under Katherine's chin. She attempted to suck in air but couldn't.

She couldn't breathe at all.

And she stopped hearing the voices around her.

— — —

"Katherine?"

Someone squeezed her hand.

There was a buzz of voices.

Doors slammed.

"You're gonna be okay, all right? Maggie, call your dad. Let him know what's happening." The voice was deep and male, and she recognized it.

Her world started to move—no, *she* was moving. Being loaded into…something. An ambulance?

"I'll stay with her," the voice said, and then he was there. Ben, frowning down at her. "I used to be an EMT," he said, and she realized that an EMT was on her right, pushing a needle into her arm.

Katherine flinched.

"It's okay. Hey, hey, keep those eyes open!" Ben snapped.

She wanted to, but it was so hard.

His fingers squeezed hers.

"Are you having an allergic reaction to something?" Ben asked her. "Did something—"

She managed to shake her head.

"Poison, drugs…" The other man was talking, but she could barely make out his words.

Her heart wasn't beating quickly now. It was beating too slowly.

A siren wailed.

Her fingers were still twined with Ben's. "You're going to be all right," Ben told her. "Just hang on. I'll keep you safe."

Her eyes couldn't stay open any longer.

— — —

Dane's eyes swept Trent Lancaster's bedroom. Nothing in the house was out of place. He'd hoped to find some evidence there that could tell him if Trent had been watched or stalked in the days leading up to his attack.

The phone on his hip vibrated. Dane put the phone to his ear. "Black."

"Get to Mercy General," the captain's voice ordered. "Get there *now*."

"What's happening?"

Mac looked over at him, obviously catching the tight note in Dane's voice.

"Maggie just called."

Maggie. Harley's daughter.

"She was at a café in the Quarter. Katherine was there—"

Why the hell would Katherine—

"Katherine collapsed. She's being taken to the hospital now. Maggie knew who she was, she'd seen the stories, and she called because she was scared Valentine might have targeted Katherine."

Dane was already running for the door.

— — —

Katherine's throat hurt. Her stomach ached, and the bitter taste in her mouth had only grown worse.

Her eyes opened to a world of white. White ceiling. White walls. A bright, white light overhead.

Someone was holding her hand.

Ben. Ben had been holding her hand in the ambulance.

She turned her head, but Ben wasn't there.

Dane was.

And he looked haggard. Dark shadows were under his eyes, and the lines near his mouth looked deeper.

But when he looked into her eyes, a smile swept over his face. "You're back."

"Where...did...I..." Oh, but her throat hurt. "Go?"

"Away from me." He leaned forward and pressed a kiss to her lips. "And I want you to promise never, ever to fucking do that again." Dane pushed the call button on the side of the bed.

She tried to shift in the bed. "How did…I…?"

"You were drugged, Katherine." Fury burned in his eyes, flashing as his hand tightened on hers. "A damn deadly mix designed to take you out. But the doctors worked some fucking miracles here."

Had they pumped her stomach? Was that why her throat and stomach hurt so much?

"You pulled through."

He kissed her again, as if he couldn't help himself. "I've never been that scared." He whispered the stark confession.

"How—" Katherine began again.

"We think it was in the drink you had. We've got Joe at the station, and Mac is going to grill that bastard."

"Not…Joe…" He hadn't even given her the café au lait, had he? It was so hard to remember.

The door opened, and a woman holding a white clipboard bustled inside. She smiled when she saw Katherine. "You're awake." Her warm brown eyes cut to Dane. "I told your detective that you would be, but he insisted on staying by your side."

Her heart was beating faster, and the monitors on the right picked up the frantic sound.

The doctor came closer. "You're going to be fine, Ms. Cole. You were very lucky. The fentanyl was mixed with several drugs to—"

"Fentanyl," Katherine repeated. The monitors were beeping like mad now.

The doctor nodded and started talking about why Katherine had convulsed. The mixture of drugs. The intensity…

Katherine barely heard her. Katherine's gaze had turned back to Dane. "He came for me," she whispered. Valentine had given her the same drug that he'd used on his other victims.

He tried to kill me?

She lifted her left hand. An IV line was hooked in the vein on the top of her hand. Her fingers rose and hovered over her heart.

She could almost feel the slice of Valentine's knife.

"I don't think he meant for you to go under so fast," Dane said. "He was probably planning to get you as soon as you left the diner."

Only she'd never made it out of the diner.

He tried to kill me.

The doctor started checking the monitors near Katherine.

"He was there," Katherine said. Her voice was stronger even as fear thickened within her. She tried to remember the customers in the diner. Others had been close to her at the counter, but she'd barely glanced at them. She'd been so busy talking to Evelyn. "Evelyn…"

"She stayed at the hospital for more than four hours, waiting until we were sure you were all right." He brushed back her hair. "I had a uniform take her back home."

Katherine didn't think Evelyn would be staying at her home long. The woman was terrified, and after this attack, well, Katherine figured Evelyn would be packing her bags as quickly as she could.

The doctor eased from the room.

"I'm scared," Katherine confessed to Dane.

A muscle jerked in his jaw.

"He drugged me." She shook her head. A bitter smile curved her lips. "I guess this means Marcus has to rework his profile." He'd always been so sure that Valentine wouldn't hurt her.

Had she been sure of it, too?

No, she'd always thought...*someday, he'll come for me.*

That day had come.

"I want you to go with Ross."

She blinked, surprised.

"He's already working on a new cover for you. I want you to leave with him as soon as you're cleared from the hospital." Dane gave a quick nod. "You'll be out of New Orleans by night-fall. You'll be safe."

Another name, another place? "He'll just find me."

"Not before I find *him.*"

"I don't want to go through this."

"I thought you were dead." The words were rough. "When I saw you in the ER, you were so still and pale, and I thought the doctors weren't going to be able to save you."

Fear whispered in his words.

"I don't want to feel that way again. I'm not using you as bait. I'm fucking not using you at all. You're going with Ross. He's going to keep you safe until this is over."

She tried to push up in the bed, and, instantly, Dane was on his feet. Helping her. Supporting her. "I go, and what happens?" She licked her dry lips. "He gets angry and goes after someone else who happened to be in my life? I don't want any more deaths on me!"

"And I don't want you dead."

A rap sounded at the door.

Dane looked up at a uniform who had poked his head in the door.

"The captain's here," the cop said. "And some more visitors with him."

Dane gave a grim nod. Like he could refuse the captain's entrance.

Then the door was swinging open, and Harley was striding inside. Ben was behind him, with his arm around the shoulders of the pretty blonde—wait, Maggie. Her name was Maggie.

What were they all doing together?

"You gave us all a scare," Harley said quietly.

"I scared myself," Katherine managed.

Ben eased away from Maggie and came closer to the bed. He had some tulips in his hand. "Maggie and I wanted to bring these to you. We hope you get out of here soon."

Ben. He'd helped her at the diner. He'd held her hand in the ambulance.

"Thank you," Katherine whispered. Her body had tensed at the sight of the flowers. Not roses, no, but she couldn't look at any flowers without remembering Valentine. Couldn't enjoy the scent or the sight.

For her, flowers were too tied to Valentine. Maybe one day it would be different but…Katherine couldn't even bring herself to reach out and take the tulips.

His head inclined toward her. "I wasn't about to let anything happen to you." He gave her a small smile. "You can count on me." Then he carefully put the tulips on the small table near the bed.

Tears threatened to fill her eyes. When she hadn't been looking, she'd found friends.

"This is my daughter," Harley said as he glanced toward Maggie. "She called the station, and you can believe we all busted ass getting to you."

Katherine's gaze slid to Dane.

"I couldn't get here fast enough," he muttered.

"Who gave you the drink?" Harley asked her. "Do you remember what happened?"

"Bits and pieces." Tiny pieces. "I spilled my first drink, and I think the waitress brought the second one to me."

Harley exchanged a hard look with Dane. "We've got techs searching that whole café, but so far, the only traces of fentanyl or any other drugs we can find were just in your cup."

"That café was packed," Maggie whispered. "So many people…"

"And some of them slipped out before we could secure the scene. The cops got as many contacts as they could, and they're interviewing all those that they were able to hold at the café. We *will* figure out who drugged you." Harley was adamant.

"But in the meantime, what?" Katherine asked. She pulled the thin hospital sheets up higher. "Dane wants me to leave, but I am so tired of running. Exhausted."

Another rap at her door. She looked up, expecting to see the uniform showing Ross inside next. With the marshal, it would be quite the little party.

But Ross wasn't there. It was the uniform, his face grim. "Flowers," he said, his voice tight.

Not just any flowers. He was holding roses in his hands.

The monitors started to beep frantically once more.

"Nurse just brought them," the cop said. "I thought—"

"Captain, stay with her," Dane snapped as he rushed from the room.

And Katherine realized that Valentine wasn't ever going to stop his games. Not until she was dead.

Or he was.

"Katherine?" Ben hadn't moved. Maggie stood by him, looking nervous.

She didn't blame her.

The sweet scent of the roses made the whole room smell of death. Nausea twisted in Katherine's stomach. "You should go," she managed to say to Ben and Maggie. "Please, you need to stay away from me."

Maggie edged back. As a police captain's daughter, she would understand just how dangerous the world could be.

Ben's heavy brows lowered.

But Harley pushed them toward the door, even as he yanked out his cell and started barking orders for others to come to the hospital room.

And the uniform kept standing there, holding the flowers.

Bloodred.

"How many are there?" Katherine asked.

The uniform blinked.

"Count the roses," Harley snapped at him.

"Eleven, sir."

Eleven. That meant one was saved, as it always was, for the victim's hand.

– 15 –

"I want you to pack your bags," Dane said as he opened the passenger-side door for Katherine. "We're going into your house, getting what you need, and then getting you the hell out of here."

The fucking flowers. The bastard had actually been ballsy enough to send them to the hospital. The nurse had told him that a flower delivery boy gave them to her, and the surveillance videos verified it. The videos had verified a fucking ton of rose deliveries. For Valentine's Day, what else were people going to send? Roses. Every damn place. In nearly every room at that hospital.

After some hard digging, they'd tracked the delivery back to an overworked florist on Chartres. The florist had the order in his books—along with more than two hundred other orders for a dozen roses—but that particular charge had been an Internet order, one that used a stolen credit card. Their techs at the office were trying to follow the IP address for that order, but so far, hell, they had nothing.

And I want Katherine out of here.

"He's going to follow me," Katherine said. "He'll *always* follow me."

She was too pale. She'd nearly died. He couldn't get the image of her still body out of his mind. "He's making mistakes. Going into the diner, using the florist—we're so damn close to having him." His fingers curled over her shoulders. "I just want some time, Katherine. Time when I can focus on the case because I know you're safe."

"And I don't want anyone else dead because of me!"

He pulled her toward the house. A cop was at her door. His orders. He wanted Katherine watched constantly. "It's not you. It's that twisted freak of a killer." How many times did he have to say the words?

"It's easy to say when the blood isn't on your hands."

He caught her right hand. Small. Smooth. "There is no blood here. It's all on him."

She pressed her lips together and slipped into the house. He followed her, staying as close as a shadow as she went toward the stairs.

He wanted to be near her constantly now. She'd come too close to death, and he'd seen his worst nightmare.

The stairs squeaked softly as they climbed, and then they were in Katherine's bedroom. The bedroom smelled of her. Sweet. Light.

He knew the worry wouldn't stop when she left with Ross. If he couldn't see her, then Dane knew he'd still be frantic. He'd only feel secure if he could keep an eye on her twenty-four seven.

Twenty-four seven.

Understanding hit him instantly. Dane wanted to keep a constant watch on Katherine so he could keep her safe.

Valentine...Valentine would want to keep a constant eye on her, too.

While Katherine was in her closet, he yanked out his crime-scene gloves. Carefully put them on.

He began to walk around the room, looking carefully in each corner, near each window.

"What are you doing?" Katherine asked.

He glanced over his shoulder. She stood in the doorway of her closet, frowning at him.

Cops had been in her house. Dozens of them. But they had been intent on keeping the killer *out*. Dane realized that the guy was already in. "He said he was watching you."

She nodded. Her right hand had a white-knuckled grip on a small overnight bag.

"He's obsessed, so he'd want to be near you all the time." He kept up his slow search, letting his gaze slide carefully over every inch of the room. "And he told you to stay away from me."

"Yes."

Was it because the bastard knew that Dane had been intimate with Katherine? Was that what had made the guy snap and attack her?

If the man knew that, then he'd been watching, all right. Watching with a view that let him see straight into Katherine's bedroom.

The techs had been over her house so carefully, they wouldn't have missed a small camera or even a bug. Not if one were hidden in the obvious spots that most of that team would have checked.

Not obvious, but…

I know you're watching.

His gaze locked on the security box on her far right wall. The green light shone, indicating the system was set. "Who installed your security system?"

"A…uh, a local company. Joe at the café, he suggested them."

Fuck. Mac had let Joe walk from the station. The guy had undergone grilling for hours, but he'd sworn he had nothing to do with hurting Katherine. The café owner's lawyers had pushed for him to be either charged or released.

They hadn't possessed any evidence to charge him.

Dane's gaze was on that security box. "Ross didn't handle it?" The guy should have.

"He checked them out. Said they were clear."

The box was bothering him. It was bigger than the box he'd seen in her den, bigger by at least four inches. And it was positioned at a direct angle to her bed and to the entrance to her bathroom.

He stepped a little closer to the box, eyes narrowing.

Sonofabitch. There was a small hole in the front of that box. And what sure as shit looked like a tiny camera lens peeking out at him.

He turned and headed toward Katherine. "Bring the bag, and let's go."

"But—"

He put his mouth near her ear. It probably looked like they were kissing, but he needed her to hear his whisper. "Don't say anything else. He's watching us."

A tremble shook her body, but she nodded.

The sick prick had truly been watching her all along. But Dane wasn't about to run over there and grab the camera. It was transmitting. If Valentine saw that they were on to him, the man would run.

But if they could trace that transmission back without alerting Valentine...

Got you.

He pulled away from her. "Let's go."

Katherine nodded. Her features were clear, showing no fear or anger. The woman really was a pretty fine actress. She hurried across the room, still clutching her bag, and hurriedly packed some clothes. She reached into her nightstand and pulled out—

"I won't be coming back for a while, will I?" Katherine asked.

He shook his head.

That woman had just slipped a gun into her bag. Damn but he could love her.

Could?

"Then I'll try to be as prepared as possible."

Hell yes.

They left the house and went back to Dane's car. As soon as their doors shut, he was on the line with his captain. "Harley, get a tech team working on Katherine's house ASAP. The bastard's been watching her. He's got a camera in her bedroom."

From the corner of his eye, he saw Katherine's hands clench in her lap.

"Yeah, yeah," he said to the captain. "I'm thinking we can trace the path of the signal. *Find* him. Stop him."

Then Katherine could have her life back.

They were close. So fucking close. Valentine had screwed up. Left them a trail of bread crumbs to follow. This was the break they'd needed. This. Was. It. The techs hadn't thought to check the security box—hell, it was the one thing most folks would assume was safe. Ross might have cleared the security company, but Dane didn't think the guy had actually gone into Katherine's bedroom. He hadn't *seen* the box.

But all the while, Valentine had been seeing Katherine.

No more.

– – –

The techs were in a van, one with the big label of a local cable company plastered on the side. Dane crouched in that van, with Katherine seated close by.

John Baylor, the tech guru at the New Orleans PD, was typing furiously on his laptop. "It's a short-range transmission."

Unfortunately, that was exactly what Dane had feared.

"Short-range?" Katherine repeated.

"No more than a mile, maybe two, tops," John said without looking up from his computer.

Katherine glanced at Dane. "He's been less than two miles away from me? This whole time?"

Dane wasn't sure just how long he'd been there. "When did you get your security system installed?"

"A year ago."

Fuck.

Harley was down at the security office, questioning the manager and every person who worked there.

"Almost got the bastard…he put up some red herrings, bouncing it, but I almost…" John slapped the keyboard. "*Got you.*"

Yes. "Where?" Dane demanded.

"Five blocks away."

"Five blocks?" Katherine's voice had risen a few notches.

Dane yanked out his phone and got the captain instantly. "We're moving."

"Five-two-oh-seven Oakland Way," John said. He was smiling.

Dane was too tense to smile. He wanted in that house. Wanted to bust his way inside *now*. But he knew the way this had to be handled. He gave the captain the address.

"Don't move until I'm there," Harley ordered. "I'm sending you backup. We go in right, and we take him *down*."

Dane shoved the phone into his pocket. He leaned forward and pressed his lips to Katherine's. "It's almost over," he promised her.

But a faint line was etched between her brows. "Five blocks? I-I thought I was safe, and he was just *five* blocks away."

"Pretty soon he's gonna be in a cage, and he won't ever hurt anyone again." With all of his kills, the bastard could get a needle shoved into his arm, or he could fry in the chair. Then Katherine's nightmare would really be over.

Katherine grabbed his arm. Held tight. "Be careful."

He always was.

She shook her head. "Don't be cocky. Be *careful*. Valentine is smart, and he won't go down without a fight."

Good. Because Dane was more than ready for the battle.

– – –

"What are you doing, Detective? Are you trying to take my Kat away?" Valentine stared at the screen. Rewound the footage. Played it again.

The detective kept touching Kat too much. He'd thought their relationship was a ploy at first.

A way of getting to me.

But Kat looked at the detective differently. Her gaze softened when she stared at him.

And she touched the detective. Kat didn't like to touch others. But she touched Dane Black. *Far too much.*

Valentine leaned forward and studied the scene once more. Something was off. He glared at the detective. The man had a past as fucked-up as Valentine's own. He would never do for Katherine.

And if he kept touching—

The detective was wearing latex gloves. *Why?* Why wear gloves if they were just running in to pack a bag for Kat?

Valentine backed away from the screen.

This scene wasn't about getting clothes.

Dane Black had been searching for something in that house. Then he'd hauled ass out of there…because he'd found what he was looking for.

Valentine watched as the detective's gaze darted toward the security box. There…*there*. Dane Black's stare narrowed.

He'd worn the gloves so the guy wouldn't disturb any evidence. And, while Katherine had been packing, Dane had—

He found me.

Valentine ran for the stairs.

- - -

The house was unassuming. Small and brick, nestled at the end of a narrow street. Darkness was coming, and heavy shadows stretched over the area.

From his position behind the patrol car, Dane glared at the house.

"Doesn't look like the place a serial killer would call home, huh?" The question came from Anthony Ross. Like Dane, he stood behind the patrol car. The marshal had been one of the first responders to rush to the scene.

"It looks *exactly* like the place a serial killer would call home," Marcus argued quietly from Dane's side. "Not like they have flashing neon signs." The profiler's voice was tight.

"Signs would make the job a whole lot fucking easier." Ross shifted his position and pulled out his gun.

Dane already had his gun ready. He was just waiting on the order from the captain. They had their search warrant—they had more than enough probable cause to bust through that door.

He just needed the captain to wave his hand. *Come on, Harley.
Come the fuck on.*

Katherine was in the van to the left of Dane. After all she'd
been through, the woman deserved to see them bring down
Valentine. When Dane had left the van, Katherine had been quiet
and tense, and he knew that she was worried.

Worried that Valentine would plan some kind of last-minute
attack. And yeah, she was right. No way would Dane buy that a
guy like Valentine would go down easy.

"Jail isn't gonna be an option for him," Marcus said, seeming
to echo Dane's thoughts. "Be prepared for anything in there."

He would be.

Any damn thing.

Harley headed toward the men. Like Dane and the others, he
was wearing a bulletproof vest. Police officers stood at the ready
around them, just waiting for the signal to begin their run on the
house.

As he approached, Harley stared into Dane's eyes. "You ready
for this?"

"Yes, sir."

Harley nodded. "Then go drag that bastard out. Make New
Orleans safe."

Dane didn't have to be told twice. He led the team toward the
house. Half would follow him through the front door. Half would
go with the marshal through the back.

The cops had the house surrounded. No one inside would
get out.

- - -

"It's all right," Captain Harley said as Katherine eased from the van and stood beside him. "Those men know exactly what they are doing."

She understood that. But knowing didn't do anything to fight the gnawing fear growing within her. "I want it to be over."

But...

She was afraid to hope.

Dane was at the front door now. She saw him motion to the men with him. Then he was kicking the door open. Rushing in. "He always has to be first," she muttered.

"Dane doesn't want anyone else to take his risks."

But she didn't want him risking his life.

Katherine was clutching her bag in her hand. The bag that held her gun. Being so close to Valentine, she wanted that gun *out*. In her hands.

Five blocks away. Nausea rolled in her stomach. Not from the remnants of the drugs, but from fear and fury. "I must have seen him," she said. While she'd been jogging. Heading to work. "I never knew."

"Probably because he looks different now. Just like you do."

New hair. No tan. And she'd lost some weight. But...it would need to be more than that for him. She would remember his jaw. His eyes. His nose. If he'd been so close, why hadn't she seen him?

The cops were inside now.

All she could do was wait.

– – –

The house was clean—almost too clean. As if no real person lived there. Magazines were neatly stacked on the coffee table. Not so much as a speck of dust on the TV tray. Books were carefully arranged—in alphabetical order—on the small shelf in a corner of the living room.

The cops were searching every inch of the first floor. Ross and his team went to the back of the house, but Dane knew where Valentine liked to work, so he headed for the basement. With a motion of his hand, he got two officers to follow him. He yanked open the door to the stairway and rushed down the narrow steps.

Dane was afraid he'd find a body down there. The same twisted scene that Valentine had played out before.

But there was no victim in the basement this time. There was no one there at all.

Dane's gaze narrowed on a small table against the right wall. A computer sat on top of that table. An image was looping and playing on that screen, again and again. Dane and Katherine. In her bedroom.

Valentine had been watching. Just a few minutes ago.

Dane stared at the screen, his body tight. *You were here. Are you still?* "Search every closet, under every bed—every damn place!" Dane barked. He tapped his transmitter. "Captain, he may have just fled the premises. Get the cops outside to start fanning out!"

– – –

The captain was shouting orders, telling his men to search the area.

"Get back in the van," Harley told Katherine as his cheeks flushed. "Stay there until it's safe."

A cop ran toward Harley, coming from the back of the small house. He had a cap pulled over his head. Harley motioned to him. "Take the south patrol! Join up with them!"

Harley turned away from the cop and helped Katherine into the van.

The cop didn't head south.

Katherine frowned. "Wait, didn't you tell him—"

Harley's phone began to ring. He grabbed it with his left hand even as his right kept pulling the van door shut. "Stay inside!" Harley told her once more.

But the cop hadn't headed south. He'd turned toward the woods.

Katherine glanced over at the tech. John looked tense, and his gaze was on the computer screen.

"John, who owns this house?"

He looked over at her. "Can't tell yet. Hell, what I've gathered, no one should own it. It was foreclosed on a year ago." His gaze shifted back to the small screen. "The lights are hooked up, gas and electricity, but it looks like the guy used three different names for those services. Tricky SOB."

Yes, he was.

Katherine glanced toward the closed van door. She kept seeing that cop head the wrong way. It had probably been nothing. Maybe someone else had told him to search in that direction, but...

It felt wrong. She reached for her bag and the gun that was inside it. Right then, she needed that security.

As her fingers closed around the bag, Katherine heard a faint a gasp, then a thud. *Like a body hitting the pavement.*

Her heart slammed into her ribs as she lunged up and grabbed the door's handle. The door rolled back, and the light from the van's interior spilled on the ground.

Showing Katherine the fresh spatter of blood that was just inches from the van.

John grabbed her. "Hey, what are you doing? The captain said to stay—"

"Didn't you hear that sound?"

He just stared blankly at her. He hadn't. He hadn't heard. She had. "He's out there." She clutched the bag tighter. "There's blood on the ground, and I'm sorry, but you have to let me out of this van." She wasn't going to sit back again. Not going to let others be risked.

John scrambled back. "Blood? Where?"

She pointed to the ground and heard his sharp inhale. "Get on the radio," she ordered him. "Valentine's here." And before he could stop her, she jumped out of the van. Katherine yanked her gun out of the bag. Harley was gone. There was no sign of the cop who'd been wearing the cap. Where were they?

She glanced around the street.

Harley had wanted the cop to search to the south.

So that just leaves north, west, and east.

Then she heard a faint groan. Pain-filled, soft. That faint sound had come from the left. *To the west.*

She ran as fast as she could. She jumped over a tall row of bushes, felt the scratches on her right leg. Tripped over someone's discarded tricycle, and then—

Harley was on the ground.

The cop with the cap was crouched over him. The cop—he had a knife at Harley's chest.

"You should have taken better care of her. I mean, you call yourself a fucking cop." She heard the words distantly. They seemed too quiet. Maybe her heartbeat was too loud.

"You're useless, that's what you are."

That voice.

"Michael." The first time she'd said his name since the day she'd found him standing over another victim. Only this time, his victim wasn't dead.

She saw his shoulders tense. The darkness was growing thicker, and it was hard to see him clearly. His cap was hiding his hair, and his shoulders—they were much bigger than they'd been before.

He didn't turn to face her, and he made no move away from Harley. Harley wasn't fighting his attacker. Just lying limp on the ground.

"You aren't supposed to be here, Kat." Michael's voice was chiding. "I saw the captain put you in the van. You're supposed to be in the van."

Valentine. Think of him as Valentine. It was the way she kept them separate. Her way of convincing herself that she'd never loved a killer.

She was good at lying to herself.

He still had the knife over Harley's chest. "The captain told you it was safe in the van."

"I also wasn't supposed to come home early that day." The gun was shaking in her fingers. "Get away from him or I'll shoot you."

He laughed. "That again, huh?"

"There are bullets in the gun this time." She'd made sure of it. "Now get away from him."

Silence. Then he lifted the knife, moving it away from Harley's body, but not dropping it. "Did you know that Harley is the one who stood by and let your detective become so warped and twisted?"

"Dane isn't warped." And he wasn't twisted. "That's you."

Laughter again. The low, husky laughter that she remembered so well. "Ah, Kat, haven't you realized you're attracted only to men like me? You see the darkness in us, and it pulls you right in."

"Get. Away. From. Him."

"You have a choice now, Kat. You can save this man. A man who stood by while a child was abused, again and again, a man who wore the uniform that said he would protect everyone…"

Harley was groaning.

"Or you can run back to that house, and *maybe* you'll get there in time to save your detective."

Her heart was beating so fast her chest hurt. "What have you done?"

"I learned from my last mistake. I'm not going to leave evidence behind again." He shook his head. She almost caught a glimpse of his jaw. Almost. She wanted to see the face that he'd been hiding behind. "That's just messy when you leave your work behind. Nothing will be taken away from that house."

She glanced over her shoulder. She could just see the roof of the house at 5207 Oakland.

"I'd say you have about two minutes. If you do go in that house…" Valentine paused. "Please be out before then. I don't want you to die."

Her cheeks were numb. "A bomb?" That demolitions training he'd had in the military. Oh, God, he *would* know how to rig the place to blow. Two minutes…it made sense. He'd set something to explode.

Her hand stopped shaking. "I'll save them all."

He stiffened. Jerked up and to the left.

She fired.

The bullet sank into his shoulder.

The knife fell to the ground with a clatter.

Before she could fire again, Valentine lunged toward a small row of trees on the right, heading for a little patch of woods that separated the subdivision from the edge of the swamp just a few yards away. He left a trail of blood behind him.

I shot him.

She rushed forward. "Captain!"

Blood trickled down his temple. There was a giant gash on the side of his head. More blood on the sidewalk. *Valentine bashed his head in.* That had been the thud she heard.

But the captain was still alive. Still breathing.

Katherine glanced at the woods. She could run after Valentine. He was hurt. This was her chance to get him. *Her chance.*

But her gaze went back to the rooftop of that house. Two minutes. Less than that now. If Valentine hadn't been bluffing, if there were explosives set to go off…

She shoved back to her feet and ran for the house. "Get out!" Katherine screamed as she raced toward 5207 Oakland Way. Some cops were already running from the house. They'd heard her gunshot. Her gunshot seemed to have drawn everyone's attention. Good.

She lifted the gun into the air. Fired again.

"*Get out!*" Katherine screamed. "The house is a trap! It's going to—"

A cop tackled her. Some uniform that she'd never met before. Her body slammed into the ground, and he twisted her wrist until the gun fell from her fingers.

"Get the fuck off her!" Dane's voice. *Dane.* Then the cop who'd tackled her was tossed to the side. Dane caught Katherine's hands and pulled her up against him. "Baby, what the hell?"

"Valentine. He set the house to explode!" Her gaze flew over his shoulder. "Get them out!"

"Out!" Dane snarled into his transmitter even as he lifted Katherine into his arms and started running away from the house. "Extraction *now*! The house isn't secure!"

The cops began to rush away from the house. Katherine twisted, trying to see the front of that place. More uniforms rushed out. There was Ross, leaping out of the front door, and then—

An explosion shattered the windows. Glass flew through the air as a wave of heat burst from the house. Flames. Bricks. Chunks of wood.

And Katherine was flying, too. She and Dane hurtled in the air and crashed down hard on the earth.

Dane was over her. His mouth was moving, but all she heard was her heartbeat. Only heard—

"Katherine, are you all right? Dammit, say something!"

She put her hand to the ground. Felt blood trickling down her cheek. "Did everyone get out?"

His lips tightened. "I don't know." He pulled her against him. Held her tight.

She looked back at the inferno. Nothing was left of the house. Just a shattered husk that was blazing.

"The captain's down!" The cry came from John.

Katherine jumped to her feet. The world swayed for a minute. Dane grabbed her. "Take it easy."

There was no easy. "Valentine. He attacked your captain!"

Dane's eyes widened.

"I saw him. I *shot* him…"

"You killed Valentine?"

She shook her head.

"I need some help!" Marcus yelled. "Get me an EMT!"

Katherine and Dane both rushed toward his cry. The profiler was crouched over the captain. Harley's eyes were closed. His chest barely seeming to rise.

"He must have been tossed in the explosion," Marcus said, his voice rough. There were deep scratches and cuts on his arms. It looked like he'd been tossed through the air, too.

"No," Katherine told Marcus, "he wasn't."

Then sirens were screaming. The EMTs who'd been just a few blocks away—held back as a precaution while the cops stormed the house—were racing to the scene.

"He ran that way," Katherine said, pointing to the trees. Night had come too quickly, but the inferno lit up the edge of the woods. "He was bleeding. If you get the dogs, you can track him. He tried to kill the captain."

Ross had come up behind her. Blood trickled down the side of his face. "Katherine, how did you know the place was gonna blow?"

Dane was sending cops into the woods and calling for the dogs.

She backed up so the EMTs could work on Harley. "Valentine told me. Said I had a choice to make. I could save the captain or the men in the house."

Ross's eyes narrowed. "He set us all up to die?"

"It wasn't about you." Valentine hadn't cared about the lives that he would take. "He didn't want to leave evidence behind." She swiped her hand over her eye, over the cut on her eyebrow that was sending blood down her cheek.

Ross gave a grim nod. "I'm joining the search."

His shirt was smoldering and bloody. Heavy patches of blood covered his shoulders. He barely seemed to be standing on his feet. "No, you need help!" Katherine turned and called for an EMT.

But when she glanced back, Ross was gone. He'd vanished into the woods.

Katherine's breath huffed out. Ross needed treatment, but she knew that, for him, the job always took priority.

She stood there in the midst of the chaos, and her gaze swept the scene. So many were injured.

Another ambulance hurried onto the street. She counted at least a half dozen cops who were bleeding and burned. One guy had a broken leg, one a broken arm, both from their impact with the ground after the explosion.

If she hadn't seen Valentine with Harley...if she hadn't fired her gun...all of those men would be dead.

Dane would be dead.

She stared back at the fire. The flames were so big and bright.

Valentine had gotten away.

One day until Valentine's Day. Just one.

He'd gotten away, but she didn't think he'd run far.

— — —

Valentine smiled as he gunned his vehicle and hauled ass away from the swamp. He'd long ago mapped out a perfect escape route through that swamp.

Always have an escape plan. He'd learned that valuable lesson, thanks to Kat.

So he'd been prepared, just like a good Boy Scout.

He could see the smoke drifting in the air. Hear the scream of fire trucks and more ambulances as they raced to the scene.

Katherine had been so afraid. She'd screamed, desperate to get those men and women out of the house.

There wasn't a timer, sweetheart.

As if he'd ever risk her safety that way. He'd never let the house blow while Katherine was close to it.

He'd had the detonator. He'd run into those woods deliberately. Then, with one push of a button on his cell phone, he'd triggered the blast.

He'd learned quite a few handy tricks over the past few years. When you had to vanish, had to discover how to become someone new, it paid to learn all the deadly tricks you could.

He'd watched. Seen the detective grab Katherine and rush away with her. He'd known that would be Dane's response, of course. *Get the girl to safety. Play hero.*

And he was only *playing*.

That bastard would pay, soon enough.

Even with his injury—sweet Kat had barely clipped him—it had been so easy to slip away in the borrowed police uniform. Now, while the cops were distracted, searching the woods that were fucking empty, he would focus on his next victim. A victim who wouldn't even see him coming.

Valentine's Day was almost here.

Time to celebrate.

Ready to be mine, Kat? Always…mine.

- 16 -

Ronnie turned off the lights in her office and grabbed her bag. It was edging close to nine p.m. She should have left hours before, but she'd hung around, hoping to get the tox screen back on Trent Lancaster. The guy running the report didn't seem to understand the concept of ASAP. Captain Harley would have to get on his ass.

Her tennis shoes squeaked on the tile floor. She passed Mr. Jarvis, the night janitor, and gave him a little nod. He had his iPod playing, so he barely glanced her way.

She exhaled and hurried toward the stairs. The day had been a bitch, and she just wanted to go home, shower, and crash into bed.

Preferably with Mac. Maybe he'd sneak over and join her. Before this damn case, they'd actually had plans for a romantic Valentine's Day getaway.

Now no one in the precinct could look at the holiday the same way.

It's about death, not love.

She pushed open the exit door and headed for her car. The Jeep waited for her under the gleaming light of the parking lot. She always left the Jeep under the light. Occupational hazard: she saw threats everywhere. Right then, she even had a can of Mace gripped in her hand.

Because I always see the dead. Everywhere I go. After the bodies crossed her table, they haunted her. Their stories haunted her.

But as she came closer to her vehicle, she realized something was wrong. Her back tire was flat. Completely and totally flat.

Hell.

Her eyes narrowed. The shower would have to wait a while. Ronnie glanced back over her shoulder at the building. She could change the flat on her own, no problem, but she wasn't doing it. No way was she going to huddle down there, alone in the dark, and struggle with that tire. She turned on her heel and began to march back to the building. She'd get someone to help her. Mac immediately sprang to mind. The man was very good with his hands.

Standing out there alone had a bad horror-movie ending written all over it. She reached for the door handle so she could head back inside the building.

Only the handle wasn't turning. The damn door was locked.

Crap.

Sometimes the lock would engage automatically. She'd complained three times to maintenance about the problem. But of course they hadn't fixed it. Maintenance had their priorities, and the back door wasn't one of them.

Ronnie grabbed her phone. She'd call Mac. He could come and meet her and help get her tire changed. Then maybe they'd leave together and…

Something jabbed Ronnie in the neck. She screamed, more in shock than pain because she hadn't heard anyone or anything approach.

She was falling. Her phone flew from her fingers. She tried to spray the Mace that she still gripped in her left hand, and a line of liquid shot out of the canister.

But the spray didn't hit anyone.

She hit the ground.

Her body was quickly becoming sluggish, the muscles refusing to obey her command to get up. To *move*.

She opened her mouth to scream, but something sticky and rough was shoved over her lips.

Ronnie struggled to keep her eyes open. Her lids wanted to sag. She couldn't see the light from the building any longer. Couldn't see her Jeep.

Couldn't see anything.

As she slumped on the hard ground, Ronnie knew exactly what was happening to her.

An injection had been sent directly into her jugular vein. Fentanyl was coursing through her system, she had no doubt.

Just like with Savannah and Amy.

She wouldn't be able to fight her attacker.

Not when he came to drive his knife into her heart.

— — —

Dane glared at the woods around him. The dogs were behind him, silent now. They'd been barking furiously at first.

Then they'd lost Valentine's scent.

It didn't fucking help that the woods backed up to an old highway. Valentine would have known that, of course. Dane was sure the fucker had planned an escape. The bomb had been in place, so, yeah, it figured he'd have a vehicle around too.

"Keep searching," Dane ordered the dogs' handlers, but he didn't have much hope that they'd turn up anything that night.

The scent of smoke was in the air, and as he headed back toward the smoldering remains of the house on Oakland, Dane saw the firefighters who'd gathered at the scene.

The captain was gone—headed to the hospital, as were at least five other cops who'd been injured in the blast.

Marcus glanced up, saw Dane, and hurried toward him.

"Was this in your fucking profile?" Dane demanded.

Marcus was pale. "He's covering his tracks. The explosion was a necessity for him, not—"

"Not like his damn pleasure kills," Dane finished, voice snapping. "So what does he do next? He came after Katherine—"

Marcus looked to the side. Katherine stood between two uniforms.

"And she went after him," Dane finished. She'd shot the bastard *and* saved Dane and his men. The woman was so much stronger than he ever realized. "I guess that blows your theory of her being involved in the crimes to hell, huh?"

"Katherine isn't what I thought."

And she was more than Dane had ever expected.

"We've got an alert out to every hospital," Dane said as he headed toward Katherine. He hated that tense look on her face. "He's injured, so if he goes in for treatment, we'll know." Cops were stepping up their searches in the city, too.

Dane's phone rang. He answered as he closed the distance between himself and Katherine. "Black."

"I need you at the station."

Dane frowned. It was Mac's voice—and it was shaking.

"I'm at the crime scene. We're not done here, man—"

"Ronnie is gone. She was taken."

"Are you sure?" *Ronnie?*

"Fucking certain. Her Jeep's still in the lot. Her back tire was slashed, no one can find her." He could hear Mac's fury and fear. Everyone else tended to think Mac was controlled, but Dane knew that when it came to Ronnie, that control was weak.

Ronnie and Mac put on a show for the rest of the station, but Dane had caught them making out a few months back. They were involved—damn deep.

"She's not answering her phone," Mac said. "She's not at home. She's *gone*."

Katherine frowned and stepped toward him, "Dane?"

"I'm on my way," Dane said. He ended the call. Glanced at Katherine. At Marcus. "He took the ME. The bastard left us here, chasing our tails—and he went after *her*."

– – –

Ronnie squinted against the bright light. She had a terrible acidic taste in her mouth and—

She couldn't move.

Her memory came flooding back, and she opened her mouth to scream. But the sound was choked back because something was over her mouth.

Duct tape.

Her hands were bound with rope, secured over her head. Her ankles were tied, keeping her immobile.

She was on a table, much like the ones in her lab. The ones she used for the autopsies.

A tear leaked from her eye.

"You're awake."

The voice was being filtered through a distorter, and it had her flinching, then turning. Her glasses were gone. Without them, she couldn't see clearly for more than two feet in front of her. Valentine was a black-covered blur.

"I was starting to think you'd OD before we could have any fun."

Ronnie's temples were throbbing. Her heart was racing.

The dark blur moved around her, skirting the metal table. "Sorry for the bruises. I'm afraid I had to drag your body inside. I wasn't exactly gentle on the stairs."

Her right wrist was throbbing. She suspected it was broken.

"But I'm sure, *Dr.* Thomas, you can understand that, sometimes, a little pain is necessary."

Ronnie squinted, trying to see more, but the light was too bright and the attacker was too far back.

Then she felt a light stroke on her arm. Just two inches below her elbow.

"Pain is necessary. In order to get things just as they should be."

She screamed behind the tape but the sound was muffled.

The knife sliced into her. *Cut number one.*

"Try not to struggle too much. It's very important that I get this part just right."

She wasn't just going to lie there and let her body be filleted. But when she tried to twist, she found that her muscles weren't cooperating. It wasn't just the ropes holding her down. The fentanyl hadn't fully worn off.

Another slice. This one deeper. Longer.

"That was a good one…"

A scream echoed in Ronnie's mind.

And the knife came down again.

— — —

The cops weren't used to turning their own turf into a crime scene. But this time, it was exactly what they had to do. Behind the death rooms, the parking lot was swarming with police. Dane saw Mac crouching near Ronnie's Jeep, and the guy's face…

His partner had to be close to breaking on the inside.

Hell.

Mac glanced up and saw Dane and Katherine. He headed toward them.

"Katherine, did you get a phone call?" Mac demanded. "He called you when he took Savannah Slater and Amy Evans—did the bastard call when he took my Ronnie?"

Katherine shook her head.

Dane didn't point out that Valentine hadn't called when Trent Lancaster had been killed. He knew that Mac was using the phone call as a sign of hope. If they got the call, it meant Ronnie was still alive.

If they didn't…

Mac swallowed. "We found Ronnie's glasses. Smashed. Right over there." He pointed toward the metal door that led into the building. "I'm thinking she saw her Jeep, saw the tire, and tried to get back in the building."

Dane moved toward that door. With his gloves on, he pulled on the handle.

The door wouldn't open.

"The stupid sonofabitch is stuck again." Mac's voice vibrated with fury. "I told maintenance again and again that the lock kept catching when the door was shut. If she'd just been able to get through that damn door…"

"I'm sorry," Katherine whispered.

Mac flinched.

The way those two were acting, they were already burying Ronnie. "She's not dead," Dane snarled, needing to chase away the fear and defeat from his friend's eyes. Mac *had* to be stronger than this.

Mac's head jerked up. His eyes narrowed on Dane. "I checked the logs. Before I called you, she'd been missing for over an hour." He yanked a hand over his face. "We were supposed to meet up, but with the case, I wasn't gonna be able to make it. I-I tried to get her on the phone. When I couldn't, I got worried—so fucking worried…" His words trailed away.

If she'd been missing for an hour before then…shit. Valentine would've had plenty of time to patch himself up from the wound he'd gotten—especially if it had just been a flesh wound—and get to Ronnie. The bastard was *playing* them.

"Just how long," Mac demanded, "do you think it's gonna take him to put his knife in her heart?"

"Usually at least four hours," was Katherine's quiet response. "That's what it took him before, in Boston."

Dane grabbed his arm. "She's alive. We just have to find her."

The lines on Mac's face were deeper. His eyes wild. "How?" Fear cracked the word. "The crime techs have been crawling all over this lot. They aren't finding anything."

"Video surveillance," Dane said, thinking fast.

"That camera has been out of commission for three weeks," Mac said, his shoulders slumping. "Ronnie left after the shift change. No one was out here. Captain had ordered all hands out to the Oakland scene. No one saw a damn thing."

Dane's phone rang. He yanked it out, not bothering to look at the caller ID. "Black."

A woman's scream echoed on the line.

His blood turned to ice. Then he flipped his phone around and stared at the ID—the call was coming from Ronnie's phone.

The bastard wasn't making his before-death call to Katherine this time.

"Let her go," Dane roared.

Mac's eyes widened. "*Ronnie!*"

The scream on the line choked away.

Her phone. Dane mouthed the words. Mac's head jerked and he hurried away, immediately yelling for the tech team to put a track on Ronnie's phone. They hadn't been able to track it while it was turned off, but now they could hit the cell towers and try to get a lock on the signal.

"Don't kill her," Dane said, lowering his voice and talking quickly now. "Let Dr. Thomas go. Just leave her and walk away…"

Laughter. The sound was grating. He was clearly using a voice distorter. Then he spoke. "She's not my usual type." The voice was as distorted as the laughter. "But I was feeling pretty pissed at you fucking police, so I decided to get some payback."

Mac huddled with the techs. They'd triangulate that signal. They'd find her.

"Why else would you call me if you didn't want me to find you? You want us to stop you."

Silence. No denial.

"So just save us all some time and tell us where you are."

"It's not your turn yet. Don't worry, you'll be dying soon."

The line cut away.

"Dane?" Katherine touched his arm.

He stared at Katherine. "He's hurting her," he said in a whisper. He didn't want Mac to hear.

"*We've got Ronnie!*" Mac was too busy yelling to hear anything that Dane said. Dane spun and saw Mac rushing toward him.

"The techs tracked her! The signal came from around Fifty-Fourth and Millway!"

He knew Millway was filled with run-down and vacant houses. The perfect place to dump a body.

"We're searching every house there!" Dane shouted to the men who were jumping to obey him. "Every single one!" The DA was there, standing in the background. He could work out any warrant issue. "Dr. Thomas is one of our own, and we're bringing her in alive!" Dane still didn't mention her screams. He just turned with the crowd and hurried toward his car. Katherine was with him every step of the way.

Every man and woman there knew Ronnie's life was on the line. They had to find her.

Before her screams were forever silenced.

- - -

"They're coming."

The smell of blood clogged Ronnie's nostrils. Her blood.

The phone was on the table beside her.

"I have to move quickly. There's no time to waste."

The knife lifted.

"I'll be long gone when they find your body."

She wasn't ready to die. She and Mac...they had plans. They'd talked about getting a house together, and one day maybe even having a kid.

I don't want Mac to find my body.

Ronnie tried to talk behind the duct tape but could still only manage weak grunts. The long, terror-filled scream that had ripped through the room moments before—

It hadn't been hers.

It had come from the crazy bitch with the knife.

Because the voice distorter was gone now. And even though she couldn't clearly see the killer, Ronnie could hear the woman perfectly.

Not Valentine.

"As if I'd let the victims actually talk." A low laugh came from the killer. "They might give the game away that a woman was holding them, not Valentine."

Now she understood why fentanyl had been in the victims' blood. Because a woman had been taking them, and the killer had needed to disable her victims.

She couldn't charm and seduce the way Valentine had in Boston.

Not fucking Valentine.

But she was about to die, and no one else would learn the truth.

The knife had just started to descend toward Ronnie's heart when she heard it. The faintest creak of a door opening. The bitch froze.

"They can't be here," the killer whispered. "Not yet…"

Someone *was* there. Hope exploded inside Ronnie, making her light-headed.

Or maybe the feeling was just due to the blood loss.

She didn't care. She just needed help. She tried screaming, but her mutters barely broke through the tape.

The bitch had spun around. She had her knife in her hand, and she was heading toward the stairs. As she stalked away, Ronnie started struggling with the ropes once more. The drug had worn off more, but because of her injuries, her arms were nearly useless.

But with blood coating her wrists, maybe she could just turn her hands and slide out of the ropes.

She didn't see the bitch anymore. The woman had gone up the stairs.

A faint breeze blew over her skin.

Goose bumps rose on her flesh. There'd been no breeze before.

She could smell fresh air over the cloying scent of her blood.

More tears filled her eyes.

Then a hand pressed against her cheek. It was gloved. The hand wiped away her tears.

Ronnie jerked.

"Shh…" It was a soft rumble of sound. "I'm not here to hurt you," a man's rumbling voice said.

Then, squinting, she saw the flash of a knife, and knew his words for the lie they were.

Valentine?

– – –

"What did the killer say?" Katherine asked as they sped toward Millway.

Dane's hands had a white-knuckled grip on the steering wheel. He kept his eyes on the road as he answered, "He was just jerking us around." Jerking *me* around.

"Are you sure he has Ronnie? Are you sure she's still alive?"

The cop cars weren't going in with sirens wailing. It was the same approach they'd tried when looking for Amy Evans. Just as before, they were afraid they'd spook the guy. And if he got spooked, he'd kill.

"Dane, are you sure?" Katherine pressed.

He told her what he hadn't told the others. "She screamed. The dead don't scream."

He could feel Katherine's stare on him. "He's luring you to the scene, just like before. It's all just like before."

It had better not end the same as before. Mac would shatter at the sight of Ronnie's body.

"Why did he call you? He'd been calling me." Her voice was confused. "Why switch now?"

"Probably because he knows that we've been monitoring your phone line. We've been preparing for the call. Maybe he thought it would take us longer to track him this way." *Plus, the prick wanted to taunt me and get in my head to piss me off.*

He had.

"We won't be too late," he said. "*We won't be.*"

Ronnie was smart. She was strong. She knew what was coming. *So use that, Ronnie. Distract the bastard. Just buy us some time.*

– – –

The ropes fell away from Ronnie's wrists. Tears were running down her cheeks because it felt like a thousand needles had just jabbed into her fingertips.

"She tied you too tight." His voice was angry. "Fucking amateur hour."

Part of her was terrified. Shaking. Screaming on the inside.

The knife sliced away the rope at her ankles. "You're a very lucky woman, Dr. Thomas."

She wasn't feeling so lucky right then.

"If your glasses hadn't been smashed and left back in that parking lot, I'm afraid you'd be experiencing an entirely different ending right now. I couldn't have you seeing my face."

She turned her head, making sure not to look toward the end of the table.

He laughed softly. "Even if you turned my way, how much would you see? I've done my research on you. Genius mind, but truly shitty eyesight."

Then he was reaching for her right arm. She flinched when he curled his fingers around her wrist. "I'm sure you realize," he said softly, "that she cut you too deeply here. If you don't stop that blood flow, you could die. Do you want to live, Dr. Thomas?"

Mac's image flashed in her mind. She nodded.

"Then you'll get off this table. You'll walk straight ahead, seven feet. *Seven feet.* You'll reach up to your left. There's an old window there. I took the liberty of leaving it open for you." He was pulling her to her feet. Holding her when her knees wanted to buckle. "I even put a box there so you could stand on it and reach the window."

He shook her. "*Focus.* The drugs are still in your system, so you may have trouble getting out on your own. You have to fight them, understand? Push with everything you've got. Get out of that window. Get away from this house. Fucking crawl if you have to do it."

She would. She'd do anything to survive.

And she still wasn't looking at his face.

He brought his head in closer to her. Ronnie squeezed her eyes shut. She could hear creaks from upstairs.

The bitch was coming back.

"Do you know who I am?" He asked in Ronnie's ear. The light whisper of his breath sent a shiver of pure terror through her.

She didn't move.

His gloved hand was over her deepest wound. Applying pressure.

Helping me.

"You're so smart, of course, you know…"

247

She only saw blackness. Her eyelids were squeezed so tightly together that they hurt.

"If you tell anyone about me, Dr. Thomas, I will find you. There is no police officer who can protect you. No lover who will keep you safe. I will find you, and then I'll make this little torture scene look like a fond memory in comparison with what I'll do to you."

The promise was unmistakable.

"Go forward seven feet. Climb on that box. Push your body through that window. Don't look back, and *don't* fucking tell anyone about me."

She nodded frantically, willing to promise anything, do anything, if she could just get away.

"Because if you tell them, I'll come for you."

He released her. Ronnie took one trembling step forward. He caught her when her legs gave way. "Crawl if you must," he reminded her, gritting the words.

She would. But when she heard another creak from upstairs, her head jerked toward the sound. Even if Ronnie escaped now, would that bitch just track her? Kill her?

"Don't worry about her," he said, and she could almost hear the smile in his words. "She'll be dead. I owe her some pain."

Then he released her. Ronnie hit the floor, and pain burst in her kneecap. The old wound had never healed right, not since it had been battered in an accident with a drunk driver. But she didn't care about how fucked her knee had just become.

She started to crawl.

Seven feet. Just seven feet.

His footsteps pounded behind her. He was heading away.

Her bloody fingers touched the box. She hauled herself up. Climbed. Fought her way to the window. Fresh air hit her face.

And, behind her, she heard the sound of a scream.

\- \- \-

Dane jumped from his car. There were five houses on this dead-end street. Old houses, abandoned, boarded up, and left to rot. Big, overgrown fields sat around each house. Nature was trying to take back the area. Trying and succeeding.

But Dane knew a construction company was scheduled to come into the area soon. They were going to bulldoze all the houses in just a few weeks. Until then, no one would be there.

The killer had chosen well.

But not well enough.

Katherine was behind him, guarded by two uniforms. Mac was leading a team toward the first house.

Not that one.

The first house was too obvious. Too easy. Dane's gaze darted to the second house. The third.

The fourth had dead roses near the door. Twisting roses that had withered in the winter.

"It's the fourth house," Dane snarled into his headset. He'd grabbed the headset and hooked up as fast as he could moments before. They were all linked now, communicating with each other as they searched.

He yanked out his gun and ran toward that fourth house. His attention was on the doors. The boarded-up windows and—

Someone was coming toward him. Crawling from the house.

Dane took aim with his gun. "New Orleans PD!" He yelled. "Put your hands up!"

But no hands came up into the air.

The figure slumped down even farther in the overgrown grass. Footsteps raced behind him as the others closed in.

"Identify yourself!" Dane demanded even as he yanked out his flashlight with his left hand.

The light fell on a tangled mass of red hair. Hunched shoulders. Bloody fingers digging into the earth.

Ronnie.

He ran to her. "I've got the doc!" he shouted, and oh, damn, she looked bad.

Carefully, he rolled her over.

Other cops approached, shining their lights on her.

He saw that her mouth was covered with duct tape. Blood was everywhere. Soaking her shirt. Drenching her clothes.

"Ronnie?" He grabbed the tape and carefully pulled it away. "Where is the bastard?" Dane whispered to her even as he saw the blood pumping from her sliced arms.

"Get the medic!" he yelled before Ronnie could speak.

Her body was shuddering against his. Trembling so hard.

"Ronnie?" Mac was there, his voice broken. Her head jerked toward him. Then she was crying and pulling away from Dane as she lunged for Mac.

Mac's arms closed around her. He lifted her up against him and held her tight. "You scared me to death."

But then her shudders deepened. Not just trembles. Convulsions. "Medic!" Dane yelled again.

Mac wasn't waiting for the medic to come to him. He turned and, holding Ronnie in his arms, ran back for the line of cop cars that waited at the edge of the road.

Dane faced the line of houses. The bastard could still be there. Dane motioned with his hand and pointed to the fourth house.

Four men and one uniformed woman immediately followed him. All had their guns ready.

The sagging porch groaned under his weight. He reached for the door.

It was already open.

So much for having to kick it down.

He rushed inside that dark cavern of a house. The others followed him, checking the room. Finding nothing but dust and broken furniture. Roaches that scurried away from them.

The floor creaked beneath Dane's feet. The other cops were fanning out. Searching the small scattering of rooms in the house. Finding nothing.

He *knew* this was the place. His instincts were screaming at him. Dane opened the narrow door to the left. *Not a closet.*

Stairs. Stairs illuminated by a faint glow that came from below.

The others had seen his discovery. They hurried to him. With the floors groaning so loudly, there was no chance they'd catch their perp by surprise.

It didn't matter if he was surprised or not. What mattered was *catching him.*

Dane led the way down the stairs. The light was coming from some old lanterns that had been set up. The basement stretched, the walls sliding into shadows. The basement was as big as the first floor of the house. And right in the middle of that basement, a large metal table stood, a table that was dripping blood onto the dirty floor.

Bloody ropes had been left on the table. He stared at those ropes, noting the clean cuts. Sliced.

Ronnie hadn't broken free by yanking on the rope or by breaking it. A knife had cut through her bonds.

Only as he looked around, he didn't see a knife at the scene. Just blood.

"The house is clear," a uniform said behind him.

This wasn't right. He kept staring at the ropes. He raised his hand to the transmitter attached to his right ear. "He isn't in the house."

Dane's gaze drifted around the basement. No pictures. No clothing. No furniture. Just the table. Just the blood.

The ropes that had been cut.

"We're sweeping all the houses," Detective Karen James replied in Dane's ear. "Sending cops and dogs into the woods."

"I want to talk to Ronnie." He turned away from the table. A live witness. She could tell them exactly what was happening.

The scene isn't right.

It looked like the killer had just let Ronnie go. Cut her, tortured her, but spared her life in the end.

His flashlight swept the floor once more. The trail of blood led from the table to the open window. A window that wasn't boarded up. Ronnie had slipped out that way. Gone through the window and dragged herself to freedom.

Carefully he walked the length of the room.

He froze when he saw the drops of blood on the fourth stair. He'd gone down those stairs so quickly that he hadn't even noticed it.

"Don't touch this area!" Dane barked. He could see blood and…shit, was that hair on the fourth stair? Stuck in the blood? It sure looked like it. A long strand of hair.

Blonde hair.

None of the victims—those they knew about—had blonde hair. And the blood hadn't left a trail. There were just a few drops on the steps, far from what he assumed was Ronnie's escape trail.

Another victim?

Or the killer? Had the killer fallen while making his escape? Smashed his head into the stairs, then rushed away, injured?

Only that strand of hair was *so* long. His heart beat faster. Maybe they weren't looking for a *he*.

- - -

An ambulance took the ME away. She was bloody and crying and didn't want to let go of Mac.

Katherine watched as Mac climbed into the ambulance with her. Mac wasn't letting go of her, either.

Dogs were hunting in the woods. Dane had come out of the house. Dogs were searching the area. Their barks and growls carried easily through the night.

It was hot, sweltering, but chill bumps covered her arms.

And she felt like she was being watched.

Katherine's gaze slid through the darkness. The house was small, and, without the air of neglect, it would have looked like any normal home. Before time had warped it, what had the owners been like?

And had a monster lived there? Hiding beneath the guise of a smiling face? Because this house—with its dead roses—wasn't random. The killer had lured them there, shown them the roses, because the killer wanted them to find something.

Not just about Ronnie. The killer wants us to see something here.

"Sonofabitch." It was Dane, headed toward Katherine with glinting eyes. "I just got the background information on this house. Wanna know who lived here for two years when she was a kid?"

Katherine's gaze drifted to the roses. Roses had been in the hands of the victims. Rose petals had been in the packages with the photos.

Dane's question echoed through her mind. *She.*

Katherine remembered a woman who enjoyed having fresh roses nearby. Roses that were always watered. Always blooming. The smell of those roses had made Katherine tense up every single time she went into that office.

Katherine shook her head. She should have seen it. All of the questions. The intensity.

Even before Dane opened his mouth to tell her, she knew who had once lived in that house.

— — —

"Hello, Dr. Knight."

The voice pulled her back to consciousness.

"Sorry for the binding," the man told her, and Evelyn realized that her hands and feet were tied with heavy, thick rope. Rope that was abrading her skin, chafing her, trapping her.

"But I'm sure you understand," he continued, his voice mild. They were in a car. No, an SUV, and she was crammed down in the back. She couldn't see him. Could only hear him. "I needed to keep you contained during the transport."

He started to whistle then. Easy, carefree.

She was covered in blood. He was whistling.

Her breath hitched in her lungs. She wanted to call out to him, but duct tape was over her mouth.

"You shouldn't have taken the ME. That was just a foolish mistake."

Her gloves were gone. He'd taken them. Taken her knife.

"Oh, I'm sorry." Now he sounded abashed. "I should probably introduce myself, shouldn't I?"

No, he didn't need to do that. She already knew exactly who he was. She knew everything about him. But...

"I'm Valentine," he said.

Her heart beat faster but that fast beat wasn't from fear. *Valentine*. She'd wanted this meeting for so long.

"And I'm afraid that you'll be dead soon."

Her elation vanished. She started to fight harder, yanking at the ropes. They wouldn't give.

He began to whistle once more.

– 17 –

Katherine watched as Dane paced the small confines of the hospital waiting room. His body was tight with barely leashed energy. Mac was with them, his hands shoved into the pockets of his pants as he leaned forward and glared down at the floor.

"She's going to be fine," the doctor said, appearing in the doorway. It was the same doctor who had treated Katherine. "But she's out. Fentanyl was in her system, so it's pretty much a miracle that she was still conscious enough to crawl out of that house."

Mac surged to his feet. "I want to be with her."

The doctor nodded.

Dane caught Mac's arm. "As soon as she wakes up, you call me."

Marcus crept into the room. "Is Dr. Thomas—"

"She's going to be all right," Dane said, rolling his shoulders. "A copycat...we were dealing with a fucking copycat killer."

"No." Katherine spoke quickly as she curled her hands into fists. "I *saw* Valentine. He's here—he was in my gallery, he was at the house on Oakland—"

"He's here," Marcus agreed, "and he wanted you to know that he killed Trent Lancaster, but with the fentanyl in the blood of the other victims..." He exhaled slowly. "I don't think those were his crimes. He realized what was happening—that someone else was hunting as him." Marcus exhaled slowly. "I was so focused on his profile that I never considered an alternative."

An alternative. Evelyn.

Marcus's gaze slid to Katherine. "With Dr. Knight's medical license, she would have access to the fentanyl," he said, voice rumbling.

My fault. "I told her that the ME had found fentanyl in the victims' tox reports," Katherine whispered. "She must have realized that Ronnie would learn more, so she went after her."

Marcus nodded.

"Evelyn is obsessed with Valentine." Katherine put her hands in front of her. Twisted them. "In all of our sessions together, she always asked about him. About what he did. Why I thought he'd committed the crimes." *Why he never attacked me.* "I stopped seeing her because I felt like she was more interested in Valentine than she was in actually helping me."

Evelyn had made her feel broken beyond repair.

A curiosity, one to be examined, studied. Journaled about.

"Did you tell her about the specific way he cut his victims? Those twenty-one slices on their arms?" Marcus asked as he pinned her with his gaze.

Miserably, she nodded. "Yes." She had thought that detail didn't matter, that it was safe to reveal to her doctor. It wasn't like she'd shared it with the press. Discussing it in therapy should have been okay.

She'd been so wrong.

Disgust tightened Dane's face. "And, thanks to the overeager press everyone knew that Valentine liked to leave roses in the hands of his victims. Roses and a knife to the heart."

Yes, everyone knew.

Dane stood close to Katherine. Just a foot away. She wanted to reach out and touch him, soothe him, because there was plenty of pain and fury to see on his face.

But she didn't move.

Not yet.

Evelyn wasn't found at the crime scene.

She had her own tension. Her own growing fears.

"So the shrink was a fan girl who wanted to be like Valentine," Dane said. "The question is…where is she now?"

Marcus was silent.

Katherine wasn't. "Where is she, and where is Valentine?"

— — —

They finally left the hospital and headed back to the station. While Dane changed in the locker room and ditched his ash-covered and bloodstained clothes, Katherine waited near Dane's desk, her fingers tapping nervously on the wood. The place was mostly deserted now. It was nearing six a.m., and she could see faint streaks of light cutting through the blinds.

A detective brushed by her as he made his way to the door. She glanced over at him—the guy was holding a big, heart-shaped box of candy. He gave a little wince when he saw her gaze drop to the box, and he tried to offer her a smile. "My wife. She always wants the chocolates."

Katherine nodded. Just because Valentine's Day equaled a nightmare for her, it didn't mean that everyone else felt the same way.

Maybe one day, it'll just be a holiday for me.

Yeah, right. She wasn't even going to try to lie to herself about that one.

"Come with me."

Her head jerked up at Dane's low words. His black hair was damp, his eyes hot.

She rose and followed him down a narrow hallway. No one stopped them. No one was even there to see them.

He opened a door and stepped back for her to walk inside. "No one will be fuckin' watching this time." He shut the door behind her. Put a chair beneath the doorknob.

She frowned at that and turned toward him. When had someone watched? "Dane—"

"*I saw the table. I saw the blood.*" His fingers came up and caught her jaw. He tilted her head back and stared into her eyes. "And all I could think was that I never wanted that to be you."

His forehead leaned against hers. "Mac was out of his mind. So desperate to get to Ronnie. I knew how afraid he was. If it had been you instead of her—"

Dane broke off, and his mouth took hers. The kiss was hot and hard and wild. No control. Just raw need.

"*I never want that to be you.*" Dane said the words against her lips.

And she realized that her nightmare had become his.

"It won't be," Katherine promised as her hands rose to curl around his shoulders. "It *won't.*"

His mouth was on hers. Tongue thrusting deep. She could feel the hard thrust of his arousal pushing at her. Warm. Strong. *Alive.*

His scent surrounded her. Fresh from the shower. The slight tang of his soap. The deeper scent that was his alone. Her fingernails sank into Dane's shoulders.

"I need you," Dane growled.

There was no foreplay. No finesse. She didn't want that. Didn't need it.

She just needed Dane.

He shoved down her jeans. She yanked open his waistband. He lifted her up. Pushed her back against the wall. Jerked her panties to the side.

Her heart was racing. Her body shuddering.

Dane stared into her eyes. *"It won't be you."*

She stared back. Saw past the fury to the fear. *And it won't be you. I won't let it be you.*

He thrust into her. Hard, strong, filling her completely. Their gazes held.

His hand slid between their bodies. Found the center of her need. Stroked.

He withdrew. Thrust back in a deep, smooth glide.

She bit her lip, trying to hold back her moan. There were no windows in the room. Only one door. But how thick were the walls? She didn't want to cry out.

He thrust again.

Her mouth opened.

He kissed her, muffling the sound.

Again and again, he thrust. Her back hit the wall, her legs tightened around him. It was basic. It was raw.

It was life.

When the pleasure crashed over her, she lost her breath. Her body tightened, her heartbeat seemed to stop, and the climax flooded through her. Not a wave. Not a pulse. Too consuming. Too deep.

She held onto Dane as tightly as she could and just felt the power of her release sweep her away. Then he was stiffening against her. Driving deep once more. Holding her with hands that bruised, but she didn't care. She was holding him just as tightly.

Holding on as if she never wanted to let go.

His breath rasped against her. She could hear the thunder of her heartbeat. Or was it his? Didn't matter.

She didn't want to let him go.

Dane kissed her once more. Light. Gentle now. Then he put his forehead against hers. "What the hell is happening? I don't do this." He sounded angry. "Not at the station. *Never* here. You make me lose control." His forehead lifted. Her gaze found his. The emotions that she saw filling his eyes, maybe they should have scared her.

Dane swore and pulled away. "*Why? Why do I want you so badly?*"

She didn't question why she wanted him any longer. She was just glad that she did. Glad that she wasn't living in a void.

I'm alive now. I'm not a ghost.

"Fuck, I didn't even use anything." Shock vibrated in Dane's words as he lowered her legs back to the floor.

Her knees were shaking. She locked her legs and pushed her heels into the hard tile. *The better to hide the tremble.*

She stiffened. "We don't have to worry about kids."

His gaze lasered in on her. "You're on protection?"

Since she'd had zero sex in three years? Um, no. "I don't need it. I can't have kids. Ever." He pulled away, and suddenly, when she'd felt lust and heat and need mere moments before, she now felt…embarrassment.

She scrambled, yanking up her jeans. Shoving her ripped panties into her pocket. Jerking on her shoes.

He fixed his clothing, but not with the same mad rush. Then his hands were on her wrists. Not hurting. Strong. Steady.

The way he usually was.

"Talk to me."

The light was too bright. Why hadn't she noticed that before? The light in the room was stark and bright. She should have noticed it.

"*Katherine.*"

Fine. He'd told her about the nightmares of his childhood and adolescence. "You know my mother abused me. My father...he wasn't exactly in the picture."

He nodded.

"I had a dozen broken bones by the time I was ten. Child Protective Services took me away from her, but they always sent me back." *Why?* She'd preferred the foster homes. Preferred anything to her mother. "She was an addict. She'd say she was clean, and maybe she would be for a little while." It had never lasted. *Never.* "One month, two, then she'd be using again."

She hated the bright light. Secrets were to be shared in the dark. Not in this stark light. They didn't need to be shared when she could still *feel* Dane inside her. Could smell the faint scent of sex.

She wanted to think about the pleasure he'd given her.

Not about the pain of the past.

There's no escaping it.

So she stared into her memories and told him, "I was fifteen the last time I saw her." She could remember it all so clearly. Would never forget. "She was high. Out of her mind. And she was the one driving the car."

"Katherine..."

No, he'd asked. He'd hear her story.

"The cops thought she didn't see the big rig. That's what they all said." But they hadn't been in the car. "My mother pushed down the accelerator. She laughed. And she turned the wheel and she *aimed* for him. I could have jumped from the car." She'd had the choice. Had the time.

He was silent. Staring down at her with a locked jaw and glinting eyes.

"But I had to try and save her." Time had slowed down. "She was my mother." ·

She could remember unhooking her seat belt. Fighting for the wheel. Shoving her foot down on the brake. But her mother had struggled against her, still laughing.

"We went through the light. The truck driver tried to swerve, but it was too late." She shrugged, but the move was a lie. There was nothing careless about this memory. "We were both pinned in the car until the firefighters could cut us out. She died on impact."

Her hand lifted to her stomach. "I had internal injuries." She'd been in the hospital for so long. "The scars are faint now." Her lips twisted. "I had a good doctor." A team of them. "But there won't ever be children for me."

He pulled her into his arms. Held her tight. Did she feel a shudder run the length of his body?

Her hands pushed at his shoulders.

He wasn't letting go. His hold tightened around her.

He smelled good. She *felt* good with his arms around her.

"You're getting inside," he whispered.

Then she heard footsteps rushing down the hallway.

"Detective Black?" a female voice called out.

She'd never been so glad to have an interruption. She'd laid bare enough of her soul.

Dane just stared at her. So she was the one to move back, push that chair away, and yank the door open. "He's here," Katherine answered.

"He's got a phone call," the uniformed officer told her. "It's Mac. Ronnie's awake." Then the brunette's gaze darted to Katherine. "And she's asking to see you, ma'am."

- 18 -

Katherine's shoes tapped over the white tile in the hospital. There was a uniform blocking Ronnie's door. He was standing at attention, but he relaxed when he saw Dane.

Katherine glanced toward the closed hospital door. She'd been told that Ronnie wouldn't talk to anyone else, that she just kept asking for Katherine again and again.

Dane opened the door. "Stay out here," he said.

She glanced over her shoulder. Dane wasn't talking to her. Marcus had come along too. The profiler nodded slowly, but the guy didn't exactly look happy to be left behind.

Hesitant, she stepped into the room. Heard the fast beep of machines. The soft rumble of a voice. Dane grabbed the thin curtain that blocked the bed and pushed it aside.

Mac was there. Leaning over the bed. Smoothing his fingers over the ME's pale cheek.

At the sound of the sliding curtain, Ronnie glanced over at Dane and Katherine. She had on a pair of wire-framed glasses, and when her gaze found Katherine's, Ronnie's lower lip began to tremble.

"Ronnie," Mac said, sounding as if he were being torn apart. "There's nothing for you to be scared of, love. I'm right here. I'll keep you safe, I swear."

Still looking right at Katherine, Ronnie said, "You can't." Absolute certainty.

Dane stepped forward. Katherine didn't move.

"Tell us who hurt you," Dane said, voice soft and gentle. "Hell, Ronnie, we've already pieced it all together anyway, we just need you to confirm—"

Ronnie shook her head.

"It wasn't Valentine, was it?" Dane asked.

"It was that bitch Evelyn Knight!" Mac surged to his feet. The machines beeped louder. Faster. "We know it was her! Screw dancing around, it's just us in this room, and protocol can be *fucked*!"

His rage and fear had obviously taken over. Katherine watched his desperate gaze slide back to the Ronnie. *He loves her.*

"We're gonna find her," Mac promised the pale woman in the bed. "She's never gonna hurt you again."

Ronnie was still looking just at Katherine. "I want..." Her voice was hoarse. Dane had said that he heard her scream on the phone. "I want to talk to her." She lifted a hand, one attached to an IV, and pointed to Katherine. "Alone."

"I don't want to leave you," Mac said immediately in a gruff voice.

Ronnie's heart rate spiked. The machines were going crazy. "*Please.*"

Katherine could tell by the expression on Mac's face that the guy would deny her nothing. He nodded and said, "I'll be right outside the door." Mac pressed a gentle kiss to Ronnie's cheek.

Dane glanced at Katherine, brows up.

"Go," she told him.

Dane and Mac shuffled out to join Marcus. Katherine came closer to the bed.

"I'm scared," Ronnie whispered.

Katherine found herself taking Ronnie's hand. She noticed that Ronnie's other wrist had been set in a cast. *So much pain.* "It's all right. After what you've been through, I think you're entitled to be scared."

But Ronnie shook her head. "Not scared because of what happened. Scared of what *will* happen."

Katherine leaned toward her. "Nothing else is going to happen to you. You're safe. You've got a guard at your door, and you have one very devoted detective who won't—"

"Mac can't protect me. No one can."

"You've been through a nightmare." One Katherine sure as hell understood.

"Only you."

Katherine leaned even closer because she'd almost missed Ronnie's soft words.

"You can stop him," Ronnie continued.

The machine was still beeping too fast, a beep that now matched the frantic rhythm of Katherine's heart too. "How did you get away?" she asked.

Ronnie's lips trembled. "I *can't.*"

"Did Evelyn let you go?"

Ronnie shook her head.

As she stared into Ronnie's terrified eyes, Katherine felt her own cheeks ice. "Someone else was there."

A slow nod.

"You saw him."

"I couldn't see much of anything without my glasses."

Katherine just stared at her.

"If I tell, I'll die." Ronnie's hand turned and clasped Katherine's wrist. "Please, help me. I don't want to die." Tears leaked down her cheeks.

"You're not going to die!" Katherine told her at once, voice sharp. "You're safe here. There are two detectives and an FBI agent right outside that door."

"They can't protect me. No one can. Not from—"

Ronnie broke off, not saying any more, but Katherine knew what she'd meant.

Not from him.

"Valentine."

A shudder shook Ronnie's body.

"He was there?"

Ronnie didn't confirm or deny it.

If I tell, I'll die.

"Is he working with Evelyn?" She was very afraid that he might be. A perfect, deadly team.

Ronnie's lips trembled, then she whispered, "I think Dr. Knight isn't…a threat anymore."

"Did he take her?" Katherine asked.

Tears were in Ronnie's eyes. Her hold on Katherine tightened.

"Ronnie, you have to tell Mac and Dane. Tell them what you saw. They can help you."

"I *didn't* see anything!" Anger gave her words power. "I couldn't see! Everything more than a foot away from me was a blur."

"You might not have seen his face, but you smelled him. You talked to him. You *know* he's out there."

Ronnie's chin dropped. "I heard her scream."

A chill skated over Katherine's spine. "Evelyn?"

A nod. "She won't be hurting anyone else."

"You have to tell Mac and Dane."

"He'll come for me. He'll kill me and maybe even Mac." Her gaze was on the bandages that covered her arms. On her broken wrist. "I don't want to be on a slab in my own morgue."

"For three years," Katherine told her, "I've been looking over my shoulder. Wondering when I'd see him again."

Ronnie glanced back up at her. The ME's eyes were so big and lost.

"You don't want to live that way. You don't want to always be glancing over your shoulder."

Ronnie pulled her hand away. "In Boston, why did he let you go?"

"That's the million-dollar question," Katherine muttered.

"Why did he save me?" Now Ronnie sounded even more confused. "He tortures and kills. Why save me?"

"Because you weren't the one he wanted." Marcus had been right. Valentine had found out that Evelyn was copying his crimes. Katherine headed for the door.

"Each time he goes after someone else, you have the guilt, don't you?"

Katherine froze. "Yes."

This is why she wanted to see me. She wants someone to under-stand why she isn't telling the police. She works with the cops, day in and day out, but she also sees the bodies. She doesn't want to wind up as a victim in her own morgue.

"How do you live with it?"

"You don't sleep. You jump at every sound. Then, one day, you walk into a police station and tell the world who you are." She glanced back over her shoulder. "Because you'll get to the point where you can't hold back any longer. You'll want to stop him more than you want anything else."

Ronnie gazed helplessly back at her. The struggle was plain to see on her face.

"You have to get to that point," Katherine told her with a sad smile. "No one can make you do it." She reached out for the door.

The beeping of the machines finally slowed. "Bring them in," Ronnie said.

Katherine opened the door and waved in the detectives. Dane and Mac entered, faces grim.

Ronnie pulled in a deep breath. "Evelyn Knight...she was the one who took me. I didn't even realize it was her at first because she was still distorting her voice, but after the phone call to you—"

"When I heard you scream," Dane cut in.

Ronnie shook her head. "That wasn't me. She never took the duct tape off my mouth. That was her scream. She said that she hadn't let her other victims scream either."

Savannah. Amy.

"She stopped using the voice distorter after she got off the phone with you. I guess because...it was time for me to die, and she wanted me to know that she was the one killing me." Ronnie swallowed. Mac eased closer to her. "But then she heard something upstairs. She thought someone else was in her house." Her voice dropped. "He was there."

"Valentine? You *saw* him?" Mac pushed.

"I didn't look at his face." It was said with shame. "I didn't want to see because if I did...I was afraid he'd kill me."

Dane glanced over at Katherine.

"He wasn't there to kill me. He was there for Evelyn. He let me go, and I heard her scream."

Goose bumps had risen on Katherine's arms.

"He's got her," Ronnie said, "and he's killing her."

— — —

Evelyn was on a table. Her wrists and ankles were still bound with rope. The duct tape was still over her mouth. Evelyn struggled fiercely. If she could just get the duct tape off her mouth, then she could make him understand.

He appeared before her. A bright light had been positioned right over her head, so, beneath that light, she could see him perfectly.

He looked different from all the pictures she'd seen online.

Not what she'd expected at all.

But Evelyn wasn't disappointed. She could never be disappointed in him.

He had a knife in his hand. He raised that knife, and she should have tensed. Should have tried to cry out.

She just stared up at him.

He won't hurt me. He'll see me for what I am. The knowledge was certain and sure within her. She knew him better than anyone else. Better than Katherine could ever hope.

The others had screamed. They'd fought.

He'd fought back.

Her struggles were gone now. Her body lay limp and relaxed on that hard table. She stared up at him, with all of her certainty and love shining in her eyes.

He brought the knife closer. "You should be afraid."

She shook her head. *No.*

"Then you're even more screwed up than I am."

He took the knife and sliced it along her left arm. When the blood started to flow, she refused to cry.

He smiled down at her, then he asked, "Do you want to die?"

Pain pulsed in her arm. It wasn't like it was the first time she'd been cut. As a teen, she'd cut herself plenty of times.

She'd felt alive then.

She felt alive now.

"Do you?" He pressed, sounding mildly curious.

She wouldn't shake her head. Wouldn't nod. If he wanted her answer, he'd have to let her talk. *Take off the tape.*

"You think you're the smart one, don't you, Dr. Knight?"

He was putting the knife down, so, yes, she rather did think she was smart.

His fingers came up, strong, long, golden, and pulled the tape from her mouth. She barely felt the tug against her lips.

"Got some last words for me?"

"Not…last." She hated that he'd drugged her. It had been so unnecessary. But at least he hadn't given her a dose that was too strong. Not like she'd given to Amy and Savannah.

I was helping them. Making their deaths easier.

He frowned down at her. She smiled back up at him. She'd enjoyed the way he looked before, but this was even better. Wonderful. Perfect.

"I know you." She whispered this secret.

One brow rose. "Do you." Not a question.

But she responded as if it were. "I know so much about you… your life…your kills."

He stiffened. "Give someone a fistful of degrees and they think they know everything."

"Not everything." She shook her head. Tried to control her smile. *It's him.* "Only you."

He wasn't reaching for the knife. He was studying her as if she were some kind of mystery.

He didn't understand yet. She was his other half. The person he needed.

Not Katherine.

"I started studying your case when I was finishing up my PhD. I read everything about you, did as much research as I could." Her words came faster. "Then Katherine—Kat—I saw her by chance one day in the Quarter. I knew who she was—the dark hair didn't change her. We started talking. I told her what I did for a living." And Katherine had been curious…and hopeful.

"Kat told you about me." Now there was *definite* interest in his voice.

She nodded. "She didn't want to talk about you." Anger cracked through the words. "But I told her it was necessary for her therapy to progress. I *made* her tell me." Evelyn had pried the details out of Katherine, one precious secret at a time.

His eyes narrowed. "You're one of them."

Now he was disgusted. No, no that wouldn't work. "Them?"

His hand lifted. Stroked her cheek. Sent a lick of heat unfurling in her belly. "Those broken women who get off," he murmured, "on fucking killers."

She flinched at that. Jerked against the rope. "No! Haven't you seen what I've done?" And she was hurt by his accusation.

She knew him so well.

Couldn't he try to know her better?

"What you've done is…" His fingers were still at her cheek. "You've stirred up the past. Started a new manhunt for me. *Killed*, pretending to be me."

Laughter slipped from her. "I gave you a present. I made everyone remember you again."

He shook his head. "You made them hunt me. Until you started, I was just a memory to most folks. You made me a nightmare again."

Ah, yes, he did understand. She stared into his eyes and whispered, "You're welcome."

- - -

Dane paced the narrow hospital hallway. Everywhere he turned, there were fucking red, heart-shaped balloons or bundles of roses being delivered to patients. They were like slaps in his face. Valentine, taunting him. "Where would he take her?" Dammit, Valentine wasn't slipping away again. "Where?"

The profiler eased up beside him. Katherine and Mac were still in Ronnie's room, talking quietly with the ME.

"Valentine is angry with Evelyn," Marcus said. "He's going to punish her."

Dane whirled to face him. "Evelyn was the one who drugged Katherine." She had been there, *right there,* in that café. Evelyn had probably slipped the drugs into Katherine's drink when she'd been distracted.

"That's what will anger him the most," Marcus said with a nod. "Evelyn tried to hurt the one person Valentine thinks he loves."

Valentine's house was gone. Blown to hell. Evelyn's house was under a lockdown by the police.

Where else would the man go?

"Evelyn made it personal by attacking Katherine, so he'll make his own attack on her have extra significance…"

Extra significance.

Dane stilled. "Her office."

Because Katherine had been there in that office, revealing all of her secrets about Valentine.

None of the staff would be there. The place had been shut down because of Trent's death. It would be empty, deserted at this hour.

And Dane already knew there weren't security cameras on that floor.

The perfect kill spot.

"Mac!" Dane stormed back into the hospital room. "I think I know where the bastard is hiding."

And killing.

— — —

"You made a mistake picking Kat," Evelyn told him. She wished he would cut away the ropes, but they'd get to that soon enough. For now, they'd talk. She'd been wanting to talk to him for so long. "She never understood you."

Frowning now, he bent over her and shoved up the sleeves of her shirt. His hands ran over her upper arms, and she knew he was feeling the old scars.

"I survived," she whispered, "just like you. Do you know what I've done for you?" she asked. "I *killed* for you."

He smiled at her, revealing perfect white teeth. "No, you did that for you. Because you're broken and twisted. You've got a monster in you. One that's been wanting to get out for a long time."

"No, no, I was helping you—"

"I heard people become shrinks because they're screwed up inside." He reached for his knife. "That's why people become serial killers, too. I mean, I know I'm twisted. I shouldn't like killing. I shouldn't *enjoy* it when I see the life fade from someone's eyes… but I do." He lifted the knife. Watched the light glint off the blade. "But what are you going to do? We are who we are."

"Don't!" He was coming at her with the knife.

"You cut yourself when you were a teen," he said, the words a dark rumble. "What set you off, Evelyn? What twisted you?"

She remembered the old house she'd once lived in. With the beautiful roses that her mother had loved. "My mother died when I was five."

He waited. Watched.

"My father remarried a few years later, and I *hated* her."

His eyes didn't blink.

"When my father was out of town, she'd have men over. I told him. He didn't believe me. No one ever believed me." Softer.

"Those men, what did they do?"

Just one man. "He hurt me." He'd been drunk. He'd caught her alone. His hands had been big and pale and freckled.

She'd bled.

Her stepmother had laughed when she told her the story. Denise with her long, dark hair and her pale, perfect skin.

Denise had stopped laughing when Evelyn had pushed her down the stairs. An accident, or so the police had thought.

They'd thought wrong.

"Have there been others?" he asked quietly. "Others you've killed?"

His eyes said he knew about her stepmother.

Did he know about the man she'd picked up at the bar on her twenty-first birthday? When she'd changed her mind about the pickup and become afraid, he'd been angry. He'd pushed for more from her. Tried to take more than she wanted to give, and she'd pulled her knife from her purse. She always kept her knife close. She needed it to feel safe.

The knife had wound up in that frat boy's throat.

"Oh, Evelyn…" His sigh was sad. "You didn't kill for me. You did all of that for *you*."

"We're alike!" she told him, desperate for him to see. There wasn't anything damaged about her. She was stronger, better, just like him. They were a match. "We survived. We grew stronger."

He nodded. "Yes."

Yes.

"I can be better for you than Kat." Her words came so quickly. "I can be just what you need. I can be *everything*—"

"Kat was abused when she was a kid. Hurt, again and again. She didn't…" His eyes were on the knife. "She didn't turn out like us."

"Kat's weak. She jumps at her own shadow. She—"

His head snapped up. Rage was boiling in his eyes. Scaring her. "She's stronger than you are. Stronger than all the others. Unbroken. Pure. She wasn't like the other women."

The women he'd killed in Boston? Or had there been even more?

Jealousy twisted her gut.

"The others didn't give a shit about anyone or anything. Kat did. Kat cared. She…*loved me*."

"No!" The denial burst from her. "She loved who she thought you were! I love you!" All of him.

"Kat's good," he whispered. "She didn't do drugs, didn't whore herself out like the others who had our piss-fucking-poor start in life. She was better." A muscle jerked in his jaw. "She made me want to be better."

"You *are* better—"

"And you tried to kill her." His eyes blazed.

Her breath caught in her throat.

"You think I didn't know it was you? You with your drugs. Such a fucking sloppy way to kill. First Savannah, then Amy. Then you went after my Kat."

Rage splintered her. "Katherine is *not* better than me!" Kat was as damaged as they came. Evelyn knew she should have killed that scrawny bitch months ago. The first time Trent had looked at her.

Trent.

"You killed Trent," Evelyn said. At first, she truly had been devastated by Trent's death. She'd never planned for him to die, but when she realized what his death truly meant—

Valentine was there.

Her pain had faded then, and she'd taken the necessary steps to eliminate Kat. Only Kat hadn't died.

"I've killed a lot of different people." Deliberately vague. He used the knife to cut open her shirt.

She wasn't afraid. "Trent Lancaster. I thought maybe Kat had done it…but it was *you.*"

"He shouldn't have hurt her."

He'd killed Trent for Kat? Her own rage blossomed. "She wasn't worth his life."

The blade of the knife pressed against her bra strap. "You hate my Kat, don't you?"

She held her tongue. *Yes. As long as she's around, you'll be tied to her.* "You don't need her any longer." Why couldn't he understand? "You have me. I won't ever judge you. I can help you. Protect you." That was why she'd become a psychiatrist. To protect herself. To learn to see the weakness in others. "Just get these ropes off me. I can offer you so much. I can—"

He drove the knife into her chest. She cried out, choking as the pain flooded her. Valentine bent and put his lips near her ear. "I know you planned to go after Kat next. I know about your stepmother, I know about the college boy, I know about the old bastard you drowned in the pool." His lips brushed against the shell of her ear. "I know everything about you, Dr. Knight. And you are *not* what I need." He twisted the blade.

"I…love…" Her fingers wouldn't move. The ropes didn't hurt any longer.

CYNTHIA EDEN

Her body felt cold. Already. She was chilled and she wanted some cover to warm her.

She'd loved him. Believed that she'd found someone who would understand...

"You thought you'd hurt Kat." The rage was roughening his voice once more. "No one hurts her."

Fixated. He was too locked on Kat.

Just as I was too locked on Valentine.

He wasn't perfect. Wasn't the man she needed. Wasn't the perfect man who could understand her secrets.

He *was* darkness. He was death.

Her lashes fell closed.

The knife twisted again, but this time, Evelyn didn't feel the pain. She was far past feeling anything at all.

– – –

Dane kicked open the door of the psychiatry office. Mac was on his heels as he raced inside.

And Dane could smell blood.

He heard a faint gurgle, a groan of sound...

He ran forward, gun drawn, rushing toward the closed door to Evelyn's office.

Another kick, and the door was open.

The scent of blood was so much stronger.

"Fuck," Mac muttered.

"Put your hands up!" Dane yelled as he took in the scene before him.

Evelyn, tied down on her own desk. Blood all around her. And a man leaned over her. The man's back was to Dane, but he seemed damn familiar.

His hands began to rise. There was no weapon in his hands because his knife was embedded in Evelyn's chest.

"Step away from her," Dane ordered.

The man backed up.

Dane hurried forward. Felt for a pulse on Evelyn's neck.

"You arrived too late," the man said. "That's what Kat did too, years ago. Always too late…"

He finally turned to face Dane.

And Dane *knew* that face.

The brown eyes. The broken nose. This guy had claimed to be Katherine's friend. This guy was dating the captain's fucking daughter.

He was staring at Ben Miller.

Sirens yelled in the distance.

"You look surprised," Ben murmured, smiling. "Kat looked that way when she found me with Stephanie. Surprised, shocked…" He took a step forward.

"Take one more step, and I'll put a bullet in your heart," Dane told him.

Valentine raised his brows. "Would you shoot an unarmed man?"

"If that unarmed bastard was you, hell yes, I would."

And he would. It was all part of the darkness that rested inside him.

Valentine smiled. "I knew you were like that. You're not the hero. Kat is so wrong about you."

Mac grabbed the guy's arms and began to handcuff him while Dane kept the bastard locked in his sights.

"Don't fucking talk about her," Dane snarled.

"Why? Afraid she'll realize you're as twisted as me? As screwed as—"

Dane lunged toward him. "I know you want me to pull the trigger."

"What *you* want." Valentine flinched when Mac tightened the cuffs. "You both want me dead. But the badges that you wear won't let you just shoot me and walk away."

Valentine glanced over his shoulder at Mac. Sweat beaded Mac's temples. "That little ME...I warned her about what would happen if she talked."

"You won't hurt her!" Mac shouted.

"Maybe I won't be the one who goes after her." Valentine shrugged. "Maybe it will be one of my fans. Take a look on the Internet. So many people out there, desperate for a taste of power. I bet I could get them to do anything for me."

And it was true. Dammit. With a few careful words, another copycat would be born. *Aim and kill.*

Mac's breath heaved. "You *won't*—"

"Valentine!" Dane snarled, drawing the killer's focus back to him. Mac was on a razor's edge. He wouldn't let his partner lose control.

And he wouldn't let Valentine take control from them.

"You have the right to remain silent," Dane began. His gaze shot to Mac's. "Call for backup. Tell them we've got the bastard."

Valentine's body had tensed.

"Anything you fucking say will be held against you," Dane continued. He was close to the killer now, and he stared straight into the guy's eyes.

But Valentine laughed. "I won't be staying in jail, so it doesn't matter what I say."

Mac shoved the man forward. "You're never getting out. They're gonna shove you in a hole so deep, you won't see daylight again."

Valentine didn't stop smiling, and as he finished reading the bastard his rights, Dane couldn't shake the feeling that this wasn't the end for the serial killer.

Not yet.

"The captain sure has a pretty daughter," Valentine murmured as they shoved him toward the door. "Not as beautiful as my Kat, but I've sure enjoyed getting to know her."

The prick. The captain was still in the hospital, in the ICU. Dane had tried to reach Maggie, but he'd been told she was out of town for a seminar.

"Though I don't know if sweet Maggie enjoyed getting to know me as much."

She's not out of town. Fuck. Dane's hold tightened on the killer. "What have you done?"

Valentine's gaze cut to him. "I guess you'll have to just wait and find out, won't you, Detective?"

— — —

Katherine tensed when the doors to the high-rise swung open. A security guard was in the lobby—he'd given Dane and Mac access to the offices moments before.

Now the man was scrambling outside. He had a radio in his hand, and it looked like he was calling for help.

"Sonofabitch," Marcus whispered as he shoved open the door of his vehicle. "They got him."

She'd been sitting in the car with Marcus. Dane had refused to let her go into the building, and Marcus had been given guard duty. But when she caught sight of three more men coming out of those swinging doors, Katherine shoved her way out of the vehicle.

Sirens screamed in the distance, coming closer and closer. Backup for the detectives, racing to the scene.

Dark shadows concealed much of the men as they walked toward Katherine. Marcus took up a position beside her, and she saw him draw out his weapon.

Her eyes narrowed as she strained to see.

Dane…Dane's strong shoulders. His determined walk. He was okay.

And—that was Mac, on the far left. Holding tight to their prisoner.

Brakes squealed behind Katherine. The cavalry had arrived.

She didn't look back. She was too busy straining to see the face of the man who was held by both Dane and Mac.

The man who—

She *knew.*

They'd just stepped under one of the streetlights. Katherine's heart seemed to stop in that instant as her gaze swept over the man's face.

It wasn't the face of the man she'd known as Michael O'Rourke. Michael had been classically handsome. High cheekbones. A straight bridge of a nose. Dark hair.

This man—he looked *nothing* like Valentine.

Maybe that was why she had seen him so many times, again and again, and hadn't realized…

Katherine was staring right at the man she knew as Ben Miller. Bodybuilder Ben with his easy smile. The guy who'd always been at the café in the morning, grabbing breakfast right after he worked out.

Always at the café…*waiting on me.*

Always there…*watching me.*

He was wearing contact lenses. That was why his eyes had been dark, not the green she remembered. Contacts *and* fake glasses. The glasses had been an extra deception to throw her off. They'd made his eyes look bigger, but now, without them, she could see that his eye shape...it was the same.

"Hello, Kat." He'd dropped the fake Southern drawl, the rumble that had always slid beneath Ben's words.

His nose was different—the bridge wider, with a heavy bump in the middle. His cheeks were fuller, his jaw more rounded. Even his lips were different. What had he done? Injected them with collagen? He'd dyed his hair. Let it grow so much longer. Long enough to curl lightly. Michael—he'd always kept his hair almost too short before.

"Did you miss me?" he asked softly.

Uniform cops swarmed him. Dane and Mac kept their grip on the killer and pushed him toward the back of a patrol car.

"I missed you," Valentine called out to her. "Missed you so much that I had to get close again."

How many times had they had breakfast together? He'd been just feet from her, all those days...

And she hadn't known.

"No one else has ever been as perfect for me as you, no one else was good enough—"

Dane slammed the door, halting Valentine's words. A uniform was already behind the wheel of the car. Mac jumped in the front passenger seat. The siren screamed on as the vehicle rolled forward.

Another patrol car was moving behind that vehicle. A motorcycle pulled in front, leading the line.

Katherine stared there, lost, stunned, as the swirling lights of the police cruisers lit up the scene.

Someone touched her shoulder, and Katherine jumped, flinching.

"Easy," Dane whispered. "It's me."

His touch usually warmed her, but right then she just felt… cold. "Where's Evelyn?"

No answer.

"Where. Is. She." A demand.

"She was already dead." His jaw tightened. "She wanted Valentine, and it looks like she got exactly what she wanted."

Marcus swore.

Cops were heading toward the building. A crime-scene van rolled up.

"The reporters are going to be here soon," Dane said. "They would have been listening to the police radio. We need to get you out of here."

Right. Only she wasn't moving.

Dane put his hands on her shoulders and pulled her toward him. "We got him, Katherine. We got the bastard."

"He looks so different," she whispered. "But before he got into that patrol car, his voice—his voice was Michael's."

Dane gave a grim nod. "We'll check his prints, compare his DNA, but the bastard confessed upstairs. He *is* Valentine."

"Then it's over," Marcus said. "His crimes end—"

But he broke off, seeing as Katherine did the hard jerk of his head that Dane had just given.

"We need to find Maggie Dunning," Dane said.

"Isn't she at the hospital?" Katherine asked slowly. "With her father?"

"I hope to hell she is by now." But Dane didn't look hopeful. "Because it sounded like the guy was taunting us upstairs." His gaze burned into Katherine's. "He wanted us to think he still had one more victim out there…"

"Maggie." Margaret Dunning.

Marcus rocked forward on the balls of his feet. "He's still playing with us."

Dane's expression was hard, unreadable, but fear had thickened inside Katherine because yes, she was very afraid that Valentine was still playing and that the deaths weren't over.

Not yet.

They had the sonofabitch.

Valentine sat, hands cuffed behind him, two uniformed guards just a few feet away, in a chair in interrogation room number one. Dane and Mac were in the observation room, surrounded by half a dozen other detectives. The DA, Henry Meadows, was there, pacing nervously. He was sweating, and the cool-under-fire DA wasn't normally the type to sweat.

"No one can locate Margaret Dunning," Meadows said, jaw locking. His light blue eyes were a stark contrast to his dark brown skin. "There was no conference out of town. No seminar. She hasn't been at work in three days, and her apartment is empty."

Dane glanced through the observation mirror. Valentine had a faint smile curving his lips. "He knows where she is."

"Is she dead, Detective?" Meadows asked flatly.

Probably. But he couldn't bring himself to say what they all feared. Margaret—Maggie. She'd always been a sweet girl. Kind to everyone she met. Far too trusting for a cop's daughter.

Meadows exhaled. "We need to know. Because I don't want to bargain with that sick prick over a dead woman's body."

"Even when it's the captain's daughter?" Mac snapped at him.

Meadows glanced through the glass. "People in this city are gonna want the death penalty for him. I know assholes just like him. Seen plenty like him over the years. Plenty of twisted freaks. He'll try to trade the woman's body for his own life. If I make that deal..."

"The captain's *daughter*," Mac repeated, sounding as if rage were choking him.

"If she's alive, I'll do anything to get her back," Meadows said instantly. "But let's make absolutely sure that Valentine has her. That the girl didn't just get pissed and run out of town or—"

"She's the daughter of a cop." Dane kept his gaze on Valentine. The guy looked far too smug. "She knows better than to vanish without telling someone where she's going." He lifted his hand. Tapped the glass. "He knows where she is. He planned for this, wanted a way out in case we caught him."

"There *is* no way out." Meadows was adamant.

"No." Dane shook his head. "Not for him." He rolled his shoulders, trying to push away his tension. He had to go in there and get the bastard to confess...to all of his crimes. He wanted an airtight case against Valentine. Wanted to nail this bastard to the wall. "Let's do this, Mac." He turned toward the door.

And found his path blocked by Meadows. The guy's lips were tight and his voice hard as he said, "You did a great job bringing him in, Detective Black, but from now on, you're staying away from him." He motioned to two detectives on the left. "Forrest, Smith, get me a confession."

"*What the fuck?*" Mac demanded.

"I'm thinking about trial," Meadows snapped right back. "You..." He pointed at Dane. "You're sleeping with the killer's ex."

"*Watch it.*" Dane's back teeth ground together.

"And you..." Meadows glanced at Mac. "The killer threatened your lover. Neither one of you two are what I'd call unbiased. If I'm getting a needle shoved in that guy's arm, then I need a confession that won't be tossed. One his lawyer won't get shredded by the judge." He exhaled and shrugged. "Sorry, men, but you're out."

"This is bullshit," Mac spat out as he stabbed a finger into the DA's chest. "*We* worked this case. Risked our lives for it, and you're shutting us out now?"

There was regret in his eyes, but Meadows simply said, "Yes."

"No way, no—" Mac began.

Dane put his hand on his partner's shoulder. "It's okay."

Mac spun on him. "How can you be so cool?"

He wasn't. He was burning on the inside. "He's cuffed. *We* got him, Mac. We got the bastard." And if they needed to step back so the deal would be sealed and a needle shoved into the guy...*I can do that.*

Because it wasn't about grabbing a headline or being the detective who was up on the stand making the big testimony before all the cameras. To him, this was about Katherine. Giving her life back to her.

About *stopping* Valentine. Making sure that bastard never hurt anyone else.

Katherine was safe. Ronnie was safe.

And I hope to hell that Maggie is, too.

"We did our job," Dane said again.

Mac gave a grudging nod.

"The perp has already flatly refused to talk to the profiler, so Marcus Wayne is back studying the last crime scene, getting us more evidence to nail this guy's coffin shut," Meadows said. "This is a high-fucking-profile case. It's gonna be on every news channel in the United States. I don't want anything screwing it up."

Dane looked over his shoulder. Forrest and Smith had just entered interrogation room one.

Valentine frowned at them, then shook his head. "Do I look like I want amateur hour?" he demanded.

You don't want anything screwing it up, Meadows? Then watch out…because Valentine lives to screw with people.

"Oh, don't worry," Smith drawled, grabbing the chair across from Valentine. "We aren't amateurs."

Valentine started to laugh. Deep, rumbling chuckles as he tossed back his head. Then, with his lips still twisting, he looked away from those two detectives and stared right at the two-way mirror. *Right at Dane.*

"I'm only talking to Dane and Mac. The rest of the detectives here can fuck off."

"It's *not* about what you want," Smith began.

Valentine kept staring at the mirror. "Meadows, are you there too?"

The guy stiffened beside Dane.

"You have such a lovely wife," Valentine said. "Sweet lady, but Tonya doesn't know about all the deals you make with killers, does she? Bad move, dealing with devils. You could get burned."

"He did not just fucking say my wife's name." A lethal intensity had entered Meadows's voice.

"Meadows, meet Valentine," Dane muttered. He had the feeling that Valentine had been ahead of the cops from the beginning.

Was *still* ahead.

Where was Maggie?

"I haven't asked for a lawyer," Valentine said, the heel of his right foot tapping back against his chair leg. "And I won't."

"Because you're a dumb-ass," Meadows growled.

"But I'm only talking to Dane and Mac." Valentine's foot stopped tapping as he leaned back in his chair. The smile slowly faded from his face. "And it's not like we really have time to waste."

Meadows was frowning. "He's bullshitting."

"Valentine *doesn't* bullshit," Dane replied. The DA should know that. "And maybe you should rethink having Wayne away from the station during the interrogation."

"Look around," Valentine said, then widened his eyes innocently. "The gang should all be here, right? But...is someone missing?"

"*Margaret,*" Meadows whispered.

Dane shook his head. "Maggie wouldn't be at the station. She never comes here." She hated that her father was a cop. Hated the danger that had stalked him for her entire life.

The gang...

Dane's gaze met Mac's. "Were any cops missing after that explosion? Was there *anyone* who wasn't accounted for?" They'd been so busy hunting for Valentine in the swamp. Had he been hunting one of them?

"The longer I wait, the less I'll share." Valentine's gaze flickered to the detectives in the room with him. "You two should just get the hell out."

"And you need to stop acting like you're the man in charge," Forrest said as he sauntered up behind Valentine. "You need to—"

Valentine lunged up from his chair, twisted, and slammed his head into Forrest's face. Blood spurted from the detective's nose. He reached for his gun.

The uniforms rushed forward, ready to restrain Valentine.

But the guy just sat back in his chair, as nice as you please. Blood was on his shirt. He was smiling again.

Meadows hit the button for the intercom. "Cuff the bastard to the table."

The door opened behind Dane. Detective Karen James came inside. Like most of the cops, she was eager to get an up-close look at the killer. Only she shouldn't have been in there at that moment—when they'd arrived at the station, Karen had been assigned to watch Katherine while Dane met with the DA.

"What happened to Forrest?" Karen asked as she leaned closer to the glass.

"Valentine," Mac answered.

Dane exhaled slowly. He didn't like that the killer was still playing his games with them. The whole scene felt wrong. "Where's Katherine?" Dane asked.

"In Harley's office," Karen replied, her gaze still on Valentine. "Don't worry, your lady's safe."

Your lady. "You need to send us in, Meadows," Dane said, his voice hardening.

"I thought you were fine with us staying out here," Mac muttered, frowning at him.

"That was before the asshole asked for us and broke Forrest's nose." *And said we were running out of time. He's still playing his games.*

Meadows loosened his tie. "I *can't*. You're personally involved. The captain should have pulled you."

"We brought the bastard in *because* of our personal involvement. If Katherine hadn't been working with us, a dozen cops might have died at that house on Oakland. She saved Harley's life. Every step of the way, she was trying to help us figure out Valentine."

Dane looked back through the mirror. Forrest had his hand shoved under his nose, trying to stop the blood flow. It looked like the guy was exercising all of his self-control to keep from attacking Valentine.

And Valentine, he was just sitting there as calm as you please.

"I'm sure my propensity for violence is listed in my profile," Valentine said, straightening his shoulders. "You don't need to act so surprised by the attack, Detective."

Listed in my profile…

Dane's eyes narrowed.

The gang should all be here.

To Valentine, just who all comprised the gang to him? Dane, Mac, Wayne…*Ross?* "Where's the marshal?"

Meadows faltered.

"Has anyone seen Anthony Ross?" Dane demanded.

The cops stared blankly at him.

Dane yanked out his phone and tried to get the marshal on the line. Ross would want to know about Valentine—but hell, when they'd brought the killer to the station, the reporters had been waiting for them. Valentine's new face was already splashed on all the TVs in town.

Ross would have heard the reports. He *should* have been there.

And Ross wasn't answering his phone.

Dane's fingers tightened around the phone. Ross had been at the explosion on Oakland, but Dane hadn't seen the guy since then. "Was he taken to the hospital after Oakland?" The scene had been chaos. So many injured cops…

No one answered. Shit. Dane called Mercy General, got the attendant to check, but there was no record of an Anthony Ross being treated.

Dane glanced around the room and saw John Baylor. He was damn glad John was there—the man was the best tech support they had. "Trace his phone," he ordered John.

"I don't think that's necessary," Meadows began. "If a man doesn't answer when you call, that doesn't mean—"

"Valentine is too smug, too damn confident for a man who should be looking at death." Dane shook his head. "Anthony Ross has been on this case for three years—*three years*—but he's not here now, when we actually have Valentine?" No, that wasn't the way the scene would play.

Sweat beaded near the DA's temples. "Fine. John, get a trace on his phone. Show the detective that he's wrong."

Dane wanted to be wrong.

"He's not afraid of us," Mac said. "That asshole *should* be afraid."

"He's not afraid because he doesn't give a shit what we think." Dane took his gun out of his holster. Put it on the table. If he was going in that room, he wanted to remove temptation from his grasp.

Because I want you dead, bastard. When he got close to Valentine, the temptation to shoot just might be too strong for him.

"He only cares about Katherine," Mac added as he scrubbed a hand over his face. "She's the only one—"

"And we just might have to get her in there." Dane's jaw ached from gritting his teeth. "He's not going to tell Forrest and Smith *anything*. We're wasting too much fucking time."

Valentine stopped grinning. "Tick, tick, tick."

Screw this. Dane shoved past Meadows and pushed the button for the intercom. "You took someone."

Valentine raised his brows. "Did I, Detective Black?"

"He's got them both," Mac said. "*Both.*"

"You're jumping to conclusions," Meadows told them, but his voice was shaking. "We have no proof that…"

John cleared his throat and put down the phone he'd had at his ear. "Sir, a trace wasn't necessary. We just located Ross's phone."

Meadows looked relieved. "I *told* you—"

"The ME found it in Evelyn Knight's coat pocket. She heard it ringing when Detective Black called—"

"*Sonofabitch*." From Meadows.

"Tick, tick, tick," Valentine said once more. "If you don't hurry, you're gonna be seeing red." His head cocked as he studied the big, round clock on the wall to his right. "And look at that, it's Valentine's Day."

Then Meadows was the one rushing from the room and heading into interrogation. Mac and Dane were with him, clearing a path.

Meadows shoved the door open, and it banged against the wall. "Do you have knowledge of Anthony Ross's whereabouts?"

Valentine nodded. "I believe I do." His fake drawl rolled beneath the words.

"*Where* is he?"

Valentine tapped his chin with his right index finger. "He's dying right now. Every precious second just ticking past." Valentine's sigh held no regret. "I kept trying to tell you we don't have time to dick around here."

"*Where*—"

"Ah, Detective Black, I figured you'd join me, if I used the right bait." Valentine's eyes held no emotion. "Now that we're all here and not pulling the ridiculous bullshit of talking through the glass, this is how the deal is going to work." He leaned forward.

"I don't deal with—" Meadows began.

"You deal with every murderer, rapist, and pedophile that you can." Valentine's voice was mild. "And you *will* fucking deal with me. Or I'll make your world a nightmare."

Meadows surged toward him. "You're *threatening* me?"

"If I were, you'd already be dead." Valentine inclined his head. "Right now, I'm dealing with you. Offering a trade. One life, for another."

"We're not letting you go, bastard." Meadows glared at Valentine.

"Then I guess that will be one life lost." Valentine didn't look like he cared worth a damn. "But the marshal was always expendable, wasn't he? It's the girl, the pretty little blonde. I'm betting she'll matter more."

Hell. Until that moment, Dane had been holding out some hope that there was a mistake. That Maggie would turn up at the hospital, rushing to her father's bedside.

The silence in the room was thick and dark and evil. Just like Valentine.

"You're fucking enjoying this, aren't you?" Dane knew it was true.

Valentine blinked, as if surprised. "Of course I enjoy my kills. Don't *you* enjoy it when you have the power of life and death over someone? When you have all the control?"

"I don't get off on killing," Dane bit off the words through clenched teeth.

Anger flared in Valentine's eyes, but the expression cooled quickly. *Control.* Yeah, that bastard wanted to have it, all right.

"Here's how this deal will work," Valentine said, his voice rumbling. "I'll take you to the marshal, in exchange for your not seeking the death penalty."

"And what will you want for Maggie's life?" Dane demanded.

Meadows had backed away from Valentine. Smart move. The guy must have just noticed the blood on the floor, courtesy of Forrest. Forrest was currently leaning against the right wall. Meadows and Smith and Forrest and the uniforms were all afraid of Valentine. Their body language and their shifting eyes screamed their fear.

And Valentine *liked* for them to be afraid.

Dane stalked toward the guy. He grabbed Valentine's chair and spun the bastard so that he had to fully face him. "What do you expect to get for her?"

Valentine blinked. "Isn't it obvious? It should be. I mean, what's the one thing I want in this world?"

Katherine.

Dane shoved his hands down on Valentine's shoulders. The pressure would ensure that Valentine didn't lunge up and attack him the way the guy had done with Forrest. Then Dane leaned closer to him and whispered, "You're not getting near Katherine."

"Then your captain will find his little girl's body." A bitter laugh. "Or maybe he won't. Maybe he won't ever know what happened to her. Maybe he'll spend his whole life searching for her bones."

Dane stared into the man's eyes. There should have been a soul there. There should have been emotions. Hate. Fury. Fear. There should have been something. "How the hell did you wind up this way?" he asked.

"Maybe I was always like this." But Valentine's eyelids flickered. "Now bring Kat to me, and let's get this show on the road."

Dane shook his head. Valentine was talking now. That was what they wanted. Step one was a success. As far as Katherine was concerned, *never gonna happen.* They'd keep the guy talking. Maybe break through that wall of ice he was using for protection, and then he'd slip up. Give them a clue to Ross's or Maggie's whereabouts.

The door opened behind him. Dane didn't glance back over his shoulder. When a snake was about to strike, you damn well didn't look away. Everyone knew that lesson. Every. One.

Footsteps shuffled toward him. Slow.

"Where is she?" The captain's voice. Weak.

Fuck. "You shouldn't be here, Harley." The captain still should have been in the hospital.

"Heard…you brought him in…had to come see…the others told me…on the way…*can't find…my Maggie…*"

He'd never heard the captain sound so lost.

"She was crying for him when I left her," Valentine said.

The captain sucked in a pained breath.

The guy had just damn well confessed to hurting Maggie, but Dane knew he had to push for more, so he said, "That's bullshit. You put duct tape over your victims' mouths. You don't let them talk or cry or beg." Maybe the guy didn't have her. Maybe—

"I let Evelyn talk. When you got there, did you see duct tape on her mouth?"

No, there hadn't been any duct tape on her.

"She confessed to killing Savannah Slater and Amy Evans." He exhaled slowly. "Such a troubled woman. Dr. Knight was so very broken."

And you're not?

"Where is…Margaret?" Harley's hand closed around Dane's shoulder. Dane let the guy haul him back.

But then…

He never expected the captain to move so fast. In an instant, the captain had his gun out and the barrel shoved right against Valentine's head. Dead center in the middle of his forehead. "*Where is my girl?*"

It seemed as if every cop in the room had stopped breathing. Except for the captain. His breath sawed in and out. In and out. Heavy and too hard.

Dane's hands were in the air. Frozen. "You don't want to do this, Harley."

"He told me…I did…nothing."

Dane took a cautious step toward the captain. The guy's body was trembling.

"I let you...get hurt...all those...years." The gun dug deeper into Valentine's forehead. "I won't...do nothing now." His finger was squeezing the trigger. "*Where is she?*"

"If you kill me, she just dies a slower, more painful death." Valentine's voice was mild and even. *He's taunting Harley.*

Harley's face crumbled. Dane lunged forward, grabbed the gun, and pushed the captain back.

"Good job, Detective," Valentine murmured. He didn't look even a *little* worried. "There just might be a hero in you yet."

Pull the trigger. The temptation whispered through Dane's mind. One quick pull, and everything would be over.

His gaze held Valentine's. *Do it.* The challenge seemed to be right there, but that didn't make any sense. Valentine was fighting to get the death penalty off the table. So why would he also be pushing for death-by-cop?

"Bring Katherine Cole in here, *now!*" Meadows yelled. He pointed his finger, a shaking finger, at Harley. "And get the captain out of here."

Smith and Forrest were only too happy to comply.

Dane didn't move. He wasn't sure he could. *Shoot the bastard.*

"Detective, you need to step back," Meadows told him.

Yes, he supposed that was what he needed to do.

"Want to pull that trigger, don't you?" Valentine whispered to him.

"Yes." His own voice was just as soft. The captain was gone. Only Dane, Mac, and Meadows were in that room.

"Making a deal with him will be a mistake," Mac rasped.

"And if I don't," Meadows said, "then a man I've known for twenty years will probably eat his gun before the night's over."

Yes, Harley would.

More footsteps were heading toward them. Not heavy this time. Light.

Valentine's nostrils flared, as if he were drinking in a scent.

"Dane?" Shock coated Katherine's voice.

Because he had a gun at Valentine's forehead.

"She's seeing you for what you are," Valentine told him with a flash of that maddening grin.

Jaw locked, Dane stepped back. He shoved the gun into the empty holster under his left shoulder.

"Ms. Cole," Meadows began. "I'm very sorry to bring you in."

"Don't be sorry." Her gaze swept the room. Lingered on Dane. Didn't even glance at Valentine. "What has he done?"

There wasn't time for sugarcoating. No time. No point. "Two people are missing. Valentine says he has them."

She finally glanced at Valentine. "Do you?"

His eyes changed, flashing with an emotion—and not that smug confidence he'd shown since coming to the station. "Yes."

"Who did you take?" she asked as she made her way to stand at Dane's side. Her shoulder brushed his arm.

Valentine's gaze darted down. Narrowed as he studied the point where they touched. *Another emotion. Anger.*

Katherine was definitely the man's trigger. But they'd known that all along.

He just hadn't wanted to use her again. He'd wanted the nightmare to be over for her.

"The marshal." Valentine's shoes rocked back and forth on the floor. "That bastard should have protected you—it was his *job.* Instead, you almost died in that café when Evelyn drugged you."

"That wasn't Ross's fault. He didn't know that Evelyn was a threat. He was supposed to protect me—from you." Katherine's

299

voice was quiet. As calm as Valentine had been before. *Before she came into the room and the guy lit up like a Christmas tree.*

Valentine licked his lips. "You've changed, Kat."

Her eyelids lowered as she pressed even closer to Dane's body. "Who else did you take?"

Valentine exhaled, as if annoyed. "Margaret Dunning. The police's captain's spoiled bitch of a daughter."

"Watch your mouth," Mac snapped.

Valentine couldn't seem to look away from Katherine. Dane stepped forward and deliberately put his body in front of hers.

Oh yeah, that was rage flaring in the man's eyes.

"Maggie Dunning is already dead," Dane said flatly.

Meadows swore behind him. Like Dane, the DA must have thought that Harley was watching from the observation room. By this point, Dane was pretty sure that room had to be packed.

"Not yet, she isn't," Valentine snapped back. "But you just keep wasting my time."

"And we're supposed to believe the serial killer?" Mac said.

Valentine spared Mac an annoyed glance. He hadn't lunged to his feet. Hadn't attacked. "Why would I lie?"

Why would you tell the truth? "To save your own skin," Dane told him, fighting to keep a tight rein on his own fury. This was the man who'd made Katherine's life hell. The man who'd killed and tortured so many women. "You'd say anything to avoid getting a needle in your arm." He kept his arms loose at his sides, a fake pose because his body was tight with battle-ready tension.

"You keep wasting so much time." Valentine sighed. "But if you just want more deaths on you, that's fine with me."

"So you admit to murdering Trent Lancaster?" Dane fired out the question. Valentine had said that Evelyn confessed to killing

Savannah and Amy, and that fit—those victims had been drugged with the fentanyl.

The drug that Evelyn had used on both Katherine and Ronnie.

But no fentanyl had been found in Trent Lancaster's tox screen.

After a moment, Valentine nodded.

"Say it," Dane snarled. "Admit what you did."

Katherine stepped forward, putting her body next to Dane's.

Valentine's eyes found hers once more. His face seemed to soften as he stared at her. "You aren't damaged, Kat. I knew what he'd said. I knew how he talked to you. He didn't deserve to be anywhere near you."

Katherine's breath rushed out. "You shoved a knife into his chest and you left him for me to find."

"He was a present."

"A dead body *isn't* the kind of present that I wanted!"

Valentine's eyes slid over her. "You needed to know that someone was looking out for you. I didn't want you to worry that you'd be a target." His voice dropped. "Never you. That's why I stayed in the gallery, so you'd understand."

"Is that why you killed Evelyn?" Dane asked. If the idiot wanted to talk, he'd let the guy bury himself. "Because she was targeting Katherine?"

"She tried to kill my Kat. She was dead the minute I knew." He sucked in a breath, as if trying to regain his control. "Besides, Evelyn thought she was something that she wasn't."

"And what was that?" Dane pushed.

"Good enough for me. Only one woman has ever been *good* enough." His shoulders rolled back. "For a shrink, the woman was pretty fucking crazy."

It takes a psycho to recognize one.

"And you set the bomb to explode at the house on Oakland?" Now it was Meadows asking the question. The guy had composed himself a bit. Good.

Valentine focused on Katherine. "I knew you'd make the right choice."

"You almost killed a dozen cops!" Her cheeks had flushed a dark pink.

"You could have let them all burn. Could have just killed me and let them *burn*."

"That wasn't a choice for me. Saving them was the only option."

Valentine lunged to his feet.

Dane and Mac both yanked out their guns.

But Valentine made no move to attack. He just stared at Katherine. "*That's* why you're different. You keep choosing life, when you should choose death. When you were fifteen, you *should* have let that bitch die in that car without a backward glance. And at Oakland, you *should* have laughed and watched the fire as the cops burned." He shook his head. "How? How do you do it? Didn't you *want* to hurt your mother? Didn't a little part of you *want* to see that house burn with all those bastards inside?"

Valentine jerked his head toward Dane. "He understands. He killed his old man, did you know that? Dane *wanted* him to die. *Why are you different from him? From me?*"

Katherine moved toward him. Dane put his arm in front of her, but she shoved it away. "Take me to Maggie and Ross, and I'll tell you why. Take us to them now, get us there while they are still alive, and I'll tell you."

Valentine's eyes lit up. "Deal."

Take me to Margaret and Ross.

"I haven't agreed to take the death penalty off the table," Meadows said, sounding a bit strained, "but you just promised to take us to the missing victims."

"Yes, I did…as long as Kat goes with me." Valentine's gaze swept the small circle in the room. "Kat. Dane, and Mac. Just them. No one else."

Meadows shook his head. "No dice, no—"

"You really think your two detectives aren't competent enough to keep me in check? Even handcuffed?" Valentine looked sad for them. "And here I thought the New Orleans PD was supposed to be tough."

"We're tough," Dane agreed. "Not stupid." The guy wanted them out of the station. Who the hell knew where he'd lead them?

"Then get a helicopter to do aerial surveillance on us as we move." Valentine sighed. "Get your eyes in the sky to keep track of us, if that makes you all feel better, but do it fast. Based on my rather extensive experience with death, I'd say one of our missing has only about an hour to live, maybe less." Then he pursed his lips thoughtfully. "The chopper should probably be one of those medevac units. Because once you find the victims, they'll need immediate medical care."

Shit.

"Deal," Meadows said, sealing their fates.

Mac shoved Valentine back in his chair. The interrogation room door opened. As uniformed cops spilled inside for guard duty, Dane followed Katherine toward the door. He wanted her *out* of there. Meadows was hurrying behind him.

They all wanted away from the grim reaper.

"Oh, Meadows?" Valentine's voice called after them.

Dane glanced back. So did Meadows.

"You *are* taking the death penalty off the table."

303

Meadows laughed. "Your dumb mistake. I told you, that wasn't part of the deal for Ross and Margaret."

"No, not their deal. But if you want to know the locations of the other bodies, then you'll make sure I live for a very, very long time."

The other bodies.

"You didn't honestly think I gave up killing in the last three years, did you? I'm sure the profiler told you that a guy like me can't just go cold turkey. He would have been right on that one point." A chilling pause. "There are bodies. Lots of them. And I'll give them to you...once you give me a deal to sign for my life."

The sonofabitch. He was just playing them. Every moment, every word. It was all a game.

Dane took Katherine's arm. Led her away. Didn't stop when other detectives called out to him. He hurried down the hallway, practically dragging her with him. He needed her alone. Had to talk to her without all the eyes and ears on them.

He shoved open a door on their right. *The same room.* The same room where he'd taken her frantically hours before. Because he hadn't been able to keep his hands off her. Because he'd needed her.

He'd been afraid of losing her. Of death. He'd been rough and hard. Always too rough and hard.

She'd deserved more. Better. Romance. Courting. Not a fast screw in an old cop room.

"Katherine..."

She shut the door, then stood in front of him, her body brushing against his.

There was so much to say to her, and he didn't even know where to start.

He stared into her eyes and wondered if he looked as obsessed as Valentine. Because he felt the same way. Like she was everything. That she was the one he had to protect from every threat. Everyone.

Have to protect her, even from myself.

Fuck, what if Valentine was right? What if he was more like the guy than he'd believed?

I've killed. I'd do it again in a heartbeat to protect her. When Valentine had risen from that chair, he'd imagined himself blowing the man's brains out.

It would be so easy.

And what will happen when we go out of the station with him? It's going to be a trap, I know it will be.

"Don't go," Dane said, because, maybe, those were the only words that mattered. *Don't go with us to find Ross and Margaret. Don't put yourself at risk.* "Stay at the station. We'll bring them back."

Alive? Doubtful. Valentine was just going to take them to find the dead bodies. *If* he even led them to the bodies.

"If I don't go, you won't find them." Her voice was soft but certain. "He wants me there. He wants me to see what he's done."

"Fuck what he wants." His fingers curled around her shoulders. "I want you safe."

"And I want to be strong." Her chin lifted as her eyes flashed golden fire. "I don't want these deaths on me. I want to *save* someone."

She was so beautiful he ached. "They're already dead. He's going to take us into the middle of nowhere, he'll try to escape, and I'll shoot him in the head." That was how this would end. "He wants you to see me as a killer, and he's setting it up so that there is no other option, no choice for any of us."

"There's always a choice," Katherine whispered. "Even if it looks like there isn't." Then she rose onto her toes and put her mouth against his. Her lips were soft, the caress so very light. Intimate. Loving.

I love her.

He realized the truth in that instant. It wasn't just an obsession. Not for him. He wanted her safe. He wanted her *happy*. And he never wanted her to fear monsters in the world ever again.

To keep her alive and happy, Dane realized that he'd give up everything.

Her arms twined around his neck. "I won't ever see you as a killer. You're a cop, you protect."

And I kill.

"I want you to know me as I am." He didn't want lies between them. No false images. She'd had all that before. "I *killed* my father when I was seventeen. I could have let the bastard live. Could have gotten him tossed in jail." Not choices he'd made. "I killed him." When his father had been coming at him with that bottle, Dane had known one thing with utter certainty...*He's not walking away. He won't ever hurt me again.* Even if his father hadn't fallen down those stairs, he would have been a dead man.

She backed away, just a few inches, and gazed up at him. "Is that supposed to change the way I feel?"

"See me as I am!" Valentine knew. He was going to use that truth against them all.

"I do." Soft, when his words had been so angry and hard. "I see a man who is brave and strong. A man who makes me feel safe, even when I'm surrounded by death. A man who makes me feel alive, when I thought I was already dead."

"Stay here," he said again, the words growling out.

"No. I want to be with you. I want to finish this, with you."

He felt like she was breaking him. This time, he was the one to kiss her. And Dane knew she needed gentleness. Knew that she deserved care, but he was too afraid.

Afraid for her.

He pulled her against him. His mouth crashed down on hers. His tongue thrust into her mouth. Desperation drove him.

Finally found her. Can't lose her. Can't.

Was that the way Valentine felt? Like his whole damn world began and ended with her?

If something happened to Katherine, just how far would Dane go to get vengeance? Just what would he do?

I don't want to find out.

He tried to gentle the kiss. Couldn't. Tried to get his hands to let her go. Couldn't.

He'd never wanted another woman with this intensity. When he'd seen Valentine in that office, Dane's first instinct hadn't been to tell the guy to freeze. To tell him to drop his gun.

I wanted to shoot. To take him out of Katherine's life forever. The squeeze of his trigger would have done it. *I fucking should have done it.*

He wore the badge for a reason. But he'd been ready to toss it away. Was still ready.

Katherine's fingers pressed lightly against his shoulders. Her mouth was moving softly beneath his, caressing his lips, and the frantic drumming of his heartbeat slowly faded.

Another kiss. Finally, softer, and his head lifted. Being close to her made him feel stronger.

He reached into his holster and pulled out the gun.

– 20 –

Dane tucked the gun into Katherine's hand. "If this goes south, if Valentine tries anything, don't hesitate to shoot him."

"I didn't hesitate before," Katherine reminded him.

Dane's fingers brushed back her hair. "I didn't expect you."

Her brows lifted even as she tucked the gun into the back waistband of her jeans. She pulled her shirt down, covering the weapon. "I didn't exactly expect you, either." But she was sure glad she'd found him.

His handsome face was tense, his eyes so deep.

"Do you trust me, Katherine?"

Trust. It was the one thing she'd never thought she'd be able to give a man again. But Dane…"Yes." There was no hesitation with her answer.

His blue eyes seemed to burn. "I swear, I won't let you down."

"I know." But did he understand what she was telling him? For her, there was no difference between trusting Dane and loving him. She trusted *because* she loved.

He'd gotten to her. Slipped past her ice and taught her that it was okay to feel again.

"Whatever happens," he told her, fingers warm against her chilled cheek, "you can count on me."

She smiled up at him. "I know." She'd known it for a while now. Her true-blue cop.

No, it wasn't the cop part that she cared about. She just cared about *him*.

Dane looked like he wanted to say more. She *wanted* him to say more. But he just gave a grim nod and reached around her for the door.

Um, *no*. She slammed the door shut. "That's it?"

A muscle jerked in his jaw.

"Do better than this," she told him, anger roughening her words because they both deserved more. "Don't shut me out. *Tell me*." Because she wanted to hear the words. Sometimes a girl needed them.

"You already know."

Katherine shook her head. "Not good enough. I want to hear them. Before anything else happens."

His pupils had grown, nearly swallowing the blue of his eyes. "Katherine Cole, *I love you*."

"Was that so hard?" she whispered as her heart ached. She wanted to smile. In the midst of the hell that was happening, her lips were trying to curl. "When we have Ross and Maggie back, when Valentine is locked in jail, I'm going to want to hear those words again."

"You'll get more than just the words." A promise. She knew Dane wasn't the type of man to easily promise anything. Only when he meant his vow. "I want to be with you, Katherine. I want us to have a chance together."

She wanted that chance.

Nodding, she turned from him and curled her fingers around the doorknob.

"Don't you have something to tell me?" His breath blew against the shell of her ear.

For an instant, her eyes squeezed shut. She thought of all the wonderful things that could be. Her. Dane. A house. Maybe even one with that perfect white picket fence. Laughter and love as the years slid by.

Then she thought of what was. A killer. Victims trapped. Death coming. Clearing her throat, she said, "You already know." And she opened the door.

Cops were bustling in the hallway. Hurrying. Voices rose and fell.

But Dane's voice was quiet behind her. "Yes, baby, I do. Because you said you trust me."

He understands.

And whatever happened next, they would deal with it together.

They joined the other cops heading toward the tech room. Dane, Mac, and Katherine were all given GPS tracking watches, a precaution in case the helicopter lost visual on them.

"The patrol car will be tracked, too," Meadows said, "but we want to have a handle on you when you're on foot."

Then Dane gave Katherine a bulletproof vest. She slid it on, and the weight should have reassured her, but it didn't. "He didn't use bullets before," she said.

"And he didn't always use bombs, either. There's a first time for everything." Dane pulled on his vest. "And the vest will make it harder for him to come at your heart with a knife."

"Please…" Harley had come into the room, slumped shoulders, bruises and cuts all over his face. His desperate gaze locked on Katherine. "Bring back Maggie."

They would. *Be alive.* Because, like Dane, Katherine wasn't sure that the woman was still living.

He didn't hurt me. Maybe he didn't hurt her.

They had to cling to that hope.

Harley's gaze swung to Dane. "So…sorry." A hoarse whisper.

The others were quiet. Watching with avid eyes.

Harley whispered, "I should have…helped you…"

Dane shook his head. "He was good at hiding who he was."

"I should have *helped* you!" Harley's breath was loud and heaving. "But James was my partner, and I didn't want to believe— I didn't want to think—"

"That you'd trusted a monster," Katherine finished for him.

"Yes." Harley's hands were shaking. His whole body trembling. "I tried to make up…for it…tried to help…but the damage was done."

Dane wasn't damaged.

Neither am I.

"No, it wasn't," Katherine snapped as her spine straightened. "We aren't who our pasts say we are. Damage doesn't define us. *We define ourselves.*"

Dane caught her arm. Pulled her close and kissed her, right there, in front of all the assembled cops. "I love you," he said against her lips.

She'd never get tired of hearing those words. "Good," she whispered. "Now let's get Ross and Maggie back." Valentine might think he was playing a game, but they would dictate the rules.

And he would lose.

"The car's been wired," Meadows told her and Dane. "Got a video and audio linkup. We'll hear and see everything that happens. You aren't going to be alone out there."

Then they walked to the back of the station. A patrol car was waiting. Mac had already slid into the driver's seat. Katherine hesitated near the passenger-side door.

Then she saw Valentine. Being led toward them. Cops all around. His hands were cuffed in front of him now, and a line of red dripped from his busted lip. He had shackles on his ankles, and they were connected to his handcuffs by a silver chain.

"Forrest…" Dane growled.

The cop on the right smiled.

Dane went toward them. Stared at Valentine. "You try to attack anyone in the car, you make any move to escape, and I'll put a bullet in your head."

"I wouldn't expect any less," Valentine murmured.

No, Katherine knew he wouldn't. The guy was counting on Dane to follow through with his promise.

Dane always keeps his promises.

"You want to die, don't you?" Katherine asked him.

Valentine didn't answer.

Dane pushed Valentine into the back of the car. Kept his gun out and aimed at the killer the whole time.

Katherine was conscious of her own weapon. So close.

She slid into the passenger seat. Glanced back through the protective glass to see Valentine smiling.

"Are the medics coming in the helicopter?" he wanted to know.

"The chopper's coming," Mac noted as he cranked the car.

"Then we're all set." Valentine's voice was mild. "Start driving, Detective, and I'll tell you exactly where to go."

Katherine already knew where he wanted to take them. *Hell.*

"Be sure to buckle your seat belt, Kat," Valentine murmured. "Cops can be such terrible drivers."

Mac cursed under his breath.

Then they started driving. And driving. Valentine gave directions in a low, calm voice. They left the city. Drove toward the swamp. The road narrowed to just two lanes, an old highway filled with potholes and heavy cracks.

"So far away," Dane said from the darkness of the car's backseat.

Katherine's sweaty palm curled around her door handle.

Dane sighed. "You wouldn't just be leading us on a wild goose chase, would you, Michael?"

Michael. Katherine flinched at the name.

"No, Detective," Valentine said in that same calm voice. "After Boston, I learned the importance of not shitting where I eat."

Her jaw dropped.

"So I keep my kills far away from my house now."

Katherine glanced back, but in the heavy darkness, she couldn't make out more than the outline of his features.

"Go about thirty yards, then turn right, Mac," Valentine said.

The car began to slow.

"You're both incredibly trusting, for cops." Now a rougher tone had entered Valentine's voice. "You let me lure you both out here, with Kat. And, Dane, I'm betting you even gave her a gun before she climbed into the car."

Katherine felt the gun in her jacket pocket.

"How do you know," Valentine asked, tone curious, "that Kat isn't working with me? That the goal wasn't to pull you both out here, and when we make that turn in a few minutes, when Mac is working hard to control the wheel because there's going to be one huge dip up there—how do you know Kat won't pull out her gun then and blow a hole in Mac's head?"

Silence.

The car was still slowing as Mac prepared to make that turn.

"When she shoots Mac, I can ram my head into your face, breaking your nose the same way I did that prick's at the station. I'll disarm you, and, while we're fighting, Kat will come around to the back of the vehicle and open the door. When you look up, my Kat will have the gun pointed dead-center at your forehead."

She didn't speak. Her heart was racing, the thunder echoing in her ears.

"All along, Kat could have been secretly working with me. We lived so close to one another, saw each other every single day…"

Mac was turning onto the dirt road.

"Does a part of you suspect her, Dane?" Valentine's dark question poured through the car. "Inside, deep down, are you one hundred percent sure that you can count on her? Is your heart racing fast? Are you nervous, are you wondering—"

Dane was laughing.

The car hit the heavy dip, jostling the whole vehicle. Swearing, Mac fought to keep the car steady.

"Save your bullshit," Dane rasped. "I *trust* Katherine."

"Funny. I trust her, too."

The weird part was Katherine knew it was true. Valentine *did* trust her.

"But what about you, Mac?" Valentine asked.

Katherine glanced toward Mac. The light from the dash barely illuminated him.

"Do you also trust Kat? Or do you keep glancing at her from the corner of your eye, every few moments?"

He had been looking at her. She'd felt his gaze slide to her more than a few times during the drive.

"Dane's fucking her, so, of course, he'll say she won't turn on him, but what do you think? Do you think she's just waiting? That she's going to attack when she has that perfect moment?"

"Stop," Dane snapped at him.

"Kat is the one who got your girl to talk in the hospital." Valentine's voice was even deeper now. "Kat is the one who sealed Ronnie's fate. I told Ronnie that she could live as long as she didn't talk, but she had to go and break the rules."

"Shut up," Mac gritted out.

"When I found her in that basement, she was crying. Tears were tracking down her cheeks. She had duct tape over her mouth and—"

"Shut the fuck up!" Mac was screaming now, his hands locked tightly around the wheel.

"Mac..." Katherine began. "Look at the road." Because it was dark. Bushes and branches were beating at the vehicle, and Mac was driving faster now. *Faster.*

"Don't say another word," Dane warned Valentine.

But that was just going to make him want to say more. She knew it would.

"The ropes were around her arms and legs. Her skin was slashed open. Her blood was dripping off the table. At first, I thought about just shoving my knife in her chest. That would have been so easy."

Katherine glanced back. Saw the shadow of Dane's gun. It was rising toward Valentine.

"But I decided to let her live. *Then.* I won't make the same mistake again. I'll go for her. I'll slip into her bedroom. I'll tie her up. Maybe leave the tape off so she can beg."

Mac spun toward him. "Shut him up, Dane! Or I'll fucking—"

"Then I'll drive the knife into her chest."

Katherine was looking straight ahead, staring in horror because she'd just tried to grab the car's steering wheel, and she realized that dark spot in the dirt up ahead…it wasn't just hard mud or a big crack in the surface of the area.

"Spikes!" she cried as they came into focus beneath the glare of the car's headlights. "*Stop!*" Her scream.

But it was too late. She couldn't reach the brake from her position. Mac wasn't even looking at the road. He turned back, too late, and jerked the wheel to the right.

The car hit the spikes. The front wheels blew out instantly. Mac was trying to control the car, just like he'd done minutes before, but this time there was no saving the vehicle. He'd yanked the wheel too hard to the right. The vehicle was spinning now, hurtling over onto its side, and the bushes had hidden the fact that on that right side was only swampy water waiting below. They were up on an incline, and as the car tumbled over and over again, it rolled down that incline.

Metal was screeching. Glass shattering. Katherine's seat belt bit into her shoulder, and the gun she'd grabbed flew from her fingers.

Someone was calling her name. Someone was screaming.

A trap. A deadly trap. One last punishment to send us all to hell.

Then the car hit the water. And the screams stopped.

– – –

"What do you mean, you 'lost them'?" Meadows demanded as he crouched behind John. "There's a brand-new tracker on that vehicle. It was installed five minutes before they left!"

"It stopped sending a signal."

"Get me someone on that chopper."

The transmitter flashed on. The call was routed through the center, then pushed into the microphone speakers. "Sir?"

Meadows stood at attention. "Tell me you have a visual on our car."

"Negative."

No fucking way.

"They turned down a heavily tree-lined road a few moments ago. We should regain aerial visibility momentarily."

No, they wouldn't regain that visibility. Because Valentine was playing his games. Trying to kill his detectives.

"The watches," he said, the word close to a snarl of desperate frustration,. "Tell me you're getting a signal from them."

"Not from Detective Mac Turner," John told him.

Shit, shit, *shit.*

"But I'm reading a signal from Katherine Cole and Detective Black," John continued, voice cracking with excitement.

Damn straight.

"Get patrols out there right *now.*" Meadows sucked in a deep breath. His gut was twisting. "Get SWAT, get whoever the hell we need. And you, flyboy," he added, because he knew the helicopter pilot could hear him, "you get these coordinates we're sending you, and you find a place to land that chopper. Give those men on the ground backup!"

Before they'd lost the radio signal from the car, Meadows had heard the screams. Heard the shriek of metal. And he'd also heard…

Laughter.

You aren't killing my men, Valentine.

Because if he did, those deaths would be on Meadows. He'd made the deal. He'd sent the detectives out with that bastard.

Had he sent them to their deaths?

— — —

Water was filling the car. Hell. Dane felt it sloshing around his legs. His head hurt like a bitch—it had slammed into the side window, and a chunk of metal dug into his side.

"Katherine?" There was so much silence…and darkness. "Katherine!"

"I'll take care of her," a voice whispered from the darkness.

Valentine.

Couldn't the SOB have just died in the wreck?

The metal twisted in his side. Dane groaned at the pain and realized Valentine was the one twisting the metal. No, not metal. Broken glass. Valentine's cuffs were gone. He'd shoved Dane's bulletproof vest to the side, and the psycho was using a giant piece of glass to saw into Dane's flesh.

"The…fuck…you…will…" Dane growled. He reached down, jerking under the water to try and find the gun he'd had before. He ignored the pain. His fingers closed around the weapon. The gun had still better fire.

The car was tilted on its side, sending all of the water pooling toward Dane. He was sinking, but Valentine was protected, his side of the vehicle was still elevated and—

Valentine's door flew open. "Get away from him!" Katherine screamed.

The glass was gone from Dane's side.

"Katherine, you're hurt!" Valentine's voice was dripping with concern. "Didn't I tell you to put on your seat belt?"

318

Then Valentine was out of the car and lunging toward her. *Valentine had the glass.* Katherine was stumbling back as Valentine rushed through the water toward her.

Dane's fingers closed around the gun. "Get back, Katherine!" he yelled.

Then he fired. The bullet plowed into Valentine's body and the man fell, face-first, onto the bank.

Dane realized that the impact of the crash must have knocked him out for a bit. Valentine—the bastard—had stayed conscious and gotten out of his cuffs, and he'd been working on him with that glass. "Mac?" he called.

No answer.

"Dane…" Katherine was there, pulling him from the car. There was no moonlight to spill down on them. Clouds blotted out the sky. But he could just make out Valentine's body, slumped over on the small bank area.

"Where's Mac?" Dane managed to ask. His left arm was wrapped around Katherine's shoulders. He was holding her tight. His right hand gripped the gun.

"He's in the car. I couldn't get him to move."

Fuck.

His gaze flew over the killer. Valentine was still slumped on the bank. Not moving.

The car was sinking deeper into the water. Dane backed away from Valentine and tried to open Mac's door.

"It won't open," Katherine said. "I tried. Mine wouldn't either. I had to crawl out. The windshield was smashed. I got out that way."

Dane wasn't going to let his partner sink. He gave Katherine the gun. Tightened her fingers around the weapon. "If Valentine so much as twitches, shoot him in the head." He ignored the pain in his side and didn't tell her about it. She hadn't seen the wound, couldn't see it in the dark.

He pushed deeper into the water. Prayed there weren't any gators swimming around because he couldn't deal with that shit, too. He climbed onto the hood of the vehicle. Made his way through the broken glass. Wrapped his arms around Mac. "Buddy, you're gonna owe me," Dane muttered as he started to pull Mac out.

The car shifted beneath him. More water rolled in, and then—

Then metal groaned. Screeched.

And the whole fucking car went totally under the water.

– – –

"Dane!" Katherine screamed when the car lurched and sank beneath the water. She ran for the bubbling water.

"You don't want to do that." Hard arms wrapped around her stomach, and Katherine was hauled back against a big, muscled body.

Her fingers clenched around the gun.

"That water is so much deeper than it looks from up on that incline, and someone might have set up some small detonations in that spot recently, to weaken things more, to make it easier for a big object to sink fast."

He'd planned *everything*?

Valentine's hand slid down and curled around the gun. "Just give this to me, Kat."

"You never intended to let Maggie and Ross go." Her lips felt numb as she spoke. "You set this whole road up as a trap for us."

"Not just for you. For *any* cop who tracked me. Got to have that exit strategy."

The water looked pitch black. She didn't see Dane.

She would only have an instant...

He laughed in her ear. "I know what you're thinking. You'll hit back at me with your elbow. Catch me off guard because I won't expect you to fight. Then you'll go and jump into that water. You'll save your hero—and go out for a fucking candlelit dinner to celebrate—on Valentine's Day, on *my* day."

Katherine swallowed back her fear. "You think you know me so well."

How long would Dane be able to hold his breath?

"You want to save the world, Kat. It's your flaw."

Not this time.

You don't know me.

She thought of all the self-defense classes she'd taken. Hours and hours, so she wouldn't be weak. So she wouldn't freeze when this one moment came.

Her fingers slipped from his, letting go of the gun. In the next instant, she was spinning in his arms—and her fingers went straight for his eyes. He cried out in shocked pain and his hands automatically went to cover his eyes.

Giving her plenty of target space.

Katherine kicked out, aiming for his groin, using as much force as she could. He'd destroyed so much of her life—of so many lives—she wanted him to *hurt*.

He stumbled back. She grabbed the gun. She'd save Dane, all right, but she'd make sure that Valentine was dead first. She wasn't going to let him come back and attack just as Dane was getting out of the water.

She lifted the gun. Aimed it at Valentine.

He was laughing.

She pulled the trigger.

And nothing happened.

He laughed harder. "That's what happens with those cheap cop guns. When water gets to them, sometimes they just don't work."

No. *No.*

He rose, and there was something sharp in his hand. She could see the outline. Bigger than a knife. Longer. Jagged. Metal? Some hunk of metal or glass?

Water sloshed behind her. Katherine jerked and glanced back. Dane had just broken the surface of the water. Mac was in his arms.

And in the next instant, Valentine had his makeshift knife at Katherine's neck. "Try to get away, try that little elbow trick again, I'll slice your throat open," he promised her. The rage was there, burning beneath his words. He'd always been so calm, so controlled with her before, but now…now she was seeing the beast.

She didn't move.

"Do you want to see how much blood can pump out of sweet Kat?" Valentine called out to Dane.

Dane was heading toward the shore.

"Shove your friend back into the water," Valentine ordered.

Dane stilled. Water poured off him. "He's unconscious." His voice carried easily. So did his rage. "Mac isn't a threat to you."

"Not now," Valentine agreed. "Now shove him back into the water!"

"He'll die!"

"Isn't that the point?" Valentine whispered to Kat. "Your cop should be smarter." His sigh blew over her cheek. "Just let him sink," he told Dane. "Then you can come out and try to play the hero for Kat. Either you'll die or I will. If you move fast enough, you might even be able to go back into the water and save old Mac before he drowns."

Katherine shook her head. *Don't do it.*

The weapon nicked her skin, and she felt the wet warmth of her blood.

"Stop moving, Kat!" Valentine barked.

"Don't let him go," Katherine said, ignoring Valentine. "Dane, bring Mac out! Save him!"

"Let him die, Dane," Valentine snarled at the same time. "It's him or Kat. You choose."

Life was always about choices. Choosing to save. Choosing to kill.

Choosing to die.

She could feel Dane's struggle. She saw his hands. They were wrapped around Mac's body. His best friend. His partner.

Mac was already hurt. If he went beneath that water, would he ever come back up?

"*I* choose," Katherine said as her right hand rose to her neck. Because, maybe, maybe this was the way it was always meant to be. It would hurt, there would be blood, but Mac would live. Dane would live.

Valentine?

It's about the choices we make.

"No," Valentine whispered in her ear. "Don't."

Because he really did know her well.

"*Please…*" Valentine was begging her.

Or was that Dane?

Both of them?

She pressed forward, heading not away from the weapon but toward it, even as she grabbed Valentine's hand and tried to shove it away to the right.

The glass sliced across her throat. Blood slid down her neck.

"No!" Dane's roar.

But Valentine had dropped the weapon. "*Katherine!*"

She sagged in his arms. Took them both down to the muddy ground. Water was sloshing. Dane coming to her. He'd better be hauling Mac with him.

Valentine's hand was at her throat. "*Why? I could have killed you.*"

Her throat hurt, but it wasn't an injury that would kill. The wound wasn't deep enough to kill. She'd pushed his hand away in time, or maybe—maybe Valentine had stopped himself.

"Choices," she told him, voice rasping. The slice might not be deep enough to kill, but it still *hurt*. "I couldn't…let Dane…make the wrong one."

Valentine leaned over her and lifted the chunk of glass. "He'll still do what has to be done."

Katherine stared up at him. Even in the darkness, she could see his pain. The hopelessness. Both were so clear to her. "Why?"

"Because I can't stop myself."

He lifted the glass over her. It looked like he was preparing to drive that weapon into her chest.

"It's Valentine's Day," he told her, voice breaking. "I love you, Katherine."

She grabbed his hand. Held the weapon back. "No you don't."

You don't go out like this.

You don't get to decide how this ends.

Dane slammed into Valentine. They rolled on the ground. She heard the thud of flesh hitting flesh. The men were pounding each other. Dane was on top, driving his fist into Valentine's face. Again and again.

But Valentine was fighting back. He still had that glass chunk, and he shoved it through Dane's right fist.

Katherine screamed, but Dane kept fighting. He rammed his head into Valentine's. Drove his left fist into the killer's stomach. The fight was brutal and bloody.

The glass flew from Dane's hand.

Mac was on the ground a few feet away. Katherine ran to him. She felt for his pulse. *Beating. Breathing. Yes.* He'd make it. Now if they could just find Ross and Maggie, maybe they'd all have a chance.

All but Valentine.

Cops always had a backup weapon, and going on a hunt with Valentine, there was no way Mac wouldn't have come prepared.

She reached down near his ankle.

Yes.

Not a gun. A knife. He'd strapped a knife to his ankle.

She leapt back to her feet and ran toward the fighting men. The knife was gripped tightly in her fist. Dane and Valentine were staggering to their feet. Getting ready to slam into each other again.

No.

It ends.

"Valentine!"

He spun at her call.

She drove the knife into his chest. His hands closed around her arms. His body shuddered. "Good-bye, Michael," she told him, voice breaking.

Because now she understood. Michael *had* wanted her help all along. He'd wanted her to save him, as she'd tried to save her mother.

Only saving Michael meant killing Valentine.

"I did it," he whispered. "I died for you." His fingers eased their grip on her. He staggered, then fell, his body slumping over.

In the next moment, Dane was there, pulling her against him. Holding her so close.

She heard a whoop-whoop-whoop fill the air, and a gust of wind blew over her face.

The helicopter. The helicopter was there.

It was landing. She could see the bright lights spilling from it.

"The...cavalry..." Valentine whispered.

Dane's gaze was on Katherine's neck. "Why the hell did you do that? He could have cut your throat wide open."

"I shoved his wrist back. From that angle, he wasn't going to be able to do much damage." She'd practiced that move before. He didn't realize how many self-defense classes she'd taken over the years. She'd tried to prepare herself, again and again, for this moment.

He pulled her against his chest again. Held tight. He was soaking wet, so was she, and she could feel the shudders that shook his body. Voice thick with fear and rage, he said, "I thought you were going to die in front of me."

She'd been afraid that she might.

"Don't ever scare me like that again," he ordered, and held her even tighter. "I think I lost about ten years of my life."

Better than losing all of it.

Better than Mac losing his life.

Mac.

She and Dane rushed to the fallen man. There were other footsteps, racing toward them now. The helicopter had landed, and the EMTs and the cops who'd been on board were running to help. *The EMTs.* Valentine had made that request deliberately, because he knew that they would be hurt. *That I might be hurt.*

Mac was groaning and trying to open his eyes. A giant cut ran from his temple to his jawline. "Did we…get him?" he asked, squinting to see in the dark.

"Yeah, buddy, we did." Dane clasped his hand.

Katherine glanced back at Valentine's body. The knife handle rose from his chest. She'd driven that blade in as hard as she could.

His blood was on her hands.

She tried to wipe the blood onto her jeans. The sticky wetness clung to her.

"Good…" Mac rasped. "Hope…bastard…suffered…"

Not as much as his victims had suffered, no.

The EMTs broke through the brush.

"Here!" Dane shouted. "We've got an officer down!"

Two men and a woman immediately ran toward Dane.

"Anyone else injured?" Another guy called out. He was coming up at the rear.

Dane backed away so the EMTs could work on Mac. "Our prisoner was stabbed." He was edging near Valentine's body. Dane had his arms at his sides.

The last EMT headed toward Valentine. "No." Dane grabbed the man's arm, stopping him. "Where's the cop with you?"

A woman pushed through the brush.

"Karen, give me your backup weapon," Dane demanded when he saw the detective.

He took the gun from her. Checked the clip, then said, "Now let's make damn sure he doesn't have a pulse."

They advanced on Valentine. Katherine didn't move. She felt as if her muscles were locking down. One of the EMTs put a blanket around her shoulders. It didn't make her feel any warmer.

Carefully, Dane crouched near Valentine. Dane's fingers went to Valentine's throat. Stayed there.

Katherine began to count in her mind.

One.

She saw Michael, as he'd been the day they first met. That wide grin. The sparkling eyes.

Two.

She saw him with the engagement ring. Down on one knee. Asking her to marry him.

Three.

She saw him in his black painting apron…a knife still in his hand. Blood. *You didn't come home soon enough.* The words whispered through her mind.

Four.

She saw him as he'd been moments before, when he'd turned at her shout. He'd seemed almost…eager as he pushed toward her. As he thrust his body right at the knife, even angling his chest so that her knife would sink into just the right spot.

Five.

She saw Dane shake his head. Valentine—*Michael*—was gone.

Dane rose and walked toward her. "It should have been me," he said, voice rumbling. He pulled her into his arms once more. "I should have been the one to kill him. You didn't need that on your shoulders."

Actually, she did. Valentine had wanted to be saved. And in the end, maybe he'd gotten just what he wanted.

Streaks of red were lighting up the dark sky. Dawn was coming now. The night was truly ending. The darkness gone.

"What the hell?" Dane growled, and his body stiffened against hers.

She turned in his arms, followed his stare. With the rising of the sun, she could just make out the battered form of a small shack at the edge of the swamp.

"Sonofabitch." Dane blew out a disbelieving breath. "He brought us to them. *He brought us to them.*"

It looked as if Valentine had kept his part of the bargain, to a certain extent. But would Maggie and Ross be alive?

She and Dane started running as one. Slogging through the mud, shoving away the bushes and branches. Dane yelled for backup.

The EMTs had loaded Mac onto a stretcher.

Sirens wailed in the distance.

She and Dane kept running.

Then he was at the shack's door. He had his weapon drawn. "New Orleans PD!" he yelled. "We're coming in!"

Then he grabbed the knob. Twisted. It didn't give, so Dane kicked the door in.

The scent of death hit her then. Blood and decay. Hell.

And she wasn't so sure they would be rescuing anyone that day. Valentine just might have taken more victims before death had taken him.

– 21 –

He didn't see blood, but he could smell it all around him. Valentine hadn't been lying when he told them about his secret little hideaway. Hell, out in the swamp, he'd probably been able to slice up his victims and feed the body parts to the gators.

No wonder no bodies had been found sooner.

It was always easier to keep the dead quiet when there were no dead to find.

The floor sloped in the cabin. Dane followed the scent of the blood. It was heaviest toward the right. The light from the growing dawn fell through the old blinds and revealed a wooden door in the right corner. Faded with time. Padlocked.

Screw the lock.

Dane lifted his foot and kicked that door open too. Then he rushed into the room.

The scent of blood was so much stronger…because there was a woman lying on a table in the middle of the room. A woman with pale blonde hair. A woman with duct tape over her mouth and with her hands and feet bound with rope.

Her arms were cut. Deep slashes that had sent blood dripping onto the floor.

Only the blood had dried on the floor.

And the woman…

Dane touched her. She flinched. Tears leaked from the eyes that she'd squeezed shut.

Katherine gasped behind him.

He knew this scene would be too familiar for her.

But this time, the ending would be different. The bad guy wouldn't win. *He wouldn't win.*

"It's all right," Dane told the blonde. *Maggie.* "You're safe." It looked like Valentine had been careful with his torture. No veins had been sliced. No tendons severed. *He was playing with her.* "It's me, Maggie. It's Dane. I'm here to take you home."

Her eyes flew open.

Gently he pulled the duct tape off her lips.

"Dane?" Desperate hope.

"Yes, Maggie. You're safe now."

Deep, shuddering sobs shook her body.

He jerked at the ropes. Twisted. Yanked. Had her hands free. She was naked and bloody and she locked onto him, holding tight.

Katherine freed Maggie's legs. Dane didn't even know where she'd gotten it from, but Katherine wrapped an old blanket around Maggie.

"You…" Maggie whispered as she blinked at Katherine. "I know you…"

Katherine's bottom lip trembled. "You're going to be safe now."

Maggie shook her head. "He'll come back. He said he was coming, that he was going to kill us."

"He's the one who's dead," Dane gritted out as his back teeth ground together. "He can't hurt anyone ever again." He hoped the bastard was fucking burning in hell right then.

Tension thickened in Dane's gut. They'd won. They'd defeated Valentine. They'd just found one of his victims—alive.

Only...

Only the scene felt wrong, and he kept remembering the explosion that had rocked the house on Oakland. Valentine had told Katherine that he'd learned from his mistake in Boston. That he didn't want to leave evidence behind.

The shack was crammed with evidence.

Valentine had planned everything so perfectly. Too perfectly?

He said he was coming, that he was going to kill us. Maggie's words whispered through his mind.

At the station, the guy had kept saying... *Tick, tick, tick.*

He'd made the house on Oakland explode because he didn't want to leave any evidence behind, and this little cabin with its heavy stench of death—it was full of evidence.

Tick, tick, tick.

Dane swallowed and fought to keep his voice steady as he said, "Katherine, take Maggie out to the EMTs." *Get out, Katherine. Get out now.*

"Ross has to be here," Katherine said, glancing around.

Dane would search for him while Katherine waited safely outside. But if he told her why he was worried...

She won't leave me.

And he couldn't leave Ross alone there. Not if his suspicions were correct.

Choices...

He was making his.

"Get her out. I'll be right behind you."

Maggie let go of him and grabbed tightly to Katherine.

Dane caught Katherine's chin. Tilted her face up to meet his. "I love you, Katherine Cole."

She smiled at him. "And I love you."

His jaw locked. "*Go.*"

Valentine had told him that Ross didn't have much time left. If the guy had been cut, bleeding out...hell, even Valentine couldn't have been that precise about the timing of the guy's death.

What had Valentine said? *Every precious second just ticking past.*

Tick, tick, tick.

Had the bastard been telling Dane exactly what he had planned?

Katherine was at the front door. She was guiding Maggie out. Katherine glanced back. Smiled at him. He saw love on her face.

I love you, Katherine.

If you wanted to get specific about a man's time of death, there was one surefire way to guarantee the kill.

Dane glanced at the door on the left. The door that Katherine had probably thought was just a closet, but he'd gauged the length of the cabin and he knew the door would lead to more secrets. More death?

He twisted the doorknob. The door swung inward easily.

The rising sun hit the lone window in that room. He could see all of the photos on the wall. Dozens of them. Black-and-whites. So many bodies. So many deaths as victims were immortalized in their last moments.

And though Dane heard no sound, his gaze was drawn to the far corner of the room. The corner cloaked in shadows. The corner where Anthony Ross sat, tied to a chair, with duct tape over his mouth.

Very, very slowly, Dane walked toward him. As soon as Ross saw him, the marshal started to frantically shake his head.

Because there was a bomb strapped to his chest. A bomb with a countdown ticking away in big, bold numbers.

Tick, tick, tick.

A mirror was positioned in front of Ross.

So he could watch the minutes of his life tick away?

Valentine had been a sadistic bastard.

And Ross had only two minutes left.

No time for a bomb squad to come in.

No time for much of anything, but death.

Dane tucked the gun into his waistband. He lifted his hand and pried the duct tape off Ross's mouth.

"Go…" Ross whispered. "No time…I'm…already dead…"

"No, you're not. You're *fucking* not."

He stared down at the bomb. Crude, but it would get the job done. Three wires. Just three. Red. Yellow. Blue.

Fuck, fuck, fuck! Which one? Which one would be the trigger?

Then he remembered something else that prick Valentine had said at the station. *You're gonna be seeing red…*

He'd thought the guy was talking about seeing blood. But, no, what if Valentine had been talking about the red wire?

He backed away. "I need a knife." His gaze fell to the left. To the row of knives that were sharp and gleaming. Knives that Dane knew had no doubt killed so many.

He grabbed the smallest one. Bent low over Ross.

"Wait!" Ross wheezed.

Dane glanced up at him.

"Do you know…what you're…doing?"

"We've got about sixty seconds, so does it even matter? I figure we got a damn one in three shot here."

Ross's eyes bulged.

The floor creaked behind Dane. *No, no, no…*

"Dane?" Katherine called. "Dane, I need—"

"*Get out!*" he roared as fear twisted his heart.

Forty seconds.

But her footsteps weren't running away. She was coming toward him. She thought he was in danger. *Coming to help. Always coming to help.*

Thirty seconds.

He couldn't let her get any closer. If he was wrong about the wires, then she'd be dead. But if she stayed in the outer area, she might make it. She might—

Twenty seconds. "Stay back!" Dane yelled.

He cut the red wire.

The countdown stopped.

Hell, yes. Dane let out the breath he had been holding.

He sliced through the ropes.

"Dane?" Katherine was behind him. Voice frantic. He looked back. She had the gun clutched in her hand. Her eyes widened, and he knew she'd caught sight of the bomb.

A bomb that he was slowly moving off Ross. Slowly... slowly...

He put the bomb down.

"Now," Dane snapped, "let's all get the fuck out of here."

They ran for the front of the cabin.

And they'd just cleared the steps when the place exploded.

- - -

The crowd of reporters surrounded the DA, watching his every move. The cameras were zoomed in close, the microphones scattered over the podium. Meadows, his face grim, stared back at the assembled group. "Our latest estimate is nineteen victims."

Stunned silence.

Then a deluge of questions erupted. Dane shifted against wall, his battered body aching, as he watched the throng attack.

Meadows lifted his hand. "Valentine didn't want anyone to know the true extent of his crimes."

No, the sonofabitch sure hadn't wanted to share his secrets.

"But our crime-scene techs are doing an amazing job of recovering evidence from the area surrounding his cabin."

Recovering evidence. Finding body parts out in the swamp that the gators had missed or just hadn't wanted.

The DA cleared his throat and said, "Valentine intended to kill Margaret Dunning and U.S. Marshal Anthony Ross on Valentine's Day, and it was only through the very swift and brave actions of Detective Dane Black that those two individuals were spared."

There was a smattering of applause. Cameras turned his way. Dane kept his expression blank. He wasn't looking for thanks. He'd just been doing his job.

Actually, the last thing he wanted right then was to be in the limelight. He wanted to be away from those reporters. Away from the station. He wanted to be with Katherine.

Katherine.

"But unfortunately, not everyone survived the deadly blast that Valentine had rigged so carefully." Sorrow softened the DA's voice. "Katherine Cole, the woman originally known to many of you as Katelynn Crenshaw..."

"Valentine's fiancée," one of the reporters said, nodding quickly.

Dane stiffened.

Meadows shook his head. "Katherine Cole did not make it out of the blast. She risked her life to apprehend the Valentine Killer. To stop the bloody trail of his kills. The department—the whole city of New Orleans—will never forget the sacrifice that she made for us."

Dane knew he was supposed to keep holding it together. Not let any emotion slip out. The killer had been stopped. The streets were safe.

But all he could think was…

Katherine.

His gaze swept over the crowd. The DA and the captain were going to give him and Mac some kind of fucking medal soon. He didn't want the medal. Didn't want the stupid slaps on the back. Didn't want his face splashed in the papers. All he wanted was Katherine.

But hadn't he realized that truth, before the explosion? Hadn't he known how much she meant to him? When he heard her come back in that shack, when she'd called out his name…

Dane forced himself to take a slow, deep breath. Meadows was looking at him expectantly. Shit. The captain was up there, too. They were motioning for him to come toward them. Right. Mac, bandaged, bruised, was already up there.

The DA wanted a big picture of them all smiling for the press.

He didn't feel like smiling.

Dane headed toward them. Positioned his body between the captain and the DA. As flashes from cameras lit the scene, Dane leaned toward Harley and told him, "I quit."

– – –

As soon as he could, Dane went back to his condo. Reporters were camped out downstairs, but a few off-duty cops were earning some extra bucks by keeping them back.

After making his announcement to the captain, Dane had packed up his desk. Harley had argued, damn near begged, but

Dane had stood firm. He didn't want to work in New Orleans anymore. Too many memories were in this city. Good and bad.

Too many memories, and not enough hope.

The elevator dinged and spat him out on his floor. The carpet muffled his footsteps as he headed toward his home. A cold, dark home. Was that what he wanted for the rest of his life?

No.

He juggled the box of his belongings with one hand and unlocked his door. So dark inside. He didn't flip on the lights. Just shoved the box onto the nearest table. Then he slammed and locked the door and—

Soft hands wrapped around him. "I was wondering if you were ever going to come home," Katherine whispered.

His whole body stiffened. "You aren't supposed to be here."

She should be gone. Flying away on a jet to some new town. To some new life. Ross had promised he'd take care of her.

Carefully, Dane turned in her arms. Oh, but she felt *good.* It had been three days since he'd held her. Three days since the explosion. Three days since they'd hurtled out of that shack. His clothes had caught on fire. She'd slapped at the flames, desperate to protect him.

He reached out one arm and flipped on the light.

"Katherine Cole isn't here," she told him as her gaze locked on his. "You can call me Katie." A little shrug. "Ross always says it's important to keep your names as close as you can to your original. That way, you can remember to answer when people call you." The faintest smile tilted her lips.

Dark red lips. To match her new dark red hair. Dark red, and cut shorter, with soft curls.

The haircut made her look even sexier than before. Hell, who was he kidding? He *always* thought the woman was sexy.

"It's the new me." Her smile dimmed. "And I hope it's the last me."

Bandages covered her palms. Where she'd slapped at the fire that had burned over him.

"You didn't really think I'd just leave town without saying good-bye, did you?" Her voice was the husky purr that would haunt him for the rest of his life.

"It wouldn't have mattered," he managed to say.

Pain flickered in her gaze, and her smile dimmed as her hands slid away from his waist. "I…ah…see…" Katherine—Katie—cleared her throat. "I didn't realize…I thought you'd want…"

He kissed her. Deep and hard. Let her feel the lust and need and *love* that were burning inside him. "I was gonna call Ross," he whispered against her lips. "I was gonna make him tell me where you were. I figured after everything, the guy owed me." And he'd planned to trade in that IOU for Katherine.

She pulled away from him. Her eyes widened.

"Wherever the hell you were, I was going there, too."

It had seemed like the perfect plan. With the explosion, Katherine Cole could disappear. She could escape all the reporters—and all the Valentine-obsessed loons out there—like Evelyn Knight—who would make her life hell. She could start fresh.

One final relocation.

One final life.

Only it would have been a life without him.

Ross had started making the plans immediately. Katherine had been taken away from Dane at the crime scene. The story of her death had been deliberately leaked to the reporters.

Everything should have worked perfectly. Katherine would have her freedom. The killer would be dead. New Orleans safe. *Should have been perfect.*

Except for one small problem. He didn't want to live his life without Katherine.

"Your life is here," she said as she gazed up at him with her deep golden eyes. "Your job. Your friends."

She didn't get it. "You *are* my life." He'd tried living without her for just over seventy-two hours. Those had been the shittiest seventy-two hours of his life. "From now on, where you go, I go."

Then he did something he'd never thought he'd do. Dane dropped down to one knee. "I don't have a ring."

She blinked. Then her eyes—those beautiful eyes that made him think of sex and love and hope—widened.

"I'm so sorry, baby, I swear, I'll buy you the biggest damn diamond in the world." Well, the biggest damn diamond that an ex–New Orleans detective could afford. "I'll buy you *anything*, just please do me the honor of becoming my wife."

She wasn't saying anything.

So he kept talking. Fast. He was holding onto her wrists because he didn't want to hurt the wounds on her hands. "I love you, Katherine. Hell, I was willing to die for you. Willing to kill in order to keep you safe."

"I don't want anyone dying for me." Her voice was so soft.

"Death is behind us." He wanted life. With her. "You want to start over. You want to begin without the baggage of Valentine? Then let's do it. Together. Let's pick a small town. I can be the sheriff. Hell, I'll pay my dues and start as a deputy if I have to. You can open another art gallery. You can paint. You can do anything you want. Just…do it with me. Start fresh…*with me*."

It looked like she might cry. He didn't want her to cry. Oh, hell, no, he hated it when Katherine cried.

"I want to wake up next to you in the morning and go to bed holding your hand each night." His jaw locked. "Katherine, marry me."

She laughed then. A sweet, light sound that pierced right to his heart. "I don't really want a diamond."

His brows lowered.

"I don't care about a ring." She dropped to her knees. Brought her face close to his. "I just care about you. I love you, Dane Black. And Katelynn, Katherine, hell, even Katie—whichever one of us you want—we'll marry you."

"I want you all." Every part of her. He wrapped his arms around her. Pulled her close. "I want you."

Her gaze held his. "Then you've got me."

He kissed her and knew he had to have her. *I need her.* He wanted to feel her body against his. Wanted to be sure that the nightmare was really over. That Katherine was alive and safe and *with* him.

Not a thousand miles away in a new town.

Not dead, killed in an explosion set by Valentine.

He lifted her into his arms. Made sure not to jostle her hands and took her into the bedroom.

This time, he wouldn't be frantic. He'd put a stranglehold on the insatiable hunger he felt for her. He stripped her, so carefully. Kissed her flesh as he tossed away her shirt and skirt.

She wore a lacy black bra and panties. Looking at her made his whole body ache. Part of him wanted to rip away the panties. To just take…

But being with Katherine was about more than taking. More than just sex.

More than fucking in the dark.

His fingers threaded with hers. He kissed her. Keeping his lips gentle and easy.

He pulled away long enough to strip off his own clothes, and he threw them into the corner.

With fingers that trembled, he slid off her bra. Licked, caressed her breasts. Such perfect breasts. He loved the way she moaned and arched up against him.

She wanted more. So did he.

He tried to be careful with her panties, but he still shredded them as he pulled the delicate lace off her hips.

Katherine laughed.

He loved the sound of her laugh.

Then he was between her legs. She was wet and ready, and he was about to explode, but even though his muscles locked from the effort and sweat slickened his back, he pushed into her slowly.

He stared into her eyes.

And he saw forever. The best dream he'd ever had.

"Give me more," Katherine whispered.

He'd give her anything. Everything. Just as he'd promised.

The rhythm started slow. The bed creaked beneath him. She tried to touch him, but he was afraid she'd hurt her hands so he lifted them up, caught her wrists in one hand, and pinned them carefully to the bed.

Withdraw. Thrust.

Her cheeks were flushed. Her eyes gleaming.

He thrust harder. A little deeper.

Her legs wrapped around his hips. "Dane…"

He loved the way she said his name. Loved the way she felt against him.

Warm. Sexy.

There was no death here. No fear.

She was moving faster. So was he. His climax was pressing ever closer, but he didn't want this moment to end. He wanted to be with her. To feel the pleasure pulse through her body, around him.

He kissed her.

She came.

He kept kissing her. Kept thrusting. He couldn't hold off his release. Not any longer.

His head lifted. He stared into her eyes. Saw her pleasure. "I...love you..."

She smiled.

And the pleasure swept over him.

He'd fucked plenty of women, but with Katherine, only with her, did he feel like he was loving someone.

"I don't ever want to lose you," he rasped as his heart thundered in his chest. He wouldn't. Couldn't.

Obsession?

Love?

Sometimes, it was hard to tell where one ended and the other began.

Valentine had crossed that line. Hell, Valentine had crossed a hundred lines.

"You won't lose me," Katherine whispered as her breath panted out.

"That better be a promise."

Her lips curled. "Detective, it's a guarantee."

He smiled. For the first time in longer than he could remember, Dane actually felt happy.

His past wasn't going to haunt him. He wouldn't let it. He wouldn't turn out like his old man. Not fucking ever.

Choices.

Katherine had been right about that part. Life was all about the choices that people made.

He stared into her eyes. *She* was his choice. The best thing in his life.

He was stronger, a better person when he was with her.

And he'd make sure, no matter what the future brought, that he stayed at Katherine's side.

For better or worse...

Hell, they'd already done the worse part.

Time for better.

Time for *life*.

No more nightmares. No more killers.

This was the way the story ended for them. Not with Valentine winning. Not with death.

With life.

With love.

EPILOGUE

A new town. A new name.

A new husband.

Katherine—Katie—walked into her home and smiled when she caught the scent of fresh flowers in the air. Then she saw the flowers waiting on the kitchen table.

Daisies. Not roses. Fresh, beautiful daisies. Her new favorite flower.

For a moment, her heart beat a little too fast as the past tried to push its way into her perfect present. She walked toward the table. Let her fingers caress the flowers.

Footsteps sounded behind her. Warm hands closed around her shoulders. She didn't jump now when she was touched from behind. Not when she knew who was touching her. And she'd always know Dane's touch.

Smiling, she turned toward him.

"I've got a surprise for you," he said, his deep voice rumbling.

They'd been in their new house for just over a week. She was setting up her art gallery, and Dane—well, he was taking over the vacant sheriff's position in town. Ross had seemingly found them the perfect new home.

But Katherine knew nothing was perfect.

I can't hope for perfect. I don't want perfect. I just want to be happy.

With Dane, she was.

She might not ever be able to completely get over her past, but she didn't want to forget where she'd come from. Darkness and scars. Pain and suffering. Everything had shaped her.

Dane led her up the stairs. There was no basement at this house. One of her rules.

No damn basements. And no roses—ever.

He opened the door on the right. Bright light filled the space. Canvases. Paints.

"I thought you might like to have a studio here. You know, for when I piss you off and you want some private space."

She smiled at that. "It's wonderful." So now she knew what the guy had been working on so hard for the past day and a half.

Dane and his secrets.

At least she knew his secrets weren't the killing kind.

He wiggled his brows at her. "Should we christen the room?"

She laughed. She was doing that more. Laughing with Dane. Enjoying life.

Maybe one day, she'd see her past through a cloudy veil. Maybe it would seem like everything had happened to someone else.

Maybe she'd just be the happy woman with the doting husband.

The woman who could live next door to anyone.

The woman who'd once had a serial killer say he loved her. In those last moments, Valentine had whispered to her, and he'd said...

I did it. I died for you.

She wrapped her arms around Dane. His warmth pushed away the cold of her past.

She was a new woman. In a new place. With a man who loved her, darkness and all.

And she loved him. So much that, sometimes, the power of that love scared her.

She'd expected love to be beautiful. Kind. Good.

She knew now that it could be consuming. Terrifying.

But even in the midst of that terror, love could bring you safety. Hope.

Dane was her hope. Her future.

And she couldn't wait to see what more life would bring them.

She was Katie Black. She lived in Anywhere, U.S.A. She knew about killers. She knew about death.

And now, she knew about love.

Thanks to a detective who hadn't been interested in dying, but more interested in living, for her.

ACKNOWLEDGMENTS

I want to thank my fabulous editor, Lindsay, for all of her wonderful insight as we worked on *Die for Me*. Lindsay, working with you is a pleasure!

For my equally fabulous agent, Laura Blake Peterson, thank you for your incredible support.

ABOUT THE AUTHOR

A Southern girl with a penchant for both horror movies and happy endings, *USA Today* bestselling author Cynthia Eden has written more than two dozen tales of paranormal romance and romantic suspense. Her books have received starred reviews from *Publishers Weekly*, and her novel *Deadly Fear* was named a Rita finalist for best romantic suspense. She currently lives in Alabama.